PENGUIN BOOKS

Lovestruck

Julia Llewellyn is the aut
Amy's Honeymoon, *The M*
Fall in Love, all publishe
Llewellyn Smith she wri
the *Sunday Times* and ma............publications. julia lives in
London with her family.

Lovestruck

JULIA LLEWELLYN

PENGUIN BOOKS

PENGUIN BOOKS

Published by the Penguin Group
Penguin Books Ltd, 80 Strand, London WC2R ORL, England
Penguin Group (USA) Inc., 375 Hudson Street, New York, New York 10014, USA
Penguin Group (Canada), 90 Eglinton Avenue East, Suite 700, Toronto, Ontario, Canada M4P 2Y3
(a division of Pearson Penguin Canada Inc.)
Penguin Ireland, 25 St Stephen's Green, Dublin 2, Ireland (a division of Penguin Books Ltd)
Penguin Group (Australia), 707 Collins Street, Melbourne, Victoria 3008, Australia
(a division of Pearson Australia Group Pty Ltd)
Penguin Books India Pvt Ltd, 11 Community Centre, Panchsheel Park, New Delhi – 110 017, India
Penguin Group (NZ), 67 Apollo Drive, Rosedale, Auckland 0632, New Zealand
(a division of Pearson New Zealand Ltd)
Penguin Books (South Africa) (Pty) Ltd, Block D, Rosebank Office Park,
181 Jan Smuts Avenue, Parktown North, Gauteng 2193, South Africa

Penguin Books Ltd, Registered Offices: 80 Strand, London WC2R ORL, England

www.penguin.com

First published 2014
001

Copyright © Julia Llewellyn, 2014
All rights reserved

The moral right of the author has been asserted

Set in 12.5/14.75 pt Garamond MT Std
Typeset by Jouve (UK), Milton Keynes
Printed in Great Britain by Clays Ltd, St Ives plc

ISBN: 978–0–141–04818–5

www.greenpenguin.co.uk

MIX
Paper from
responsible sources
FSC® C018179

Penguin Books is committed to a sustainable
future for our business, our readers and our planet.
This book is made from Forest Stewardship
Council™ certified paper.

For Lizzy Kremer.
Thank you for everything

Prologue

They lay on Jake's bed, breathing heavily, bodies inter-twined and sweaty under the rumpled sheets. Daylight streamed in through the curtains; outside, cars were honking and birds singing.

'We've been up all night,' Jake laughed.

'We need to get some sleep,' Rosie agreed.

He leaned forward and kissed her on the nose. 'Night, then.'

'Night.'

Giggling, they both shut their eyes. Rosie could hear her heart thudding. She tried to slow down her breathing, to black out. She had to be exhausted; she'd been up all night. But she wasn't: her body was purring like a Ferrari at traffic lights, ready to spring off again. She could sense Jake looking at her. Her eyes popped open.

'Cheat!' she yelled and they both burst out laughing.

'I couldn't help it. You're so gorgeous, I just had to watch you.'

Rosie was embarrassed. 'You're just saying that.'

'I'm not.' Jake reached out and stroked her cheek lightly. 'The second I saw you last night . . . You're the most beautiful girl I've ever seen. There's something about you. I've never felt like this about anything, or anyone.'

'You're just saying it,' repeated Rosie, dipping her gaze, though she wanted to cry out: '*I feel the same way too! I love you! Let's get married this afternoon and have a baby in nine months' time.*'

'I am not. I swear. You're incredible. I think . . . Rosie . . . Rosie, what's your surname?'

'Rosie Prest,' she laughed. 'I'm such a slut! Christy and I always agreed we would never even kiss a boy unless we knew his middle name.'

'Well, I'm not telling you my middle name in a million years,' said Jake. Her curiosity was piqued, but before she could pursue this, he continued: 'Rosie Prest. I love you. I know I've only known you for . . . what? . . . eight hours, but I am bowled over. I am besotted. I am lovestruck.'

Silence, except the sound of a bus engine revving.

'You're just saying all that,' Rosie said again. 'You're an actor. You're playing a part.'

Jake sat bolt upright. There was almost no hair on his chest, Rosie noticed, blinking. She'd missed quite a few details as she'd ripped out her contact lenses several hours ago when they became too scratchy to tolerate. Although he was skinny, muscles rippled under his torso. She reached out and touched him, as he said, 'I know how I must sound. But I mean it. I've never been so sincere about anything in my life. We are going to be together forever. I just know it. I'll have to convince you to feel the same way but . . .'

'You don't have to convince me,' Rosie said quietly.

Then she felt terrified. Rosie Prest was a hesitant woman. She didn't believe in throwing caution to the winds, in making grand declarations and gestures. These things could get thrown back in your face. It was better to go through life quietly, not expecting too much, because that way you couldn't be disappointed. That had been her philosophy. Until now.

Now she felt invincible.

'Do you mean that?' Jake gawped at her, then pulled her towards him. 'Really? You feel the same way?'

She didn't answer; she just started kissing him. Her lips melted into his and she was twisting, twirling into space, like a balloon come untethered. They rolled over, so she was on top of him. Normally she'd have been shy in such a position with a brand-new man and the cold light of day upon her. But right now Rosie felt proud of her naked body, her face smudged with last night's mascara, her bird's-nest hair. It was like falling from a great height, but she wasn't scared. She was invigorated.

'I love you, Rosie. We'll be together forever. And I am going to make you so, so happy. I'm going to give you everything you ever wanted.'

I

It took an hour and a half to travel from Rosie and Jake's old two-bedroom flat on the grimy fringes of the North Circular to the Village nestling on a bend just south of the Thames. The Village, which had a duck pond, an ancient church with a steeple you could climb on Sunday afternoons, an array of gift shops selling wrapping paper at five pounds a pop and coffee parlours competing to serve the best chocolate brownie. The Village looked its absolute best on this breezy day in early spring, with almond blossom blowing from the trees like candied pink snow.

'That restaurant on the corner just got a Michelin star,' said Jake, nodding at a whitewashed Victorian cottage with wisteria growing round the door and no sign whatsoever it might be open to members of the public. 'We should go.'

'Definitely,' Rosie agreed. 'As soon as I find a baby-sitter.'

'Or we could take the boys,' Jake said, as Toby hollered from the back seat, 'Get off, George! Stop hitting me.'

'Maybe not,' Rosie smiled.

'Look!' yelled little George. 'A kite!'

Indeed, there were two little boys in cord shorts and chambray shirts holding a kite string, not squabbling over it as Rosie's boys would have, but smiling delightedly as they ran along. A Labrador barked excitedly. A pretty mummy with long dark hair in a floaty summer dress watched, beaming. A daddy, also in shorts and a violet polo top was shouting encouragement. It was like the old Peter and Jane books that Rosie had learned to read from come to life. Did the Village tourist board pay them to stand there?

'Can we fly a kite?' George asked. 'Today?' In Neasden the only place to fly a kite was on the patch of grass next to the four-lane A road decorated with disused needles and dog shit.

'Not today, love, because we'll need to buy one first. But once we have one, yes, every day.' Remembering George was apt to take promises literally, Rosie hastily backtracked. 'I mean, most days. Now we'll be living so close to the Green.' Another thought struck her. 'We might even be able to fly it in the garden; it's big enough.'

'We're going to have a trampoline in the garden,' Toby reminded her. 'You promised.'

'I know. I've ordered one. It'll be delivered next week.' It had been a pinch-yourself moment clicking on CONFIRM. Imagine, a trampoline in the back garden. Rosie knew virtually all kids had them these days, along with tutors and ADHD, but it was still a dream come true for someone who had grown up in a cramped three-bedroom flat above a bookies with no outdoor space at all – it was still a dream come true.

'Mummy!' shrieked George, the suggestion of bouncing having obviously been the last straw. 'I'm going to be sick.'

'Oh no! Slow down, Jake.' Poor George suffered horribly from car-sickness. Rosie had spent a small fortune – probably the cost of two trampolines – on acupuncture wristbands and homeopathic remedies to tackle the problem, but since she always forgot to administer them before they set out on a car trip, she had no idea if they worked or not. Likewise, she never remembered to bring plastic bags as vomit receptacles. 'Jake, slow down!

'We'll be there in just two minutes.' Jake always said this. It drove Rosie mad.

'Slow bloody down!' she hissed, craning round. Her two-year-old son had turned an alarming shade of green.

'*Slowdownforfuck'ssakeJake!*'

But it was too late. George had hurled his breakfast Weetabix and raisins all over himself and the back seat of their elderly Passat.

'Mummeee!'

'Uurgh, Georgie, you stink!' Toby bellowed as the car belatedly halted in front of the high iron gates that protected their new home from the outside world.

'Don't stink!'

'Toby, don't be mean to your brother. Jake, I told you

7

to stop!' But Jake wasn't listening, he was fiddling with his new key ring. He pressed a button and the gates slowly opened.

'How cool is that? I'm like Blofeld,' he crowed as they drove through them, crunching to a halt on the gravel. Rosie leaped out of her seat, opened the back door and yanked George out of his car seat. Puke splattered over the drive.

'Welcome to our new abode,' laughed Jake.

'Take off my clothes,' George sobbed.

'Oh, sweetheart,' Rosie said, gingerly pulling his T-shirt over his head, so his reddish curls were streaked fetchingly with complementary orange vomit. 'Poor you. We'll change you as soon as the removal van arrives with all your clothes. And while we're waiting you can have the first bath in our new house.'

'That's not *fair*,' protested Toby, whose life was a series of never-ending injustices.

'You can share it,' Rosie amended, holding her son's reeking clothes by the tips of her fingers. 'Or have a bath of your very own.' After all, there were six bathrooms to choose from, as she recalled.

Whooping, the boys ran up the front steps that led to the glossy black front door, which was flanked by two stone sleeping dogs, statues of Lampard and Di Canio, Louis and Samantha's, the previous owners, beloved Rhodesian ridgebacks.

Rosie and Jake stood gazing up at the house. Three storeys of dark red Georgian brick studded with white-framed sash windows. Like the heartbreakingly pretty homes inhabited by characters in Jane Austen novels (at least in the telly versions Rosie had watched). The kind of house that today was the domain of rock stars, bankers, famous sportsmen – the rich.

Because, not quite overnight, but within the past year or so, Rosie and Jake had become one of that number.

'It's beautiful, isn't it?' Jake said.

'I can't believe this is really happening.' Nor could Rosie believe she was standing in front of her dream home holding a selection of puke-splashed garments, but never mind.

'Mum, Mum. I need a weeee!' Toby yelled. '*Open the door.*'

'Oh Christ.' Jake started fumbling with the key ring again. 'Not vomit *and* wee on the same day, surely?'

'That's pretty good going. We need to add some blood and crap into the mix for it really to get exciting.'

'Which key goes in which lock?' Jake panicked, examining the brand-new set of keys that Fripley and Farquhar's couriers had biked round that morning.

'Hurry, Daddy! I'm bursting.'

'Nearly there.' Jake pushed the huge brass door knob and the door swung open revealing the marble hallway. Without Louis and Samantha's reproduction furniture, it was even bigger than Rosie remembered. The burglar alarm started bleeping.

'Oh fuck, what do we do?'

'I have the code!' Rosie smiled. She was the calm one in their partnership. 'Nine nine four two.'

'Let me!' yelled George, but Jake had already stabbed in the numbers.

'Daddd-eeeeee.' George started weeping at this betrayal.

'Oh, George, it's OK.'

'Where's the toilet?' Toby wailed, clutching the front of his trousers.

'You'll have to say "loo", now, my son,' Jake teased. 'We're not in Neasden any more.'

'*Mummy* says "toilet".'

'Yes, and Mummy will always say "toilet",' responded Rosie cheerfully. Words like 'toilet', 'lounge' and 'pardon' were her mother-in-law Yolande's pet hates; she and Jake always joked about it.

'C'mon,' Jake said. 'It's over there. I'll race ya.'

They ran into the little hallway that led to the kitchen, yelling with delight. Rosie knelt down and put her arms round George in his skimpy underpants. They looked up at the double-height ceiling: supported by twirly Corinthian pillars.

'What do you think, schnooks?'

'It's big.'

'Shall we go up to the bathroom? To one of the many bathrooms,' Rosie giggled, struck yet again by the amazing change in their fortunes. Would she ever get used to it? 'We'll get you washed. Maybe in the jacuzzi.' There was a jacuzzi in her and Jake's peach-coloured en suite, not to mention glass his 'n' hers sinks. They planned to fill it with foam up to their necks and then drink a bottle of Moët in it to christen the new house.

'Waaargh!' bellowed Toby, re-emerging from the loo. 'Come on, Georgie. Let's play. Kill, kill, kill!'

'We're going up for a bath and then you can play.'

'The gold taps will have to go,' said Jake, following him. 'And the water in the loo's still blue. Sam must have had her cleaner give the place a final once-over before she left to give Marbella a good spring clean.' He put his arms round Rosie's waist and kissed her gently on the lips, smiling down at her.

'We've done good, Old Bean,' he said. He had called her that since he'd had a tiny part in a fringe Jeeves and Wooster play, just after they met.

'*You've* done good. I just married the right man.' Rosie hugged him close. 'Is it really ours?'

'It's one hundred per cent ours. Cash. No mortgage.'

'No mortgage,' Rosie breathed. She thought back to her childhood, when some months she and Nanna had to literally search for coins down the back of the sofa to pay the rent. 'Our bricks.'

'Our gutters.'

'Our ivy.'

'Our light switches.'

'Hopefully not for much longer,' grimaced Rosie. Samantha and Louis's light switches were gold-plated, very eighties, another detail that strongly evoked her best friend Christy's childhood home. Twenty years ago

Rosie had thought Christy's parents were the ultimate sophisticater, even if her mother was horrible. Now, of course, fashions had changed completely. Rosie was planning to rip out everything, make the house contemporary and stylish.

'We're going to grow old and die here. Though we'll have to install a Stannah. Two Stannahs. Our Stannahs.'

'Four. Two for each staircase. His 'n' hers. Designed like thrones.'

Hand in hand, they walked into the 'reception room' as Samantha called it. Yolande would have corrected her, told her it was the 'living room', Rosie thought, smiling.

The dusky-green carpet was brighter where the kidney-shaped glass coffee table and white leather sofas had sat, and the lavender walls had faded patches where the Warhol-style oil portraits of Louis and Samantha had hung. They'd left the curtains: voluminous maroon swags held back by lap-dancery tassels, and there were huge holes in the walls, relics of the cabling for Louis's vast home-entertainment system.

'Sam did all of this,' Louis had said when showing them round (he'd refused to let the man from Fripley and Farquhar have a look-in) and instead of immediately issuing her husband with a writ for libel Samantha had nodded proudly. She was an ex-model, huge in the seventies apparently, with a cloud of ash-blonde hair and a penchant for tight leggings and low-cut tops, revealing an only slightly raddled cleavage. Rosie instantly liked Samantha, passion for antiseptic wipes, air freshener and all. She and Louis, who had finally retired from running a chain of bookies, had downsized to their second home in Spain, but they'd promised they'd visit whenever they returned to the Village to see their friends.

'You're going to have a great social life here, babe,' Samantha had promised. 'Do you want me to put you in touch with my bridge club? They'd love to have you on board.'

The hideous decor didn't matter. Something in the bones of this house spoke to Rosie from the instant she saw it, making her want it so badly it was like a chasm opening in her chest. She'd imagined herself making scones on the Aga (she hadn't a clue how Agas worked and didn't even much like scones, but never mind). She envisaged the boys playing cricket in the garden (they'd remove Louis's greenhouse), while she – in a lineny dress like one she'd admired a few years ago in Jigsaw but couldn't then afford – would wander out with a wicker basket to gather raspberries from the bush in the far corner to make into jam. They'd be happy here, she knew it.

Mind you, she and Jake had been very happy in the cramped flat in Neasden. But they were outgrowing it and then, virtually overnight, they'd had the money to buy – not *any* house they wanted – they still couldn't have afforded a maisonette in somewhere like Knightsbridge – but their dream house, their forever house, in a lovely area, with a huge garden and rooms going spare.

She still couldn't believe how simple the process had been. Rosie had said she wanted the house and Jake agreed (though it helped that his mother had also proclaimed it an excellent investment). They'd offered the asking price and been immediately accepted. All those years of scrimping, trying not to turn on the heating until November, buying nappies from Lidl, no holidays and suddenly this. Overnight, almost. Extraordinary.

'Our Ikea furniture's going to look so ridiculous in this room,' Rosie grinned, looking around the cavernous space.

'Looks better without all the crystal ornaments on the mantelpiece, though.' Jake hugged her. 'But you're right. We'll need to buy some new stuff. Get rid of those horrible curtains, put in shutters.'

Rosie pulled back the curtains and looked down at the garden. A garden with planning permission for a swimming pool. As a child she'd always wanted a pool, considering it the acme of luxury. Though they'd have to wait a few years to install it – good Lord, could you imagine George around it? But when the boys were older, it would be a different matter.

They could have a dog. They *could* have another baby, but Rosie wasn't interested. She was so grateful and thrilled that she'd been able to jack in her job and spend more time with the boys, but at the same time the reality of being at home with small children wasn't quite living up to her fantasy. It was messier than she'd imagined, noisier, more boring and sometimes more lonely – though of course there were brilliant bits too. Still, the first item on her to-do list was finding a good nursery. Then she'd have mornings off, time to . . . she didn't know. Well, do up the house obviously. She'd drive to antiques markets that started at dawn and scour eBay for finds just like people did in *Living Etc*, people whose children were called things like Indigo, Thorn and Bushfire.

But then? Take up pottery? Start training for entry to *The Great British Bake Off*? Study for a PhD in Spanish literature? Who knew? At least she wouldn't be strap-hanging on the Bakerloo line, beating herself up because Toby had a rash and she'd said nothing about it to the nursery staff or having to deal with dreary Cillian at the next-door desk complaining about his adenoids.

Only eighteen months ago that had been her life. She'd been working in that little office in Paddington for Tapper-Green IT Consultants, earning OK-ish money, but money that all seemed to be going on nursery fees Jake was a struggling actor, often doing gigs for free, just to get his face seen. Rosie was exhausted from rushing from home to nursery to work to nursery to home again, too grumpy and tired to really enjoy the boys. But just as she was teetering on the verge of a nervous breakdown, about to beg Jake to jack in the acting dream and find a proper job, he got the part in *Archbishop Grace*.

It was an overnight sensation. From being a nobody, people had started pointing and nudging at her husband as he walked down the street. They asked for autographs when he was standing in the queue at Tesco's. A man had approached him the other day in Oxford Street and picked him up and licked his face. People filmed him peeing in public toilets. Everywhere he went, people yelled out his catchphrase: 'Not under *my* patio.' Everyone thought this was hilarious. Rosie had trained herself to smile when they did it, even though the joke had long lost its lustre.

He was interviewed constantly for every publication imaginable. He had four hundred and fifty-three thousand-odd followers on Twitter and had closed down his Facebook page because so many weirdos were jumping on there. He had been to the pub with Ricky Gervais after filming a comedy quiz show and had Jonathan Ross's email.

He was just about to start rehearsing for a West End version of *Twelfth Night* – not the glitziest choice, and certainly not the best paid, though the fact that Ellie Lewis, star for years of the insanely popular, brainy and glamorous American drama *O'Rourke's*, was going to be Viola, had given the enterprise a load more sex appeal. Not to mention, Christy Papadopolous, Rosie's best and oldest friend – and as it happened, her husband's agent, but that was another story – had assured Jake the play was the best step to take if he wanted to be regarded not just as a sitcom star but as a serious actor. And Christy knew what she was talking about.

Anyway, Rosie thought, as she moved from the

reception room to the 'snug', which, despite its name, could contain their old flat, the end result was suddenly money had been pouring into Jake's bank account. She wouldn't call herself rich, because she didn't feel like a rich person. Rich people spoke like the queen and spent their nights out at Boujis or Annabel's, rather than in front of a Love Film DVD. She didn't look rich – her shoulder-length hair was always pulled back in a practical ponytail and she hadn't had time to have her highlights done for six months and she wore no make-up. Again, when would you find the time to apply it when the boys were displaying their kung-fu kicks? Her jeans were from Gap (bought with a thirty-per-cent-off voucher). Her trainers were FitFlops (*not* cool but *so* comfy). Her top was River Island. Then there was her turquoise necklace purchased on that holiday with Christy in Rimini, when they'd danced until dawn every night.

'Happy?' said Jake behind her. He slipped his arms over her shoulders and rubbed himself against her bottom. Jake would have to be in a coma not to want to have sex. Rosie slapped his hand gently as it moved towards the zip of her jeans.

'Stop it, you sick pervert. We have a vomit-encrusted child to bathe.'

'Later?' he whispered in her ear. 'To christen the bedroom?'

'Of course later,' Rosie grinned.

'Mummy!' shouted Toby. 'The moving van is here.'

She ran back into the hallway and peered through one of the windowpanes that flanked the front door. Sure enough, the van was drawing up.

'Better put the kettle on.'

'Can I help them?' Toby cried.

'Well . . . You can perhaps help unpack something.' She'd originally said they'd do the unpacking themselves, but Jake had overridden her and said they'd pay the premium and have the removal guys do it. Why not? They could afford it. He was always saying that these days.

There was just one thing she needed to do before making cups of tea. She pulled out her old Samsung – as soon as she had a moment she'd get round to finally upgrading to an iPhone – and jabbed out a quick text. Two recipients: Christy and Sandrine.

> We're finally here! So excited. Can't wait for you to come and see it. xxx

She opened the door and as she stepped outside into the spring sunshine, her phone tringed. Sandrine.

> So excited for you, honey-bunny. xx

Rosie smiled. Truly, there was no one lovelier than Sandrine. She imagined her pootling around her kitchen in Hebden Bridge in her huge shabby slippers and one of her baggy sweatshirts, cat rubbing against her ankles, while her partner June pottered in their little herb garden. Rosie hoped she'd visit soon. She'd die of laughter when she saw the gold taps, but it would be kind, supportive laughter.

The inbox showed another text. Christy. Rosie's best friend since she was seven years old.

Can't wait to see the results of all my hard work! Xx PS Bottle of Moët on the way. Let me know if it doesn't turn up.

'Oh, Christy,' Rosie grinned. She showed the text to Jake.

He smiled wryly. 'That woman and Moët. She's getting more *Ab Fab* by the second.'

Rosie smiled up at him. Sometimes she felt like she was standing in a rainstorm, being pelted with the force of her love for Jake. She was so lucky. She had everything – her wonderful husband, her two boys and now all this. And her best friend who'd helped her achieve all this. When they were kids, she'd always made up little stories about living in a huge house with a beautiful garden and now . . .

'All right?' asked Nicky, head of the delivery squad, winking as he climbed down from the driver's cab.

'Never better,' Rosie replied. 'Just need to unpack the soap, some boys' clothes, the kettle and we'll be raring to go.'

2

It was very early the following morning. Rosie and Jake were lying in their tiny double bed. It had barely fitted into their old room in Neasden, but which in their new bedroom with its dressing area looked like a bread-crumb on a dinner plate.

Between them lay George slurping from his sippy cup of milk. In Neasden they'd had to dash across the hall into the kitchenette to warm it in the microwave. Here, at six a.m., Rosie had had to go down two storeys and pad in bare feet across the kitchen's acres of freez-ing flagstones, then go all the way back upstairs again.

'I think we'd better wean Georgie off his morning milk soon,' she said.

'Nooo! Mummy! Love my cuppy.'

'Poor little Georgie,' Jake agreed annoyingly. He loved to do this, side with the boys to be the fun dad. It wound Rosie up that she was always the misery guts, saying 'No' to everything.

'Well, then, you go down for his milk tomorrow. Either that or we're going to have to have a microwave in the bedroom. We'll need to keep a stash of nappies in here too,' she added, patting her son's damp bottom through his pyjama trousers.

'Try not to make it six tomorrow, Georgie Porgie,' Jake pleaded. Rosie glanced at her husband in the sunshine, streaming in through a gap in Samantha's peach curtains.

She loved the way he looked in the morning: his black hair rumpled, chin stubbly, touchingly vulnerable without his glasses. Jake wasn't traditionally handsome; he was too tall and skinny for that, and his face wasn't symmetrical: his nose a little too large, his mouth too wide and . . . whisper it, because it was a subject on which Jake was extremely touchy . . . his crown was showing just the earliest hints of balding. But he had a gangly charm to him – one that Rosie thought she'd been the only one to appreciate, but which, according to dozens of Internet forums and, freakily, one 'tribute site' set up by a mystery admirer, thousands of women shared.

'I'm full of beans!' George replied proudly. Granny Yolande had told him this and he never tired of repeating it. George was a mini-Jake: dark and vital with rosy chipmunk cheeks. Toby was so much more like Rosie: pale and inclined to fade into the background.

'Did you like sleeping in your new bedroom, Georgie?' Rosie asked.

George drained his cup. 'Want breakfast now!'

'Oh, George, it's so early.' And Rosie and Jake had been up until past midnight, finishing Christy's Moët, which had arrived as promised, and then christening the rooms in the house. They'd done the lot, bar the boys' bedrooms, and it had been hilarious, even if

Rosie's bottom and back ached from all the cold stone floors.

'Full of beans!'

Jake laughed. 'I'll take him down,' he said, just as the buzzer signalling someone was at the front gates hummed like a huge bumblebee.

'Who the fuck is that?'

'I don't know. It's . . .' Rosie peered at her phone, unable to see much without her contact lenses. 'Just gone seven.'

'Who the fuck!' sang George. Rosie cringed.

'I'll go and see.' Jake jumped out of bed and grabbed last night's pants from last's night's discarded clothes on the floor.

'You can't open the door like that,' Rosie laughed.

'Why not? It might be the paparazzi. Let them have something decent to take a picture of for once.' Just after *Archbishop Grace* was first screened, they'd left the flat in Neasden one Monday morning pushing the double buggy when a man with a huge camera had jumped out from behind a bush and started snapping away. It had been a bit scary, but then funny – the pictures were so dull they'd never made the papers and word had clearly got round that the Perrys weren't worth bothering with, as after that they'd been left well alone.

'Come on, Georgie,' Jake said, as the buzzing started again. 'Let's see who it is.'

'It might be burglars!' Rosie cried as the pair dashed down the stairs, no doubt waking Toby in the process.

She ran into the hall in her pair of horrible old pants, which had turned yellow from too much washing. She peered over the balustrade, with its view down two storeys into the hallway. Jake was peering at the little screen by the intercom.

'Surprise!' it crackled.

'Mum, bloody hell. What are you doing?' Jake pressed the button to open the gates. Seconds later, there was banging on the front door. Rosie ducked down below the banister.

'You know me and Dad,' bellowed her mother-in-law as she marched into the hall. 'Early risers, us old folk. It's the hormones going doolally. So we thought: Well, they'll be awake soon, and we jumped in the motor – hello, my little chickadee, yes, Granny *is* pleased to see you – so here we are.'

Rupert was looking around him. 'My word, Perry. It's a mansion.'

'I told you,' Yolande said smugly.

'Mummy!' cried Toby from his room on the floor below. 'What's happening?'

'Don't worry, darling!' replied Rosie, still crouching down. 'Granny's just here early, that's all. Go down and see her.'

'Come and get me, Mummy.'

'I can't, darling. I have to get dressed.'

'Morning, Rosie!'

Rosie peeked through the railings. Yolande stood in the middle of the hall, resplendent in a primrose-yellow top and Not Your Daughter's jeans, ash-blonde hair perfectly highlighted and coral lipstick ('It makes your teeth appear so much whiter') applied. Her slightly sarcastic tone suggested it was nearly noon, rather than literally the crack of dawn.

'Morning, Yolande, be down in just a sec'.' Rosie started crawling back to the bedroom. She hoped Rupert didn't look up.

'What are you doing, Mummy?' George yelled. Rosie ignored him. Safe in the bedroom, she pulled on yesterday's jeans and top. Oh, Yolande and Rupert. Why were they five hours early? Couldn't they give them just a little more space? She hadn't seen her own mother for years, but this was taking things to another extreme altogether.

Jake had two siblings, but his mother often seemed to forget that. Fraser the oldest was, at forty-three, a surfing addict, who spent his life travelling from beach to beach in pursuit of the perfect wave, supporting himself through the occasional bartending job. Becki, the second child, led a blameless existence as a teaching assistant and slightly smug mother of four in Swindon.

But Yolande clearly longed for glamour and excitement in contrast to her own respectable but unexciting life as an accountant, and her hopes for this were all invested in Jake. At school, he'd told Rosie, his mother had attended every single football, cricket and rugby match he took part in, yelling 'Kill them!' from the sidelines. There were days' worth of video footage of Jake in every school and uni play and, after uni, it had been Yolande who'd persuaded him to reach for the stars and audition for drama school.

Every review from every fringe play Jake had been in, no matter how ropey or obscure, was pasted into a scrapbook. As break after break eluded Jake, Yolande had been the one to insist he kept plugging away, never gave up hope. And so now fame had finally, belatedly, arrived, she was ecstatic. She'd taken charge of their new wealth, investing Jake's money, urging them to buy the biggest property they could. Rosie was a little bit apprehensive about listening to her – after all, not that long ago, she'd lost virtually all of the family's money in some dodgy pyramid scheme; they'd only kept the house because it was in Rupert's – a retired dentist – name. But Yolande had learned her lesson, she told them repeatedly, and property was always a safe bet.

Her interest was touching really, Rosie told herself as Toby screamed, 'Mummy! Come and get me! I'm scared!'

'Oh, Tobes.' Rosie hurried out of the room and down the stairs and long corridor to Toby's room. Her son was sitting in his bed, duvet pulled around him, his earnest little nose poking out. 'What is it?'

'It's scary in this room. Something lives in that cupboard.'

He pointed at the huge built-in wardrobe, which Rosie had fallen in love with. No more toys scattered all over the floor. She obsessed over storage like she'd obsessed over pop music as a teenager. It was one of the many freaky ways in which motherhood had changed her life.

'Nothing lives in the cupboard, Tobes. Shall I look for you?' She opened the door. 'See? Nothing.'

Toby's expression was dubious.

'Oh, darling.' Rosie picked him up and carried him to the cupboard, enjoying the warmth of his body against hers, the smell of tousled mousy hair. 'See?'

'OK.'

'Granny and Grandpa are downstairs. Shall we go and see them?'

In the kitchen Rupert was sitting at their tiny Ikea dining table reading the paper. He was wearing a beautifully ironed blue shirt that set off his eyes, and his grey hair was immaculate. Rupert was a very handsome man, but surprisingly low-key for someone so good-looking. Yolande was reading something on her iPhone.

'I see Billy Whitely's got a part in the new Trevor Nunn musical,' she said to Jake. Billy Whiteley had been the star of Jake's year at drama school and had long been a thorn in Yolande's side. 'But the last thing he did bombed, so he needs a hit.'

'Billy's all right, Mum.'

'What about Julianna Frost? Haven't seen her in anything for ages.' Yolande tapped ferociously into Google. She visited the IMDB site about nine hundred and twenty-seven times a day.

'Julianna's just had a baby,' Rosie said firmly. She liked

Julianna and refused to encourage her mother-in-law's aspersions.

'Your lawn needs cutting,' said Yolande, putting down the phone and turning towards the French windows that led into the garden. 'We should have brought the mower; Dad could have done it.' She began walking around the room, proprietorially sweeping imaginary specks of dust off the Shaker units. 'This is lovely, but gosh, they could have left it cleaner.' She bent down to kiss Toby. 'How is Granny's boy? Granny's bought you some sweeties for later. Mind you, it's all dependent on you eating a good lunch. Do you know, I was talking to your Auntie Becki and she says when Noah was nearly five, he *loved* nothing more than broccoli and salmon and roast potatoes. Do you think if Granny cooked broccoli and salmon and roast potatoes for your lunch you could eat it all up and we could tell Noah what a good boy you are?'

'No,' said Toby.

'I was planning on doing pasta for lunch,' Rosie said.

Yolande wrinkled her nose. She didn't consider pasta a proper meal – where was the meat? 'But I've filled the freezer already with home-cooked meals. Just like I used to. Remember, Perry, when you were a bachelor boy? That'll take the pressure off, won't it?'

'That's so kind of you.' Rosie's heart sank. She hated Yolande's cooking. It was all overdone roasts and soggy vegetables. But some battles were simply not worth fighting.

'Think nothing of it. Now – and you needn't thank me for this either – I have a little surprise for you all. Well, actually, quite a big surprise. Rupert go and fetch it, love. Perry, you can help.'

'Why does Granny call Daddy "Perry"?' Toby asked as the men went outside. Out of the corner of her eye, Rosie could see them unloading things from the back of the ancient Range Rover. Oh no. Oh help.

'Mummy, *why*?'

'Darling, you know the answer to that.' Oh bugger. Not that hideous carpet that looked like a homage to a Tarantino shoot-out.

'No, I don't!'

'You do.' She smiled. Toby loved hearing the same things again and again; it reassured him.

'It's his real name, love,' Yolande said. 'Peregrine. Peregrine Merlin Jake-Clements. I loved the name Peregrine when I was pregnant, it reminded me of a falcon sailing through the skies. We all called him Perry when he was a boy. Grandpa and I still do.'

'But why is he Jake Perry now?'

Less posh, Rosie thought, as her mother-in-law explained. 'Shorter. Peregrine Jake-Clements is a terrible mouthful for people to have to remember.'

'So his real name is Perry?'

'Yes. But he's been Jake for ages. Since he was twenty-two and went to drama school.'

'But *I'm* Toby Perry?'

'You're Toby Perry, love,' Yolande agreed. 'Daddy

changed his name by something called deed poll. And George is George Perry and Mummy is—'

'And Mummy is Rosie Prest,' Rosie said firmly. She'd always vowed never to change her name if and when she got married. It was the most pointless, old-fashioned exercise she could imagine. Yolande shook her head as if George had said something cute.

'And Mummy *was* Rosie Prest until she married Daddy.'

'She's still Rosie Prest,' Rosie said firmly. 'Yolande, have you seen the house yet? Do you want Toby to give you a tour?'

'Come and see the lounge, Granny.' Toby pulled at Yolande's arm.

Yolande blenched. 'Living room, darling.'

Rosie concealed a smile, as Rupert in the hallway yelled: 'Come and look!'

Just as she'd feared – a pile of ancient furniture sat there. Well, that was going straight to the tip.

'We really don't need all this any more,' Yolande said. 'But it'll be so much help to you in this enormous space.' She picked up a pair of violet flowery curtains that Rosie dimly remembered seeing in their spare bedroom. 'Look at these. We thought we'd get shutters in that room but they'd be ideal for you. Look what good-quality they are. Lined and everything.' She waved a fake gold vase in the air. 'And this'll be useful for all the flowers everyone's sending Perry.'

'This is good too,' said Rupert proudly, patting a

huge dark mahogany dressing table. 'Excellent quality. Antique. It'll be murder to get up those stairs, mind. Still, I think I'm fit enough. Did I tell you I've joined a new gym? Shall we try after lunch, Perry?'

The boys were beating each other round the head with ancient tennis rackets with half the strings missing.

'You could get those restrung easily and then the boys could start learning. I'm sure my friend Dorothy's granddaughter already does toddler tennis. It's never too early, you know.'

To garner ingredients for Yolande's lunch, they took her for a walk around the Village.

'It's delightful!' cried Yolande as they stood at the Village pond, the boys throwing handfuls of grain (which cost an extortionate fifty pence a bag, chucking in old bread crusts was strictly forbidden) at the overfed ducks, who showed no interest whatsoever in their bounty. 'Thank goodness you're out of that horrible place.'

'I didn't mind Neasden, actually,' said Rosie. All right, it had had its rough edges, but she loved the feeling of so many people from all over the world living so closely together and largely getting on, the way nineteen different languages were spoken by the children at the nursery. The Village, she could see already, wasn't like that at all. Nearly everyone, apart from the men who served them in the little Sainsbury's Local was fair-skinned, and the shops all sold elaborate cards and fridge magnets, instead of yam and persimmon.

'So much better for the boys being here,' said Yolande, though her words were almost drowned out by a Boeing overhead, coming in to land at Heathrow. 'Loads more fresh air for them. Now have you thought any more about schools?'

Rosie braced herself. 'We've put Toby's name on the waiting list for the local primary but it's full, so we'll just have to hope a space comes up.' This had been her main reservation about moving to the area – no school places for September, but Jake and Yolande had overridden her, saying surely a family would move out and, anyway, they were rich enough to send the boys to private schools now.

Rosie couldn't really get her head around private schools. Her own school had had its grim sides, like the handful of girls who disappeared around GCSE time, whom six months later she bumped into at Cribbs Causeway pushing buggies, but she'd emerged OK. She found the idea of buying a better life for your child strangely repellent, especially when that child was only just four.

'The private schools round here are excellent. Have you called them yet?' Yolande persisted.

'No. I will.' *Suppose they look at me and don't like what they see? Suppose they see a girl from a cramped flat in St Pauls?*

'You should at least take a look. We educated Perry privately and look what an advantage it's bought him. You can't entertain these silly notions about fairness when you're a mother. You want to do what's best for your children.'

'Mmm.' Time to change the subject. 'Boys!' she called. 'Shall we go and find the playground? We'll be spending a lot of time there.'

'You haven't forgotten the party in June?' Yolande said anxiously. 'For Fraser?'

'Of course not.' Yolande had been planning the party to welcome the prodigal son (briefly) home for months and checked with Rosie at least once a month that it was in the diary. 'I can't wait.'

'The neighbours are all very excited Perry will be there. Tell him to start practising his autograph.'

'I think he's already pretty good at that.'

From: Yolande_JakePerry@messages.com
To: Rosie.Prest@emayle.co.uk

Dear Rosie,

So kind of you to host us this weekend. Your house is delightful, as I always knew it would be, and Rupert and I are thrilled for you and Perry. With a few homely touches it will be even nicer. I'd hang those curtains in George's bedroom.

Don't forget not to waste too much time before looking at schools – we want our Toby to have the best possible start in life, after all. I know your financial circumstances did make it hard for you to do anything but send him to nursery when he was so little, but let's try to make it up to him now, shall we?

On which note, Granny was a little bit concerned about his and George's eating this weekend. I never had any trouble with my three and I do think a firmer line is needed. Tell them I went out with my friend Dorothy yesterday and her little granddaughter, who is only two, ate sweetcorn (half), two roast potatoes, peas and tiny bit of chicken followed by treacle tart. At four thirty p.m. she had a snack of raisins, two crackers, an apple and a beaker of milk. Having said that, she still doesn't speak in sentences like the boys, or indeed any of my grandchildren, did at this age, but that is not her fault – after all they are exceptionally advanced.

With much love,
Yolande

PS DON'T FORGET ABOUT THE SCHOOLS.

PPS Tell Perry that Miles Hogan, who was in his year, has just been cast in rep in a Pinter revival in Doncaster. 'One-nil to the Perrys.'

   PPPS PLEASE double-check you haven't booked anything else for the weekend of our party. Fraser is now saying he may be at a surf competition in Mexico, but 'the show must go on' with or without him.

3

The three-day heatwave that had had everyone talking excitedly about staycations and barbecues was over. Now the grass on the Green was waterlogged. Buggies' sun screens had been replaced by rain hoods. The skies were light blue and dappled with clouds as Rosie, Toby and George crossed the Green, en-route to the Conifers and the first birthday party of their new lives.

Rosie had been so excited when the boys came running out of Wendy's, their new nursery school, waving the white envelope.

'Mummy, Mummy, we've been invited to Santos and Michael's birthday party.'

'Wow, boys, that's great. Who are Santos and Michael?'

'Them,' said Wendy darkly, standing at the nursery door, gesturing towards two boys in matching blue corduroy knickerbockers and striped shirts with Peter Pan collars being shepherded out of the gates by two nannies. Rosie had been aghast the first time she spotted them, not only because there was a nanny for each child, but also because they were wearing grey uniforms. Had she stepped back into the nineteen thirties?

'Twins?'

'Mmm hmm,' said Wendy, and then, out of the corner of her mouth, 'Fertility treatment, obviously.'

'Ah!'

Wendy was a very tall Kiwi in her sixties. She wore lots of make-up in shades of coral that matched her tightly permed hair. She almost never smiled and appeared to have no interest in children whatsoever, though she did like to gossip about the parents and in the past three days had already informed Rosie that Isla's parents were in the middle of a bitter divorce (Rosie had no idea which one Isla was), and that she thought Freddie's mummy should go easy on the snacks (Rosie had spotted Freddie because he was, indeed, slightly on the chubby side). Who knew what she was telling the other mums about Rosie?

Wendy didn't appear to like children much either, making her an ideal candidate for running a nursery. So why had Rosie chosen to send her two precious children to such an establishment? Because it was the only nursery within a fifteen-mile radius with vacancies. Call her a bad mother, but Rosie simply wasn't convinced that if in thirty years' time her sons lay on the couch of a serious-looking lady with interesting jewellery it would be because of the three hours daily they spent as toddlers playing with Lego at Wendy's, which had places available, as opposed to the Montessori down the road with ninety-eight children on its waiting list. After all, the boys seemed happy enough there. Wendy didn't actually beat them, even if she didn't smile at them much, and her failings were compensated for by the rest of the staff, who were all cuddly, smiling ladies.

'It should be quite a party,' Wendy said. 'Patrizia and Gary aren't short of cash. He's a major hedge-fund manager. She's a Brazilian heiress.'

'How . . . nice.' Rosie clapped her hands as if she were auditioning for a CBBC presenter job. 'Come on, children. Home we go!'

'I'd make sure the boys are looking a bit smarter than usual,' Wendy said, turning back inside.

Outside the gates, Rosie ripped open the invitation. It was on stiff white card, like a wedding invite, with a multi-coloured, childish raised font.

Santos and Michael
invite Toby and George
to their fourth birthday party!!!
On Saturday at 3 p.m.
See you there!!!!

There was a mobile number for RSVPs. As soon as they were home Rosie sent a text accepting. She was excited. She tried to kid herself it was because the boys were making friends, but really it was because of the potential the party offered her. Now she was a full-time mum she needed to make mum chums to hang out with.

So far she'd been too shy so far to pluck up conversation with any of Wendy's mums at the gates – not that there were many mums around. Pick-ups seemed to be done mainly by bored-looking nannies (although Santos and Michael's were the only ones actually in uniform) and au pairs. The couple of mothers she had clocked had looked like illustrations from a *Sunday Times Style* article about mummies, right down to their Acne Pistol boots, as opposed to the exhausted creatures in suits splodged with baby sick that Rosie used to bump into outside Happy Tots in Neasden. But in Neasden everyone was a working mum and the nursery – open from seven a.m. to six p.m. – was their lifeline.

Wendy's, on the other hand, with its three-hour morning sessions, existed clearly in order to allow mothers a window in which to shop, have facials or torrid sex with the gardener.

Rosie missed her Happy Tots posse. Parvaneh, who'd been her best friend at uni, who'd turned up, living just down the road, who always cracked open the wine during play dates (for them not the children), and Nola, who lived two doors down, whose kids reassuringly always slept even worse, ate worse and behaved worse than Rosie's – though Nola was moving to the countryside anyway, so wouldn't have been around for much longer.

They'd forged a lifelong bond, navigating the trenches of early motherhood together. After maternity leave, she hadn't seen as much of them as she'd have liked but they were always there for her at weekends when Jake had been away filming or appearing in a fringe play in Lancaster.

They'd gone to the pub to bid Rosie farewell and drunkenly promised stay in touch forever. But they all privately knew they wouldn't. It was a question of geography. Before Rosie was a mum she had friends all over London. In the evenings and at weekends, they all jumped on tubes and met up in Soho and caught night buses home, but now it would only have been marginally tougher to trek to the South Pole than to cross the capital and back with two small boys, who needed to go to bed at around seven. Rosie's horizons had narrowed to the surrounding streets and she needed to comb them for buddies. The party would be a start.

So now it was Saturday, ten to three. Two junior science kits had been ineptly wrapped (Rosie hoped the Brazilian heiress would note she'd given both boys a present, rather than measly joint one – an educational yet fun present too, she thought), and the boys were in their only smart trousers, which Rosie had actually ironed – so eager was she to make the right impression.

She was in a gingham sundress with a huge flared skirt that she'd bought for an enormous sum in Selfridges a couple of days before she finished at Tapper-Green, when she was at the height of her *Mad Men* fixation. Rosie wasn't much of a one for dresses, wasn't much of a one for fancy clothes generally, let alone hairdos and elaborate make-up – she was too cack-handed to do any of that properly and, anyway, dolling herself up brought back queasy memories of her own mother doing the same before disappearing all night with whoever the latest boyfriend was. But the Betty Draper dress seemed the kind of thing mums in the Village would wear, though when she put it on she found she moved more carefully than normal and was more reluctant to have the boys wipe their sticky faces against her.

'Have fun!' yelled Jake, who was slumped on the sofa watching the cricket, delighted to discover he had the afternoon off.

'Sure you don't want to come?'

'Positive. A load of mums saying "Not on *my* patio." No, thanks. I'll be just fine here, drinking beer on my lonesome ownsome and suffering the Test match.'

The Conifers was a ten-minute walk away on the other side of the Green, surrounded by high white-washed walls like those of an enlightened Norwegian prison. The gates, with a unicorn crest woven into the metalwork, were decorated with fat silver balloons. They stepped through them on to the drive of a house that made Rosie and Jake's place look like a cottage and which was jammed with shiny four-by-fours. Little girls in smocked party dresses with little ankle socks and patent Mary Janes. Boys in chinos. All staggering under huge, clearly professionally wrapped parcels. Suddenly the science kits didn't seem like such a great idea any more.

They climbed the front steps and passed through the

front door, which was being held open by a uniformed maid. Rosie's stomach lolloped. A maid. She thought she was living in a grand house, but not retainer-style grand. The fact they were going to have to employ a cleaner had been daunting enough for her.

'Through there,' the maid said, nodding across the vast hallway – again, it made the Perry's entrance look like an aeroplane aisle. Ahead of them was a beautiful cantilevered oak staircase rising up to the heavens. To the left were open double doors. George charged through them, Toby held back.

'No, Mummy! I'm scared!'

'Nonsense, darling, it'll be fun!'

Rosie was petrified too. She'd never enjoyed making entrances.

'No!' Toby squawked.

'It'll be all the children from Wendy's. All your friends.'

'They're *not* my friends. Everybody hates me.'

Rosie felt as if she'd been pushed into a freezer. This was news. Wendy had said he was settling in well. 'They *are* your friends, sweetie,' she said firmly, and holding tightly on to his hand she led him into the room. It was gigantic with wall-to-wall cream carpets. Two low-slung cowhide sofas sat in the middle around what looked like a chunk of driftwood and the walls were covered in huge abstract splashes. Not a toy or a children's item in sight, nor a single book. Houses without books always made Rosie uneasy, quite unreasonably. The first things she'd unpacked had been her own huge collection of paperbacks, even though they looked tatty on Louis and Samantha's pristine shelves.

In the far corner, a clown was playing a guitar and singing, with a group of children kneeling in front of him, including George. Near the door stood a group of women, all in skinny jeans and floaty tops, some of whom Rosie recognized from the Wendy's gates. Immediately she knew her gingham dress was all wrong. Cymbals clashed uneasily in her chest. Everyone looked so polished, like furniture in a showroom.

'Hello,' said a small lady in jeans (white) and floaty top (sort of scarlet and brown). Her black hair was in a severe Louise Brooks bob. Despite a totally creaseless face, Rosie would have put her at early fifties. 'I am Patrizia, the twins' mother. Welcome! And you are . . . ?'

'Toby and George's mum,' Rosie said, holding out a hand. 'Rosie. Thank you so much for inviting us – I mean, them. This is Toby,' she added, indicating the child clinging to her leg.

'Pleasure, pleasure, welcome to the Village. Love the dress! Giorgio Armani?'

'No, Giorgio at Asda,' Rosie quipped.

Patrizia looked puzzled. 'Wendy told us all about you,' she said after a second's hesitation. She looked over Rosie's shoulder, disappointment flickering in her brown eyes. 'So, no husband?'

'Um, I didn't know he was invited.'

'But of course, we all wanted to meet him so much.

We're such fans. "Not on *my* patio."' Patrizia laughed uproariously, then snapped to attention. 'You don't have a drink.' She waved at another uniformed minion, who approached with a tray of flutes. 'Champagne?'

'Thank you.'

'There are nibbles.' Patrizia looked around crossly. 'Where's that girl gone? I hope you like sushi, we had our friends at Nobu prepare it.'

'I *love* sushi.' Though she hated the word 'nibbles'; it was in the category she reserved for 'crease', 'sassy' and 'hubby'. Inwardly Rosie was panicking. It was George's birthday in July, Toby's in October, and she'd been thinking along the lines of a few kids coming over to bounce on the trampoline. Was she now expected to host a party complete with sushi chefs? She looked around. 'I love those paintings.'

'Saatchi tipped us off about the artist; he's very hot. Such a shame your husband couldn't make it.'

'Yes, well, I'm here!' Rosie smiled again, as a Chinese-looking woman drifted over.

'Patrizia, you're looking so well!' Air kisses were exchanged. 'Have you lost weight?'

'I had lunchtime lipo on Thursday.' Patrizia sounded as nonchalant as if she were mentioning popping into Boots for shampoo. The two women started talking animatedly about a waiting list for a bag – Patrizia was twenty-seventh, while the other woman was jealous she hadn't even been able to get a placing. No introductions were made, so Rosie after a second or two standing

43

twisting her hands, bent down to Toby and said: 'Shall we go and see what Georgie is doing?'

'No! Stay here.'

He'd always been like this at toddler groups, refusing to interact with other children, screaming if one of them tried to 'share' toys with him and rushing back to Rosie, who, on her one day off from work, would be trying to make polite conversation with a stranger. George on the other hand had no problem mucking in. Right now, he was picking his nose and occasionally prodding the little boy beside him, who was dressed in a fawn pullover and fawn cords. Rosie wagged a finger at him and sat on one of the rock-hard cowhide sofas. She tried to place her champagne flute on the driftwood table, but the surface was too uneven for her to risk it. Toby sat at her feet.

'The wheels on the bus go round and round,' sang the clown, whose name badge read Gary Guitar, 'round and round, round and round.'

'Hey,' said a toothpick-slim woman in a wrap dress, sitting down beside her. 'I'm Caroline. I hear you're Jake Perry's wife. "Not on *my* patio." God, I love that programme.'

'Rosie.'

'Your husband's working today? Gosh, even mine manages to take Sundays off. Turns off the iPhone for a couple of hours. Financial pages are banned.'

'He has a big show coming up in the West End,' Rosie said, thinking of her big-shot husband slumped in front of the cricket, blinds drawn, hands no doubt in his comfort position down the front of his tracksuit bottoms.

'What's the show?'

'It's Shakespeare. An updated version of *Twelfth Night*. Starring Ellie Lewis.'

'Ellie Lewis! Oh my God. What's she like?'

'I've no idea. I haven't met her.' Of course she'd been badgering Jake for gossip every day but he had none. He said Ellie was very professional and spent all her time offstage in her dressing room, never socializing with the rest of the cast and crew.

'Ellie Lewis in Shakespeare. I'd love to see that. Can you get us tickets?'

People always asked this. 'Er, it's probably better to go through the box office, so you can go the night you want.' Luckily Caroline didn't press the point, unlike the random mum at Tiny Tots whom Rosie had never exchanged a word with, who out of the blue demanded two front stalls tickets on a Saturday night to see Jake in his tiny bit part in *Flutes and Rosalinds* in the West End, the play that got him noticed by the woman casting *Archbishop Grace*.

'Five green speckled frogs, sat on a yellow log.'

George's hand had wandered down the front of his pants, just like his dad's when he wasn't concentrating. Rosie glared at him but he didn't notice. Suddenly the children gave a collective shout of delight. Rosie looked around. Behind Gary Guitar, an enormous Peppa Pig had appeared, who started gyrating vigorously to the music.

'Peppa, Peppa, Peppa!' The children leaped to their feet and flocked around her, as if she were Jesus giving his Sermon on the Mount. Gary looked distinctly put out and started strumming louder. Peppa's dancing became even more flamboyant. The children fought to high-five her. Gary stopped playing.

'Peppa,' he said between gritted teeth. 'Would you mind terribly waiting your turn in the other room? Just until I've finished.'

Peppa attempted a high five.

Gary loftily ignored him. 'Please, Peppa?'

With a sulky shrug, Peppa ambled off. The children shrieked in disappointment.

'Well, children. How about "Zoom, zoom, zoom. We're going to . . ."'

'Waaan' Peppa!'

'Well, you're getting Gary,' Mr Guitar said over brightly.

'Sorry, I lost you for a moment there,' said Patrizia, sitting down beside Rosie. 'So how are your boys settling in at Wendy's? I know some people say it's not up to the standard of the Montessori, but have you been to that place? The atmosphere is so restrictive. Wendy's children are creative, who cares if they don't get as many children into St Botolph's? The Montessori children all have tutors to pass the assessment.'

'They're loving Wendy's, but they're bloody hard

work when they get home at the moment,' Rosie replied truthfully, wondering what St Botolph's and 'the assessment' was. 'They're both really playing up at bedtime. It takes hours to get them from the bath into bed and then I'm too frazzled to do anything more than have a glass of wine and collapse myself.'

Patrizia tried and failed to raise an eyebrow. 'I never have this problem with my boys. I insist on total calm for an hour before bedtime. You know, reading, perhaps listening to classical music.' She winked like Sarah Palin. 'Try it. You'll be surprised.'

She wafted away from the fight that was rapidly developing between Gary and Peppa, leaving Rosie reeling. In Neasden when you said something like this it was a cue for the other mum to comfort you by retorting: 'Think that's bad? My kids are both up on charges of GBH.' Like when you said: 'I'm so fat,' your friend was supposed to reply: 'Oh no, you're not. *I'm* so fat.' But Patrizia obviously wouldn't. Patrizia would say: 'Well, have lipo then, like me.'

She downed her glass in one. 'We're not in Neasden any more, Rosie,' she told herself, and took some sashimi on a skewer from a waitress. She dipped it in the soy sauce. It splattered all over the Betty dress.

4

A week had passed. It was Sunday morning and the family were in the car, coming off the M4 into Bristol, for the monthly visit to Nanna. *Silly Songs* tootled out of the ancient speakers and Rosie's eyes were watering: the enormous bouquet she'd bought Nanna that morning was giving her hay fever. But who cared? It was so exciting to be able to treat her grandmother.

'Why can't Nanna come and see us?' George asked, kicking the back of Rosie's seat.

'She's too old, darling, it would be too tricky for her.'

'She could get in the car.'

'She doesn't have a car.'

'We could buy her one. We're rich now.'

Rosie and Jake exchanged glances. The boys had been making a few remarks like this. They needed to be nipped in the bud.

'She's too old to drive,' Jake said. 'She's eighty-nine.'

'Will she live to be a hundred? Will she get a birthday card from the queen?'

'I hope so,' Rosie said. 'And I hope she does come to visit us one day. I'll pick her up and she'll stay for a week. I want her to see the new house.' She didn't mention her secret dream, that maybe one day Nanna would be persuaded to leave the little flat above the now-bankrupt bookies and move in with them. She'd earmarked the 'boudoir', as Samantha had called it, on the ground floor with a view of the garden for transformation into a Nanna flat with en suite.

'Did you really grow up, here, Mummy?' George asked, as they left the city centre with its Costas and branches of Paperchase and carried on into St Pauls with its derelict-looking terraces, tower blocks and scary-looking pubs.

'Certainly did,' Rosie said cheerfully. She had made a firm decision some time back to never be ashamed of her origins. She'd suffered throughout school, but she was over it now.

'If we keep on visiting, then I think we should put the idea of a new car on the back burner,' said Jake. 'Something fancy will be wrecked in seconds.'

Toby panicked. 'Is somebody going to hurt our car?'

'No, darling,' Rosie soothed, nudging her husband. 'Everything is going to be just fine. And of course we're going to keep visiting.'

'Of course we are. Sorry, I didn't mean it like that.'

Nanna lived up two steep flights of stairs.

'How can she manage with her shopping?' Jake asked.

'I know. I'm going to see if Ocado deliver here.'

'Let's hope the delivery men wear flak jackets.'

'Enough!' Rosie snapped. She glared at Jake. He was annoying her today.

Nanna had been watching them park from behind her net curtains and was standing at her front door.

'You're early! Were you sick, lover?' She chucked George under the chin. Nanna called everyone 'lover'; it was a Bristol thing. 'No? Well done.'

'Couldn't wait to see you, Marjorie.' Jake kissed Nanna on the cheek. Rosie smiled. She'd been in love with Jake from the second she laid eyes on him. But when she'd taken him to visit Nanna (he hadn't said rude things about St Pauls that time, in fact he'd clearly been rather impressed that his girlfriend had grown up in something resembling a 'hood) she'd known it was forever. He'd chatted to Nanna so warmly, rather than tolerating her like her ex, Adam, would have done – not that Adam would ever even have agreed to give up a weekend of hangovers and football to visit an old lady.

'Come in. Kettle's on. I've got chips in the oven for you, boys. I know even you love chips, fusspot Toby. And a Mars Bar each for afters. Oh my goodness gracious, Rosie Prest. Is this for me?'

'Who did you think it was for?' Rosie handed her the bouquet, trying to hold in a sneeze. Her flower allergy had never been an issue until Jake became famous, but now someone seemed to send them a huge bouquet virtually every week and she was getting through boxes of tissues like Elvis devoured cheeseburgers.

'I don't have a vase for it,' Nanna said, pretending to sound cross, though you could tell she was delighted.

Rosie glowed. This was what this sudden burst of fortune was all about – being able to treat your loved ones.

'I thought of that!' Rosie stepped back into the tiny hall and returned with the huge crystal vase she'd bought yesterday from an extortionately priced gift shop in the village. It reminded her of the one Christy used to have in her sitting room.

'Oh, you! There's no space for it.'

'Oh.' Nanna was right. 'It'll fit on the counter top if you move the bread bin,' Rosie said dubiously, handing it over.

'All right,' Nanna said, taking it. But when she stepped backwards the vase dropped on the floor, smashing into a million pieces.

'Oh bugger it!' Nanna slammed her fist on the counter.

'Never mind, Nanna. Sit down. I'll tidy up.' Rosie took a dustpan from the cupboard under the sink.

'I'm so sorry, lover.'

'Don't be mad, Nanna. It's a vase. I'll buy you another one. A smaller one.' She started sweeping up. Nanna sat at the kitchen table. She looked devastated; in fact, she was trembling. Not like her at all. Rosie looked at her more closely. Her skin was very pale, her eyes seemed larger and her cheekbones more defined than on their last visit.

'Nanna, you're losing weight still. Are you OK?'

'Never better.'

'This place is tiny. Did you really live here, Mummy?' Toby was incredulous.

'Toby, you know I did,' Rosie said crossly, still sweeping, as Nanna replied calmly. 'She lived here until she was eighteen. She did all her homework at that table, while I cooked.'

'And my mum slept,' Rosie said more sharply than she'd intended.

'Well, she was usually working nights.' Nanna always defended her only daughter when Rosie criticized her. 'I don't know how we managed, but we did. Now, who wants a beer? Then tell me about Ellie Lewis.'

Nanna was an *O'Rourke's* devotee. Rosie had given her the complete box set for Christmas and she watched the episodes again and again. She couldn't believe her grandson-in-law was actually spending every day with the most glamorous cast member.

'There's nothing much to tell,' sighed Jake, who was bored of this line of questioning. 'She's having trouble learning the lines, she spends every break on the phone to the US and she doesn't socialize with us.'

'Does she have a fella? Someone as beautiful as her must.'

'Not that I'm aware. Like I say, she doesn't talk to us mortals. She's not really coming to grips with Shakespeare.'

'Well, why would she be? She's comes from Nowheresville, Ohio, not Stratford-upon-Avon. And how's your beautiful new house? I'm so looking forward to seeing it.'

'I'll show you photos,' Jake said, pulling out his phone. While Nanna peered at the shots of the house – 'How will you keep it clean? Oh, you'll have a cleaner will you? And a gardener? Well, yes, you'll need one' – and the boys watched CBeebies on the telly in the corner, Rosie wandered to the window and stared out at the boarded-up shopfronts across the way.

When she'd lived here there'd been, respectively, a fish and chip shop – they must have been its best customers – and a hairdressers. Rosie remembered sitting in that chair, a scratchy black gown on, having her first professional cut aged thirteen – before that Nanna had always done it with a pudding bowl and, God, it had shown.

There'd been a newsagents and a corner shop too. All gone now, destroyed by the power of Cribbs Causeway and the Internet. Nanna had to walk a mile both ways in each direction now, when she ran out of fags.

She turned back to the room. Nanna was chatting to Jake as she chucked frozen peas into boiling water. On the stained wall beside her was a poster of Snoopy and Charlie Brown lying back to back. 'All You Need Is Love' was the slogan. For years Rosie had thought it the cutest thing she'd ever seen. Next to it there was a photo of Rosie the summer after GCSEs. God, she looked awful, she thought. That unfortunate bleached mop of hair, the horrible peachy lipstick, the terribly applied fake tan — fake tan had dominated those years, she'd ruined so many sheets with the stuff. The grey and yellow T-shirt from Jane Norman too — whatever happened to Jane Norman? Did it still exist? What nonsense that your teens were your salad days. Every single thing about Rosie's life was better now. The only good thing about that photo was she wasn't wearing her horrible black-framed glasses — when she was fourteen Christy had nagged her into getting contact lenses, which Rosie had paid for with the funds from her paper round.

She owed it all to Christy. And to Nanna, for making sure she met Christy. Brightman's, their school, was on the other side of town, and even though they lived nowhere near the catchment, Nanna had wangled her a place by working for the feeder primary Mount Seward for a few terms as a dinner lady. Nanna was always looking out for her.

Mount Seward wasn't a particularly special school either, but compared to the local primary it was Eton College. Rosie's journey there involved two bus rides, which she loved because she spent them reading: something that was very hard to do in the flat with Mum's music always turned up full blast. Christy had lived just two roads away from Mount Seward.

She didn't really hang out with Christy at first. Christy had been best friends with Belinda Crighton, who was the class golden girl. But when Christy turned eight, twelve of them were invited to her birthday party. Rosie wore her best dress, which Nanna had bought her in the Tammy Girl sale – a sailor number with a huge sailor collar shot with gold thread and – after some nagging from Rosie – money was found to buy Christy a splendid colouring book that Rosie had coveted for herself. Christy, who answered the door to Rosie, beaming, was in a white frilly dress – the antithesis of the kind of thing she wore now – which emphasized her round tummy. Her brown curls hung round her cheeks in ringlets like Nanna's old dolly Violet.

'You're here!' she cried. 'Mummy said you might not come. She said your grandmother might not be able to afford the bus fare.'

'Of course she could afford the bus fare,' Rosie replied, immediately defensive.

But Christy just laughed and held out her hand. 'Let me give you a tour. That's what Mummy always does.'

Rosie couldn't get over the size of Christy's house. It was on two storeys, with a huge, mature garden, and the furniture was all new and white. Everything was immaculate: cushions were plumped, surfaces were dust-free. Christy had a gorgeous dressing table in her bedroom, white with a massive gilt-edged mirror and draped in hot-pink taffeta like something from the Sindy bedroom set Nanna refused to buy Rosie, because it was too expensive. Maybe they *were* poor then. An empty perfume bottle – 'One of Mummy's old ones,' Christy had said – sat on top, next to an lacy embroidered tissue-box cover and a silver-backed mirror.

Rosie had gasped, gazing around. 'This is so beautiful. If I lived somewhere like this, I'd never feel sad again.' In the hallway Christy opened a little door that revealed a tiny washroom with pink walls. 'Even your toilet sparkles.'

'So you must be Rosie,' said a cool voice behind them. It was the first time Rosie had seen Christy's mother Sandra Papadopolous. She was tall, taller than Christy's dad, with bobbed brown hair, and was wearing a cream shirt dress, like a mother from a book. Mum always wore combats and T-shirts that revealed her tattoos. Rosie knew Sandra was a doctor at the local hospital; Nanna had made some remark about how both Christy's parents were doctors and how they couldn't have any money problems. She looked Rosie up and down slowly. Rosie shifted from one foot to another and looked down to check her dress wasn't stained, then glanced in the mirror to see if her face was dirty. Something was wrong with her, Sandra was making that quite clear.

'Come along,' she said. 'The party's starting.'

The party was in the lounge. There was a big vase on the side table with criss-crosses etched into it. Christy said it was called a harlequin pattern. Three nights a week, she said, her mother filled it with fresh flowers. There were pink and white shiny balloons everywhere, and the table was laden with plates of cupcakes – brilliantly iced and decorated with little silver beads. There was a cake in the shape of a princess with a purple dress latticed with silver. They played games like pass the parcel and grandmother's footsteps with Nick Papadopolous being grandmother and wearing a silly orange wig. Rosie decided she liked Nick far more than Sandra.

The other unnerving presence had been Barron – Christy's older brother. Rosie had been dimly aware of a brother, but Christy had said something about him being at boarding school, a concept that Rosie had found so exotic – and frankly unbelievable – she'd simply put it out of her mind.

But there he was standing in a corner, hands in pockets, watching proceedings with dark eyes concealed by a too-long fringe. He was about twelve, Rosie recalled, but very tall for his age and he was fat too – not obese, but definitely chubby, and you didn't often see chubby children back in those days. Rosie was a little bit scared of him. Sometimes he tried to join in, but he got over-excited playing musical statues and knocked over Billy Wildman, who'd cried and cried, and Sandra, who'd been tidying up in the kitchen, appeared in a stripy pinny and said 'Barron! Sit down and behave!' in a soft voice that nonetheless chilled.

'But, Mum, it was an accident,' Barron protested in a growly voice, as Billy – who was a terrible wuss – continued to scream.

'I am not hearing any more from you today, Barron,' Sandra hissed. She never spoke to Christy that way. To everyone's horror Barron began to cry too – a twelve-year-old boy! Large, drippy, snotty-nosed sobs.

'Go to your room!' Sandra ordered. None of the children moved.

'Sandy,' Nick tried.

'I have had enough,' she said coldly to her husband. 'We should have sent him to a holiday camp. Go to your room.'

Barron left, shutting the door quietly behind him. After a moment, the party resumed. Everyone got a going-home present of a little packet of felt tips, some sweets and a tiny bouncy rubber ball. Sandra gave Rosie a special slice of the birthday cake that included the princess's crown. Rosie was overwhelmed. On the way home, next to Nanna on the bus, she'd vowed that one day she'd live in a house like Christy's and give all her guests little packets of treats when they left.

'You never told me about Barron,' she said to Christy on Monday.

'What do you want me to tell you? He was born with a funny ear and he didn't hear well until he had grommets put in. Mummy says he's difficult and so he had to go to boarding school.'

'Oh.'

'Shall I draw you a picture? I can't wait for your party.' Christy reached into her school bag.

'What are you looking for, *Christine*?' sneered Belinda, who'd just walked into the classroom. 'A tissue to wipe your brother's tears?'

'He's a cry baby,' said Julie Anderson, snatching the bag from Christy.

'Give it back, please,' Christy said calmly.

'Give it back, please,' Belinda mimicked.

'Don't cry,' Rosie said quietly. 'Take it back.'

Christy made a grab for it. Belinda and Julie started throwing the bag at each other over her head. 'Piggy in the middle. Your party was rubbish.'

Rosie dived in and snatched the bag. She handed it back to Christy, who sat at her desk stony-faced. 'Here you go. Leave her alone, you bullies.'

'Ooh, bullies,' mocked Belinda, as Miss Bryne entered the classroom. The teasing abruptly stopped, only to recommence at break time. From that day on, Christy ignored Belinda and she and Rosie were best friends.

'You're not with us, love,' Nanna said now, snapping her fingers under Rosie's nose. 'I was asking. So what are you going to do, living in this mansion as a lady of leisure?'

'I'll be busy with the boys, Nanna. They're only at nursery three hours a day.'

'Still three hours you have to fill. And then Toby'll be at school in September and George the next year. What will you do then?'

'That's a while off. I don't know, Nanna. Something will come up. I might start my own business.'

'Well, make sure it's not baking your own cupcakes, like those yummy mummies in the magazines.'

'It won't be cupcakes,' said Rosie.

Nanna stared at her fondly. 'I can't imagine you not working, love. You've always been such a grafter. Talking of which, any news from your mum?'

'She hasn't been in touch with you?' Rosie chewed a cuticle. It infuriated her the way her mother didn't keep tabs on Nanna.

'She called me a few weeks ago. Couldn't stop talking about you. Well, about Jake . . . She's very proud.'

Nice if she were proud of me, rather than who I married, Rosie thought. Time to change the subject. 'You're coming to the play, aren't you, Nanna?'

'Wild horses wouldn't keep me away,' Nanna said. 'I've written the first night in my calendar, and I've already booked a hairdo. I need to stun Ellie Lewis. What are you going to wear, lover?'

'I'm thinking of my dress from New Look.'

Nanna wrinkled her nose. 'You can do better than that. Don't worry, I'll scout out something for you next time Maureen gives me a lift over to Cribbs.' She clapped her hands. 'Boys, are you ready? Sausages and chips time!'

5

It was around six in the morning and she and Jake were lying in bed. George nestled between them slurping on his milk and tunelessly singing the 'bum-bum song', which he had recently composed. Normally she would feel flat and exhausted, but today was different.

Rosie was excited. Tonight Christy and Sandrine were visiting. Sandrine was travelling all the way down from Yorkshire and was going to stay for the next couple of nights. It was the first time they'd had people over for dinner, and Rosie had been planning it for days.

She'd bought lamb shoulder from the Village's butcher. (A butcher! *Her* butcher. Recipe books always said 'Ask your butcher' and she'd always snarled back, 'Where do you think I live? Little Snoring?' But no longer.).

She'd been soaking chickpeas overnight to make her legendary (immodest but true) side dish from a recipe torn from a copy of the *Lady* in the GP's waiting room. She was planning a huge tomato salad scattered with basil. They'd eat in Louis and Samantha's conservatory with its views out over the garden, and laugh and talk and toast their new home and Rosie would be floating on air, with her children asleep upstairs and her oldest friends and her husband all together in her forever home.

Jake said, 'Listen, Bean. Sorry to be a pain in the bum-bum, but I can't be here this evening.'

Rosie's insides turned cold: 'Why not?'

'This American agent is in town and he really wants to have dinner with me.'

'But Christy and Sandrine are coming! You knew that.'

'I know, I'm gutted. But I'll be back in time to see them. I'll just be out for dinner.'

'See him another time.'

'He's only in town tonight. I really do need to meet him. He's one of the biggest players in Hollywood. If he takes me on we could be talking sky's the limit. Bean, I'd rather be here with you than with some American bore eating gluten-free and raising his eyebrows when I have a glass of wine, but that's my job.'

'I thought your job was prancing around pretending to be someone else. Why didn't you tell me earlier?'

'Christy emailed me last night about it and I saw it when we'd just got back from your nanna's and it was chaos getting the boys into bed. I meant to tell you, but I forgot.'

He was so transparent: he meant he knew he'd get into trouble, so he'd decided to ambush Rosie at the last minute, when it would be too late to rearrange. What was Christy thinking of? She knew she was coming over, so why arrange an appointment that would clash? But then maybe Christy had done it on purpose. Maybe she saw enough of Jake at work, and wanted girl-time for the three of them?

'Off you go,' she said crossly.

Jake beamed in relief. 'You're a star, Old Bean. Thanks for being so understanding.'

'You didn't give me a lot of choice,' she mumbled.

'Sorry?'

'Nothing.'

In the afternoon, the boys played on the trampoline, without fighting too much, and Rosie cooked. By the time Jake headed off to Claridge's, the house was filled with appetizing smells and she was feeling rather proud of herself. This was her new life as a roaringly successful hostess. First, Christy and Sandrine, next the whole of the Wendy's mums for a buffet supper, then perhaps Simon Barry – *Twelfth Night*'s director and his German supermodel wife, Brunhilde von Fournigan – then Ellie Lewis and the rest of the cast, then the Obamas . . .

'I wish I didn't have to go out,' Jake said again.

'Oh, bugger off and have a lovely time.' Rosie kissed him on the cheek. He'd shaved, which she always loved, his skin felt so soft and raw.

He put his hand on her bottom. 'I wish no one was coming over. I wish I could just stay home alone with you.'

'Get off.' Rosie removed his hand. 'You don't want to be late for Mr Hollywood and I have to get the boys in the bath. Sandrine'll be here any minute.'

'Tell her I'll see her in the morning. She can cook me a fry-up.' He pulled an innocent face, at Rosie's mock-outraged expression. 'What? She does run a bloody B & B.'

'Just go!'

Half an hour later, the boys were in their pyjamas with their faces pressed to Toby's bedroom window that looked out over the drive. 'Sandrine!' yelled George. 'I can see her car.'

They dashed down the stairs, a whirlwind of arms and legs, to the front door. 'Hey!' cried Rosie as Sandrine's wide face loomed in the entry-system screen. She hit the button that opened the gates. Two seconds later, Sandrine was climbing out of her orange Renault and they were hugging each other hard. Rosie stepped back and looked at her. Sandrine was in jeans and a flowery top, she'd guess came from Evans in Manchester, which was Sandrine's favourite shop, catering, as it did, for the larger lady. Christy occasionally bought her something from somewhere like Brora, but Sandrine never wore it or shrunk it in the wash. Her hair was longer than before and she was wearing pink lipstick and purplish eyeshadow.

'How are you doing? Was the drive OK?'

'Piece of cake,' Sandrine replied, in her funny deep voice. 'About four hours door to door. And no worries about parking at the destination.' She grinned. 'Your own gated drive, lady. Now that's what I call fancy.'

'I told you,' Rosie giggled.

Toby pulled at Sandrine's arm. 'Come and see the garden. We've got a trampoline.'

64

'OK, my darling.' She gestured at her tiny wheelie case. 'Shall I just put this in my room first? I can't believe it. An actual bed. No more futon in the living room for me.'

A horn honked, as a silver Audi – Christy's – turned into the drive. Christy parked adeptly beside the Renault and jumped out. In so many ways she'd hardly changed since those Brightman's days. Same chestnut hair (with just a few highlights added) that she used to tie back in a ponytail, but which now framed her face in a chin-length bob, her curls tamed with expensive and time-consuming straightening treatments. Same big brown eyes and pointy nose, same alert expression as she gazed around her.

She was wearing a dress with a black skirt and a top with a pattern of exploding red flowers and flat pumps in a red that reflected the colours. The effect was very French. As soon as she'd broken free from her mother and her fondness for frilly frocks, Christy had always dressed like a grown-up: jeans and T-shirts had never been her thing.

'Chris!'

'Ro!'

More hugs, first for Rosie, before the customary bottle of Moët was retrieved from the passenger seat and handed over. Rosie hid a smile as she accepted it. She remembered well how Christy used to say champagne was just fizzy pop, that people who insisted on designer French labels instead of Cava were arse-wipes. But that was a long time ago before she realized a bottle of French vintage stuff was the best way to woo A-list clients.

Christy turned to Sandrine. 'Hey, sis!'

'Hey!' They hugged, then Christy turned and looked up at the house. A slow appreciative whistle. Rosie had always envied Christy's ability to whistle.

'Yowza! It's even bigger than it looks on Street View.'

'Shall I give you a tour? Isn't that what your mum always used to say?'

'Please don't say you're turning into my mum.'

They giggled as they ascended the stairs into the hall, climbing over Rosie's sons, who were huddled over the iPad that they never failed to unearth, no matter how carefully she hid it. 'Hi, boys,' Christy said,

'Nrrr-ffm,' they mumbled. The boys had never warmed to Christy like they had to Sandrine, even though she lavished them with generous presents at birthday and Christmas time. 'Sandrine, come on the trampoline. Now!'

'Don't you want to do the tour, Sands? I can tell them to leave you alone?'

'I'm staying the night, aren't I? I can have the tour later. Come on, boys.'

They dragged her towards the garden.

On the wide landing, Christy looked around her happily. 'Well. I see what you mean about the decor. Straight from my childhood home.'

'That's what I thought!'

Christy laughed. 'That's probably why you wanted this place so badly. You always used to say you wanted to live in my house. Before you realized it was run by a psychopath. But we can sort this out.' She pulled out her phone and scrolled rapidly through her contacts. 'I'm going to ask Eliza for her decorator's details.'

'Eliza?' Eliza would be a hot star on Christy's books. Christy always did this never-mentioning-surnames thing, to show how close she was to the person in question.

'Eliza Wragg? You know, the actress. She was in that ITV police drama. You don't? Shit, I need to work on raising her profile. She has this amazing house in Wimbledon. She's got kids too, but she manages to make it look as if they don't exist. I really recommend her guy. He's hugely in demand but if you mention my name, he'll fit you in, I'm sure.'

'I wasn't planning on a decorator. Didn't you once say people who employed decorators were people who were colour-blind and had money to flush down the toilet?'

'I used to think that, then I saw the effect these pros can achieve. Lover, seriously, when are you ever going to find the time to decorate this house yourself? Believe me, go for this guy. It'll so be worth it. He can get you discounts on everything, so in the end it'll pay for itself.' Christy looked around the hallway. Evening sunshine slanted in through the high windows and pooled on the tiles, like a golden puddle. In the garden, Sandrine and the boys were whooping. 'Yes, I've done good. I really have.'

Behind her back, Rosie rolled her eyes. She loved Christy, obviously, but her smugness about Jake's – about their – change in fortune, was slightly tiresome. Yes, she had got him the *Archbishop Grace* audition and had negotiated some great deals for him, but ultimately it was all about Jake's talent. Any agent could have pulled off something similar.

'We don't have a swimming pool,' Rosie pointed out.

'You will have, before long. Trust me. There's so much interest in Jake; it's just amazing. I guess the only thing is that it may not be long before you move to Hollywood.'

'Hollywood!'

'Why do you think he's meeting this agent? So many movie parts on offer, not to mention mini-series.'

'But I don't want to live in Hollywood.' Eurgh. It would be everything that unnerved Rosie about the Village, only a million times worse. Most importantly, she'd be thousands of miles away from Nanna.

'It's the centre of your husband's industry,' Christy said gently. 'Ultimately if you want to be a star it's where you end up. Think of the house you could live in there. Maybe the Beckhams' old mansion?'

'Don't be daft. We're not exactly Beckham-level, are we?'

'The sky's the limit, lover,' said Christy in her

strongest Bristol accent, defusing the tension by making Rosie laugh.

George came dashing in from the garden. 'Mummy, Mummy. Come and see the new bum-bum dance.'

'Your what?' Christy looked appalled. Rosie always remembered her expression when she'd once casually sniffed Toby's nappy-clad bottom to see if he'd done a poo. People without children just didn't get it – and why should they?

George giggled. 'Our bum-bum dance. We boing on the trampoline and show you our bums while we sing the bum-bum song. It's really funny. Come and see it, Mummy, please!'

Post bum-bum dance, which Christy watched pretending to be thrilled (admittedly she had to do enough of that humouring her adult clients), the boys went to bed. Sandrine read them four stories. Eventually they sat down to dinner.

'Cooking dinner in a room where you can stretch out both your arms and not touch the walls,' gloated Rosie as she dished out the chickpeas – they didn't look as appetizing as usual, but then everything came out a bit differently from the Aga. 'It makes me feel like a grown-up.'

'It's an amazing place,' said Sandrine. 'Like something on telly.'

'I know. It's the sort of place unfeasibly gorgeous people live, who do something unspecified that brings in huge wealth and leaves loads of time for rumpy-pump with the gardener and plotting to murder their spouses.'

'All you need is a chihuahua called President Muh-gah-bay, who'll touch nothing but Beluga and will only wear a diamond-studded collar and you'll be made.'

'I'll put one on my shopping list.' They laughed.

'Shame Jake's not here,' Sandrine said, as Rosie removed Christy's Moët from the fridge.

'He drinks far too much champagne as it is,' Rosie said, then couldn't resist a mischievous, 'Blame Christy, she scheduled this meeting with the American agent for tonight.'

'Sorry, Rosalba fucked up.' Rosalba was Christy's slinky PA, who tended to get the blame for an awful lot. 'I thought of asking her to cancel but this guy is the key to Hollywood.'

Hollywood. That sick feeling hit Rosie again.

'You're his agent, why are you introducing him to another?' Sandrine asked.

'We'll work in cahoots. He has the West Coast link. I have London. Powerful combination.'

'If your clients keep doing this well, you'll be able to buy yourself a mansion soon, sis,' said Sandrine teasingly. 'Have your very own gold taps and jacuzzi.'

'Stop taking the piss out of the gold taps,' Christy retorted, as Rosie popped the cork. 'Rosie's going to get rid of them.'

'Eventually,' Rosie cautioned. She poured the fizz into three wine glasses.

'I can't believe you don't have champagne flutes,' Sandrine teased. 'Well, now I know what to get you for your birthday.'

'Yes, please,' said Rosie, proudly removing the lid of her new Le Creuset casserole she'd ordered from John Lewis. Le Creuset in the kitchen. Molton Brown in the bathroom. Scatter cushions in the living room. Cake ingredients in the cupboards. She had finally become a grown-up. But was the lamb OK? It had shrunk strangely since she'd last seen it several hours ago.

'Mmm!' Sandrine cried, as Rosie frowned over the diminished offering. 'Smells yum.'

As she dished out the lamb, she told them about Patrizia's comments about how to bring up her children. 'Fair enough, they are pretty feral,' Rosie concluded, sounding cheerful, though the usual pincers of doubt about her mothering abilities were squeezing tight. Maybe she shouldn't be a stay-at-home mother? What did she know about bringing up kids?

'She sounds like an idiot,' Sandrine said firmly.

'No. I am rubbish at controlling them.' Rosie took a bite of the lamb. It had a bitter, charred taste. 'Oh God, sorry. This really isn't very nice.'

'It's fine,' said Christy, pushing the food around her plate.

'I had a moment of wishing we'd never moved here,' Rosie suddenly confessed. Until that moment, she didn't even know she'd harboured this thought. 'Why are we starting from scratch all over again? We should have stayed in Neasden and just bought a bigger place. Then I could still see all my old mates.'

Christy looked outraged. 'Rosie, the only large place you could have bought in Neasden would have been the boys' reform school. The place you have now is *amazing*. I can't believe you're complaining about it. You always said if you lived in a lovely house your life would be perfect. You have everything you ever wanted.'

Christy's fantastic memory again. 'I have no problems about the area – or the house – I just miss things about the old neighbourhood.'

'Like litter blowing up and down the high street and yellow police signs about stabbings at the tube station? God, people would kill to live in the Village.'

'It takes time to settle into a new place,' said Sandrine, who usually had an enormous appetite, but whose plate now was only half touched. 'It took me at least six months to feel happy in Hebden. You've only been here – what – a month?'

'You're right. I keep pinching myself. I can't believe it's real.'

Christy sniffed, vaguely appeased.

'I'm sorry, Chris. I know I sound ungrateful, but sometimes it all seems overwhelming. The guy who cleans the windows rang the bell the other day and said he had a deal with Samantha to come once a month for two hundred pounds. I mean . . . how much is that! But cleaning the windows would take all day here and there's no point owning this beautiful house and not looking after it. But, it's just so . . .'

'I know,' Christy said, her tone and expression softening. 'I understand. I've seen it so many times before, you know. Jake's going to be away a lot, and all your routines have been overturned. There are all sorts of new people hanging around, wanting a piece of him, which is why you're so lucky *I* am your agent, rather than some money-grabber. I'm going to make sure both you and Jake are looked after.'

She paused triumphantly. It was Rosie's cue to sound grateful, and reluctantly she filled it. 'I don't know what we'd do without you, Chris. Anyway,' she continued hastily, 'what's the news with the Papadopolouses? How's Nick?'

Cuddly, jovial Nick had long retired from his work as a paediatrician and was living in Australia with his second wife, Bettina.

'He's good,' Sandrine said. 'He pulled a ligament the other day jogging, but at least he's trying to keep fit. They're hoping to visit next summer. I might go over there at Christmas.'

'Cool!' Christy exclaimed. 'I might go with you. Though God knows how I'd manage to get the time off.'

'You'd need to be with Mum, wouldn't you?' asked Sandrine, and then after a tiny pause in a quieter voice. 'How is she?'

'She's fine,' Christy said. 'She's on a sports kick too,

determined to get her handicap down again. Oh, and Bryan's thinking of running as a council candidate for UKIP.'

'You're not serious! Anyway, how can he? They live in France.'

'You've never met Bryan. He'll know a way. He's got the villa all wired up to get British telly, he reads the *Daily Mail* online every morning first thing and red-arrows other people's comments, and he's found a supermarket that sells Marmite and HP Sauce. He collects ale glasses. He wears Reactolite sunglasses. They make him look like a paedophile.'

'I was thinking of writing to her,' Sandrine said. 'It's her seventieth this year. I was hoping . . .' She tailed off.

Christy caught Rosie's eye and cleared her throat. 'Be careful, Sand, don't get your hopes up. You know what Mum's like. Delicious pork, Ro. I knew you were wasted in IT.'

'It's lamb, actually,' Rosie giggled.

'Whatever. You should have been a chef. Though you need to watch the portion sizes with Jake.'

Rosie put down her fork. 'Are you serious? Jake's skinny as a pencil.'

'I know, but he still has to watch it. I mean, he's not out there to play the romantic leads, fortunately he's more of a comedy actor, but still . . . these LA people don't do fat. They think you're morally lacking if you're just a pound overweight. So best go in for the low-fat yoghurt and fruit for now.'

'I . . .' Rosie opened her mouth to protest, then shut it again.

'I know I sound like a twat,' Christy said. 'But that's the way these people think.'

'I'm completely full,' said Sandrine, pushing her unfinished plate away.

Rosie burst out laughing. 'With me cooking there's no chance of Jake getting fat, Chris. I really wouldn't worry.'

'That's not what I meant . . .' Christy began, but she was drowned out by Rosie and Sandrine's laughter. Christy laughed too, before asking: 'So how's your mum?'

'In Corby shacked up with her boyfriend, as far as I know.' Rosie shrugged. 'Still the worst mum in the world, basically.'

Now Christy laughed. 'No, that's my mum.'

'Excuse me, but my mother is way worse than yours.' It had been their own, private joke since year eight when they'd heard Belinda Crighton and Shanna Vaughan competing about who had the best mum in the world.

'And your nanna?'

'We saw her yesterday. Still on top form. Though for how much longer, who knows. Which is why I ain't moving to LA.'

'Think what kind of care you could afford,' Christy said.

Rosie had had enough. 'Chris! It's not about affording care. It's about being there for her.'

'OK, OK,' Christy said hastily. 'I'm sorry, I didn't mean to upset you, I know you love your nanna.'

Rosie smiled, grateful to her for changing the subject. 'Yolande's as obsessive and doting as ever. I think she goes into chat rooms under made-up names and defends Jake from trolls. I know she wrote his Wikipedia page.'

Sandrine and Rosie giggled, but Christy looked horrified. 'That woman is awful. You can get in loads of trouble for that!'

'Don't worry, she knows. She did it in an Internet café, so they can't trace the ISP.'

'All the same.' Christy tapped a little note into her iPhone. Then she was distracted by an email. 'Oh Christ,' she muttered. 'Sorry, girls, just got to dash out a response to this.'

Sandrine winked at Rosie. 'So how about you, Christy?' she asked. 'Work going well obviously. What's up with your love life?'

'What?' Christy was still frowning at the screen, pretending not to hear them. Christy discussed her love life about as often as giant pandas mate. Sandrine and Rosie grinned at each other again. Rosie felt so radiant with happiness a bunch of campers could have gathered around her and toasted marshmallows. So what if she couldn't cook? So what if Christy was scaring her with LA talk? She was happy in the here and now. She was in this perfect house, with her two oldest dearest friends. If only she saw more of them.

Me and My Travels with Jake Perry

Perry, 34, is best known for playing Reverend Keith Bong ('Not on my patio.') in BBC1's hit sitcom Archbishop Grace. *He stars alongside Ellie Lewis in the upcoming West End production of* Twelfth Night. *He lives in north-west London and is married to Rosemary, 44. They have two children.*

Great Holidays . . .

Which was your best holiday?

A trip to Phuket in Thailand was amazing. I loved getting out on the sea to explore the islands. Sometimes I'd sleep on a boat overnight so that I could watch the sunrise. There's a spirit to Thailand – an energy – that calms me down the moment I arrive.

And the best hotel you've stayed in?

I can't remember its name but it was a little beach shack in Phuket. No running water, cockroaches on the floor. Perfection.

What do you need for a perfect holiday?

Now: a good kids' club.

What do you always take with you?

A pile of books. Next on my reading list is Bring Up the Bodies *by Hilary Mantel. I adored* Wolf Hall *and can't wait to check this one out.*

What's your best piece of travel advice?

Just go with the flow. Delays happen, plans change – it's all part of life's rich tapestry.

Where do you want to go next?

I'm a bit of an art fan, so I'd love to go to Saint Petersburg and discover the treasures in the Hermitage

. . . and Disasters

Which was your worst holiday?

About ten years ago I went to Belize with my then girlfriend. We had to change flights in Miami and when I grabbed her bag from the luggage carousel, I twisted my lower back. The pain was excruciating. Then I picked up an ear infection snorkelling. The last straw was getting about fifty mosquito bites! I've not been back to Belize since.

Which is the worst hotel you've stayed in?

It was in Hamburg about fifteen years ago with my then girl-friend. The door of our hotel room had been kicked in and wouldn't lock. All that was on offer in the hotel restaurant was salami with noodles. Horrible.

What do you avoid on holiday?

I don't really avoid anything. I take the holiday as it comes. Years ago I was in Barcelona, watching a show with my then girlfriend and this guy called me up on stage and said, 'Walk across the stage with a ten-cent piece between your butt cheeks and then drop it in that glass over there.' The reward was a free cab back to the hotel. I'll never forget my girlfriend's horrified expression when I dropped my trousers. We got the free cab ride, though.

What do you hate about holidays?

I'm always working, so when I do get a holiday I surrender to it. However, after two weeks I'm ready to get back to the coalface.

6

Sandrine returned to Hebden after two blissful days of wandering round the Village together and long laughter-filled dinners. The next morning, Rosie was reimmersed in her new life: the cleaner, who used to work for Samantha, was starting.

'She's only nineteen, but an absolute treasure,' Samantha had said during their cup of tea after their offer had been accepted. 'She lives just down the road, so the job's convenient for her.' But for the past three weeks, the treasure had been on holiday, with an agreement – conducted over text – to start the day after her return.

Rosie imagined a rude girl from the estate, headphones round her neck, orange tan, probably the daughter of a single mother. She'd treat her very kindly, mentor her, encourage her to return to education.

Nanna had done a lot of cleaning over the years and Rosie had heard so many stories about bad clients. There were the ones who never had any cash on them and said they'd pay her next week. The nutters who wouldn't let her use 'unnatural' cleaning products, insisting she scrubbed the toilet with bicarbonate of soda and an old toothbrush. The ones who'd expected her to take care of children at the same time as de-linescaling the shower. There was one woman who used to hold out a bin bag to her without meeting her eye. There was another whose Filofax Nanna had once sneaked through to see if she was listed under 'M' for Marjorie or 'P' for Prest. She was under 'C' for Cleaner.

On her return from nursery Rosie dashed around, tidying up and wiping surfaces. She'd always been super-tidy herself, the result of living in that tiny flat with no room for mess, but Jake was the opposite – he was a hoarder, who kept everything in old shoeboxes that had all been faithfully removed from Neasden and transplanted here. There were old school play programmes, ticket stubs, birthday cards. Rosie had tried to chuck some out during the move but he kept rescuing old film magazines from the recycling, asking what she thought she was doing and didn't she understand the sentimental value? She'd have another crack at it soon.

The doorbell rang. Rosie ran to answer it. 'Dizzy, hello,' she said, smiling. Then she stopped short.

Dizzy was indeed about nineteen years old. She was also six foot tall with shiny bobbed auburn hair that spoke of a lifetime of nutritious meals and bi-annual trips to Verbier. She had a make-up free face and was dressed in a Barbour, jeans, a yellow gilet and riding boots.

'Hello,' she said in pure Cheltenham Ladies College tones, holding out a gracious hand. 'Dizzy. You must be Rosie. So pleased to meet you.'

'Er, likewise. Come in.'

Dizzy marched in, pulled off her Barbour and looked around her. 'Where's the coat rack gawn? Oh, God, of course, Samantha's taken it?' She pulled off her riding boots and picked up a piece of Lego from the floor. 'I *love* Lego.'

'I'm getting around to furnishing the house properly,' Rosie said. 'We were in quite a small flat before; it's a bit of a leap.'

'Yes, it must have been.' Dizzy looked at her with pity. 'Well, don't worry, you're going to *love* living in the Village. I've lived here all my life. It's *so* lovely. We're in Conifer Gardens, just round the corner, so I know everything. If you need any tips, just ask.'

'Thank you,' Rosie said humbly.

'No problem.' Dizzy winked. Was she really nineteen or was she fifty-two? 'Looks like you need me, so I'll get to work. Do you think you'll replace Sam's Aga? Mummy has a Falcon range. Honestly, they're so much better; I'd really recommend one. By the way, you know tonight is my night?'

'Sorry?'

'I always doggy-sat for Samantha and Louis on Tuesdays when they went to bridge. So called. I was sure they were swinging.' Dizzy snorted at her wit. 'So, for you, I'll babysit. You can go somewhere lovely with your husband.'

'Oh!'

'Try Gepetto's in the Village. My friend Miranda is a

waitress there. They do fabulous pizzas – yum. Try a four seasons, you'll *adore*.'

The thought was extraordinary. She and Jake go out for dinner, just for the hell of it – on a week night, with no birthday or anniversary to celebrate? There'd never been any room in their old lives for 'date nights', it had all been such a hamster wheel. Rosie had returned from work, utterly frazzled, and before she'd even removed her coat had had to start preparing meals and laying out bags of clean nappies and clothes for the following day's nursery. There'd been no time for conversations about anything, except had Jake remembered to send Becki a birthday card? Even if she hadn't been so shattered, how could they have afforded it? Forty-odd pounds to the babysitter, plus her taxi home, just to spend another eighty-odd pounds in a restaurant where all they'd talk about was the children and how broke they were. But now money was not an object. Someone was being insane enough to volunteer babysitting.

'I *love* kids,' Dizzy said, as if reading her mind.

'Why not?' Rosie exclaimed.

'Great,' said Jake, when she called him. 'Why not? But not some tacky pizza place in the Village. Let's go a little swankier.'

'I don't think the pizzeria's tacky. It looks cute.'

'We can do better. Try the one-star Michelin place I pointed out the day we moved in. Listen, got to go, Simon's calling us back into rehearsals.'

Rosie hung up, annoyed. She wasn't a fan of fancy

restaurants. She liked discovering cosy neighbourhood haunts – and Gepetto's, from what she'd glimpsed of it when running errands in the high street, seemed exactly her kind of place. But whatever.

She called the one-star Michelin. At first, the woman at the end of the phone hummed and hawed, then she said she could squeeze them in at seven. 'But we'll need the table back at eight thirty,' she added severely.

'Fine,' said Rosie.

'I'll need a credit-card number for the reservation.'

Annoyed, Rosie fumbled in her purse and pulled out their joint card – a new thing since she'd given up work, which she still felt guilty about spending. She gave the details.

'And the name is Prest?' asked the receptionist.

'Well, yes, Ms R. Prest and Mr J. Perry, my husband.'

'J. Perry?' The voice altered. '*Jake Perry*? We'd heard he'd just moved into the area.'

Rosie was even more annoyed now. 'Um, yes, that's my husband.'

'You should have said. No need to give the table back. We look forward to seeing you at seven, Mrs Perry. Or later if need be. No worries.'

She hung up crossly, but before there was time to muse on how she felt about this new level of treatment, the phone rang again. Withheld number. Heart in mouth – she still associated withheld numbers with scary phone calls from the bank, even though those days were long gone – she answered. 'Hello?'

'No need to sound so scared. It's me, Patty!'

'Patty! How are you? How's everyone?'

Patty was the office manager at Tapper-Green, where Rosie had worked until their lives had so miraculously changed. An ultra-efficient PA, with a sharp, red Mary Portas bob and a bottom the size of Rosie's old flat, which she always showed to best advantage in tight leggings and sleeveless tops. In her spare time Patty was a beautiful bodies campaigner, who went on anti-fattist marches, chanting slogans like: 'Say it Out Loud, We're Fat and We're Proud.'

'We're all good. We miss you, though. You'd have loved the other night. We all went to the Dangler's after work and Matt got shitfaced and puked in Julie's handbag. It was hilarious. And there's a rumour that Siobhan fancies Alun; she's been coming in early and staying late, all dolled up.'

'Really?' Rosie's heart twanged with nostalgia. When she'd quit the job, it hadn't occurred to her how much she'd miss all that officey stuff. The boys were lovely, but they didn't provide gossip fodder and when they puked (often) it was far from hilarious. 'Brilliant, I wish I'd been there.'

'Oh no, you'll be having far more fun now with those little bundles of joy. Anyway, you won't care about all our gossip now. I was just calling because I saw that "Me and My Travels" thing today. I didn't know Jake was your toy boy.'

'He's not!'

'"His wife Rosemary, forty-four",' it says. 'You're looking good for your age – I never knew. I had you down for about thirty-five.'

'I'm thirty-four. And my name isn't Rosemary, it's Rosie. Short for nothing.'

'Are you sure?' Patty said teasingly. 'I can check the personnel files, you know. I was a bit surprised. You should get on to them, ask them to correct it.'

'They never correct,' Rosie said, speaking from experience. 'And I'd just have a reputation as a vain nightmare.'

'They should interview me. "The Real Rosie Perry by Patty Belshaw".'

'Rosie *Prest*, Patty.'

'We can't call you Prest. No one would know who you were. Oh shite, I'd better go – Cillian's calling me.'

'Cillian,' said Rosie nostalgically. 'Still dribbling snot everywhere?'

'Oh yes, and telling us all how noble he is to come in with his cold and then hacking all day into a single tissue. Bless. Anyway, love, if you're ever in the 'hood drop in and see us. We miss you. No one to tell us what the stars are really like. Give us the dirt on Ellie Lewis.'

'I'd love to.' Rosie was sincere about this. 'Maybe we should have—'

'Gotta go,' Patty squeaked and the line went dead.

*

Rosie worried the boys would be upset at the concept of a new babysitter, but Dizzy had their number straightaway. 'Right!' she bellowed. 'I'm going to chase you round the house three times and anyone not in bed after the third round is a stinky poo and will be flushed down the loo.'

'Flushed down the loo,' the boys screamed in ecstasy.

'Now chop-chop. Off you go,' she ordered Rosie. 'Try the duck, it's absolutely delish.'

'Great,' Rosie said. The restaurant was just ten minutes walk away through the Village and she revelled in the sensation of being out in the evening alone, unencumbered by buggies, nappies and irrational demands to pat a mangy dog or pick an ugly flower. She could stop off at a pub and have a drink – but she wouldn't because Jake would be on his way from the theatre and she didn't want to keep him waiting.

She pushed open the restaurant door. It was a small, bright room with a fire – not strictly necessary on this warm spring evening, but still very cheering – crackling in the corner. A handful of tables were set wide apart and some serious-looking couples were dining. No sound at all. Right. One of those places where everyone whispered: too intimidated by the menu to dare have a good time.

'Hello,' she said to the man behind the desk. 'We have a reservation. Perry.' She winced slightly.

'Perry?' He sounded French. He frowned as he stared at the book. Rosie leaned over, keen to help him. She saw their name. Beside it, someone had written *Semi-VIP*.

'Ah, yes, madam. Welcome. So glad to have you here. Please, we have a lovely table for you. Quite private. I hope you enjoy it.'

Oh do shut up. Still, as she was led to a secluded table near the crackling fire, Rosie couldn't help smiling at the semi-VIP tag. So that was where Jake sat on the pecking order. Slightly above the rest, but hardly in the Beyoncé or Chris 'n' Gwyneth league. That would keep him in his place. She couldn't wait to tell him about it. She glanced at her phone. A text had arrived from him.

Sozza. Just leaving now. Got held up.

For Christ's sake. Jake finished rehearsals at five. He should easily be home by six, with a copy of the *Evening Standard* that Rosie virtually snatched from him, her umbilical cord to the outside world. But, more and more, he was coming later and later, calling to say he was buzzed after all the rehearsing and was going to wind down with a 'quick drink' with Simon, who instead of wanting to rush home to Brunhilde von Fournigan and their three perfect children often ended up encouraging Jake to stay for two or three more 'quick drinks' before continuing to Soho House for a 'quick bite', while the meal Rosie had so carefully prepared as part of her new housewife incarnation ended up in the bin.

'Are you OK?' asked a waitress. 'Would you like a drink while you're waiting? A newspaper to read?'

Rosie smiled. 'Yes, that would be lovely.'

A few seconds later, she had a large glass of Merlot and a copy of the *Sentinel*. Yippee. She *loved* this paper, though she'd never have admitted it. Usually she only dared glance at it online when George was napping and Toby glued to C-Beebies. She flicked through the pages, enjoying some scandal involving Justin Bieber, another involving Prince William and his dogs, and, suddenly, there it was . . . half a page, featuring a ridiculously flattering photo of her husband, minus glasses, leaning with his chin on his hand, wearing . . . could it be *eyeliner*? Oh crikey, it was the article Patty had called about. She'd meant to look it up, but things were so frantic after nursery she'd clean forgot. She gestured to the waitress. 'Could I have another glass of wine, please?'

My then girlfriend, Belize. My then girlfriend, bloody Hamburg. My then girlfriend, Barcelona. Jealousy poured through Rosie's veins like poison. It wasn't so much about the ex (or exes, it wasn't clear), it was the mention of all these exotic holidays. The only holiday she and Jake had ever had had been their honeymoon in the Lake District, when she'd been seven months pregnant and it had rained every day, not that they'd cared as they'd spent all of it in bed. Mad but true. Two sons, a huge house, but they'd never been on an aero-plane together.

It had all happened too quickly for that. Rosie had pairs of tights she'd owned far longer than she'd been with Jake. The night they'd met at Christy's little drinks party – Christy was always having little drinks parties full of important people – Rosie had been very low. She was thirty, she hadn't gone out with anyone since Adam, and she was coming to terms with the certainty that she'd never meet anyone, that she'd have to abandon dreams of kids, and instead buy a cat and become an IT-support businesswoman supremo who wore tightly belted macs and went to spas in Mauritius.

But then there was Jake, standing in the corner, smoking a cigarette out of the window, and he'd turned and they'd made eye contact, and her body had jolted like it was plugged into the national grid.

Christy had appeared waving a bottle of champagne and cried, 'Rosie, you must meet my amazing client, Jake. Jake meet my oldest and bestest friend, Rosie!'

Two hours later they were in his unmade bed in the shabby, untidy flat in Neasden and by the morning they were officially in love. After that, it was all a blur. Holding hands in old men's pubs that to them seemed not rank but amusing and retro. Walking in the park. Hours in bed together, gazing into each other's eyes. They'd just started to emerge from their cocoon, to introduce each other to their friends, when Rosie had noticed that her period hadn't come and their world changed forever . . .

There'd been no holidays post-kids; they couldn't afford to go abroad and the hassle didn't seem worth it. They went to Yolande's for long weekends and the boys jumped in cow pats and rolled into nettle bushes.

Rosie had hoped they'd go away this summer, but now Jake was flat out with rehearsals. Her dream, in fact, was to take the boys to Disneyland. She could still recall the pain in her chest when she'd heard that Christy, aged ten, was going there – the dull recognition that Nanna would never be able to treat her to something like that in a million years. But now they could do it easily. Though, in the meantime, here she was reading about her husband swanning around Thai islands, no doubt with a supermodel. OK, she knew her husband wasn't a virgin when they'd married. She'd been on holiday with several boyfriends herself. But all the same, he'd never told her any of this.

No point brooding on it, Rosie figured. This was one of the reasons she'd given up work, precisely in order to get to know Jake. It sounded bonkers, how could you not know your husband? But they'd moved so fast from crazy infatuation to harried parenthood that there hadn't been time to really spend time with each other. This was what their new date-night regime would be all about.

'Sorry, Bean. Sorry. Sorry. Sorry!' Every diner's head whiplashed as Jake hurried across the room. He wore his grinning yes-yes-you're-very-kind-but-I'm-in-a-hurry-otherwise-I'd-love-to-talk expression, which he now always adopted in public. Rosie sighed. She'd hoped the village would be so sophisticated they wouldn't blink an eye at Jake. In Neasden, towards the end, he'd became a local curiosity. Crowds followed him to the Tube and someone once left a nasty note on their car calling them 'cheapskates' because Jake hadn't put money in the charity box outside the corner shop. 'Sorry!' Jake repeated, sitting down in front of her. 'Yum, I'm starving.'

'So am I.' It came out more grumpily than she'd intended. Rosie coughed, then repeated with a smile on her face, 'So am I. Let's eat.'

It wasn't quite as easy as that, though. First, they had to order drinks, then the menu arrived, then – when the waitress returned ten minutes later – they had to listen to a never-ending explanation of how the dishes were locally sourced, not to mention ask several questions about what *annatto* was, what *cacao porcelana* was, and what white *kiwicha* was. Rosie thought of the pizza restaurant and her stomach rumbled so loudly she had to disguise it with a cough.

As always in restaurants, Jake was dithering. His indecisiveness drove Rosie up the wall.

'I think I'll have the soup. No, hang on, does it have cheese in it?'

'I don't think so,' smiled the waitress, doing a job of hiding her regrets at not having studied harder for A levels, like her parents had warned her.

'Would you mind checking?'

'What are you doing?' Rosie hissed.

'I'm trying to avoid cheese.' Jake looked pained. 'Ellie says it's the best way to lose weight.'

'Ellie Lewis?' He nodded. 'Fucking hell, Jake, the way she loses weight is by consuming nothing but bottled water from a spring on a Patagonian mountaintop and working out for two hours every day.'

'She eats like a pig. She keeps ordering in McDonald's.'

'And chucking it up down the loo.'

'Don't be mean!' Jake said defensively.

'There is some cheese in the soup, yes,' said the waitress, returning.

'Ah. OK, maybe the *kiwicha* with Amazon fish then. No, no! Sorry, the beetroot salad or—'

'He'll have the beetroot salad,' Rosie said firmly. The waitress backed off, resolving to look into mature student options in the morning.

'What's all this?' Rosie said to Jake. 'Are you actually listening to Christy and this losing-weight stuff?'

Jake was leaning forward, ready with a confession. 'I think I need a personal trainer.'

'Really?' She tried to keep the incredulity out of her voice. This was the man who'd laughed until he'd almost burst a blood vessel when he'd been telling her about how one of his new celebrity chums – Ricky Gervais, was it? – had weekly facials.

'And . . .' His voice lowered another five notches. 'We may have to look into a hair transplant.'

Now Rosie couldn't contain her hilarity. She clapped her hands together. 'Oh, now I've heard it all.'

'Christy thinks it's a good idea,' Jake said huffily. 'There are fewer parts for bald men. The Americans are big on all this.'

'Oh, we're not talking about the Americans again? I've told you, Jake, I don't want to go there.'

'But they could offer millions. There's all these deals in the pipeline. You could fly home any time to see Nanna.'

'I know, but . . . It wouldn't be the same as every month. And what about the boys? I don't want them growing up as 90210 brats.'

'I'm sure Beverly Hills is no worse than the Village.'

Rosie decided distraction was the best technique. 'Shall we get back to holidays? I thought your ideal holiday was Saint Petersburg. The Hermitage.'

'You must be joking. Freezing Russia and an art gallery? Fuck that for a game of soldiers.'

'That's not what you told the *Sentinel*,' she said slyly, as the waitress deposited two square plates in front of them, each containing a thumbnail of green leaves.

'Your amuse-bouche,' she smiled. 'Enjoy!'

'Well, this will help you lose weight,' Rosie said, thinking longingly of a four-seasons pizza.

'What about the *Sentinel*?' her husband asked, swallowing. 'Urgh. I'm not entirely sure about that. What do you think it was? The chef's toenails?'

'Oh, don't! "Me and My Travels" with Jake Perry.'

'Oh that. Is it out? Can I see?'

'Why did you say you wanted to go to Saint Petersburg?'

'Because it makes me sound sophisticated, of course. Where's the article?'

'I'll show you later. And what was all this about adoring *Wolf Hall*? I thought you said Hilary Mantel was middle-class brain porn to make people feel important, because they'd read a book that was longer than five hundred pages.'

'It is. You know I'm a Jack Reacher boy through and through.'

'You're such a hypocrite!' She was going to mention the 'my then girlfriend' thing, but was distracted by her starter being placed under her nose. It looked horrible. Garlic bread and thick-stuffed crusts, where were you now?

'I know. But I don't want to tell the world the truth. I want to keep my distance from them. I don't want them knowing the real Jake Perry. He's reserved for you.' He smiled at her in that winning way of his, but Rosie wasn't looking, her eyes were on the middle-aged man in chinos and a blazer, standing behind him.

'Er, Jake.' Her husband looked round.

'Excuse me, I'm most terribly sorry, but can I have your autograph?'

'Sure,' said Jake. 'Do you have a pen?'

'Terribly sorry. Don't you?'

'Sorry!'

'I have one,' said Rosie, reaching in her bag for the beautiful black fountain pen Christy had given her for her twenty-first. It was one of her favourite possessions, along with the bracelet Jake had given her when she was pregnant with George.

'Do you have a piece of paper?' Jake continued.

'Terribly sorry, I thought you might have?'

'Sorry! I came out for dinner with my wife, not to pass an exam.' Jake was trying to sound jokey, but somehow it came across as peevish.

'Thanks for nothing,' snapped the man. He turned and crossed the room, rejoining his wife. He spoke to her rapidly and she gasped audibly. Both looked daggers at Jake and Rosie, as if they'd informed him their hobby was having sex with meerkats.

'He's still got my pen!' exclaimed Rosie. 'I'm going to get it back off him.'

'No, don't.'

'I bloody am.' Rosie jumped up and crossed the room. 'Please could I have my pen back? It has sentimental value.'

'I used to like your husband,' the man said, reluctantly handing it over.

'Trevor,' his wife cautioned, as he pulled out his phone and began jabbing something into it.

Rosie returned to the table, face flaming. 'We should never have gone out,' she hissed.

'Don't be ridiculous.'

'He's probably on Twitter now, telling the world what an arsehole you are.'

'That's his problem,' Jake said calmly. 'You just have to rise above it.'

But Rosie could feel the man's eyes on them, as they tried and failed to relax and talk normally.

Jake pushed his plate away. 'This is horrible.'

'It's not that bad,' Rosie protested, but her duck was actively nasty. Disappointment engulfed her. She must have been counting on this evening to somehow change something between them more than she had realized.

'Next time we'll go for a curry,' she said, trying to sound comforting.

'There won't be a next time,' Jake snapped. 'Sod this. In future, we're staying in, or I'm going out in Soho where no one blinks an eyelid.'

'And where does that leave me?' Rosie exclaimed. 'Stuck at home with the boys?'

'You can come and join me in Soho,' he said, but he didn't look at all certain. 'Let's get the bill.'

Perry Nice – The Daily Comet *Interview by Fabian Osmond*

It's hard to find a moment to talk to Jake Perry between rehearsals for his new theatre role in Twelfth Night. *When we eventually meet in his dressing room, I find a tall, thin, surprisingly shy man. In his jeans and a military jacket – complete with long fingers, haunted look and dark, only slightly thinning hair – he could still pass for the drama student he aspired to be during his boyhood at a Midlands comprehensive. He's slow to open up, but when he does, a thoughtful, gentle person emerges.*

As a child, Perry loved fishing, cycling and wildlife. It wasn't until he was sixteen that he joined a local youth theatre – so often a magnet for creatives and misfits – and loved it. 'I was a bit of a loner oddball at school,' he recalls, 'but that gang from youth theatre, they're still my closest friends.

'I dreamed of going to drama school, but my mother didn't consider it a proper education, and insisted I went to uni instead. Amazingly I got into Oxford, but I was a fish out of water, so to make things easier for myself I got involved with every drama production going.' On graduating he went into 'character stand-up on the cabaret circuit . . . a way to break into acting – which took ten years'. He supported himself via numerous temp jobs, working at Pizza Hut for a couple of years, followed by night shifts at a mortuary.

But now, at the relatively ripe old age of thirty-five, Perry's name is everywhere. After his breakthrough role in TV sitcom Archbishop Grace *last year ('Not on* my *patio.'), quickly followed by the equally stellar* Private Wives, *there's* been a scramble to sign him up. He's got two British films in the diary, another Archbishop Grace *to be released next month, two more British dramas in the can, and Hollywood is slavering at his door.*

But for now he's concentrating on his first love – stage – with his role as Malvolio in a hotly anticipated version of Twelfth Night, *featuring* O'Rourke's *star Ellie Lewis. Perry absolutely refuses to be drawn on this fashion for 'stunt casting', only saying, 'It's a joy to work with Ellie. She's really impressed me.'*

The show opens in November at the Criffon Theatre in the West End. 'When I was a kid I only went to the theatre once a year to the panto, so to be in the West End every night, next to a bona fide movie legend. It's a dream come true.'

These days, despite the fame, Perry lives with his two children in down-to-earth Neasden in north-west London, taking his family to a patch of woodland in Essex, 'to learn to love the natural world like I did and to camp out'.

Compared to film and TV, theatre is modestly paid. But when I ask Perry if he's now made enough money to do what he likes, he laughs. 'No, I'm not in any position to retire and do things for the love of it. But I want to better myself as an actor, which you do by doing things like this. I'm not bothered particularly about making money. People are so greedy these days. I'm disgusted by our culture allowing the big companies these tax loopholes, while taking benefits away from the people who need them most. It's all them, them, them. Nobody ever has enough. I just don't feel that way. So long as I have my family and my job – wow, that's more than enough for me.'

7

The email landed in her inbox when she was sneakily reading about Victoria Beckham's alleged cellulite in the *Sentinel* online, instead of investigating a school for Toby.

> Hi Rosie,
>
> It's Patrizia, the twins' mom!!! Remember me? I saw 'Me and My Travels' with your handsome husband and it made me think of you. ☺ Anyway, haven't seen you at Wendy's for a while – mind you, I've been pretty busy organizing a charity ball (hope you and hubby will come – maybe he could offer some signed DVDs for the raffle or, even better, give a speech??!!). But in the meantime do you wanna come to a book club? Thursday. My place. 7.30. We're reading The Help. *See you there!!!*
>
> Xx

Rosie was embarrassed at how excited this made her. She still hadn't made mum friends in the Village; she rarely spotted anyone at the nursery gates and when she did was too shy to strike up a conversation. When the boys were invited on play dates, they were always hosted by nannies, who were very sweet, but usually ten years older or ten years younger than Rosie and with a limited grasp of English. Jake was rehearsing all day and not coming back until late and she missed adult company.

Book club would be her opportunity, not to network – that was *another* vomit-inducing phrase – but simply to meet new people, to start to feel part of the community. She dutifully read *The Help*. Her margins were covered in notes. She'd even put 'Civil Rights Movement' into Wikipedia and swotted up on all the cogent issues.

Finally the day had come and she was in her new skinny jeans and one of the floaty tops she'd bought on ASOS. She'd applied make-up following guidelines from a YouTube video, but then lost her nerve and scrubbed most of it off again. She'd tried to do something with her too-thin brown shoulder-length hair but given up and pinned it in a loose topknot. The boys were curled up in front of CBeebies on iPlayer when her phone rang. It had better not be Jake saying he was going for a drink with Simon.

'Hello?' she snapped, then seeing it wasn't her husband but Bosey his oldest friend, repeated more softly: 'Hello!'

'Oh, hello, Rosie. You all right? I'm calling you because I know Mr Famous will be hanging out in Soho House with Jonathan Ross where no cell phones . . .' he pronounced the last phrase with an atrocious American accent '. . . are allowed.'

'Actually. I hope he's on his way home from work, because I'm going out.'

'To the Groucho Club to hang out with Fearne Cotton? So, listen, I was having my post-work pint and I picked up the *Evening Comet*.'

'Because the *Guardian* wasn't to hand, of course.'

'I'd have preferred the *Economist*, but yes, needs must. Anyway, there's an interview with Stooks.'

All Jake's old schoolmates called him Stooks, their stupid nicknames were a minor-public-school thing, like smashing up restaurants after a few drinks. Rosie could never remember what Bosey's real name was. Anyway. 'Oh, right?'

'An interview saying he was an oddball and bullied at school. Comprehensive school. Total fucking bollocks. He was fucking head of house at our *private* school, head of orchestra, head of chess club. All right, so he never had a proper girlfriend until he met you, unsurprisingly with a face like that, but Christ . . .'

'The journalist probably made it all up to have a better story,' Rosie said firmly, reaching for her phone to google the *Comet*.

'Do you think?' Bosey sounded mischievous. 'I don't. I think it's Stooks trying to play the plebeian card. Anyway, tell him from me, he's a prat and to call me.'

'I will. Actually, listen, Bosey, I've been meaning to get in touch. You and Stella must come over soon. It's been ages.'

'That's because Stooks is always so busy hanging out

with Jonathan Ross and Alan Carr.' Was there an edge to Bosey's voice? Before Jake had shut down his Facebook account some of his old school friends had been rather snarky about his change in fortune. The landline started ringing. 'Bosey, I have to go, there's a call waiting. I'll text Stella and put a date in. Hello?'

'Rosie,' said Yolande's voice. 'Have you read the interview with Perry in the *Comet*?'

'Um, not yet. I've only just heard about it. I'll have a—'

'Comprehensive school, indeed! He went to the best school money could buy, and thrived there. We put all our money into the children's education, that's why . . . well, never mind. And why do they say you're still living in that horrible Neasden? Did he do the interview before you moved?'

'Journalists make things up,' Rosie said, still trying to google the darn thing but her phone had misread 'comet' as 'comic'.

'But surely not to this extent!' Yolande exclaimed. 'I mean, did he really say he was a fish out of water at school? He was so popular.'

'I have no idea what he said. I wasn't there.'

'He was desperate to go to Oxford,' Yolande continued. 'I remember him working all summer holiday before he applied to have the relevant experience. And the stuff about him not fitting in there . . . he adored the place. Still, it's a lovely photo of him. They've done something to his hairline . . . and how lovely that he's been taking the boys into the Essex woodlands, I didn't know he did that.'

'*What?*' Jake was the man who thought nature was all about sticks and things that sting you, whose idea of entertaining the boys was to hand over the iPad and then lie on a sofa with an eye mask on. Her phone was beeping again. 'Sorry, Yolande, that'll be Jake on the other line, I have to go . . .'

'Just tell the boys that I went out with Dorothy and her little granddaughter the other day. It turns out she's learning the piano. Not Dorothy. The granddaughter. Have you thought about Toby taking up the piano, only—'

'Yolande, I have to go, we'll talk about piano another time.'

'It says he has all this work lined up. He doesn't. Only the next *Archbishop Grace*. He's keeping his options open.'

'Like I said, papers get loads of things wrong.'

'You are still coming to the party? Fraser will be there after all. We rearranged his flights for him.'

'Of course! Sorry, I have to go. Hello?'

'Oh, hello, Rosie?' A woman's voice. Light, friendly. Probably one of the book-club mums.

'Yes,' Rosie replied warmly. 'Sorry if I sound a bit harassed, I was talking to my mother-in-law and—'

'Mothers-in-law, oh tell me about them. It's Isobel Orchard from the *Sentinel* here.' She spoke as if Rosie were an old, old friend. 'How are you?'

'Fine. Um. Do I know you?'

Isobel ignored this pertinent question. 'I was just hoping you'd be able to help me. I'm writing a feature on cougar wives and I thought you'd be perfect to comment on what it's like to be married to a much younger man. We'd need a little chat on the phone – I can call back if now's not good and then we'd take a lovely photo, with a stylist and make-up artist and everything. We'd make you look really young. So—'

'I'm not married to a younger man. They got my age wrong.'

'Oh. Are you sure? Because on IMDB it says that Jake is thirty-five and if you're forty-four then . . .'

'I'm not forty-four. I'm thirty-four. Just. It was my birthday a couple of months ago, so I'm not even thirty-four and a quarter.' Christ, she sounded like Toby.

'Oh.' Isobel's genial tone had vanished. 'Are you *sure*?'

'Feel free to check.' Rosie's face was burning. This was outrageous, she'd done nothing, nothing, except fall in love with Jake when he was an unknown and wash his pants for years, but as a result this cheeky mare thought she had carte blanche to insult her. She heard the front door opening. 'Sorry, I have to go.'

'Rosie, wait! How about an interview anyway? How It Feels to Be Married to Patio Man?'

Rosie hung up, as Jake sauntered into the room. 'I have to go!' she snapped at him.

'Oh. Right. Lovely to see you too, my darling. Boys OK?' He added as a kind of afterthought.

'Fine.' Fuming, Rosie grabbed her bag and dashed out of the front door, across the drive, down the road, and crossed on to the Green. It was still light; the days were getting longer and people were out walking their dogs and sitting on benches contemplating the ducks on the pond.

An unfamiliar nanny/maid – there were about eight on rotation – opened the Conifers' front door. 'Hello, come in.'

'Am I late?'

'Yes, they're all in there.' She nodded towards the room where Gary Guitar and Peppa Pig had last been seen battling for supremacy. Rosie hurried through. A cloud of perfectly highlighted heads turned from the uncomfortable white sofas.

'Rosie!' cried Patrizia. 'Last but, of course, not at all least.'

'Sorry! Jake was late home.'

'Husbands.' Everyone shook their head understandingly. 'Darling, you should have told me, you could have borrowed one of my girls,' said Patrizia. 'Or if you need someone more permanent I've just heard of an amazing Filipina who's on the market. She refuses to take a day off, can you imagine how wonderful? She doesn't even have a problem with Christmas and she works from six to nine every day, Sundays too.' The room mumbled in approbation. '*Plus* she costs a pittance. She's bound to have been snapped up, but you never know, if you offered her six pounds an hour rather than five . . . Champagne?'

'Great, thank you.' There was a bowl of peanutty-looking things on the table. Rosie couldn't resist; she was starving. She should have eaten with the boys. She stuffed a handful into her mouth, then spluttered, coughed and gasped.

'Are you all right?' asked a Chinese woman, one Rosie dimly remembered from the birthday party, chatting to Caroline about lipo.

'Just a bit . . .' Rosie tried to enunciate, eyes watering. 'A bit hot.'

'Wasabi peanuts,' Patrizia explained. 'Spicy. Suppresses the appetite.' She clapped her hands. 'So, introductions. Everyone, this is Rosie. Rosie, this is Caroline, Bella, Elise, Minette'

'Hi.' Rosie waved.

Minette was the Chinese woman and Caroline the one who'd asked for tickets to *Twelfth Night*. Bella was in a tracksuit, but not the sort mums wore to the school gates in St Pauls, but the kind Gwyneth donned to work out with Madonna. Elise had a black bob splattered with grey streaks, an indignant face obscured by huge glasses, and was in a sleek, bronze-coloured shift dress.

'So shall we all start?' Elise asked impatiently.

'Before we begin,' said Caroline, 'I must just say that the bit when she split up with her fiancé so reminded me of how I felt when I left Johann. I mean, the pain was indescribable for him, but also for me. The guilt, the heartache. But like the heroine of this book, sorry I forget her name, I know I am pursuing the right cause.'

The others exchanged glances. Clearly such comments were par for the course.

'She was trying to aid the Civil Rights movement,' said Elise. 'My issue with this book was that it was trash. Trash dressed up as serious stuff, but trash.'

'I quite liked it,' Rosie said softly, and Elise shot her a fierce look.

'Too heavy going for me,' said Minette, fingering her earrings. 'I have an idea for next month. *Fifty Shades of Grey*.'

'Everyone's read that already,' Patrizia objected.

'God, if I had been married to Christian Grey instead of Johann, my life would have been so very different,' Caroline chuckled.

'I think *The Help* explored some really interesting themes, relating to friendship,' said Rosie, glancing at her notes.

'Can I make a confession?' Bella said. 'I didn't actually have time to read the book. But I did watch the DVD!'

Elise harrumphed. 'Personally I think we may need to introduce a new rule. Anyone who hasn't read the book is not allowed to attend.'

'I've been re-reading *Harry Potter*,' continued Bella. 'Maybe we should think of that? Then we could help our kids as well.'

Elise sighed. 'So. I was very interested in the role of the narrator. Is she entirely reliable?'

'Um, excuse me!' Caroline called to one of the

servants, tapping her glass meaningfully. Everyone's glass was topped up. Rosie glanced at her watch, wondering if she could invent an excuse about one of the boys being sick just as Elise's phone rang.

'Oh shit, excuse me,' she said. 'Office. Better take this outside. Hello, Brian. Yes, I'm actually on my way to a work dinner with one of the clients . . .'

The other women looked at each other significantly.

'No wonder poor Charles is so mixed up,' Patrizia said softly. 'His mother is never there. Always talking to the office.'

'She says she has to work, to pay the school fees,' Caroline said. 'Her husband's a painter, but she has her heart set on Gadney's. Rosie, what are your thoughts on schools for your little boys?'

The air rustled, as the women all turned to Rosie, twitching with eagerness to get stuck into what was clearly their favourite topic.

'Well, I thought about Jacqueline France but they've no places.'

'That's as well.' Minette shook her head. 'The children from the *estate* go there.'

'But it seems like a lovely school.'

'I did consider a state school for Ben,' said Bella contemplatively, as Elise re-entered, apologizing. 'No need to say you're sorry, Elise, what you do is amazing. I know I couldn't.'

'Don't be silly,' Elise replied. '*You're* amazing. There's no job harder than being a stay-at-home mum. I could never cut it. I'd be bored; it's not where my analytical talents lie.'

'*I'd* be exhausted going to work. It's so important to have someone keeping the home ticking along.'

Compliments batted back and forward like a ping-pong ball, then Bella cleared her throat and said, 'Anyway, Elise, we were talking about schools. I was saying I considered state for Ben as I thought it could be very good for his development to mix with ordinary people. But in the end I decided he needed to be prepared to go to Eton, or maybe Winchester. Chinese contacts, you see. That's where they're all sending their children and they're the future.'

'Glad you think so,' Minette laughed. 'I do sometimes get tired of speaking Mandarin to Nicholas, but it will pay off in the end.'

'You're going to send your son to boarding school?' Rosie tried not to sound incredulous.

'Not until he's seven, eight perhaps,' Bella replied breezily.

'You could give Gadney's a call, but I would try King's Mount,' Patrizia said to Rosie. 'It's very good for boys, especially rather tricky ones, like Toby.'

'Though it only got nine into St Botolph's last year,' Caroline warned, as Rosie failed to formulate a response to this.

'Yes, but apparently everyone's numbers for St Botolph's were down,' Minette said animatedly. 'I did a spreadsheet. They must be taking more boys from state primaries or something, and I heard about boys with full-time private tutors being flown in from Bhutan to take the exam. It's a jungle out there, I tell you.'

'Give King's Mount a call,' urged Patrizia. 'Mention my name. They may be able to fit him in – boys drop out, parents relocate.'

'Ladies, ladies, back to the book!' Elise cried exasperatedly. 'So, did we think the lack of male role models was interesting?'

'That Jessica Chastain in the film is absolutely stunning,' said Minette. 'So skinny, though. I worried about her.'

'She was in that film about Osama Bin Laden, what was it called?' Bella said. 'God, you know, I used to sometimes wonder if Johann was a spy, he was so mysterious about what he did at work.'

'Daniel Craig, now there's a spy.' Minette sighed.

All pretence at literary criticism was over. The next hour was spent discussing which James Bond was their favourite. DC won by a country mile, though Rosie made them all laugh by voting for Roger Moore. For a second she relaxed. This was more like the girls' nights she used to know. But then:

'Your husband must know all these people, yes, Rosie?' Caroline smiled.

'I don't think he knows any of them.' Rosie felt herself closing up like an anemone.

'Oh, shame,' said Bella, who was quite obviously drunk now. 'So who does he know? C'mon, spill the beans.'

'He doesn't know anyone. I mean, he's met people but . . .'

'I'd *love* your life.'

'It's really not that exciting.'

'Sorry,' said Elise. 'But who *is* your husband?'

'Um, his name's Jake Perry.'

'Is he on telly? Never watch it. No time. Occasionally a film, though no Hollywood junk.'

'He is, I'm afraid,' Rosie said humbly. 'On telly, I mean.'

'He's hilarious,' said Patrizia. 'He was in *Archbishop Grace*. "Not under *my* . . . garden, was it?"'

'Oh my God, *him*?' exclaimed Minette. 'He's on my bucket list. Like five famous men I totally have a free pass to fuck. The others are Ben Affleck, Louis Theroux, then . . . I forget. Anyway, they're all kind of geeky. I love geeky men. I can't believe you're married to him. Wait until I tell my husband someone on the bucket list is a Wendy's daddy!'

'He's in that show with Ellie Lewis now, isn't he?' interjected Caroline. 'There was something on TV about it when I was on the treadmill. That must be pretty freaky, your husband and the most beautiful woman in the world working together.'

'It's just the way it goes.' Rosie shrugged. She wasn't actually unnerved by Jake working with Ellie. She knew her husband. He was the faithful type – not least because he was too wrapped up in his own insecurities to notice that much about the people around him.

'*I'd* be worried,' Minette said.

'I trust him,' Rosie said calmly. She felt a pang of unease, like a stab in her side. She wished she wasn't here being interrogated. She wished she was with Christy in the flat in Chelsea, with Sandrine – or Barron as she used to be – in Bristol, squeezed on to the sofa together watching *Neighbours*. People who knew her, whom she knew, with whom she'd been through so much and didn't have to make an effort.

'Er, gossip later, ladies,' sighed Elise. 'Now, please. Back. To. The. Book.'

8

1993

Slowly Rosie opened her eyes and myopically took in the dim bedroom lit by flaccid winter sun creeping through a chink in the curtains. This wasn't right. This wasn't her room. What was this baggy white T-shirt she was wearing and – Oh God – who was this in bed with her? Someone with blonde curly hair, who was snoring gently. What had she done last night? Had she slept with a stranger? Had she had a . . . *one-night stand*, like she'd read about in *J-17*? She'd been so drunk she could hardly remember anything. Tentatively she pulled herself up on to her elbow and gently prodded the warm body. It mumbled and shifted slightly.

Oh, thank God, it was Christy. She was in Christy's bedroom. Last night they'd been . . .

From downstairs came a crash. Rosie sat bolt upright, terrified, as if something had been jammed into her chest.

'You fucking arsehole. Don't you know how hard this is for me?' Sandra screamed.

Rosie lay back down again. Last night they had been to the Mistletoe Ball at the Royal Lancaster Hotel in London. Last night her eyes had been plastered with blue Rimmel eyeshadow and Boots mascara, and her mousy hair had been sticky with an excess of hair gel.

What had they been doing attending a ball? She hadn't dared tell Nanna, let alone Mum – they would have laughed their heads off. It had all been Christy's idea. She'd been reading Sandra's *Tatlers* and announced that this was where the fun was at.

'I'm bored of hanging out with the Carlsedge boys,' she'd said over lunch in the canteen. 'I want to meet different boys. Better boys.'

'We can't go to a ball you read about in *Tatler*,' Rosie argued. She'd love to. Sandra subscribed to *Tatler*, *Vogue*, and *Harpers & Queen*, and she and Christy spent hours poring over the pages, reading about people with names like Venetia wearing party dresses that cost three thousand pounds to a twenty-first on a yacht moored off a private Greek island. The idea that they could actually in some way cross paths with such a world was about as likely as Rosie's mum becoming a nun.

'We can. We buy tickets. Our money's as good as anyone else's.'

'Sounds good to me,' said Belinda. By the beginning of year eight their friendship with Belinda had rekindled A wary friendship, but a friendship all the same; based on worshipping Kylie Minogue; thinking *Four Weddings* the funniest film ever made and *The Shawshank Redemption* the most profound; knowing that Oasis's lyrics far surpassed anything written by Shakespeare and despising the teachers for not seeing it; and on drinking pints of Bacardi and/or Malibu and Coke, and then throwing themselves at boys they'd otherwise have been far too scared to talk to.

Belinda was certainly a good enough friend to come to the ball. Tickets were thirty pounds, an unthinkable amount, as Rosie gently pointed out, but Christy had said she'd buy her a ticket. Guiltily, but gratefully, Rosie had accepted. She wished she could make it up to her friend in some way, but she had no idea how. Then there'd been the question of what to wear. She'd saved up from her paper round and found a black clingy dress in Miss Selfridge but she wasn't convinced it worked.

The previous evening in Christy's bedroom, Christy and Rosie had leaned into the illuminated mirror on the dressing table, applying make-up and threading huge earrings through their pierced lobes.

'I'm getting sick of Blur,' Christy sighed, as 'Country House' blared in the background. 'Everyone's listening to Oasis. I'm going to buy their new CD.'

'Will you tape it for me?'

'Course. God, I'm busting for a fag. Do you mind if I smoke?' Smoking was a new pursuit of Christy's. Rosie hated it. She saw how fags made Mum and Nanna cough and stink. Without waiting for permission, Christy opened the casement and was pulling a Silk Cut out of the packet, just as an odd gruff voice at the doorway said: 'Hello.'

Rosie turned round and her heart almost stopped in surprise. Barron was standing in the doorway. Not the

Barron Rosie remembered – the tall, clumsy, thick-lipped, stubbly teenager – but a totally different Barron. Still tall, still hairy, but wearing white trousers and a flowery blouse. Hair clips were holding back his coarse black locks that had grown to chin length. His enormous lips were emphasized by pink frosted gloss.

There was silence apart from Damon Albarn warbling through the speakers about his very big house in the count-reeeee. Barron waved one of his enormous hands in greeting.

After what seemed like hours, but must have been seconds, Rosie took hold of herself. 'Hi, Barron. I didn't know you were here. How are you?'

'Fine, thanks, Rosie. And you? How was your term?' Polite as ever.

'Fine, though I wish I hadn't decided to do physics GCSE. You've been in California, haven't you?' After Barron had left his weird boarding school, he'd gone to the USA to stay with distant relations.

'I have been, but my visa ran out one time too many. Anyway, I was homesick. I missed my family.'

'Oh.'

'So where are you going? You both look very lovely. I love the shoes.' He pointed at Rosie's electric-blue pumps from Jane Norman.

'Thank you. Er . . .' She glanced at Christy, who usually spoke for both of them, but she was standing there frozen. 'We're going to a ball. In London. It's a bit silly, really, but it might be fun.'

'A ball. How amazing. Will you waltz the night away?'

'Balls aren't like that any more,' said Christy acidly, then her tone softened. 'Barron, listen. If you are going to carry on dressing up like a girl, please try to do it properly. That lipstick is revolting, it's like something Krystle would have worn in *Dynasty*. And the hair clips make you look ludicrous.'

'Oh.' Barron stared meekly at his shoes.

'I just don't want you . . .' The look of concern in Christy's eyes was heartbreaking. 'I don't want people laughing at you. I want you to do this properly. So you feel comfortable. Do you want us to sort you out?'

Barron looked up, beaming. 'Would you?'

With a sudden whoop, Christy grabbed her Mason Pearson hairbrush. 'I'll do the hair. Ro, you're on nails duty.'

Suddenly they were all giggling, though Rosie's mind was still a whirlwind of confusion. Blur was replaced with Abba's 'Dancing Queen'. Barron's black, rather greasy locks had been teased into winsome curls and held in place with a wheeze-inducing blast of Elnett. His nails were ineptly filed and painted a pale pink by a nervous Rosie. 'Classy,' Christy opined. 'Do a kissy mouth,' she instructed her brother.

Barron pursed his lips and his sister dipped her lip-brush (she'd read in *J-17* that lipstick should be applied with a brush, so she'd gone to Superdrug that day to buy one) into her tube of Boots No7 Plum Beautiful. 'Much more discreet. And then we'll wipe the muck off your eyes. You want a sort of beigey shadow.' He sneezed as she waved her powder brush over his cheeks. 'This'll sort out the grease, but you need to use a decent face wash.'

'I'll buy one tomorrow,' Barron said. 'What do you—'

He stopped talking. Agnetha and Frida carried on singing about the Summer Night City. Rosie who was sitting on the bed, selecting a good mascara, looked up.

Sandra was standing in the doorway, arms folded across her chest.

'Hello, Barron,' she said.

'Hello, Mum,' Barron whispered.

A short pause. 'Aah ahh,' the Swedes crooned.

Then Sandra said, 'Don't do this. Ever again.'

'Mum, we're having fun,' Christy protested, but Barron was already on his feet.

'I'll take it all off, Mum.'

'Please do.'

Barron seemed to shrink as he scuttled out of the room. Rosie and Christy stood motionless. Out of the corner of her eye, Rosie saw Christy's hands twisting furiously behind her back, as she stared defiantly at her mother, chin tilted.

'Don't encourage him, Christy,' said Sandra softly. Then: 'Your father's waiting for you. You need to get on the road now, if you're going to make it to London for seven thirty.'

*

118

The toilets of the Lancaster House Hotel were filled with skinny confident public-school girls who touched up their make-up and hoicked at their black taffeta dresses from Monsoon, dresses like Rosie's but somehow better fitting. Rosie and Christy stood side by side at the mirror, tubes of Plum Beautiful at the ready.

'So what's going on with Barron?' Rosie said out of the corner of her mouth. She'd sat the whole way on the M4, bursting to ask.

Christy stared in the mirror. 'He doesn't want to be my brother any more. He wants to be my sister.'

'*What?*'

Christy shrugged. 'He wants to be a woman. He came back from San Diego just before Christmas and told Mum and Dad. He wants to be a she. So now he – or she – is seeing a shrink at Mum's insistence.' She paused and sighed. 'It's a bit *mierda*.' That was one of their favourite occupations, looking up rude words in the dictionaries in the school library.

'Poor you,' Rosie said.

'Not poor me. Poor Barron. Why would anyone choose to do this to themselves? Mum's beside herself with fury; people point and laugh when he walks down the street. But he says he has to do it, he has no choice.'

'Poor both of you.' Rosie was stunned. She knew this kind of thing happened, sometimes, somewhere, but surely not to someone you knew.

'I just want him to be OK, Ro. I don't want him being a freak.'

She hadn't looked so desolate since Belinda had taunted her all those years back. Rosie's heart swelled like an airbag. She wanted to protect Christy and Barron so badly – but had no idea how to. 'Come on,' she tried. 'Let's go and dance.'

From that point, everything became a blur. Now, lying beside Christy, Rosie remembered boogying manically to 'Let's Talk About Sex'. Arms waved, hips gyrated, knickers flashed. On velvet sofas shirts were untucked, skirts hitched up. Mascara-streaked girls sat on sweaty boys' laps; a few lay horizontal. The pair of them hadn't talked to any boys, posh or otherwise, just got drunk on bottles of wine they'd smuggled in and danced some more, but the last time she'd seen Belinda she was writhing on the floor under a boy in a dinner jacket.

And now it was morning. Rosie was in Christy's bed and the Papadopolouses were fighting. It all began to come back to her. Barron wanted to become a woman. That wouldn't go down too well with any parent – but especially not Sandra. What would they say at her golf club?

She lay there, listening to the yelling, hoping it wouldn't wake Christy. But she urgently needed the loo. She rolled out of bed and crept into the bathroom next door – another thing that she'd never been able to recover from was the number of bathrooms in Christy's house. Out of the little window she saw Sandra sitting on a bench in the wintery garden. Ice had formed on the little stone statue of a nymph bearing a basket that

Rosie always thought so pretty. Sandra was still in her pale-green dressing gown, inhaling hard on one of her menthol cigarettes and, without her usual make-up, her hair in a bird's nest, looking suddenly old.

Nick came out of the French doors in the kitchen and approached her. Gently, prepared to duck and run, Rosie lifted the latch and pushed opened the window just an inch. She knew it was wrong, but she wanted to hear this conversation.

'Look, Sandy. We have to talk about this. There must be some way we can get through this.'

Sandra shook her head. 'I love him. I don't love you. That's all there is to it.'

Him? Was she talking about Barron? Sandra had never shown the faintest sign of loving Barron. Rosie's head started throbbing. Sandra continued: 'I'll stay with you until Christy leaves university. But then I'm out of here. We only have one chance at happiness in this life. I am going to take it.' Her lips puckered again round the cigarette.

'But, Sandra . . .'

'*That* is the deal.'

'Would this have happened if Barron hadn't . . .'

Sandra raised her hand to stop him. 'I don't want to talk about Barron.'

Someone knocked on the door. Rosie jumped.

'Let me in!' Christy yelled. 'I'm busting for a wee.'

9

'George, angel, please drink from your beaker,' Rosie pleaded.

'No! Want to drink from a big boys' cup.'

'If you do, you'll get it all over your lovely shirt. And I know how much you love that shirt.'

Rosie sighed. Every weekday morning was the same: she ran around wrestling the boys into cleanish clothes, begging them to have a spoonful more Weetabix, cajoling them to brush their teeth and generally having a mini-nervous breakdown at an hour when, pre-children, she'd have been blow-drying her hair in order to impress the new bloke she fancied in HR.

Jake, meanwhile, tended to wander in, pour a bowl of cereal and then disappear into Samantha's boudoir overlooking the garden, which he'd designated his office, in order to write emails until the car that took him to rehearsals arrived. In Neasden he'd have had nowhere to hide, but in the new house it was different.

'Jake. Jaaaake! Come and help find Toby's shoe,' she tried now. Surprise, surprise. No reply.

Rosie's phone started ringing. Exasperatedly she grabbed it. Christy. Typical. Oblivious to the timing of the nursery run. She considered ignoring her, but then decided just to get it over with.

'Hi, Chris. How are you?'

'*So* busy, you have no idea. And you?'

Toby started to scream. 'Mummy, Mummy, Mummy, Mummy!'

'Er, busy too. Toby, what is it, darling?'

'It's show and tell today. Did you forget again?'

'Oh, well remembered! What letter is it this week?'

He thrust Wendy's weekly letter, the fount of all information, into her hand. Rosie peered at it. 'F. What can we bring in beginning with "F"? Christy, we need an object beginning with "F".'

'Fig? Fennel? Fur?' Typical Christy. 'No? Fruit?'

'We have no fruit,' Rosie said, looking at the hideous empty glass fruit bowl Patty had given her as a wedding present and that she would never have the heart to get rid of. 'Oh bloody hell, Patrizia's kids will be bringing in a Ferrari.'

'Or a Ferragamo bag. Maybe Fendi?'

They giggled.

'I know!' cried Christy. 'Fluff!'

'Fluff?'

'From your tumble dryer.'

'Christy Papadopolous. You're a genius.'

'I know. So, listen, are you busy?'

A hollow laugh. 'What do you think?

'You know what I mean. Later. After you've taken the boys to nursery?'

'Um, well, I have bits and bobs to do, but . . .'

'Good,' Christy said firmly. 'I have to visit Eliza in Putney, remember Eliza? Did you ever call that interior designer of hers I recommended? But I've a couple of hours before that, so I thought we could maybe have a coffee. You could show me your new haunts.'

'Oh.' A tiny part of Rosie felt resentful. All right, so she had nothing much to do except continue putting photos in her collage, but how did Christy know that? Why did Christy always expect her to be free? But she was being silly. 'OK. Great. I'll be back home about nine fifteen.'

'I'll pick you up and we'll go out for breakfast.'

'I've already . . .' But Christy had hung up.

By the time she returned, Christy's Audi was in the drive.

'We could have coffee here,' Rosie suggested.

'What, with your coffee-making skills? No, thanks, we'll go into the Village.'

'You'll have to walk there,' Rosie teased back. 'Can you cope?' Christy prided herself on never going anywhere she couldn't access by car; the last time she'd travelled on the tube was around the Millennium.

'I'll be fine,' she said crossly.

The sun was breaking through the clouds as they strolled down to the Green and along the high street. Groups of women sat outside coffee shops chattering, dogs sitting obediently at their feet, babies sleeping in three-thousand-pound buggies.

'Where are all the men?' Christy asked.

'In the City, earning a crust.'

'Hello, nineteen fifties!'

'Someone has to bring up the children.'

'I guess.' Christy looked around her bemused. 'It's another world, though. Where are the under thirties?'

'In Soho, drinking cocktails and discussing the Finnish film they saw last night.' For a second Rosie thought of Jake's avowal only to go out in Soho from now on. She distracted herself by looking into one of the many boutique windows. 'Hey, look at that dress. Isn't it gorgeous?'

Christy looked. It was a gold number, made of a kind of starchy taffeta, draping artfully round the neck and down to the knee. 'Go and try it on.'

'I couldn't do that!'

'Why not? You need something like that to wear to all the posh dos you and Jake will be attending.'

Rosie laughed. 'We never attend posh dos. Well, he does sometimes, but I'm at home with the boys.'

'He said you had a babysitter now. You should get out more.'

'Thank you for your concern.' Her sarcasm wasn't lost on Christy.

'Jake is getting all these invitations and you should be by his side. It's not good for him, or for you, if you're never together.'

'But it's not good for the boys if I'm always attending the launch of a new brand of tissues when I could be reading them bedtime stories.' *Unlike my own dear mother*, she thought. She knew a lot of her desire to spend time with the boys was to be as unlike Marianne Prest as possible.

'There's a balance,' Christy said, pushing open the door of the boutique. It had wide polished floors and a few spartan clothes racks. 'Come on, let's take a look at the dress.'

One was hanging right by the door. Rosie fingered the glorious material. It sparkled in her hand. Then she looked at the price tag. 'Fuck me. Two thousand and five pounds.'

Christy laughed. 'Your Bristol accent was very strong just then.'

'Sorry. But bloody hell!'

'But it *is* beautiful. Try it on.'

'It is lovely,' said the woman at the till. Rosie turned round and clocked her. It was Minette from book club.

'Oh, hi! Is this your shop?'

Minette nodded. 'Adrian bought it for me. I've always wanted a shop. I do have an eye for fashion, though I say so myself. I thought I recognized you. Treating yourself? Go on. You'll need something pretty to wear at all the events your hubby must be invited to attend.'

'Mmm,' Rosie smiled. She turned towards the small children's section. 'Oh, but what about this shirt for George?' She held up a little check number.

Christy yawned. 'I'm sure George doesn't need any more shirts.'

'But he always has his brother's hand-me-downs.' Rosie looked at the price tag and her expression changed. 'Um, actually, maybe not.'

'You don't need to be so careful, you know,' Christy whispered, as Minette eyed them curiously. But then Rosie showed her the price tag. 'Oh God. For a child? No bloody way. If you're going to treat someone, buy something for a person who won't grow out of it within three days.' She picked up a dark blue cashmere jumper and stroked it lovingly. 'This would suit Jake.'

'Have you seen how much it is?' Rosie hissed.

'You can afford it.'

'But it's not *my* money.'

'But he'd never get round to buying it himself,' Christy said. 'You're doing him a favour.'

'I guess you're right.' Rosie picked up a soft yellow cotton shirt folded beside it. 'He could do with one of these too. Oh, and a pair of trousers.' She shook her head. 'I'm not sure I'll ever get used to this. Depending on Jake. It always used to be the other way round.'

'You give him as much as he gives you.'

'I hope so. I'll have to try.' Rosie had chosen six garments and was just about to pay when Christy, plucking the gold dress from the rack, said warningly, 'Ro. Don't forget yourself.'

'The colour would really suit you!' Minette exclaimed. 'It's Vivienne Westwood. There's never been anyone like Vivienne.'

'When would I wear it? To take the boys to nursery?'

'Enough of the dowdy housewife bollocks. Try it on.'

In the changing room, Rosie pulled off her T-shirt and jeans and tugged the dress over her head, zipping it at the side. It was a beautiful dress, but not her style at all, far too flouncy, and whoever wore gold for heaven's sake?

'Oh.' Christy peeked round the curtain. 'Oh yes.'

'It's . . . nice,' Rosie admitted, gazing at herself.

'You *have* to get it. It's amazing.'

'But it's so expensive.'

'I've told you, relax, you can afford it.'

'I know, but . . .' As her head emerged blinking through the neck, she thought of her school days and how there'd never been enough money for her to have new shoes, so the old pairs had pinched her toes, and how she'd always had second-hand uniforms, and flicked through Sandra's old *Vogues* in a haze of envy and desire. 'Are you sure it doesn't make me look like a Quality Street wrapper?'

'You all right there?' called Minette.

'Just trying to persuade my friend she should buy this beautiful dress!' Christy hollered back.

Minette appeared. 'Oh my word, yes! Stunning. Absolutely.' Seeing Rosie was tempted, but struggling, she hastily added: 'I hope I mentioned it's ten per cent off all dresses today.'

That did it. Rosie could never resist a discount. 'OK, then,' she said. 'But I'm blaming you,' she added pointedly to Christy.

'OK, I hear you. I'll work even harder than I do already to make your husband even richer!'

Ten minutes and several thousand – thousand, this was crazy – pounds lighter, they emerged into the mid-morning sunlight.

'Thank God I bought all that for Jake or I'd feel terrible,' Rosie said. 'She did say I could bring it back within a month, so if I change my mind . . .'

'Relax, you nutter. Enjoy it.'

'I don't get it,' Rosie said, as they plonked themselves down outside a café – just like real Village women. 'Why the sudden desire to make me shop?'

'You always used to go on about how it was your dream to drift into a posh clothes shop and buy whatever you like. You should get some new make-up too. Go to one of the counters in the big department stores, they do makeovers. Have them transform you.'

Rosie remembered them messing around at the Clinique counter, aged about twelve, at Bristol House of Fraser, doing the 'computer' test to work out what kind of skin they had. They'd thought it ludicrous then, but that was a long time ago. As Christy grew older, she'd begun collecting make-up almost obsessively, convinced there was a product out there that could solve any problem. 'Yeah, I'll think about it,' Rosie said. 'It's just a question of finding the time.'

They ordered: Rosie a cappuccino, Christy, who always maintained milk was only for babies, her usual Americano. They sat back in their metal chairs, the sun bathing their faces and for a moment were silent, then Christy said, 'So, am I right in thinking your in-laws are having a party for Jake soon?'

'Next weekend. God help us. It's meant to be because Fraser's back in town between surfing contests, but really it's so Yolande can show off Jake to all her village buddies.'

Christy stirred her coffee. 'Do you want me to come?'

'You? What on earth would you want to attend a Perry family gathering in the middle of nowhere for?'

'Moral support. Sounds grim. If I was there we could have a laugh.'

Rosie thought. She wasn't looking forward to the party remotely and it was really kind of Christy to volunteer herself, but she couldn't make her leave her bed on a Sunday morning and drive all the way to the Cotswolds. After all, it wasn't like the olden days when they could have hidden themselves in a corner and laughed at the other guests; she'd be constantly having to police the boys, and make sure they weren't too rowdy and didn't stuff themselves with too much trifle from the buffet.

'You're really sweet, but honestly no need. You'll be bored silly.'

'All the same,' Christy persisted. 'I'd like to see where Jake grew up. I'm doing so much work for him at the moment and all the little details really help.'

'I'm sure Yolande would be overjoyed if you came. But you'd be nuts to. Seriously.'

'Will you ask her?'

'If you like.' Rosie said, as Caroline, jogging past with two handsome red setters trotting behind her, waved. 'Hey, Rosie.'

'See, you're settling in. You know everyone.'

'I'll get there. It takes time.' Rosie gulped down the rest of her coffee. 'I have to run or I'll be late for pick-up.'

'Wear the gold dress.'

Rosie laughed. 'Not today. Maybe tomorrow.'

Coffee morning at Caroline's next Wednesday after drop-off! No need to bring anything except your beautiful self. Goodies provided. ☺

10

'Do you know anything about King's Mount School?' Rosie asked Dizzy in the morning. She'd had her head in the sand about the school situation, but she could ignore it no longer. At pick-up yesterday even Wendy, who normally took no notice at all of her charges' welfare, had remarked acidly that it was 'very unusual' for a child only months before 'graduation', to have no school place sorted out.

Dizzy laughed. She was in orange pedal pushers today with her shirt knotted at her rather large waist like Doris Day. 'God, yah. Both my bros went there before Stowe. They absolutely loved it. It has the most wonderful cricket pitch with views over the river. I think one of Mick Jagger's kids goes there, or is it one of his grandkids? It has a helicopter landing pad, great fun on sports' day when all the Russians arrive. Are you thinking about it for the boys?'

'Possibly. Since they haven't got a place right now at Jacqueline France.'

'Jacqueline France?' Dizzy screwed up her nose. 'That's dog rough. K. M. is the business. Or there are lots of other schools.'

'Um, I was wondering. The cleaning is a short-term

133

thing presumably. What do you really want to do?' Rosie had been dying to pose this question for ages. After all, what had been the point of Dizzy's expensive education? 'Aren't most of your friends at uni?'

'Uni's not for me. I'm happy cleaning. I make far more money than I would working in a shop. I pay no tax. Mummy cooks for me and does my washing. One day I'll do something else.'

'Like what?'

'I don't know. Work in the City? My uncle will help me find a job.'

While Dizzy crashed around in the kitchen, Rosie googled King's Mount. The website was full of pictures of beaming boys – one token black, the rest all solidly Caucasian – in blazers and ties. *We believe King's Mount School is a very special place*, she read. *We are a school with a warm family atmosphere, where children feel safe and happy*.

'Well, you would say that, wouldn't you?' Rosie muttered. 'What school's going to say their children are bored and can't wait to leave and go to be cleaners?'

But she mustn't be cynical. She should at least go and have a look. After all, at this stage, what was the alternative – home-school? She picked up the phone and dialled.

'Hellairgh,' said a voice so posh, it made the queen sound like she had been brought up on a council estate.

'Oh, er, hello,' Rosie said falteringly. 'Um, my name's Rosie . . . Prest and I was wondering if you could help. My son's starting reception in September. He's very sweet . . . a bit naughty sometimes, but you know, that's boys, and, anyway, I wondered if you had any places . . . ?'

There was a stunned pause.

'In *September*?' She was Lady Bracknell, enunciating 'handbag'.

'Yes, I mean . . . I know it's soon, but we live quite close and I thought someone might pull out at the last minute . . .'

The woman laughed. 'Mrs Prest, King's Mount boys are usually registered at birth.'

'Oh. I see.'

'Some are even registered pre-birth, as soon as have people have the twelve-week scan.'

'*Really?*' All Rosie could think about around the time of her scans was where her next Snickers bar might be coming from.

'It's a very popular school. After all, it does feed the top public schools. I'm sorry to disappoint you. I can take your details and send you a prospectus, and then if you take a tour you could register for an occasional place, though I must warn you we do assess for these.'

'Oh, I see,' she said again. Assess? Assess what, Toby's Lego-building skills? It was all bollocks, but Rosie gave her address. At least then she could tell everyone she'd tried.

'Oh!' the lady said. 'You live *there*.'

Suddenly Rosie saw the light. 'Yes, we've just moved in. Dizzy Mackenzie-Stuart recommended I call you and Patrizia . . . er . . .' She couldn't remember Patrizia's surname for the life of her. 'Brazilian Patrizia!' She took a deep breath, hating herself but knowing she had no choice if Toby wasn't to end up school-less. 'And my husband's name is Jake Perry. The actor.'

'Oh!' The woman's tone had definitely changed. 'We'll be in touch very soon, Mrs Perry. Last-minute places do come up fairly regularly, you know. London being such a cosmopolitan city, people move all the time. Thank you so much for your enquiry.'

Ten minutes later, the phone rang.

'Hello.'

'Mrs Perry, it's Daphne Riversdale from King's Mount. Wonderful news! It seems there might be a place available after all. Would you and your husband be able to come in shortly for a tour?'

Seeing she was on a roll, Rosie put her discomfort to one side and resolved to phone Eliza whatsit's decorator. The fantasies she'd entertained of rising at five to visit Kempton Antiques Market were losing their appeal and her mood boards, composed of pages from her precious magazines, were becoming more and more schizophrenic. She couldn't work out if she wanted a shabby-chic vibe for the house, or a hip Balinese look like the ex-wife of a rock star was 'channelling' in this month's *Livingetc*. Or maybe a Scandi pared-down neutral look would be better, with everything in shades of stone? But then she really fancied a Versailles-type bed with a rococo headboard. Christy was right, she was beginning to concede. If the house were to live up to its potential, she would need help.

'David Allen Robertson,' trilled a woman who sounded like Dizzy's long-lost sister. 'How may I help you?'

'Oh hello, my name's Rosie –' she paused a second, making up her mind, then decided – 'Rosie *Prest* and I was wondering if I might be able to make an appointment for David to come and see my house.'

'David is *very* busy,' the woman replied. 'Could you give me your address, so I can see if he's working in the area any time soon?'

Rosie heard tapping, as she told her. Checking them out on Streetview. Sure enough . . .

'I see,' she said. 'Well, as I say, I can put you on our waiting list and if a slot comes up – it probably won't be for a year or so, though – I can arrange for David to come and interview you.'

'Interview *me*?' *Didn't she interview him?* 'OK,' Rosie said meekly.

'So let me just take down a few details, Mrs Prest.'

'No, thanks,' Rosie said shortly. 'I can't wait two years, I'm afraid. By the way, Christy Papadopolous recommended I call you, because her client Eliza . . . whatsit used you; I forget her last name but she lives in Putney.' Another deep breath, then cringing she said: 'My husband's Jake Perry.'

'Oh. You should have *said*.' She sounded as if Rosie had informed her that both Santa and the tooth fairy were actually real. 'Christy said you'd call. So sorry, we do get so many requests, but David's such a fan of your husband's, not to mention he adores Christy. I'm sure you'll have so much fun working together. So, tomorrow morning would work for him, if it would be OK with you? Nine thirty all right?'

Rosie hung up feeling faintly grubby. She hated the way she was using Perry to queue-jump. It made her feel pushy and grabby; it wasn't even her name – she was like a WAG, but without the benefits of a boob job and Botox and a *Strictly Come Dancing* glitter ball. She picked up the phone once more, this time to call Nanna. She needed to hear a Bristol accent, to be reminded of her roots. But then she saw the time and realized Nanna would be at bingo and, more pertinently, if she didn't run she'd be late for pick-up and incur Wendy's wrath and King's Mount would be alerted that, famous husband or not, she was a useless mother and her sons would end up flipping burgers.

The following morning, Rosie tidied the toys, hid her piles of magazines under the bed and placed Jake's battered uni copy of *Roland Barthes and the Art of Deconstruction* on the coffee table in the living room. She put the vase Patty had given them for their wedding present in a wardrobe, though – whatever David Allen Robertson's verdict, she knew she'd never be able to bring herself to throw it out. Rupert and Yolande's tat however . . . now there was a different matter.

She glanced at her watch. Just time to call Nanna. As

the number rang, she smiled, imagining her grandmother turning off the telly after her morning fix of
Holly and Philip and preparing to go to bingo.

'Hello, only me!'

'How are you doing, lover? Settling into that lovely
house of yours? Any more thoughts on what you'll
wear to Jake's show?'

'Yes, I bought something with Christy the other day.
Vivienne Westwood. It's gold, very flouncy. I'll email
you a photo. So, what's your news?'

'Oh, not much.'

But something about Nanna's tone belied this. 'Is
everything OK?' Rosie asked, alarmed.

Nanna sounded grumpy. 'Yes. Fine.'

'Nanna!'

'I have to go to hospital,' Nanna said crossly. 'Just for
a scan. But it's a pain. It's over the other side of town
and I'll have to miss my aqua zumba at the sports
centre. It's ever so much fun, did I tell you about it? We
have this hilarious instructor called Cherelle. Mind, she
could do with losing a few pounds, so maybe it's not all
it's cracked up to be, but we do have a laugh.'

'Scan? What for?'

'I've just been feeling a bit tired lately.'

'Oh! Is that all?' Rosie felt vaguely reassured. 'You
shouldn't go out on the razz so much, Nanna,' she
teased, telling herself not to worry, as the gate buzzer
went. 'Nanna. I have to go. Someone's here. A fancy
interior decorator. I'll call you later. Love you.'

Still, her heart was thudding as she answered the door. Scans were never good. What was going on? She did her best to focus on David Allen Robertson, who was freakishly tall, youngish, with close-cropped gingery hair and a sharp suit, and Felicity, who was willowy, blonde, early twenties, and wore a patterned minidress.

'Mrs Perry! Or may I call you Rosie? David.' He held out a hand, smiling winningly. 'So thrilled to meet you. What a house.' He looked around the hallway and did a low wolf whistle. 'What space. What potential.'

'Well, yes, I hope so . . .' Rosie began walking to the lounge – no! living room – and they followed. 'I mean. It needs work, obviously. It's a bit nineties at the moment. The curtains,' Rosie said, seizing on her particular bête noire. 'Any advice on what to do about the curtains?'

The pair gazed at the curtains, as if they were the Turin Shroud. Then David turned to Felicity. 'Are you thinking what I'm thinking?'

'I'll say,' she grinned.

'It's *got* to be scarlet.'

'Scarlet!' Felicity screamed like Meg Ryan in the orgasm scene in Katz's Deli.

'It would bring *such* vibrancy to the room. Bring it completely up to date. Lose the gastropub look, all the junk.' He nodded at the chesterfield sofa, Rosie's pride and joy bought in an auction when she was pregnant with Toby.

'Not that anything in here is junk,' said Felicity hastily, noticing her expression.

'Of course not!' David cried. 'The furniture shows you have exquisite taste. It's the decor. Did a footballer live here before? Now show us around, darling, and we'll be able to explain all the things we can do for you.' Showing them round, Rosie felt very self-conscious. The vast rooms echoed, most of them still unfurnished, their cheap, scruffy furniture incongruous in these grand surroundings. She was suddenly acutely aware that the dream house hadn't lived up to her expectations, so far: it felt like a mausoleum, rather than a home.

David had very pronounced views. Rip out the kitchen and install a new one from a company called Plain English: all distressed units in ethereal shades of green and blue. The Aga needed to go too and be replaced with another Aga, but one you could text, telling it when you were going to be home, so it would start warming your dinner, as if you were a feckless teenager and it was your cross mum.

'But I never go out,' Rosie pointed out.

'Ha ha ha.' David clearly thought she was joking. Little did he know.

The bathrooms, obviously, were for the skip – the jacuzzi, of which, actually, Rosie had grown rather fond, to be replaced by freestanding baths with claw feet. There'd be special bunk beds with slides attached for the boys – well, they'd love that. Huge abstract canvases for the walls – David showed Rosie a selection on his iPhone, which he could apparently acquire as a job lot. Rosie wasn't at all sure she liked them, but she made polite noises anyway.

He moved on to the garden, suggesting a playhouse for the boys, at a cost – with discount – of 'only seven thousand pounds, and they'll love it.' He also had plans for the lawn.

'We'll get rid of it.'

'What? We can't do that!' Rosie had visions of austere York stone stretching as far as the horizon. She didn't want that. She wanted grass flecked with daisies, apple trees, rose bushes.

'We'll replace it with fake grass. You can't tell the difference and no more mowing for your gardener. I take it you will be employing a gardener?'

'I don't know yet, I was kind of looking forward to doing it myself. It was one of the reasons I gave up work – to get my hands dirty. Ha ha.'

'Right.' Felicity looked like she'd ingested a pint of sour milk.

'You can still do all that; you just don't want the hassle of lugging around a lawn mower. Think about it. We're not here to force anything; we're here to make your home perfect. There's some brochures I want to go through with you about home cinemas. You could definitely turn the den into a proper cinema – tip-up chairs, popcorn dispensers, you name it. It would be a big build, but we could turn the conservatory into a pool and the dining room into a gym – no one uses dining rooms any more, they're totally over. You could have a dance floor with flashing lights in the far end of your living room.'

'We'd never leave home again,' said Rosie, dazed.

'Well, that's kind of the point,' he said. 'Your husband's famous now. And all my clients tell me again and again that when you're famous you can't go anywhere; it's not worth the hassle. I mean, you can go to parties with other stars and whatever, but going to the pub? Forget it. Your place becomes a bit like a prison, so you have to at least try to make it a nice prison.' He saw Rosie's stricken face. 'Sorry to sound negative, I don't mean to be. Look on the bright side. You're going to have a lot of fun spending hubby's money.'

Suggestions from David Allen Robertson Interior Designers

Dear Rosie,

We so enjoyed meeting you today and we're drawing up a proper document for you and your husband to peruse at your leisure.

However, here are some suggestions for you to be mulling over. Links and a price list attached.

How about a walk-in pantry? Also, a temperature-controlled wine cellar? For the garden, a swimming pool with underwater speakers? A cinema room with popcorn dispenser and, despite your mentioning turning the 'boudoir' into a granny flat, we think its location and dimensions would make it ideal for a very masculine study.

Check out the images for some ideas of the amazing worlds we could create for you.

Very best,

David and Felicity xx

11

Rosie stared at the email in disbelief. It was all nuts. No one needed their own cinema room with a popcorn dispenser, and what was with the 'very masculine study'? That was going to be Nanna's room.

She wanted to discuss it with Jake, but he was out late again, being wined and dined by another American agent. The boys were in bed, and she couldn't be bothered to cook for herself, so she'd stood at the fridge door gnawing at an old chunk of Cheddar.

She was missing Jake's presence around the house. He wasn't even about in the mornings any more, because – as threatened – he'd started personal training sessions with Rolla, a Slovenian former Olympian, who looked like the love child of Diane Kruger and Eddie Redmayne. He left just after seven and came back sweaty and already exhausted at half past eight when Rosie was bundling the boys out the door.

Throughout their marriage there'd been periods like this – either Jake had been around continually, driving her up the wall, or away – doing a play or making a series. But in the new house she felt his absence more acutely than ever before. In the evenings she was downstairs, the boys were sleeping two floors up, and the echoing rooms unnerved her. It was shameful and anti-feminist to admit, but she hated having to do all the little things that were normally Jake's domain – taking out the bins, changing light bulbs, investigating creepy noises. It wasn't that they were men's jobs, they just weren't her jobs – and it wasn't as if he'd taken over the washing and cooking.

Most evenings when she found herself alone she'd watch either an old box set like *The West Wing* (she and Jake had been in the middle of *Breaking Bad* when rehearsal started, but she couldn't watch it without him) or old episodes of *O'Rourke's* on cable. She adored *O'Rourke's*. It was a hugely classy drama set in the forties about an American family in meltdown, but it was very hard to imagine Ellie, who played the former virgin turned wild child with a secret heroin habit, in the role of Viola. But time would tell. If they had the cinema room, she'd be able to watch a giant Ellie emoting on a giant screen while she sat back in her giant leather tip-up seat, scoffing popcorn from the dispenser.

But tonight she wanted a change from telly. She sat at the kitchen table (again, tiny in this vast marble space) and set back to work on her photo collage which she wanted to frame and put in the downstairs loo, and yah boo sucks if David Allen Robertson declared it a taste crime.

Rosie had hoped to be able to do the collage with the boys but this dream had proven fruitless. They'd launched themselves at it screaming 'Me! Me!' and within about two seconds a photo of Toby as a newborn had been ripped in two. So now it had become her new evening activity. She dipped into the box of photos she was trying to arrange tastefully and pulled out a tiny rectangle: a snap from a photo booth. Her and Christy's heads together – one blonde, one mousy brown – both in the ugly maroon Brightman's uniform. Rosie's eyes were crossed; Christy was pulling the corners of her mouth out with her fingers. Why could only kids do that? When did faces lose their elasticity?

It was the first and only time Christy had come to the flat for what would now be called a play date. They were in year seven and had just started at Brightman's. Christy was no longer fat, though neither was she the skinny minny she would become. Sandra sent her to school with packed lunches of Ryvita and lettuce leaves, which she ate uncomplainingly, unbothered by Rosie scoffing school-dinner chips. 'You have a high metabolism, I don't,' she said philosophically.

Sandra had always made excuses for Christy not to come and play – she had homework to do and riding, ballet, tennis, violin lessons, though of course it was fine if *every now and then* Rosie visited them.

But Sandra was attending a conference in Glasgow and jolly Nick had been absolutely fine when Christy had put the plan to him. He'd be working until late, but Christy suggested that Barron come to collect her at six and escort her home on the bus.

'Isn't Barron at school?' Rosie asked, as they waited at the bus stop outside Brightman's. They hardly ever mentioned Barron. Ever since Christy's party when he'd cried and Belinda Crighton had laughed, it had been as if he didn't exist, but Rosie somehow knew that Christy was secretly worrying about him.

Sure enough, the question made Christy's face scrunch up with concern. 'His school's always on holiday. Mum complains about it all the time, how she pays so much in fees and they're never there. But she can't do anything about it. Barron didn't want to go in the first place. She made him.'

'Do you miss him?'

'When Barron's back he annoys me, but when he's away I miss him. My house is always so quiet. Unless Mum and Dad are fighting.'

Rosie was curious. 'What do they fight about?'

'Mainly about Barron.'

On the way from the bus stop, they made a detour to Woolworth's and flicked through the CD singles, discussing the music they loved. Rosie wanted to buy 'So Emotional' by Whitney Houston, but she couldn't afford it. Christy had some money – she always had some money, Rosie was beginning to realize – so she bought herself 'What Have I Done to Deserve This?' by the Pet Shop Boys.

'Shall we?' Christy asked, nodding at the photo booth in the corner.

'What for?'

'For fun. I'll pay.'

So they'd squeezed into the booth, giggling as they swirled the plastic seat up and down and eventually fed Christy's coins into the slot.

'Different pose for each one,' Christy yelled. 'Silly!'

They thumbed their noses. The flash exploded.

'Angry!'

They grimaced.

'Happy!'

Lunatic.

'Best friends forever.'

Heads together smiling cheesily. After a long wait, the machine regurgitated the photos.

'I'll have sweet and silly,' Rosie decided as they laughed at them, walking home. 'You have angry and happy.'

Nanna was waiting nervously at the door, wearing an apron — a clean apron too. This was odd.

'Why are you in a pinny, Nanna?'

'Where've you been? I was getting worried.'

'Relax.' Rosie didn't usually speak so cheekily, she was showing off. 'We just stopped off on some business.'

Nanna had also gone to the trouble of laying an oilcloth on the table. There were Mr Kipling French Fancies instead of the usual slice of bread and Iceland cola instead of highly diluted orange squash. She hovered over them as they ate, clearly dying for a cigarette but not daring to light up.

'This is brilliant,' Christy had said. 'Mummy never

lets me eat food like this. Mrs Prest, did Rosie tell you what Mrs Washington said today?'

Christy rattled on about the events of the day – what the chemistry teacher was wearing, what they'd said to each other in the changing rooms before netball, until Nanna, clearly flagging, asked if they'd like to watch *Neighbours*.

'I'm not allowed to watch *Neighbours*,' Christy apologized.

So Christy and Rosie spent the afternoon drawing. Rosie was hopeless but Christy had some talent. With Rosie's old felt tips – many of which were missing lids, she noticed to her shame – Christy quickly sketched the head of a girl with mousy brown hair and a wide, guileless smile.

'That's me!' Rosie exclaimed.

'Yup. Now. What would you like to be wearing?' She looked Rosie up and down in her maroon Brightman's uniform. 'Not that, I take it?'

'Nooo.' Rosie was dubious about this. She liked the uniform, it made her feel she belonged at Brightman's, where some of the girls had ponies and Belinda Crighton even claimed to have a swimming pool.

'How about this?' Christy sketched a stone-washed denim jacket and added a psychedelic design. Matching jeans. Pink Doc Martens.

'What do you think? Trendy Rosie.'

'Oh, yeah. Brilliant.' Actually, Rosie thought she looked ridiculous, but she was grateful to Christy for trying to transform her. Christy drew Nanna with pearls round her neck and in a pinstriped dress with a sailor collar.

'Look at me,' Nanna smiled, emerging from the bedroom where she and Mum had been conversing in low voices.

'I saw that dress in Mummy's *Vogue*. It suits you,' Christy said firmly. 'You should get one like it.'

Nanna laughed. 'I'll save up for it.'

Then they listened to Marianne's old records in Rosie's bedroom – she had a huge collection of LPs from all those eighties bands like Madness and The Specials and The Jam and Elvis Costello. Rosie had a bit of a thing about Elvis, even though he was skinny and nerdy with huge glasses. It might not entirely be coincidence that she'd ended up with a man who looked very similar. He sang a song that they both loved, called '(I Don't Want to Go to) Chelsea'.

'Where's Chelsea?' Rosie asked.

'It's in London,' Christy said. 'It has a big street running through it called the King's Road. Mummy says it's brilliant for shopping. Mummy loves shopping.' She paused for a moment and then said: 'I want to live there one day.'

'We could both live there,' said Rosie a little bit shyly. 'We could share a flat.' She'd read somewhere that this was what friends did.

'Yeah! A little flat in Chelsea.' They giggled. 'We'll do that. We'll go shopping on the King's Road.'

'I'd love to live somewhere nicer than this,' Rosie

said yearningly. 'It's so scruffy. All the furniture's falling apart. Nanna can't afford new stuff. I'd love more space. Big high windows. A garden.'

'One day you'll have all those things,' Christy said firmly.

'I don't see how. Unless I marry Prince William.'

'You'll do it yourself. Or I will. We'll make money to do it. I'll see to it.'

Rosie laughed. She admired Christy's determination so much. It wouldn't happen, of course it wouldn't; you couldn't move from St Pauls to a flat in Chelsea. A flat in a nicer part of Bristol would be enough in all honesty.

There was loud banging at the door.

'Barron!' Christy said.

They emerged from the bedroom to see Nanna opening the door. Rosie's stomach twisted. She remembered the huge clumsy figure knocking over Billy at the party, then crying when Sandra bawled him out. He'd made her nervous then and she felt nervous now three years later.

'Hello.' He had a deep voice but with an odd lisp. He was even taller than Rosie remembered and even fatter, his hair long, black and straight brushed his shoulders. His chin was stubbly.

'I'm Barron. I've come to get Christy.'

'Come in, come in. Would you like a . . . cola, er, Barron?'

'Better not. Need to get my sister back. Come on, Chris.'

'Oh, Barron!' Christy wailed.

'Come on. You know Mummy doesn't want you to be here.'

'Doesn't she?' Nanna folded her arms indignantly across her bosom.

'Sorry, I didn't mean it like that. It's just . . . it's St Pauls and it could be dangerous travelling at night. But sorry, Mrs . . . I don't know your name.'

'Mrs Prest,' sniffed Nanna, somewhat appeased. 'But you can call me Maureen.'

'What a lovely cosy room,' Barron said.

'Thank you.' Nanna touched her hair. 'So you . . . er, Barron, you're at boarding school, Rosie tells me.'

'Yes. I go to a place called Crewkerne. I don't really like it, though.'

'Oh?'

'It's all boys. Mummy thought it would toughen me up.' The childish word was so incongruous coming from this bulky man's mouth.

'Did it?' Nanna asked. 'Are you sure you don't want a drink?'

'No, thank you. Really, you're very kind, though. No. It didn't sadly. Not yet anyway. But I can leave after my GCSEs.'

'What will you do?'

Barron shrugged. 'Expire with relief, probably. Come on, Christy, we must get going.'

Later on Rosie heard that Sandra had found out about the play date, and there was a huge row at the

153

Papadopolouses with Sandra not talking to Nick for a week and then blaming it all on Barron for doing his father's bidding.

'Mum blames everything on Barron,' Christy said. 'Why?'

'I don't know. She says he cried all the time when he was a baby, that he never did what he was told. She says he's impossible. That she's given him every chance.'

'He didn't seem impossible.' Nanna had adored him, and kept going on about what a polite young man he was.

'He isn't impossible.' Christy started sharpening a pencil. 'It's just Mum that thinks that.'

Christy never came to play at her house again. But that was fine. It was nicer at Christy's anyway, even though they were only allowed raw carrots and water for their snack. She used to enjoy reading Sandra's old *Vogues* and *Ideal Homes*. They gave Rosie ideas about a world outside Bristol, about . . . Rosie's eyelids grew heavy, she was dreaming about Sandra Papapdopolous pointing and jeering at her, when suddenly the house fell down. *Crash*. Thump.

'Hiya, what's the news?' In the dark Jake bent down and kissed her. 'Urgh, have you put on that really stinky face cream? It tasted rank!'

'You bought it for me,' Rosie retorted sleepily. 'Christy told you to; it's the best for slaying wrinkles.' She sat up suddenly, wide awake.

'Listen, King's Mount say if we're interested in a

place we need to go for a tour as soon as possible and I don't know when—'

'Hey! Hey! Slow down.' Jake burped loudly. 'I have something for you!'

'Oh?' Rosie blinked as a bedside light went on. Jake was holding out a small black box. She took it and opened it. A pair of crystal earrings. Huge and blingy, they would have been perfect for Joan Collins attending an event on a Russian oligarch's yacht.

'Thank you,' she said faintly.

'I saw them in a shop window; I thought they'd be perfect for you. So I had the funniest evening.' He plonked himself on to the bed, yanking off his socks. 'I met up with Rich and he took me to a James Blade gig at the Union Chapel. It was hilarious. I saw Issy – remember Issy from drama school? She played second maid in that Spielberg Jane Austen film? Anyway, she was so off her tits she fell flat on her face and chipped a tooth.'

'Brilliant,' Rosie said unenthusiastically.

'What's up with you?'

'Oh nothing.' She rolled over so he couldn't see her expression. 'It's just . . . sometimes I feel like such an idiot, hearing about your antics. When I've been stuck at home wiping bottoms and begging the boys to eat my macaroni cheese, while you're out painting the town red. I never do that. I never say I'm just going for a quick drink and then end up crashing in at four.'

'You could. Why don't you? I'd babysit. Or Dizzy.

We could get her to come in the morning too, to get the boys up. Or better, get Mum to stay over. She'd love it.'

Rosie sighed: 'That's not the point.' She couldn't articulate that she didn't actually want to go crazy in Soho. She hadn't before having the boys and now she had to be a devoted mother, to prove history didn't repeat itself. 'What I want,' she tried to explain, 'is to *want* to stay out late. I want to go out and have fun, not just pretend to have fun while all the time I'm thinking about what to bake for coffee morning and wishing I could slip off. I want to be out partying, not even giving a thought to when I might come home. But I can't do that. I can't ever be free. And you can, you go out and you forget all about me and the boys and live in the moment and I can't do that any more. I'm a mum. It's like being in prison. I can't ever escape my responsibilities.'

She stopped, shocked at this outburst, but Jake seemed not even to have noticed, sliding his hand up Rosie's thigh and under her JoJoMaman Bébé cotton breastfeeding nightie. A perfectly good nightie. No need to bin it now those days were over.

'*Jake*. I was talking to you!'

'Rut like beasts first, talk later.'

'Sex, sex, sex, it's all you ever think about,' Rosie said in her best Virgin Mandy in the *Life of Brian* voice.

'Like you don't,' he teased, then seeing her expression sulkily said. 'All right.'

Anger whooshed through Rosie like an avalanche.

This was his house, his children. Why did he make out it was such a big deal to have to discuss the nitty-gritty they entailed? Bloody Yolande, Rosie thought, for spoiling him so much that he thought everything would just come to him, for not understanding that effort was involved in creating a comfortable life. She exhaled as she reached for the print-out of David's plans.

'I don't know what to tell him. It's going to cost nearly five hundred grand, but then David does say he'll be getting us nearly a hundred grand's worth of discounts. I mean, we don't need to do all of it but . . . So he's suggesting a light fitting like this in our bathroom.'

She held up an image of a cluster of silver balls.

'Gwyneth has one, apparently. But I'm not sure. I think it's a bit naff. And he thinks we should have what he calls a "reading niche" on the second floor.'

'What, a hole specially for reading? Sounds daft to me.'

'I think so . . . though it could be cosy,' Rosie added dubiously. 'The boys might start loving books.'

'They should love books anyway. But a cinema room. Yes! How cool will that be? And the swimming pool and gym, wicked. And an office for me. Dark wood panelling. Tobacco upholstery. Very *West Wing*.'

'That's not happening,' Rosie said firmly. 'I wanted that room for Nanna. David says put her upstairs, but he hasn't grasped she's an old lady. And the prices seem insane . . . Oh, and another thing is David says we need a gardener, even with the fake grass. Jake, are you listening to me?' His eyes had closed and his breathing was growing heavier.

'Sorry, sorry. Today was just grim. Ellie was two hours late again. Simon's starting to tear his hair out – what's left of it. And, anyway, I can't get that excited about the house – who knows, we may not be here for long. We may be moving to LA.'

'We are not moving to LA. That is final and you know it.' She paused for a moment, breathing heavily, her heart thrashing like a trapped bird under her nightie. 'So I still need to get back to this guy. And also King's Mount. And we need to set up a date with Bosey and Stella. I said next Thursday, is that OK?'

'Next Thursday?' Jake reached for his iPhone and squinted at the calendar. 'No, not all right. Dinner with agents.'

'Jake! You're always having dinner with agents. This is your best friend. He hasn't seen the house yet.'

'But Bosey can come any time. Anyway, we'll see them at Mum's party. I won't be missing that. More than my life's worth.'

'Of course not, mummy's boy.'

She stopped, appalled. She'd always succeeded in keeping her true feelings about Yolande under wraps. But Jake seemed completely unbothered, merely squeezing her bottom hard.

'What time is it?' she snarled.

'Not late. One.'

'One! George will be up in *five hours*.' Not so long ago

Rosie wouldn't have cared. Once they would have stayed out until four, then had sex until dawn and she'd have made it into the office by nine – a bit shaky but nothing a couple of espressos couldn't cure. Even post-children she'd survived hangovers with help of her best friend CBeebies babysitting the boys, while she dozed on the sofa. She hadn't understood her friends who'd said they were too tired for sex. How could anyone be too tired for the best thing in the world? But now she was beginning to understand what they'd been talking about.

'I'll get up with the boys,' he promised.

'Really?' Rosie was suspicious. 'You'll *definitely* get up with them?'

'Of course. Might even take them rambling in the Essex woodlands.'

'Oh, shut up.'

She knew that when she came down, the kitchen would be wrecked, the boys would have eaten fifteen bowls of Cheerios and be dressed in nothing but their oldest underwear and watching a horror DVD. But for a couple of bonus hours in bed, it'd be worth it. She reached for him, smiling, relieved things were nearly back to normal. And once they started it was as good as ever, even though Rosie's mind continued to wander all over the place, like a drunk in a go-kart, as she assessed David Allen Robertson's endless options.

Jake was caressing her. 'Take your nightie off,' he begged.

'Do I have to?'

'I want to feel you naked.'

But if I take it off I'll have to put it on again in a minute and that would be such a waste of time. 'I like it like this,' she tried.

'Please.'

She compromised by pulling it up round her neck, where it nestled like a snood worn by Pepsi and Shirlie in the eighties. She moved on top of him.

'Grab my balls,' Jake groaned.

'Say please,' Rosie retorted automatically. Her attention had been far away on the pros and cons of King's Mount and a cinema room.

He stopped. 'What?'

'Just joking,' Rosie said hastily.

Jake was moving faster now, so she did too, but fantasizing all the while not about orgasms but about her lie-in.

My Favourite Places by Jake Perry, London Living Magazine

Hatha Yoga Institute, London E19

Yoga keeps me sane. This place has good teachers and is in a beautiful building with large windows overlooking a park. When the morning light floods in you could be in California.

Help Gallery, London E2

I love to wander over here every so often and pick up a piece of original jewellery for my wife.

The Rectory Hotel, Tetbury-upon-Stowe

Before children, this used to be a top weekend retreat. Gorgeous gardens, great food and service, and bracing country walks. Also a great spa, my wife tells me.

Halepi, London SW18

The best Greek restaurant I've eaten in – and, luckily, not too far from us. Earthy and basic, with big fat radishes dipped in baba ganoush and tabbouleh. It's delicious, inexpensive and near Wimbledon Common for a long walk afterwards.

Anahi, Paris

Whenever I'm in Paris I eat at this tiny restaurant on Rue Volta. It has a fabulous laid-back vibe and they treat me like a local.

Milo and Olive, Santa Monica, Los Angeles

Simply the best pizza in LA, but possibly in the world too. I love a relaxed lunch there when I'm visiting Hollywood.

Made by Bob, Cirencester

This is near where I grew up in the Cotswolds. Cirencester has quirky open-air and covered markets, and this place in the Corn Hall is perfect for a simple, tasty lunch.

1 2

It was Sunday lunchtime when the car pulled up in the small driveway of Yolande and Rupert's sprawling half-timbered house, which was set down a pretty Cotswolds lane. George tumbled out, as ever covered in vomit. Jake's sister Becki, in a slightly too short red party dress and high heels, was standing in the doorway, tapping at her watch.

'What time do you call this? Mum won't allow us to pile into the buffet until the guest of honour is here and the children are starving.' Even though Becki's children were twelve, ten, nine and five, they still adhered more or less precisely to the Gina Ford routines of their babyhood, with Becki convinced the sky would collapse if there was more than a twenty-minute deviation from lunch at twelve thirty, tea at six, lights out at eight thirty and so on.

'Sorry, George was sick and . . .' Rosie was keen to ignore her sister-in-law and chuck his stinking clothes in the washing machine.

Becki was shaking her head, delighted at an immediate chance to display her amazing maternal skills. 'Forgotten to bring a change for him, have you? Never mind. Auntie Becki has some clothes of your cousin Joe's that you can wear.'

'Joe!' cried George in ecstasy. Both boys hero-worshipped their five-year-old cousin.

'Thank you, Becki,' said Rosie abjectly. She'd long learned that complete humility was the only way forward with her sister-in-law. Loud strains of jazz floated through the air. 'There's a band!'

Becki nodded disapprovingly. 'Mum's really gone to town. We'll all go out and take a look in a minute. But first, upstairs, Georgie! Auntie Becki will get you washed and tidy.'

'I wish I was as organized as you, Becki.'

'Well, I do have some experience in this field, you know. Having four of the little monkeys. Ha ha.'

George went upstairs with his aunt. Rosie followed Jake round the side of the house into the back garden, which was completely covered with a huge white marquee. Inside, the entire village was clinking glasses and bellowing at each other over the noise of a saxophone and a voluptuous lady crooning 'Moon River'.

This must have cost Yolande and Rupert a fortune, thought Rosie. They were supposed to be trying to economize, to make up the shortfall in their pensions after the Disastrous Investment. Rosie wondered how much of a contribution she and Jake had made towards the party, then stopped herself. It was Jake's money. If he'd wanted to help his parents throw a party, then why not?

Where was Jake? Aha, of course, over there surrounded by menopausal women in Marks and Spencer
Autograph, hooting with laughter at his every utter-
ance. Yolande was in the far corner in a lemon trouser
suit issuing orders to a petrified-looking uniformed
waitress behind a groaning buffet table. Rupert was . . .

'Hey, Rosie!'

'Bosey!' She kissed her husband's best friend. 'How
brilliant that you made it!' She waved a little gingerly at
the small woman with her hair in bunches standing
behind him. Her arms were folded over her tiny chest,
and she was in a flimsy sundress in a – no, yes – Hello
Kitty! pattern. Well, if you worked in a tax office you
needed to kick back somehow. 'Hi, Stella. How are
you?'

'Fine, thanks,' said Stella crisply.

'Good. Good.' Rosie bent to kiss Stella on the cheek.
Something about Bosey's latest girlfriend always made
her uncomfortable. Partly it was because she was so
dainty she made Rosie feel like a clodhopping giant,
partly it was because she was so young, and partly it was
because Bosey's girlfriends always thought they'd found
'The One' only to be dumped two years in, and Rosie
could no longer be bothered investing any serious
energy in getting to know them. 'How lovely to see you
both.'

'Finally,' Stella said sweetly.

'God, I know. Sorry. Jake's been so busy rehearsing,
he's been terrible . . .'

'Gwaaargh!' cried George, rushing over dressed head to toe in Joe's immaculately ironed clothes and with a tiger mask covering his face, no doubt something Becki had created with her children during one of their craft afternoons. 'Gwaargh! I'm a fierce, scary *beast*.'

'Oh, God, no!' yelled Bosey, cowering in mock fright. 'Don't eat me.'

George bellowed with laughter. 'I'm gonna *kill* you.'

Stella stood there, arms still folded, lips pursed. 'Shame we haven't made it round to your new residence,' she said. 'We hear we could fit our flat into your downstairs toilet, didn't we, Edward?'

'Edward! So that's your real name!' Rosie exclaimed. 'I was trying to remember.'

Stella looked puzzled, while Bosey chuckled as George bounced on his back. 'Yup, all we old Cartonians have to change our names; it's the law of the land. Hence Mr Stooks Perry. Ah, speak of the devil.'

They all turned as Jake advanced, holding out a hand to Bosey. 'All right, maaaate! *Ringa pakia*.' He bent down and slapped his hands against his thighs.

'*Uma tiraha*.' Bosey stood up and thrust out his chest.

'*Ka mate! Ka mate! Ka ora! Ka ora!*' Delightedly George danced around their feet.

'What are you two like?' Stella sighed.

'What are you like, mate?' sniggered Bosey. '"My favourite restaurant is in Paris; they treat me like a friend." KFC Paris, would that be?'

'Oh, is that the "My Favourite Places" article?' Jake asked. 'Christy told me what to say. Like I'd have a favourite place to eat in Paris if it bit me in the arse.'

'How many bedrooms did you say your new house has?' Stella asked Rosie.

'I didn't, but six,' Rosie apologized. 'But Jake's family do come to stay a lot – well, I mean, they haven't so far, but they probably will.'

'Don't see what's wrong with a futon in the lounge.' Stella twisted one of her pink sparkly hair bobbles. 'So I suppose you've heard what's happened to Edward?'

'No, what?'

'Well, he's only gone and lost his job.'

'Oh no! How awful.'

'Mmm.' Stella took a glass of champagne from a passing tray. 'It's very difficult,' she added as Bosey galloped up to them with an ecstatic George on his back. 'Giddy-up, giddy-up, horsey! Wahey!'

'Sorry to hear your news, Bose— er, Edward,' Rosie said. She turned to Jake. 'Bosey's lost his job.'

'Oh, mate.'

'Well, these things happen.' Bosey shrugged. 'Another one'll be along in a minute. Like buses. Though it's not a great time for IT sales at the minute.'

'Suppose another job doesn't come along, Edward?' said Stella. 'Then what will we do?'

'Something will.' Bosey looked faintly annoyed now. 'Don't go on about it, bunny-boo.'

'It just seems so unfair,' Stella said, popping a canapé

between her pink lips. 'That you can work for years at your job and one day – whoosh – it's gone, like that. Whereas other people get all this money for learning a few lines and saying them on telly.'

'Anything I can do to help, mate,' Jake said awkwardly.

Stella snorted. 'Are you suggesting Edward becomes your driver or something?'

'Fucking—' Jake stopped, as Rosie glared at him. 'I mean, I hope not, given the amount of points on his licence.'

'I'm clean at the moment,' Bosey beamed, forking a whole roast potato into his mouth. 'So what about you, Perry? Still hanging out with Ricky Gervais?'

'I don't hang out with him. I had a drink with him once.'

'And several other people,' Rosie interjected.

'But you couldn't make it to Bundle's stag. He was well gutted.'

'I would have loved to go to his stag, but I was filming in Liverpool that weekend. I couldn't get out of it.'

'Hey, guys!' It was Fraser. Tubbier than Rosie remembered him and with his former goatee now wispily brushing his knees.

'Frase!' exclaimed her husband, slapping his brother on the back. 'You look like a hillbilly. Where's your bloodhound and your trailer?'

'I'm entering a lot of beard competitions,' said Fraser in his pseudo-American accent. 'I'll show you some pictures.'

Rupert was approaching, slim and smiling in a pale grey suit. 'How wonderful! All my family together.'

'Great to be here, Dad,' said Jake, as a soft but firm voice behind them suddenly said: 'Hello!'

'Christy! I'd forgotten you were coming,' said Rosie.

'Charming,' Christy laughed. 'I texted you to say I was on my way. Didn't you see?' Before Rosie could reply that her phone was in her bag, she stepped forward and shook hands with Rupert. 'Hello. Christy Papadopolous. I'm Jake's agent. I remember you from the wedding . . . a long time ago now.'

'Oh yes, hello, Christy.' Rupert did have a very nice smile. 'How kind of you to come all this way.'

'All right now?' asked Becki in Rosie's ear. 'We sorted little George. I know it's hard to be organized but I would recommend you pack a going-out bag as soon as you get home and keep it near the front door. Then when you next go out it's there and waiting for you. No hurry. No panics.'

'Brilliant, thanks, Becki. I'll do that. Thank you.'

'Sorted out Toby's school yet?'

Oh, not you too. Though inevitably Becki would ask a question like that. 'We're hoping a place will come up at the local school, but it's getting a bit close to the deadline now, so we're looking at a prep school next week.'

'I see.' Becki pursed her lips.

'You went to a private school, Becki.'

'I know. But . . . Perry just has it all now, doesn't he?'

She glanced at Rosie slyly. 'Have you a lovely holiday booked?'

'No. We can't go anywhere because of the play.'

'Jessica was saying it's her life's dream to go to France for her holiday, but we can't afford it. What with four children and both of us working for the state. It's tough.'

'Yes, I can imagine.' What was Rosie supposed to do, offer to pay for their holiday? That was down to Jake. One of the best things about suddenly having money was being able to share it with loved ones, but she wanted it to be in the form of gifts; blatant demands like this left a sour taste. Happily they were interrupted by a fork tinging on a glass. The jazz instantly stopped and the chattering ceased, as Yolande climbed on to a little stool.

'So, everybody, thank you so much for coming today. The weather's been on our side and I am honoured to share my home with you on the day we welcome our son Fraser back to the UK – at least, temporarily. And also . . .' she continued, as heads turned to peer at Fraser '. . . many of you have noticed a familiar face on the goggle-box recently. He was born and brought up in this little village and it's an honour to have him back home with us. His name was Perry Jakes, now it's Jake Perry . . .' Everyone laughed at this as if Yolande were Woody Allen. 'He's become very recognizable recently, but it's taken years of hard work and dedication, so we're all really proud of Perry. Or Jake. Whichever. Here's to Jake Perry.'

At the applause and cries of 'Jake!' and 'Perry!' Jake pretended to look bashful. Rosie looked at Becki, who was standing expectantly, clearly waiting for her turn in the spotlight. But Yolande had stepped down from her stool and been swallowed up in a crowd of envious neighbours. Rosie was horrified. It was always plain that Yolande preferred boys to girls, but still this was ludicrous.

Suddenly a glass tinged again. Rupert had mounted the stool. 'And, of course, as her father, it's up to me to mention how incredibly proud we are of our lovely daughter, Becki, who does such wonderful work teaching the next generation – really the most important job in the world. Becki, you're a star.'

'Becki!' everyone roared.

'Really, it's nothing, what I do,' Becki said loudly. 'I feel very privileged to help shape the next generation.'

Guilt poured over Rosie. When they'd first met she'd hoped Becki would be the sister she'd always yearned for, but she'd quickly realized her sister-in-law had far too much on her plate to develop any kind of close relationship. But perhaps now they could fix this.

'Your birthday's coming up, isn't it?' she said to Becki.

'Unfortunately. Another year gone in the blink of an eye. Where's it all disappeared to?'

'Well, I had a thought. Maybe you and I could go

away on a girls' weekend to a posh hotel. With a spa. I'd treat you, of course,' she added hastily as a confused expression passed over Becki's face.

'But what about the kids?'

'They could cope without us. Dave can take charge of your lot and Jake of mine.'

'Huh. Last time I left Dave in charge, they ended up going to Pizza Hut for dinner.' Becki made this sound as if her children had been made to eat dog meat. Becki was very keen on meals prepared from scratch. 'And would Perry really have a clue?'

'Think about it,' Rosie said, now enamoured of the idea. 'The children will survive. And we could have a great time. Just think – massages, jacuzzis, boozy dinners. Lie-ins.'

'It's tempting, certainly,' Becki said, as Bosey approached her, arms outstretched. 'But you need to put the children first.'

'But a happy mum means happy kids,' Rosie said, as her sister-in-law disappeared into a bear hug.

13

The Wendy's mums were sitting round Caroline's oak kitchen table, drinking coffee from her Nespresso machine and studiously ignoring the plate of freshly baked pastries in front of them.

'Eat, eat!' Caroline cried, frantically waving the platter under the women's noses. 'They can't go to waste.'

'I'd love one but I'm gluten-free,' said Elise, immaculate in a black trouser suit. 'Did you really bake them, Caroline?'

'What can I say? I love baking. I find it so *connecting*.'

'I can't, darling, I'm on one of my fast days,' Patrizia apologized. 'Five: two. It's harsh, but, my God, I'm seeing results. I may never have to have lipo again.'

'You do look amazing, Patrizia,' Minette agreed. She turned to Rosie, who was longingly eyeing a Danish. 'So how are you getting on with the Westwood? I'm hoping to see you in the pages of *Grazia* at some celebrity bash. Rosie bought my Vivienne Westwood,' she told the room.

'Oh, what, the one you couldn't shift and were about to mark down?' exclaimed Bella. 'That's fantastic! Ow! You just kicked me.'

Patrizia sighed. 'So any joy with the schools, Rosie?'

'We're going on a tour of King's Mount next week. They say they may have a place.'

The women looked at each other meaningfully. 'I seem to remember when Brangelina were in town, they found room for their boys pretty quickly too,' Caroline said. 'Though I think they rejected the place.'

Rosie laughed. 'Jake and I are hardly Brangelina!'

Patrizia nodded vigorously. 'Of course you're not; you're nothing like them. But you never know.' She clapped her hands. 'So what are everyone's summer plans? We're going to Brazil, of course, but I thought maybe a stopover in the Caribbean. Any recommendations?'

'Just make sure you fly British and not Virgin,' said Bella with a shudder. 'They call it Upper Class, but frankly I wouldn't send the dogs anywhere with them. Dreadful.'

'I agree, but then Adrian maintains if Emirates doesn't fly there, you shouldn't bother going at all,' Minette chipped in earnestly. Rosie wiggled uncomfortably on her see-through plastic Ghost chair, another item on David Allen Robertson's must-have furniture list. She wished she was back in Neasden, talking about stretch marks and how her children refused to eat anything not smothered in ketchup. She would never fit in here. She couldn't help judging these women for being so carelessly rich. Even though she was now one of their number, she knew deep down she was nothing like them. They led such privileged lives, yet none seemed very happy. Patrizia's house was gorgeous, but she'd only really be happy when they'd dug out the basement and put in a gym. Elise's housekeeper had just left after a row about pay. And so many of them seemed so angry with their husbands, although their gripes were always couched lightly.

But then Rosie lived in a large house and didn't feel as happy as she should. She was cross with her husband too, most of the time. What was happening to her?

'So any more coffee, ladies?' cried Caroline. 'Bella, you haven't had any. That's not like you. Have a macchiato.'

Bella blushed prettily. 'I'd kill for one, but I can't. I'm off the caffeine.'

'Why?' Caroline asked casually and then: 'No! You're not . . .'

'I am,' she grinned.

'Aaagh!' The women all descended on Bella and started kissing and hugging her.

'Congratulations, babe. That's epic.'

'I'm pregnant again,' Bella explained to a bemused Rosie. 'I've been trying for two years; I was just about to sign up to IVF.'

'That's wonderful!' Rosie beamed.

'Thank you!'

'So you have to book my maternity nurse,' said Patrizia, scrolling through her phone. 'She will have the baby sleeping through the night in one week. How pregnant are you?' She studied Bella's pancake stomach. 'Four months?'

'I've just had the twelve weeks scan.'

'Mmm. Yes, well, usually people book Jacqui as soon as the test comes up positive, but you never know.

Someone might have had a miscarriage and then you'll get lucky.'

That afternoon Rosie had decided to bake with the boys. If Caroline could do it, then why not her? But things hadn't gone according to plan. She'd forgotten to add the eggs to the mix, so had to pull the cake out of the oven after ten minutes and hastily whisk them into the already settling goo. Then when the time was up, the so-called cake had stuck fast to the tin and had to be prised out in about a million pieces. Both boys had looked disgusted.

'Eurgh!'

'I'm not eating that.'

Rosie had exploded. 'There are children in Africa who walk twenty miles barefoot to school every day and you're turning up your noses at a delicious cake.'

'School and cake have nothing to do with each other,' Toby pointed out with unerring logic and it had been all Rosie could do not to chuck the whole wretched mess in the bin. Instead, she'd forced herself joylessly to eat a huge slice that probably contained about forty thousand calories, while the boys watched her pityingly. She'd cleaned her teeth afterwards, but the charred lumpen taste still lingered.

Now the boys were in bed and she was sitting in the snug, a large glass of Pinot Noir at her side and *O'Rourke's* playing silently in the background. She saw far more of Ellie Lewis now than she did of her husband. She was about to call Nanna – the hospital appointment was tomorrow and she wanted to wish her luck. But just as she was picking up her phone it rang, making her jump. Nanna calling her. A psychic thing. But no, it was Christy.

'Hiya, sorry I haven't been in touch for ages. I'm just *so busy.*'

'Again,' Rosie muttered. Christy ignored her. 'But I thought we could have a chat since Jake isn't home tonight.'

'How did you know Jake isn't home?' Rosie asked crossly. Jake was indeed out yet again, 'cheering up Simon', who'd apparently had yet another rough day with Ellie Lewis.

'I just saw him in Soho House with a whole gang of people. Told him he should be home with you. He said he'd have another pint and be on his way.'

'Oh. Right.'

'Rosie, don't sound so pissed off,' Christy said.

'I'm not pissed off,' Rosie lied. 'I'm just tired . . . you know, with the boys and everything.'

'I know Jake's been coming home late a lot. He feels bad about it. But it's part of the job at the minute, the schmoozing. It's what allows you to live in your beautiful house and not go to work, like you always said you wanted.'

'I know,' Rosie said. She hated the way Christy made her feel so ungrateful. She knew she'd always said she wanted those things, but it was a long time ago. There were other things she wanted more now.

'He loves you and the boys so much, you know. He does everything for you three.'

'Sure.'

'Are you OK?'

Rosie tried to come up with a good reason for her grumpiness. 'I'm stressing about this weekend away with Becki. It's only a couple of weeks away now.'

'Oh, bugger. Yeah, I'd be stressing too. But listen, how bad can it be? Just flex your credit cards. The spa's meant to be incredible, so spend as much time chilling in there as possible.' Christy ploughed on. 'Anyway, listen, I have exciting news. I've tickets for the three of us to go to a film premiere. On Thursday. Jordanna Coughlin's new one. Can you come?'

All sulkiness was forgotten. 'Ooh! A premiere! Fuck, yeah! Thanks, Christy.'

'You're welcome. It'll be fun. There's an after-party at the Roundhouse. Book your babysitter.'

'I will. Dizzy will love it; I could get her Jordanna Coughlin's autograph.'

Christy coughed. 'Ahem, please, that's very unprofessional.'

'I'm *not* a professional.'

Christy hesitated for a second, but then laughed and said: 'Fair enough. Bring your autograph book. Clooney's going to be there.'

'I'll wear the gold dress.'

'Brilliant, you do that. Sorry, I have to go – LA's on the line.' Christy vanished.

Conversations with her always ended like this these days. Sometimes it upset Rosie, but now she sat grinning like an imbecile. A premiere. She'd always wanted to go to a premiere. All right, she wasn't a huge fan of Jordanna Coughlin, who was a pointy-nosed girl-next-door blonde but still . . .

She picked up her wine. 'Here's to me,' she crowed and took a large gulp.

14

Rosalba, Christy's PA, called her in the morning.

'So, Rosie, don't get me wrong,' she said in her nasal voice, so totally out of keeping with her slinky appearance. 'You're a beautiful woman, but we don't want you to feel intimidated on the red carpet with all those stars posing, so we'd recommend you go a bit more high-maintenance than usual for the premiere.'

'Oh?' Rosie's heart thudded.

'Mmm. I'm going to email you an approved list of hairdressers our clients use. Select one and I can book you in for highlights and a blow dry. They can also do you a fake tan – nothing *TOWIE*, very subtle, but it'll give you a glow – Christy says you need one.'

'Oh does she?'

But Rosalba didn't do sarcasm. 'Yes, she does. A manicure the day before. And we'll send a make-up artist round. Christy says she's helped you select a dress. A lot of cameras will be on you. At least that's the plan – it's a big moment for Jake with the show coming up. We want his picture everywhere and that's more likely with a glamorous woman by his side.'

'Well, then it's not going to happen,' said Rosie cheerily, but Rosalba didn't laugh.

'I'll send the email with the schedule now.'

'No pressure,' Rosie said, continuing with the joking tone, but the line had gone dead.

'What do you think?' Rosie did a twirl for Jake. Her hair had been coloured and styled at Melly & Lyne in Knightsbridge, and her new, slightly shorter cut had created previously non-existent cheekbones, while the light brown streaks somehow made her eyes brighter. A tight-lipped Indian lady had given her a spray tan, a very gay man a manicure. Ten minutes earlier, she'd put on the gold dress. It felt a bit tighter than it had in the shop that day, but with her trusty ancient M&S control pants underneath she reckoned she could just about get away with it.

On her wrist was the gold and diamond bracelet Jake had bought her when she became pregnant with George. On her feet were her nude L. K. Bennett sandals, her only smart pair of shoes that went with everything. OK, so they were a bit Kate Middleton visits a hospice, but her calves ached simply at the prospect of wearing anything fancier.

'Hey, sexy lady.' Jake started to perform 'Gangnam Style', then flopped back on the bed. 'Dizzy's just arrived, so we can get going.'

Dizzy was sitting on George's bed, reading two rapt boys *The Tiger Who Came to Tea*.

'Enjoy!' she called out. 'I went to a couple of premieres with my friend Muggy – her dad's a drummer; he worked with the Rolling Stones and Duran Duran. They were really boring. You had to sit around for ages while the stars went up the red carpet and there weren't even any adverts to watch.'

'Outsmarted again by our cleaner,' Rosie sighed, as they got into the waiting car. She loved these waiting cars, it was definitely the best thing about their new existence. No more having to carry her heels in an old Tesco's bag, so she could walk to the tube, and do an awkward change just before she arrived. Their very own car, sent by the film distributors, because they were on the VIP list. VIPs apparently being urgently needed to give the movie 'buzz'.

'No longer semi-VIP,' Jake pointed out.

They high-fived each other.

'Baby, we've made it.'

As the car carried them out of the Village and towards central London, the air heady with lemon-scented freshener, Rosie pressed her face against the tinted window. A lightning flash of happiness zipped across her. Those frustrations she'd voiced the other night about being imprisoned by motherhood could be forgotten. Tonight, she was a free agent again and she intended to relish every second of her parole.

'We're having another date night,' she said, squeezing Jake's hand.

'A date with all of the industry,' he frowned. 'Christy says I have to be on my best behaviour and schmooze.'

'You may have to. I don't!'

Jake looked appalled. 'What are you planning, Old Bean?'

'Nothing much,' she teased.

'You must behave. All the Disney people will be there.'

'What do you mean, Disney?'

The look that came over Jake's face when he knew he hadn't quite got away with something appeared. '*You* know. I told you about Disney.'

'You didn't. *What* about them? Are you up for a part as a talking elephant or something?'

'They're planning a huge family franchise – a series of eight comedy-action films. I'm up for the role of the dastardly villain.'

'Wow.' Rosie digested this.

'Not the handsome hero, oddly enough. A bit hurtful but I'll cope.' He paused. 'If I do this, it'll be our pension. I'd never have to work again. Though I'd want to, obviously, but it would give me freedom to choose parts. Can you imagine?'

'Where would this be filmed?'

'In Hollywood. Probably. If it happens.'

'Oh.' *I don't want to go to Hollywood*. Like Elvis Costello not wanting to go to Chelsea. But the film world was so flaky, it might never happen. 'Who will the hero be? Daniel Craig?'

'God, I hope not. I hope it's someone very ugly and a million years old.'

183

'That sounds likely.'

'Anyway, a load of the execs will be there tonight, so you will behave, won't you?' Jake said anxiously.

'Whenever have I not?' Rosie was indignant.

'Well, there was the time we got back from Stooks's party and I found you wedged between the fridge and the kitchen units, with your skirt over your head.'

'I shouldn't have drunk that whisky.'

'Or that time you needed a wee so badly when we were coming back from the pub at Mum and Dad's you did one in the lane, and sat on a nettle.'

'Shh. The driver will hear.'

To end the conversation, Rosie pulled her phone out of her little gold clutch bag. She wanted to try Nanna again. She'd called her twice, and texted her too with a photo of the dress – Nanna would love to see it – but there'd been no reply. Still, Nanna often didn't answer the phone if she was watching telly, though she was too proud to admit she was too deaf to hear it ring over blaring *Corrie*.

'Hey, Nanna. It's me. We're on our way to a film premiere, can you believe? Jordanna Coughlin's latest. What do you think of her? What did you think of the dress? Call me when you have a second, and let me know how it went today. Love you.' She turned to Jake. 'I hope she's OK.'

'Mmm,' he said, staring out of the window.

'Jake! Did you hear me? I am talking about Nanna.'

'Sorry, Bean, sorry. I'm just stressed.'

'What are you stressed about?' Rosie asked slightly impatiently. 'You're a VIP being carried to a fancy awards ceremony in the West End!'

'I'm so scared about this play, Bean. Everyone's going to realize what a fraud I am.'

'You *are not a fraud*. You are a fantastic actor.'

Jake laughed wryly. 'You're kind, but you're a terrible liar. You're not a fantastic actor and neither am I.'

'But . . . Ow!' The sandals were starting to rub against her toes. She fumbled in the little gold clutch she'd bought and pulled out a plaster. Moshi Monsters of course. Well, it was all she had and it was better than blisters. She stuck it on her sore toe, then looking up saw they were drawing up outside the theatre. Christy was standing on the pavement in a blue jacket and black cigarette trousers, waving tickets above her head. Panic lurched in Rosie's chest. She was totally overdressed.

'Finally,' Christy huffed, as they piled out of the car. 'I was worrying you'd be late. Quick, this way to the VIP entrance.' She squeezed Rosie's arm in one of her sudden bouts of warmth. 'It's so nice to have you here. Normally you're always stuck at home with the kids.'

'The kids!' Rosie's irritation at Christy's patronizing attitude was replaced with worry about her sons. She fumbled in her bag for her phone. 'I should call Dizzy, check they're OK.'

'They'll be fine,' Jake said. 'She'll call you if there's a

problem.' He yawned loudly. 'Come on, let's do that red-carpet thing.' They approached a burly suited man with a clipboard and a I-work-at-the-Gap head-mic.

'All right, Jake?' he smiled, waving him through. Rosie tried to follow but he stuck out his arm. 'Sorry, love.'

'Hey!' Jake turned.

'Oh sorry, mate, is she your plus-one? Off you go then.'

I'm not his plus-one, I'm his wife, Rosie fumed silently. Ahead was a rather grubby red carpet filled with people giving each other exaggerated air kisses and laughing. Penned behind metal barriers, a huge crowd was screaming, waving pens, scraps of paper, camera phones and even – disconcertingly – cute babies. Behind another fence, flashbulbs popped and photographers screamed.

'Oi, Denise, love that dress! Hey, Holly, smile won't ya, darling? Amanda, hey, Amanda, over here!'

'There's Jordanna!' Rosie shrieked, pinching Christy so hard that she yelled.

There indeed was the star herself, radiating narcissism in a floor-length silver gown, talking intensely into a bevy of microphones.

'God, she's hideous,' Christy said. 'Made entirely of plastic. Shagged the director to get the part.'

Rosie giggled. 'She speaks highly of you too.'

'Jake, Jake!' the reporters were bellowing. 'Not on *my* patio. Not on *my* patio.'

'I'd better get this over with,' Jake sighed, stepping forward and switching on a megawatt smile. Christy stopped to talk to someone, so Rosie followed Jake.

'Oi!' shouted a photographer. 'Get out of the way, love.'

'Who the fuck's she?' yelled another.

She heard two women in the crowd, waving cameras above their heads. 'I don't like that Jake Perry; he thinks he's all that.'

'He looks rank,' agreed her friend. 'Who's that in the stupid dress?'

Rosie looked away, blushing. They obviously thought she was in the pages of a magazine and couldn't hear them. A sudden breeze made her shiver, and her hair flapped round her face, a lock sticking to her glossed lips.

'Dunno. What is she wearing?'

Rosie stood as the crowds mingled around her, feeling like a mouse trapped in the pathway of a Sherman tank. Everyone seemed to be talking to someone, throwing back their heads, laughing. Only the stars were in dressy dresses like hers, most people looked as if they'd come straight from the office and hurried straight into the cinema, gabbling into their phones. She felt both horribly conspicuous and totally invisible. She wanted to lie down and be rolled up in the red carpet. Then she saw Christy, turning around, looking for her. She waved and teetered towards her as fast as her heels would allow.

'Hey, Christy!' exclaimed Ellie Lewis. Rosie gaped. She was even more beautiful in the flesh than on telly: face smooth as a mirror, eyes round and blue, hair like golden candyfloss and wearing a green dress that was modest but displayed a perfect body. She longed to whip out her phone and take a photo for Nanna, but she knew what Christy would have to say about that.

'Ellie!' shrieked Christy, instantly in professional mode. 'Darling, you look amazing. Darling, do you know, Rosie? Jake's wife.'

Rather alarmingly Ellie held her arms wide open and pulled Rosie to a generous bosom, completely at odds with her skinny body. 'Rosie. Great to see you again!'

'Er, we haven't met.'

Ellie stepped back as if she'd been irradiated. 'Oh my God, I'm so sorry. I, like, say that to everyone because usually I have met them and I've, like, forgotten and then they're insulted and think I'm a stuck-up bitch. But it's so great to meet you.' She looked down at Rosie's feet. 'Great shoes. Hey, and I love the toe decoration. Cute.'

'Oh!' Rosie glanced at the Moshi plaster. 'Thank you.'

'So nice to meet you,' Ellie said firmly, before moving swiftly away. Rosie stood there, waiting to be rescued. To avoid looking like too much of a lemon, she started counting facelifts. She'd reached fifteen (nine women, six men) definites and three maybes by the time Jake returned.

'Done that,' said Jake. 'It's so weird. They ask you things like what's your favourite breakfast cereal and are you a fan of Jordanna.'

'I hope you said yes!' cried Christy, popping up behind him as a uniformed woman tapped Rosie officiously on the shoulder.

'Take your places for the film now! It's starting in five minutes.'

'They always lie about five minutes,' sighed Jake, as they sat in semi-darkness in hot scratchy seats while the big screen showed footage of Edith Bowman on the stage outside, interviewing any old random star who could be pulled off the carpet, before Jordanna finally deigned to talk to her. 'It'll be at least half an hour before this kicks in and then we'll have all the tedious speeches and arse-kissing.'

'I much prefer normal films,' agreed Christy.

'You sound like Dizzy. Look, we've got a free bag of popcorn,' Rosie pointed out. Though she daren't eat it in case she exploded out of her dress. 'And a bottle of water.'

'Bless you, so easily satisfied.'

'As the bishop said to the actress.' Rosie was determined no one should ruin this for her, even if the glamour of the occasion was rather spoilt by the huge fly that kept buzzing around in front of her, bloated from gorging itself on the popcorn strewn all over the floor.

'You two are just spoiled,' she added for good measure, as finally the lights dimmed. Suddenly Rosie shivered. What was she doing here? How had she made it from that tiny flat in St Pauls to this? She was very lucky. She needed to appreciate it more.

15

1993

They were in Christy's bedroom, lying on the floor, heads propped up on pink cushions. Next to them was a plate of digestives. Christy always got them out for Rosie from Nick's biscuit tin. Sandra and Christy didn't touch them – but in case they were ever tempted Sandra had stuck a Post-it to the lid proclaiming the calorie count: seventy-one!

But Rosie could eat as many as she liked without putting on an ounce, and right now she was doing exactly that. Nanna had forgotten to give her lunch money again and she resented using her paper-round wages, which were reserved for treats like clothes from Miss Selfridge, so she'd gone hungry again. On the CD, The Shamen were playing.

'OK, stop, stop!' Rosie waved her biro in the air.

Christy pressed pause and dictated the lyrics.

Rosie confirmed them gravely, scribbling on a piece of paper supported by Christy's defaced GCSE set text of *Tess of the D'Urbervilles*. They were determined to produce the definitive transcription of the lyrics. 'No wonder the BBC banned it.'

'We should suggest singing it in the school concert to Mr Ashdown,' Christy said dryly.

Shrieks. 'Can you imagine the parents' faces?!'

'Do you remember that time Mr Ashdown had us singing "I Am a Gay Musician"?' Christy snorted.

'What was he thinking of,' Rosie giggled, 'teaching that song to a class of fourteen-year-old girls?' She spoke as if fourteen-year-girls were babies, rather than a mere two years younger than them, the sophisticated sixteen-year-olds.

'And assembly. Having us sing about purple-headed mountains.'

'"All things bright and beautiful",' Christy trilled, then suddenly stopped at the noise of more yelling downstairs.

'*He is not going to live in my house.* I've told you, not in a million years.'

'Sandy, he's our *son.*'

'He is not my son any longer. He is a freak.'

A door slammed.

'Oh fuck,' said Christy. She almost never used words like that.

'Barron?'

After the row at Christmas Barron had been packed off to Australia, but now he was due home again.

'Mum has this stupid idea that if she keeps sending him away, he's going to change his mind,' Christy sighed. 'But he won't. It's something he has to do.

He's told me he feels like he's a prisoner, trapped in the wrong body.'

She sighed again. Christy so rarely let go of her guard, but right now she looked exhausted and utterly crestfallen.

'Mum won't have him living here, but where else can he go? He failed all his A levels, and no one would give him a job anyway because he looks so weird. He's not good at anything. He's going to have to go on the dole and get a council flat.' She saw Rosie's expression. 'I mean, not that there's anything wrong with that but . . . you know.'

'I know.'

'Dad wants to support him, but Mum says they have to wipe their hands of him until he comes to his senses. But he can't. He won't.'

At home that night, there were other troubles. While Rosie and Christy had been listening to The Shamen, Marianne had been announcing to her mother that she was moving in with her new boyfriend in Weston-super-Mare. Arguments about this had been rumbling for a while, with Nanna pointing out that she needed Marianne's housekeeping contributions from her current job as a barmaid at the bingo hall to keep afloat.

'You'll have a spare room,' she was telling Nanna, as Rosie walked through the door. 'Take in a lodger.'

'I don't want a stranger in my house. And who the hell would want to lodge here anyway?' Nanna lit a

Rothmans. 'You're so selfish, Marianne!' she exclaimed as she exhaled. 'It'll be over with this Ricky within a month and then you'll be begging to come back. It's not like it's the sodding first time.'

Rosie tried to move unobtrusively past them – impossible in a kitchen the size of a bathtub – and into her bedroom, where she could tackle her maths homework. But then an idea struck her and she swivelled round. 'I've thought of something!'

'Always was the brainbox,' Marianne muttered sourly. 'Mind you, things could have been very different for me, if I'd not made the mistake of having you. I could have stayed on at school.'

Rosie ignored her. She was far too familiar with such outbursts. 'Remember Barron, Nanna?' she said.

'The gay boy?' Marianne lit her own cigarette.

Rosie fanned away the smoke. 'He's not gay. Just . . . diffrent.'

'Such a nice boy,' Nanna purred.

'He is, isn't he? And I think he might need a place to live. At least for a while. So he could move into mum's room!'

And so it was that Barron ended up living with them. Nick paid a small rent and Barron helped Nanna with her shopping and chores while he searched fruitlessly for a job. He also made regular visits to the doctor.

'What exactly is it you're hoping for, Barron?' Nanna asked, that first evening over a tea of pie and chips.

Rosie cringed, but it was never in Nanna's nature to beat around the bush.

'Well,' Barron said, clearing his throat. He must have been about sixteen stone at this stage, with a huge beer belly that hung round his gut like a lifebelt. People crossed the road if they saw him walking down the street at night, but he was the gentlest man imaginable. 'The doctor's giving me hormones.'

'Hormones?'

'That's right. I don't want to be a man any more, you see. It's the first step to turning me into a woman.'

'Ah.' Nanna got up, took her handbag from its peg behind the front door and removed the Rothmans pack. She lit up. She inhaled. She appeared to be examining what barron had just said carefully, like a piece of steak on special at Iceland.

'What else do you have to do then?'

'Well,' Barron said. 'I also have to live like a woman for a year. To prove I really, really want this. Because obviously once they do the operation –' Christy flinched at the mere mention of this – 'there's no turning back.'

'I'll say!' exclaimed Nanna, almost choking.

'So you're going to live as a woman?' Rosie asked. She'd be lying to claim she wasn't horribly embarrassed at the prospect. The neighbours would point and nudge each other even more than they had already.

'I don't know,' Barron lisped, wiping thick gravy from his even thicker lips. 'I don't know. Because the thing is I asked, "What do you mean live like a woman?"'

And he said: "You know, wear a dress when you walk round Tesco's." And I said: "I won't wear a dress. I don't believe in all that. I'm a feminist." '

There was a second's pause and then Nanna snorted with laughter. As she began to bellow, so did Rosie. Then Barron started. It was infectious; they giggled and giggled, wiping tears from their cheeks, pushing away their half-eaten pies and clutching their aching sides.

'You're a feminist!' Nanna shrieked.

'I am. I'm bloody Emmeline Pankhurst.'

'I don't think I've had such a good laugh since I seen *Life of Brian*, lover,' Nanna told him when they'd all – sort of – calmed down. 'You can stay with me for life.'

So Barron started taking the hormones. But the stand-off over his feminism remained. He refused to wear dresses, so the therapist refused to refer him for an NHS operation.

'She says it's such a serious operation, she can't possibly do it unless she knows one hundred per cent I'm serious. But I am,' Barron wailed. 'I just have principles.'

'Can't you bend them principles a bit, lover?' Nanna asked. Much as she and Rosie adored Barron's unfailing good nature, his handiness with a duster and the funny little tunes he warbled in the shower, they were getting rather tired of this circular argument. 'Compromise, my ducks. Just wear a dress out and about in public a bit and then you'll get your op.'

'It wouldn't be being true to who I am,' Barron objected. 'That's the whole point. I've struggled for so long to be true to me; if I back down on this, I might as well throw in the towel.'

It was frustrating but Rosie kind of admired him. And she loved having Barron living with them, he was so much sunnier to have around the house than Mum with her constant moodiness, forever falling in and out of love and refusing to help Nanna with the house-work – 'Because I've just had my heart broken, can't you see?' It also meant that, for the first time since they were eleven, Christy was a visitor to the flat, coming over at least twice a week. It hadn't seemed it at the time, with exams looming and Rosie nursing an unre-quited crush on Pete Langridge who was in a joint-school drama production of *Guys and Dolls* and Nanna blow-ing her top about enormous phone bills, but looking back at how close she and Christy had been, without careers or children getting in the way, it had been one of the best chunks of her life.

16

The present

'So?' whispered Christy as, after what seemed like centuries, the credits rolled and the audience broke into rapturous applause.

'*Scheisse*,' Rosie replied, as they shuffled in the dark out into the aisle.

Christy picked up on the reference instantly. 'I know, *merde*.'

'*Poshel na khui, suka, blyad!*' They both giggled uproariously.

'What did you think?' Rosie asked Jake.

'Brilliant. Work of genius,' he said loudly. He lowered his voice. 'When I went to that Gillian Anderson film I loudly told Rosalba how crap it was and Gillian's mum was sitting behind me and went mental . . . Rhiannon! Hey, sweets. Loved it! Brilliant. Well done, darling.'

'Did you like it?' asked Rhiannon, with justified suspicion. She was about Rosie's age, in a silver trouser suit. Maybe Rosie needed a silver trouser suit to complete her life.

'Darling,' replied Jake enigmatically. He turned to

Rosie. 'This is Rhiannon Barnes. She cast the film. Brilliantly. For *Disney*. This is my wife, Rosie.'

'Hello.' Rhiannon glanced at Rosie as if she'd been asked to calculate her VAT. Then she straightened Jake's collar, smiling up at him. 'So are you coming to the party?'

'Course. Though why does it have to be in freaking Camden?'

'I know. When will they realize we'd be happier in the Hippodrome, so we could just walk across Leicester Square, show our faces and be done with it?'

Complaining again, Rosie thought. While talking, they'd left the building via a side door and emerged into the chilly night air of Leicester Square. Rosie shivered and hugged her thin jacket close. *How do the stars cope with all that posing in their skimpy frocks?* She giggled at such a Nanna-like thought.

'The car's waiting round the corner to take us to the party,' Jake said, putting his arm round her. In her ear, he whispered. 'Rhiannon is such a cunt.' Rosie stifled a laugh.

Fifteen minutes later, Rosie, Christy and Jake entered the gigantic space of the Roundhouse, which was decked out as an Aladdin's cave of wonders. Dry ice floated through the air, enormous latticed lanterns hung from the ceiling and veiled nymphettes in belly-dancer costumes waved plates of what look like oysters studded with pomegranates under their noses.

'Wow. This must have cost thousands.'

'Worth it in terms of publicity,' Christy said sagely, grabbing a glass of something purple from a tray. 'Hey, have one of these, I think it's a pomegranate Martini.'

'Ooh, yeah. Maybe take two?'

Christy laughed. 'Calm down, love. Don't behave like a competition winner.'

'But I feel like one. This is brilliant!'

The three of them clinked glasses. 'Hooray for Rosie being here!' Christy cried, beaming.

'I agree,' said Jake.

'Excuse me,' said a woman – about twenty, tight hot-pink dress, reddish curls piled high on top of her head. 'Can I have a picture please?' She handed her phone to Rosie and draped her arms round Jake's neck.

'Uh, sure.'

Rosie peered at the phone. She wasn't too good with these. She clicked what she hoped was the right button.

'Oh God, I don't believe this,' gasped the woman, slumping against Jake. 'I think I'm going to faint.'

'Are you OK?' Rosie gasped. She turned to Christy. 'Quick! Get some help.'

''S all right.' The woman straightened up and snatched her phone from Rosie. 'Thanks.' She headed off into the crowd.

'Well,' Rosie said. It was as if Jake were no longer her husband, but public property that she shared with the world. Jake shrugged as a crowd of people suddenly swarmed around him, including Simon the play's director, who was balding, a bit tubby and a good six inches shorter than Brunhilde von Fournigan, who in person looked less like a supermodel and more like a rather bored alien.

Jake introduced them to Rosie, but they both looked bemused at the very sight of her, and instantly backed away. Rosie found herself being pushed further and further away from Jake, who made no sign of coming to her rescue. After a few moments, she decided she'd had enough. She wandered off to gaze at the dance floor, where a few people were making unimpressive shapes to CeeLo Green. She turned to Christy.

'Come on!'

'I can't dance!' She looked horrified. 'A client might see me.'

'Chris! This isn't you talking.' Rosie snatched her empty glass and placed it on a table, then grabbed two more from a passing man in purple harem pants and a bare chest.

'C'mon, Chris. Down in one.'

'Coming from you, Mrs Oh-No-I'll-Have-to-Get-Up-for-the-Kids.' But there was a sudden glint in Christy's eye that Rosie hadn't seen for years.

'If you can shake off your inhibitions, I can too.' Rosie nudged Dame Maggie Smith with her hip as she headed determinedly towards the dance floor. 'C'mon. Dare ya.'

*

An hour later, Rosie was drenched and sweaty, bare-foot, having long lost her shoes. Jake tapped her on the shoulder.

'Bean, it's time we made a move. It's nearly midnight.'

'Not yet,' she yelled over the pounding beat. 'Come and dance with me.'

She reached for him, but he stepped backwards, hands raised, as if fending off an angry bull. 'Absolutely no way!'

'Aaah. C'mon.' Jake usually loved to strut his stuff, though he was no Anton Du Beke.

'Bean, no. Someone will film me on their phone and put it on YouTube. It's time to go.'

'I'm not finished yet,' she protested, just as the first bars of 'Single Ladies' struck up. 'C'mon!'

Jake took another step back. Christy stepped in between them.

'You go home,' she instructed Jake. 'Rosie and I will stay on. Girls' night, eh, Rosie?'

'Yeah!' Rosie shook a fist in the air. 'Put your hands up!'

Jake looked troubled. 'How will you get home . . . ? I can't keep the car waiting all night for you.'

'On a night bus!' shrieked Rosie. 'Never used to bother me.'

'I'll put her in a cab,' said Christy. 'Now off you toddle.'

'Are you sure about this?'

'Go!' Christy ordained. Jake obediently slunk off into the crowd.

Two hours later, exhausted-looking bouncers having begged them to leave the party so they could go home, Rosie was on the dance floor of a nightclub off the King's Road dancing to 'Where Is the Love?'. And a top-notch effort she was making, though she said it herself. Basically, if Fergie retired she could step in tomorrow, no problem. And here was her own personal will.i.am replacement in the form of a Brazilian transvestite called Georgia.

'My son's called George,' she informed him, as he twirled her under his arm. 'And my best friend's sister is a transsexual. Who's over there. Not the transsexual, the friend. Is that what you want? To be a transsexual? Or do they say transgender now? Are you gonna have the op?'

'*O que?*'

'Nothing,' Rosie yelled, waving her arms in the air as if it were still the nineties.

A new tune came on. She had no idea what she was dancing to, all her knowledge of popular music had vanished exactly three years, nine months and six days ago when Toby had emerged from her butchered nether regions.

She grabbed a random water glass on the table beside her and took a huge gulp. The hangover that had been bubbling under for the past ten minutes or so was threatening to surface, but she didn't want the night to end yet. It was so great to have turned the tables, to be the one out having fun, the one who was going to crawl in, wasted, as dawn broke.

'Thank you!' she screamed at Christy, who had reappeared from the loos and was gyrating beside her.

'Just think!' Christy shouted. 'If you move to LA, you could really enjoy the party lifestyle.'

Suddenly the noise was now officially too loud and strange, the lights too bright, the people too weird – and young. Didn't they have homes to go to?

'You know I don't want to go to LA,' she hissed.

'It would set you up for life.' Christy took a step back, as if preparing herself for a nuclear explosion. 'Just saying,' she added lightly. 'Of course it's up to you and Jake.'

'It would set you up too,' Rosie snapped, plonking herself down on a shabby leather banquette.

'I'm fine the way I am,' Christy said, sitting beside her. 'I'm thinking of you.'

'I'm fine the way I am too. It's about Nanna.' Oh God, Nanna. She pulled her phone out of her bag. She still hadn't returned her call. Well, now wasn't the time to chase her up. Rosie stood unsteadily. She was going to have huge blisters tomorrow. 'Let's get going. The sun must be up.'

'Want to stay at mine?' Christy asked. 'It's just round the corner. It would be like old times.'

'I have to get the boys up in the morning.'

'Jake can bloody do that.'

Rosie was tempted. She had a flashback to the old

204

days, when they'd shared that flat in Chelsea before Christy had bought it for a song from the landlord and she'd moved in with horrible Adam. Giggling late into the night, listening to Radiohead, watching *ER*. 'I could come back to yours for a coffee and then get a taxi home.'

'Will you?' Christy looked thrilled.

Since the time they'd both lived there, Christy's block had changed beyond recognition. Then it was a crumbling sixties monstrosity, now – thanks to huge investment by the developer who'd bought the freehold – it had been re-coated in gleaming steel. The lobby, once a bleak concrete space, was now carpeted and modern art (replicas from Ikea but anyway) hung from the walls. The lifts that used to stink of piss and broke down were shiny and swift, the corridors dimly lit with David-Allen-Robertson-style fittings.

'You were so clever to buy this place.'

'I know. It's worth a bomb now. It'll be my pension.'

Inside, the walls that used to be covered in lurid seascapes from the landlady's native Cyprus had been painted an austere dark grey. The furniture was all modern Danish – sourced painstakingly from auction houses – the books were alphabetized on the shelves in the corridor, and the bed was always neatly made as soon as Christy got up in the morning. In the kitchen, all stainless steel and exposed pipes, a single mug sat washed up next to the empty sink.

'It's amazing,' Rosie marvelled. 'You go out and you

come back and everything is exactly the same as you left it, because no sticky fingers have been throwing things all over the floor.'

Christy snorted, as if Rosie were joking. 'Coffee? Or a nightcap?'

'Nightcap,' Rosie decided. Christy opened a cupboard and selected a bottle of Bailey's. Unlike the bottle of Bailey's in Rosie's house, it wasn't seventeen years old and covered in a thick layer of dust, *and* she had two gleaming shot glasses to hand.

'You regularly serve guests tumblers of Baileys, rather than just buy it on a whim in Ibiza duty free and never touch it again?'

'Our achievements are all relative,' said Christy, as they clinked the tiny tumblers. 'You've given birth.'

'Do you want to give birth, Chris?' Rosie asked cautiously. Normally they avoided this subject like a drunk in the street. Christy had never treated Rosie in quite the same way since the boys were born, and Rosie could never work out if it was because she wanted her own children so much it hurt to go there, or if it was because she was so appalled by the prospect she no longer felt the pair of them had anything in common.

'Not in the traditional sense of the word,' Christy said. 'You know that.'

'Oh yes, you'd have an elective C-section, like your mum.' Sandra was always banging on about how she'd worked on the Friday morning, then gone into hospital at lunchtime, had Christy removed surgically and was back at work a fortnight later. 'I've seen what childbirth does to a woman's body,' she used to tell the girls grimly, while driving them somewhere in that white Volvo. It was thanks to her that Rosie had been petrified of childbirth first time round, another thing she held against Sandra P. after the appalling way she'd treated Barron. 'But do you think you want kids?'

'Not much chance of it at the moment,' Christy said grimly.

'With this guy you're seeing?'

There was a slight pause and then she said: 'Mmm.'

'He's married?' Rosie almost added, but she stopped herself just in time. 'Is he worth it?' she asked instead.

Christy chuckled wryly. 'Oh, definitely.'

'Will he leave his wife?'

'Maybe. I don't know. He wouldn't want more kids. He's already got them.'

'You wouldn't rather be with someone who was free?'

For a second she thought Christy was about to really talk but then she said: 'No, I want to be with him.' She sighed and pulled her knees up to her chest. 'It was so good to be out tonight. Do you remember that time in Italy?'

Rosie felt a tinge of frustration. It had always been this way. She came to Christy with her problems but Christy never seemed to have a care in the world – and if she did, say with all the Barron/Sandrine business, she didn't like to mention it. Still, the kids question wasn't worth pursuing. Instead, she giggled: 'We didn't realize we were in a gay resort.'

'We wondered why we were the only girls on the beach.'

'And we thought it was an Italian thing, all the men walking around holding hands.'

They both shrieked with laughter.

'No wonder they made such of a fuss of us in that disco, plying us with free drinks. We were probably the only women ever to set foot in there.'

Tears poured down Rosie's face at the memory. 'I miss you,' she said suddenly.

'I miss you too,' Christy said softly.

'You know, it's weird because if it wasn't for you I'd never have met Jake and had the boys and everything but . . .'

'. . . it all means we can't see as much of each other. I know. But things will change. The boys will get bigger and you'll have more free time.'

'But you'll always be Jake's agent?'

'Well, I hope so,' Christy said. If she'd picked up on Rosie's hint, she didn't acknowledge it. The little carriage clock on her mantelpiece struck three. Rosie started.

'Fuck! I have to be up in three hours. Fuck! Fuck, fuck.'

Christy laughed. 'I'll call you a cab, Cinderella.'

17

There was a brief hiatus as Rosie struggled to open the gates and then tried to insert the correct keys in each lock of the front door. Finally she was in her house. She managed to pull herself together just enough to stumble into the kitchen and concoct that old magic potion of two Berocca and a pint of water, then drag herself up to the bedroom, stumbling over George's monkey on the stairs.

'Oops.'

Daylight illuminated the tiny Ikea bed where Jake lay sleeping. Rosie fell on top of him.

'Whaa . . . ?'

'I love you,' she slurred. 'I love you so much.'

She yanked at his boxer shorts. He pushed her away.

'Aaah, c'mon.'

'Bean, what time is it?'

'Nearly five,' she giggled, still trying to grope him.

'George will be up in about an hour. Gerroff.' He rolled on to his side and started snoring. If the fans could see him now.

Rosie fell on to her back, slightly put out. But then a diorama of the night started jiggling in her head, and she smiled. She loved Christy, why was she ever cross with her? Los Angeles talk and married men aside. She needed more nights like this. She'd have to see what could be arranged.

Two and a half hours later, Rosie felt less enthusiastic about such nights, when a little tongue started licking her face and a shrill voice cried: 'Mummy, morning time!'

'Waaarrugh.'

'Mummy, Mummy. With a big, fat bummy.' The boys had learned this hilarious line from Horrid Henry. So much for the benefits of reading to your children.

'George, darling, Mummy's very tired. Could you just get into bed and keep the noise down? Shall we all play at going to sleep?'

'No! Let's play lions.'

'Oof.' Someone was whacking Rosie over the head with a hammer as she attempted to balance on a dinghy in treacherous seas. Last night was the stupidest activity she'd ever participated in. What had possessed her?

'Grraaargh, Mummy! I am *king of the jungle*.'

'Jake,' she pleaded. 'Can you take him downstairs, let me have a little lie-in?'

'I can,' Jake sniggered. 'But we have to be at King's Mount for our tour in just over an hour.'

'Oh fuck.'

'Mummy!' they both exclaimed delightedly.

'Sorry, I mean fudge. But I'm about to die,' Rosie protested.

'We reap what we sow,' Jake said cheekily. 'I did ask Cinderella to leave at midnight but you wanted to go pole dancing.' He paused and then said: 'Wasn't that what you were whining about the other night, never throwing your cares to the wind, never shedding responsibilities?'

'I *wasn't* whining. And I wasn't pole dancing.' Though she'd have loved to, given half a chance, she acknowledged to herself.

'Downing shots then.'

'Christy made me,' she groaned. Her brain was a burnt-out engine stuck in a bog. Then she remembered something. She grabbed her phone from the floor. Oh, thank God, a text from Nanna.

All fine, luvr. Don't u worry bt a thing. Luv the dress. Can't wait
2 hear all bout preemeer. Did u meet Ellie? Seen her in the *Sun*
this morning, looking gorge – saw Jake too, none of u. xx ☺

'Oh, thank goodness.' She fell back on her pillows and then sat bolt upright. The room tilted. 'Ugh.' Rosie forced herself to roll out of bed and stumbled to the en suite, where she caught sight of herself in the mirror. Oh help. A shower would sort her out. That and some Touche Eclat. They'd had better.

King's Mount was a towering Gothic pile that they approached through tall gates and up a leafy, winding drive.

'It doesn't look like a school; it looks like a hotel!'

'Pretty impressive, no?' said Jake, parking beside a Lamborghini. 'Think of how much more fun it would be for Tobes to go to school here than that cramped little place down the road.'

'Mmm.' Rosie was too weak to argue. She wanted nothing more than to be lying in a darkened room.

In the school lobby, lined with portraits of severe-looking men in mortar boards and notices covered in gold writing listing scholarships to Eton, three other mothers and two fathers were waiting. Covertly Rosie surveyed them. Everyone said the friendships you made at the school gates bonded you for life. These were women she would laugh and cry and grow old with. One was in a houndstooth suit, carrying a brief-case and tapping her foot impatiently. Another was in a tracksuit, hair pulled back in a ponytail and actually hopping up and down as if she couldn't wait to bound away and start jogging again. There was a couple: he in a suit, frowning over his BlackBerry, and she in a floaty summer dress, looking very pale.

'I feel sick,' the woman said confidingly to Rosie, as they poured themselves coffees at a trestle table.

'Me too,' Rosie smiled. 'I was out until three, getting wasted.'

The woman looked at her, horrified. 'I didn't mean that. I'm sick with nerves to see if Ruben gets in here. We only moved here when he was two months and I was worried I'd be too late.'

'You'll be fine,' said Rosie, hurriedly returning to

Jake with the coffee. He was talking to a man who'd just walked in. In contrast to her husband, who, at her insistence, was in a smart pair of trousers and a shirt, he was in combats and a baggy shirt. He was slightly unshaven, radiating the message I-do-something-arty-that-I-can-fit-around-the-kids.

'Hello,' he said, holding out a hand. 'I'm Kim.'

'Rosie.'

'So who's your boy?'

'Um.' In her hungover state, it took Rosie a moment to remember.

'He's called Toby,' Jake said impatiently.

'This is Shane.' He pulled out his phone and showed them a photo of a tousle-mopped tot.

'Aah, bless,' Rosie gushed. 'How old is he?' The old chestnut that she'd always pulled out at dire baby groups when she'd wanted a trapdoor in the floor to open up and deliver her from her exhaustion. As if she cared. Nothing was more boring than a stranger's child.

'Nearly two. We've almost certainly left it too late to get in here, but Shannon and I thought what the hell, give it a go. Unfortunately, Shannon couldn't come to look round. She's at Barclays; it's pretty full on. So what do you do, mate?'

'I'm an actor,' Jake said slightly frostily.

Rosie squirmed. Did her husband expect everyone to recognize him now?

'Oh yeah? Been in anything I'd have heard of?'

A tall lady in a tweed suit marched into the hallway

and everyone stood to attention. 'Good morning!' she yelled, or so it seemed to Rosie's delicate ears. 'Welcome, welcome to King's Mount. Are we all here?' She glanced at a list. 'Mr Hobbs?'

'Yes,' Kim barked.

Down the list, she went. 'Mr and Mrs Perry?' she finished. Everyone's heads turned and the suited husband muttered something to the anxious wife. The tweedy lady's expression softened. 'Thank you so much for coming', she cooed.

'Er, pleasure!' Rosie glanced down at her top. It bore a huge sticker emblazoned with a smiley face and the message I'VE BEEN A GOOD BOY. George's Wendy reward from yesterday. Shit. With as much dignity as she could muster, she ripped the sticker off and stuffed it in her pocket.

The tour commenced. Brightman's had smelled of cabbage and soap, but King's Mount reeked of lavish flower arrangements.

'This is like Anne Hathaway's hotel suite on Oscar night,' she muttered to Jake, as they were led into gleaming labs that might put NASA to shame.

'I've just realized your husband's Jake Perry,' Kim said in her ear. 'Not on *my* patio.'

'Ha ha.' Rosie seriously thought she might be sick any second.

'I hated him in *Private Wives*. I didn't think he was funny at all.' He shrugged. 'Hope you don't mind me saying. Constructive criticism's always so useful, I find.'

He smiled, as if they'd been exchanging pleasantries about the weather. It never failed to astonish Rosie how people thought it was acceptable to criticize your spouse, because they'd seen him on telly. Did they think actors and their families weren't real people, that they only existed on a screen? Did he think Rosie would pass on his 'constructive criticism' and that Jake would be grateful for it?

'Do you think he'd sign a DVD for my mum?' he continued.

She could only ignore this. 'So you're the . . . uh –' Rosie didn't want to say house husband, it sounded so politically incorrect, so she tried – 'the primary care-giver in your family?'

'That's right,' he smirked. 'After Lalage was born, I decided to downsize, so I could fully participate in my children's formative years.' He shrugged. 'I suppose I just love my children.'

And other people didn't? Who was this man? Penelope Leach disguised as a dad from a building-society advert?

'So you must know all the gossip,' said the nervous mum, suddenly slipping in beside her as they exited the building through a side door and strode across a wind-swept playing field. 'Is Ellie Lewis a total bitch? Is she still with that guy, what's his name? Oh baby brain! Darling, who was that handsome young man who played the French painter in that film we saw when your mum babysat that one time?'

'I don't remember,' her husband snapped, still studying his phone. 'You're the one who dragged me to see it.'

'Your husband's so funny,' the woman continued. 'The first time I saw him I thought he was gay but . . .'

Rosie laughed weakly. 'Obviously not.'

'Well . . . no.' The woman didn't look convinced. They were standing outside a classroom now: through the glass in the door Rosie could see rows of neat little boys in blazers, heads buried in textbooks. Would Toby really fit in here? Not to mention the far wilder George.

'It's amazing,' Jake said to her softly. 'We have to get the boys in here.'

'What do you think?' asked the businesswoman under her breath. 'I'm not that convinced. They only offer German as a second language and that's from the age of ten. What about Mandarin? What about Spanish?'

Rosie's stomach churned. There was a very tempting bin just there . . .

'Excuse me,' she said. Leaning over it, she deposited three cocktails, two shots, a selection of canapés, three glasses of champagne, two slices of dry toast and five cups of coffee.

18

The tweedy lady called to say she was so sorry about Rosie's food poisoning and she'd be in touch very shortly about any last-minute vacancies.

'Well done for cocking that one up,' Jake had snapped as they drove home, windows wide open, to lessen the chances of Rosie hurling again.

'I'm sorry,' she said abjectly. 'I couldn't help it.'

'You could have not stayed out all night and got wasted. This is our sons' future on the line.'

Rosie stared at his profile in astonishment. Jake laughed at people who said things like that. They'd agreed early on that they were laid-back parents. They mocked couples who Gina-Forded their babies and poured scorn on Baby Einstein DVDs. But he certainly wasn't laughing now.

'I'm sorry,' she said again.

'At least I was there,' Jake said. 'Hopefully I made a good enough impression to pull us through.'

'Hopefully you did.'

'Don't be sodding sarcastic.'

'I'm sorry,' she said. 'I'm sorry I got so drunk last night. It's just . . . You know I don't go out much any more.'

'Whatever,' Jake snapped.

Rosie's face flamed and her body stiffened. Jake continued driving, looking angry. How could he speak to her like that? She started dreaming up rebukes, but she simply didn't have the energy. Instead, she dwelled on the most slow and painful ways of torturing her husband, who was muttering to himself about the bad traffic and how he'd be late for rehearsals. Indeed, traffic was so slow that by the time they reached the house she had to abandon her plan of half an hour in front of Jeremy Kyle with a bar of Galaxy and more or less rush straight out to pick up the boys from nursery.

'Mummy,' George said as they ambled home, 'I didn't sleep very well last night. My bum was all itchy and bothering me and Dizzy says she thinks I must have worms.'

So now the three of them were in the chemist across the road. The chemist held a special place in Rosie's heart. Its stock made a supermarket in Siberia in the nineteen seventies look like the Grand Bazaar in Istanbul, consisting of two packs of nappies, three of sanitary towels, a couple of toothbrushes and three bars of soap. It was run by the world's grumpiest woman, who took positive pleasure in humiliating her tiny band of customers, who were too elderly or too desperate for a cure to be able to walk further afield to the smarter chemist by the Green.

'Do you really think you should be on the pill?' Grumpy had asked Rosie a couple of weeks previously in front of a queue of pensioners. 'It can't be doing your body much good. Anyway, at your age are you sure you really need it?'

It was impossible right now to see how the shop made any money. Rosie was certain it was a front for international arms dealers. But there was no alternative. Head high, shoulders back, deep breath.

'I'd like some treatment for threadworms, please.' She couldn't face the ticking off she was going to receive for not making her children wash their hands more, so she found herself adding: 'For my friend.'

Grumpy smiled, relishing the conversation they were about to have. 'Sorry? What did you say you wanted?'

'My *friend* wanted.'

She snorted. 'Right. *Friend*. What did you say your *friend* wanted?'

'Worm pills,' Rosie muttered. She should have gone to the Green.

Grumpy shook her head. 'You must tell your children to wash their hands more.'

'They're not *my* children. Child. It's just one child. And my friend.' Rosie's imagination was running riot now. 'And the au pair, she's . . . Bulgarian! And the husband – he's Spanish, he's a . . . bullfighter! Retired now. So we'll need treatment for four.'

Grumpy smirked. 'And how old is this *other person's* child then?'

'Hang on . . .' Rosie made great show of trying to remember. 'Um, four, I think.'

'Oh! Same age as *your* little boy!'

As they were leaving with an expensive packet of pills ('Remember you need to treat the whole family, all four of you and again in a fortnight if you want to say goodbye to itchy bottoms.'), a teenager appeared from the back room. Rosie couldn't bear to imagine Grumpy One procreating but the girl had a boss-eye squint that meant she must be her daughter.

She looked Rosie up and down and then said, 'Is it true you're Jake Perry's wife?'

'Um, yes.'

'Wow! That's amazing. I love Jake Perry. Will you tell him I said hello?'

'Sure.'

'My name's Shanice. You'll be sure to tell him that, won't you? Shanice. God, I can't believe you're married to Jake Perry.' She looked her up and down again. 'I mean . . . are you *sure* you are?'

'Last time I checked. Ha ha.'

'Amazing,' she breathed, shaking her head.

'Thank you.'

'Sorry about the kiddies. You know, having worms and everything.'

'It's a friend's child, actually.'

'Oh sure, and I'm the bride of Dracula,' she snapped back as Rosie hurried out of the door. Her phone was ringing. Jake. Calling to apologize, no doubt. About time too.

'Hey, how's it going? God, we've just been mortified in the chem—'

'King's Mount called me.'

'Oh?'

'They've found a place for Toby. He can start in September. Isn't that great?'

'Oh.'

'Well, sound a bit more pleased, won't you?' Jake snapped. 'I thought you'd be overjoyed after your performance this morning . . .'

'It's great, I suppose.'

'You suppose? You go and hurl in front of the head of one of the best prep schools in the country and they still offer our son a place, despite it allegedly being booked up for years. It's amazing news. Toby's a made man.'

Rosie looked at Toby, who was squatting down, poking something no doubt vile on the pavement with a stick.

'He's a made man?' she asked incredulously. What was happening to her husband? Next minute, he'd be insisting the boys went to Eton like all the Wendy's mums. Followed by a spell at Sandhurst.

'I have to go, Simon's calling us back into rehearsals. I'm sorry you're not more pleased about this.' Jake was gone.

Rosie swayed slightly. Was she going to be sick again?

'Come on, boys, let's get home. It's a telly day.'

'Wa-hoo!' they cried.

19

Becki's birthday weekend away had finally arrived. In the end it hadn't taken much persuasion for her to leave the kids in Dave's charge, after all he was hardly Kurt Cobain. She'd huffed and puffed a bit about how she'd have to cook all their meals in advance and leave a minute-by-minute timetable, but Rosie could tell she was excited at the prospect of a break and that made Rosie excited too.

She, however, had different childcare problems. An unscheduled Saturday rehearsal had been arranged, meaning Jake couldn't look after the boys. Dizzy was going to a cousin's wedding. So at the last moment she'd had to ask Yolande to help out.

'I'd love to!' she had trilled.

Now it was Saturday morning. Rosie had been up since six with George, as usual, and had spent two hours packing – not for herself, for the boys, obviously – as both insisted on taking every toy they owned.

She'd finally succeeded in strapping them into the car. She'd actually remembered the anti-sickness wrist-bands. The only task remaining was to say goodbye to Jake, who was in his tracksuit doing lunges as he waited for Rolla to arrive.

'So you'll drive down to your mum's after the rehearsal?'

'I said so, didn't I?' Jake replied, red in the face as he touched his toes.

'Yes, you did. Sorry. Just . . . I've never left the boys for this long before. It makes me anxious.'

'You have nothing to be anxious about. You're going away to have a wicked time.' He stood up and pecked her on the cheek. 'We'll speak tonight. Bye.'

'Bye,' Rosie said. 'Don't forget to make sure the boys brush their teeth. And when you come back bring Snuggle Bunny.'

'I will.' Jake's phone rang. 'Gotta take this. Have fun. Hi, Christy . . .'

On the drive to the Cotswolds Rosie felt discomfited. Ever since the King's Mount fiasco, she and Jake had been so brusque, so businesslike, with each other. When they'd just met every parting had been exquisitely painful, every reunion unspeakable bliss. But now it was all, 'Do this, do that, don't forget, see you.' Of course relationships couldn't always exist at giddy heights, but some affection would be nice, some meaningful conversation. There hadn't been any of that for weeks.

'Mummy!' cried Toby. 'Play us "Happy".'

Pharrell accompanied them on a loop for the rest of the drive. Despite the wristbands, George was sick twice. Upon arrival, Rosie had had to break the news to Yolande that toast had been deleted from Toby's 'like list'.

'He says he doesn't like bread and this is just warm bread.'

'So what does he eat for breakfast now?' Yolande was rightly appalled by this news.

'Dry Weetabix.'

'No milk, Granny. I hate milk, remember.'

'We'll try you on bacon and eggs in the morning,' Yolande had said, winking at Rosie. 'I know it's hard for you career girls to cook a full English.'

'I'm not a career girl any more –' Rosie began, but then gave up. 'Be good for Granny!' she said to the boys, but they had already run off into the garden, without even a backwards glance.

'We're going to have a lovely time,' Yolande reassured her. 'I've baked them a huge tin of cakes and I'll bet my life by the time you return I'll have Toby eating baked beans.'

Rosie smiled. 'Very good, Yolande.'

She drove across country down to Berkshire, enjoying adult voices on Radio 4, instead of pop on a loop and 'Wheels on the Bus'. She'd picked Becki up at Taplow station and they'd completed the last bit of the journey together along winding country lanes, then through the high estate gates and down the tree-lined drive, past the great fountain in the form of a giant shell with stone goddesses rising out of it, before finally pulling up in front of the magnificent house in the shadow of the evening sun, uniformed doormen flanking the great doors.

'Now this is what I call a hotel,' said Becki, eyes sweeping appraisingly over the eighteenth-century mellow-stoned façade. 'Better than the B & B in Dawlish where we went last year.'

Their room was in a wing overlooking the swimming pool, in the infamous walled garden where, back in the fifties, government ministers had cavorted with hookers. There were two single beds easily the size of Rosie and Jake's old double, a vast telly, a sofa to flop on, tasteful prints hanging on the walls and a bookcase full of old leather-bound volumes that Rosie automatically knelt down to inspect.

'Well, thank you, Perry, for bringing me here,' said Becki, tweaking her hair in the mirror.

'The pleasure's all *ours*,' Rosie said pointedly. It had nothing to do with Jake – well, all right, his money had paid for it but it was her idea. 'Dinner's starting, shall we get ready?'

'We're going to have fun,' Becki crowed, fingering the thick curtains proprietorially. 'Do you think we'll see anyone famous?'

Rosie shrugged. 'How would I know?'

'Surely you could find out via your contacts? Girlfriend, you're not working this superstar lifestyle.' She pulled her bottle of Charlie out of her bag and began dousing herself. 'I always thought I should be an actress,' she added musingly. 'But then I had the kids instead. Far more satisfying ultimately, even if life is hard.'

'Oh yes,' Rosie said obediently.

The dining room had dark panelled walls lined with portraits of Victorian beauties. They sat at a linen-clothed table and studied the menus.

'I think I'll have the sirloin steak,' mused Becki. 'Oh no, hang on, the fillet is more expensive. I'll have the fillet. And oysters to start with. What wine shall we choose?'

Once dinner was in full flow, Becki sat back happily in her chair. 'I guess you get to stay in places like this all the time.'

'Hardly,' Rosie said. *Stop being so snappy.* 'You know we never go anywhere; Jake's always working.'

'Unlike you.'

'Sorry?'

'Well, who cares if hubby's working? You've had it all handed to you. Unlike some of us.'

And breathe. Rosie smiled sweetly. She was going to rise above this. But Becki was in full flow on her favourite topic of how tough life was with all these children, how challenging life was for teaching assistants, how they never had any spare cash. All true undoubtedly, but what could Rosie do?

Becki's diatribe carried her all the way through to dessert, when she had had two brandies. Back in the room, she opened a whisky from the minibar and drank it in a long steamy bath filled with all the miniature goodies. Rosie got into her bed and tried her hardest to go to sleep before her sister-in-law re-emerged. Why was she doing this? She missed the boys so much. At home, all day long, she'd be yearning for ten minutes alone, but now she had a whole weekend she was desperate for a sticky hug or a sniff of their dirty hair.

She sat up in bed and called Jake. She wanted them to have a tender conversation, like old times, before she went to sleep.

Voicemail. Well, rehearsals hadn't finished that long ago; he was probably well on his way to the Cotswolds. She called Yolande.

'Is everything OK?'

'Wonderful,' Yolande replied. She sounded ecstatic. 'The boys are fast asleep; they've been no trouble at all for *Granny*. And, guess what, Toby ate some cauliflower cheese!'

'That's great.'

'I knew Granny's cooking would win them round.'

Rosie sighed with longing. 'Kiss them for me. Tell them I'll call them in the morning.'

'They haven't asked after you once.' Yolande couldn't keep the triumph out of her voice.

'And, uh, is Jake there yet?'

A tiny pause. 'No, love, he said he fancied a few drinks after rehearsals, so I said don't come down tonight, come in the morning.'

'Ah.'

'Nothing wrong with that,' Yolande said defensively.

'Of course not. Bye, Yolande.'

She tried to sleep, but it was impossible. Bloody Jake, out drinking again with Simon, letting his mum pick up the pieces. Of course Yolande was loving having the boys all to herself, but that wasn't the point. *Stop it, Rosie*, she told herself, sitting up and reaching for the remote. Telly would be preferable to entertaining these thoughts. She was channel-surfing when Becki emerged from the bathroom in a thick towelling robe.

'This is lovely. I'm going to take it home with me. I've always wanted one of these.'

'If you do, they'll bill us for it,' Rosie said.

Becki shot her a sly look. 'So? You can afford it, can't you?' Becki reached for the spa menu. 'Ooh, look. I can't wait to have some treatments. I mean, I know you do this stuff all the time, but it's a luxury for me. Maybe I'll have a nude sand jewel body scrub or the rose scrub clay body envelopment. I'll book it all in the morning.'

'Oh, look!' Rosie stopped zapping. 'There's Jake.'

It was a repeat of a panel game show he'd filmed just after the first series of *Archbishop Grace* when he was starting to make his name. A group of actors and comedians and one token woman with long blonde hair and big bosoms had to answer silly questions about telly, but mainly their role was to banter and display their wit to the world.

'So what do we say about these benefit cheats?' asked the compere, Rufus Shammas, a bulky potato-nosed comedian, holding up a photo of a couple with nine children, whom the press had just revealed to be living in an entirely state-funded three-million-pound mansion with a tennis court in Crawley.

'I don't see the difference between them and the bankers whose accountants put them in a one per cent tax scheme,' said Jake. Cue rapturous applause and wolf whistles from the audience.

'Do you want to watch this?' Rosie asked. But Becki had the duvet pulled up over her head and was snoring loudly.

She woke annoyingly early, around six. The whole point of being away from the boys was to have lie-ins, but she simply couldn't get back to sleep. Why hadn't Jake gone to Yolande's last night? she wondered. Why did he think he deserved a night off? He said he was sick of the play, of the cast and crew, so why was he hanging out with them, rather than bothering to drive to be with his sons? She considered calling him and bawling him out, but she felt too weary. She had another day and night to get through with Becki; she wanted to save her energies for that.

In the end, she put on her dressing gown and went out in the dawn to the walled garden. Birds were singing and dew was on the grass, as – using the key they'd given her at reception – she unlocked the door in the brick wall and padded across the grass by the outdoor pool and opened the door of the conservatory that sheltered the indoor pool. It was empty and she swam up and down thirty times, enjoying the ozoney smell and the noise of the water splashing against the tiles.

When she returned to the room Becki was standing

in front of the mirror in her nightie, turning this way and that way, admiring Rosie's gold and diamond bracelet that she'd worn to dinner the previous night.

'Er, hello.'

'Hiya!' She showed not a trace of embarrassment. '*This* is nice.'

'Yes, it was a present from Jake. So shall we go to breakfast?'

Becki pouted. 'I thought we'd have it in the room.'

Rosie thought of the fifteen-pound charge for room service. Ridiculous. 'Let's go down. You'll be dressed in a minute.' Then she added, 'We're here to treat ourselves, aren't we? We might see some stars in the dining room.'

'True.' Becki headed to the wardrobe. 'Can I wear this top? Black isn't a good colour on you anyway.'

'Sure. But please can I have my bracelet back?'

After a second Becki grudgingly unfastened the clip.

Breakfast was in the dining room again. By day you could appreciate the ravishing views over the manicured grounds and down to the river.

Becki droned on. 'You have no idea what a break this is for me. You have no idea how hard life is – working, four kids . . . It's non-stop.' She glared at Rosie over her full English. 'It's OK for you, isn't it? You just sit around in that big house of yours, with the cleaner.' Rosie had made the mistake of revealing they employed Dizzy.

'Jake works hard for us to live in that house,' Rosie said defensively. 'It didn't fall into our laps.'

'Acting isn't work,' Becki snorted. 'It's playing.' Then she froze, a mouthful of bacon halfway to her lips. '*Oh my God*. It's Ellie Lewis.'

Sure enough, in the corner, eating alone, a book propped up in front of her, sat Ellie, eating a grapefruit. She was even more dazzling than Rosie remembered.

'So it is.'

'Well, at least we know she's not shagging Jake.'

'Becki!' Rosie was horrified. Was this what everyone thought? 'She'd never even look at Jake. And Jake hates her anyway.'

Becki shrugged. 'Let's go over and say hello!'

'*No.*'

'But you know her.'

'No, *Jake* knows her. I've met her once and she wasn't exactly friendly.'

'You know her,' Becki repeated firmly. 'It would be rude not to tell her we're here. She'll be lonely all by herself. Do you think she is by herself? Is she still with that guy? The handsome one. What was his name?'

'She's probably desperate for a break.'

'But I could get an autograph.'

'Becki, you're forty-two.'

'Forty-one. My birthday isn't until Thursday.'

'Forty-one. What on earth are you going to do with an autograph?'

'Sell it on eBay. Isn't she gorgeous?'

'Please! Leave her alone.'

'Just going to the loo.' Becki jumped up and beetled towards Ellie's table.

Face burning, Rosie stared at the toast rack. This was horrible. What was she saying? Jake would kill her. Seconds later, her sister-in-law returned beaming.

'More tea please, waiter. She's going to give me an autograph! And she says she'd love to get together while we're all here.' She raised her glass of freshly squeezed orange juice in Ellie's direction, but Ellie appeared to be engrossed in her book again.

'No!'

'Why not?'

'It's embarrassing. I don't want to hang out with a woman I don't know and I sincerely doubt she wants to hang out with me.'

Becki shook her head. 'I don't know what's happened to you. You're married to my baby brother, who used to sit on my knee, but now you both think you're better than the rest of us.'

'No, we don't!'

'I remember how excited you were when Jake got cast in *Archbishop Grace*. I bet you were asking all the cast for autographs. But look at you now.' She took a mouthful of toast and, spitting out crumbs, added, 'Anyway, I told Ellie we were here for her, if she wanted to talk about her relationship problems.'

'You did what?!'

'You'll see. We're going to end up spending lots of

time with Ellie Lewis. Mark my words.' Becki tapped her nose in that infuriating way of hers.

And, as things turned out, they actually did end up spending quite a lot of time with Ellie Lewis. They bumped into her in the swimming pool and they all ended up having lunch together in their bathrobes, sitting at a little table outside the café.

'Of course I remember you from that *pre-meer*,' Ellie had gushed, taking both of Rosie's hands in hers and holding them for what seemed like a long, long time – not least because Rosie realized how gnarled her hands were compared to Ellie's lily petals. 'I only wish I'd had more time to speak to you that night. But now we have a chance. It's really nice to have someone to chat to. I'd thought I was being really brave and alternative coming here on my own, but I've felt a bit lonely. I mean I had my book.' She held up a copy of *Anna Karenina*. 'I love these French writers. I really wanted to get stuck in last night but I fell asleep. I was tired. I'm always tired at the moment. I've been going to bed really early. Anyway, as I said, I was feeling lonely . . .'

'Aah, you've got us now,' Becki said.

Ellie squeezed Rosie's hands again. 'Now when you move to LA we can hang out. It'll be like the best fun. You have kids, don't you? Jake's always talking about you and your little girls.'

'Boys. But I'm not sure if you'd like to hang out with them.' Rosie tried not to smile as an image of George performing the bum-bum dance for Ellie Lewis flashed into her mind.

Becki's face lit up. 'Move to LA? When? I didn't know about this. That'd be wicked. I've always wanted to go to Disneyland and Universal and that place where the stars have their handprints in the pavement. Get a place with a pool and that's our holidays sorted for life.'

'We're not moving to LA,' Rosie said firmly. 'In a million years,' she added just to clarify.

'Oh? He told me it was like a done deal with the Disney guys. You *should* come; we would have the best fun hanging out together.' Ellie glanced at the Rolex on her dainty wrist. 'Oh my God, it's, like, nearly two. I have a massage and facial booked. But, ladies, I'm enjoying your company so much. You're both so . . . *real.* I don't meet many people like you. Shall we do dinner tonight? In my suite, so we have some privacy? I can ask them to prepare something with wheat and dairy for you, if you'd prefer.'

'Really, I don't . . .' Rosie had started to say, as Becki exclaimed, 'We'd love that! You're on!'

20

That afternoon, Rosie was booked in for a manicure and pedicure – basically an excuse to have a break from Becki, who was having the full-body massage.

She sat in a comfy chair and allowed the beautician to file her toenails, as she leafed through glossy magazines that didn't feature Ben 10 or ZingZillas, but which did contain perfume samples. (Rosie surreptitiously pocketed a couple, plus one mini Estée Lauder foundation.) She flicked through a *Homes and Gardens*, but instead of entrancing her, as such magazines always used to, she found herself feeling oddly jangly reading about other people's apparently perfect lives. She brightened, however, at the feature on Simon Barry and Brunhilde von Fournigan at home in their Oxfordshire rectory ('They also have a house in London's Shoreditch.').

Barry preserved the staircase and exposed the joists. Other pieces, from the vintage escutcheons scavenged at Ye Olde Scrappe Yard to the many reclaimed doors they're affixed to, were found at antique fairs but made to look like they have been there forever. 'It was just a matter of uncovering a bit of charm. And Brunny did all the colours,' explains Barry,

surrounded by walls painted in his wife's favourite hue:
Fetching Blue from Unusual in Paris. 'You'd never guess a
supermodel could be so down-to-earth, but my wife is. And
she eats like a pig, more than me – I swear! Her favourite
food is bratwurst.

Not so long ago Rosie would have felt inspired. She'd
have googled the suppliers of Brunhilde and Simon's
shabby-chic furniture, she'd have reeled at the cost of
one pot of Fetching Blue. But now she just felt jaded.
They had looked so miserable when she'd spotted them
at that premiere party and she knew from Jake that
Brunhilde could talk about nothing but the fact that
Octavius was in nappies aged four and that Richenda
had failed to get into *the* east London prep school, despite two years of intensive tutoring.

She thought back to her and Christy lying on Christy's
bed with the frilly white valence – how Rosie had
yearned for a valence – reading about people like that,
thinking about how perfect their lives must be, how
they could never have any worries at all. But now, she
supposed, she was one of them and nothing funda-
mental had changed. She lived in a bigger house, she
could wear more expensive clothes, but she was still
worrying about Toby's eating habits, still bonkers about
the boys but at the same time occasionally finding a day
in their company utterly stultifying, still in love with her
husband . . .

Still in love.

As much as she used to be? Course she was, she thought crossly. She didn't want to think about it. Here was an article about Ellie Lewis. Excellent! She could refresh her memory before dinner tonight. Rosie started reading avidly. A beauty queen from the Midwest, she'd stunned everyone by winning the pivotal role in *O'Rourke's*. Her critics thought she couldn't possibly tackle such a meaty part but she'd won a string of Emmys.

Despite her dazzling beauty, she was perpetually single. 'Will London be the city where Ellie finally finds romance?' blared the article, over a photo of Ellie looking aloof in a belted mac and shades. Rosie wondered if she could pull off an outfit like that – it made Ellie look like a blonde Audrey Hepburn but she feared on herself it would be more Karren Brady in *The Apprentice*.

'Doing your homework for tonight?' shrilled Becki from the doorway. Rosie jumped.

The manicurist sighed. 'Your polish is smudged now.'

Ellie was staying in the Lady Astor suite,

'Bloody hell, Rosie, it's about the size of our house! Why didn't you book us into one of these?'

'I'll know for next time.' Rosie was looking around. The room was stuffed with antiques and old portraits – including one of Lady Astor herself. Above the crackling fire (not strictly necessary on a balmy June night) there was an elaborate overmantel carved with exotic creatures. A door led out on to a vast terrace, with heart-stopping views of the manicured gardens sweeping down to a glinting bend in the Thames.

'What a perfect place to eat!'

'Actually, I'm a little chilly, so do you mind if we stay indoors?'

'Oh, sure,' said Rosie, trying not to sound too disappointed. She sat in one of the stuffed armchairs and eagerly eyed the bottle in its cooler.

Ellie caught her eye. 'Elderflower wine. I'm not drinking right now. I hope you don't mind.'

'I hope you don't mind' was a bit of an Ellie phrase, Rosie was realizing, said with the sweetest, but steeliest, smile. She smiled back as Ellie continued: 'Of course you can order anything you like. Why don't you have a bottle of champagne?'

'Sounds like a top idea,' Becki said. 'Shall I call down to room service?'

Oh crikey, a bottle of champagne would cost hundreds of pounds. Was Ellie paying, or Rosie?

'My treat,' Ellie said smoothly. Rosie blushed. Could she read her mind?

'Oh no, no . . .' she tried, but Ellie raised a hand.

'Please! Don't insult me. You're Jake's wife. And, like I say, I'm thrilled to get to know you better. I haven't gotten to know Jake as well as I'd like; he goes out drinking a lot after the show, and, as I said, I'm not drinking right now and—'

'I'm so proud of him,' Becki interrupted. 'Hey, I forgot to say when I was having my pedicure: I was checking out pictures of him and the pair of you at that premiere the other week. People say some nasty things online, don't they? Why do they have to be so bitchy?'

'Oh tell me about it,' Ellie said airily, as Rosie – knowing she shouldn't go there – asked: 'What did they say?'

'Oh, you know, they couldn't believe a bird like you'd pulled a hunk like Jake. Didn't like your hair. Thought your knickers were showing under your dress. Nasty, petty stuff.'

Rosie felt sick. Were people really so horrified by her appearance they'd been going online to log their outrage?

Ellie saw her face and shook her head disapprovingly. 'Don't go there. Don't go there or you'll go crazy. Never read those comments. I learned that way back when everyone said I was too pretty to play Dolores. Just do your own sweet thing and fuck the rest of them.' She was about to say more, but her phone rang.

As she looked at the caller ID her expression changed. 'Sorry, I have to take this. Hello? Hello, LaTonza? How is he? Oh . . .' She listened. She looked very serious. A voice at the other end gabbled. 'I see,' said Ellie. 'Oh God. Oh, LaTonza. I am so sorry. I do understand. I know, I wish I could be there to see him, but I'm stuck in the UK for the foreseeable future. I don't know when I'm going to get a window long enough to fly to Ohio . . . Uh-huh . . . Keep me posted . . . Thank you, thank you, LaTonza. You're an angel, you know that?' She hung up. 'Shit.'

'What is it? I mean, if you want to talk about it.'

'It's my dad.' Ellie was clearly close to tears. 'He's not been well for a long time. He has dementia. His carer says he's gotten worse these past few days. He's refusing to eat, he keeps calling for me and swearing at her. He calls her a "black bitch".'

'How awful!' Rosie exclaimed. 'You poor thing.'

'Sally Ellis – she's such a hoot normally, the things she did on our karaoke night – she has a problem like that,' said Becki, as Ellie's phone rang again.

'Sorry!' She held up an apologetic hand. 'Hello, oh, hi, Sharon . . . No. Tell him I won't speak to him. No! It's over. And, anyway, I've heard what he's been saying about me all round town. Bad-mouthing me. Did he think it wouldn't get back to me?'

She hung up. 'Fuck him.' Her chin began to wobble.

'Are you OK?' Rosie asked. 'What happened?'

'Men!' said Becki. 'It reminds me of the time Dave forgot to take out the recycling. Did I ever tell you about that, he—'

'Becki . . .' Rosie warned, as her phone rang. 'Oh! It's Jake. Excuse me. I'm sorry, I'll be back in a second.'

'Say hi,' said Ellie distractedly, as Rosie stepped out on to the balcony. She leaned against a heavy stone urn. 'Hello, stranger,' she said rather tartly.

'Hiya, how's it going?' Jake sounded chirpy. In the background she could hear the boys yelling.

'Fine. Good. You'll never guess who I'm—'

'It's been a nightmare here,' Jake interrupted. 'I

240

picked the boys up from Mum's this morning, and drove them home and they fought all the way and then Georgie was sick and now they're fighting again and I thought you said it was hair wash tonight, but they say not.'

'It *is* hair wash!' Rosie was outraged. 'Little fibbers. They have to have clean hair for nursery tomorrow or Wendy will blow her top. Anyway, listen, you'll never guess—'

'Toby! Don't do that to your brother. I said *don't. Don't!*' Another heart-piercing yell. Suddenly Rosie was glad to be standing on this sun-drenched balcony. 'Sorry, they're trying to kill each other. I gotta go. I'll see you tomorrow. You'll be home by lunchtime?'

'I'll do my very best.'

'*Please*, Old Bean. I've got to be in rehearsals at two, it would be good to see you before I go.'

Rosie was flattered. 'I'll see what I can do. Give the boys a big—' But the line had gone dead. Rosie went back into the room. It was scorching in there, the fire burning more fiercely than ever. Becki was leaning forward in her armchair, talking intently.

'So then I said: "Well, if you don't want her to study ballet, even though she's clearly extremely talented, that's fine, go and play golf on Sundays instead." And he said—'

'Rosie,' said Ellie, who looked somewhat dazed. 'Everything OK at home?'

'Fine. I'm so sorry about your . . . break-up.'

'It's been stressing me out so much,' said Ellie, clearly overjoyed to be given a cue.

Rosie racked her brains, trying to remember what the spa gossip mags had said about her love life. 'I'm sorry. Was it that guy who played the pool boy in series two?'

'We'd been together ten years,' Ellie continued. 'So even though I ended things, it's still really tough.'

Becki patted her on the shoulder. 'Beautiful girl like you, you'll meet someone in no time.'

'It's been a long time coming,' Ellie said. 'Things haven't been right for years now. There was this new HBO series that I totally would have got if he'd pushed hard enough, and he didn't even manage to get me an audition for the new Woody Allen movie.' She stuck out her little chin with its heart-shaped dimple. 'I can do better.'

'Yeah, girl!' Becki cried.

'You're talking about your agent?' Rosie exclaimed.

Ellie nodded, her chin quivering. 'No wonder it's been so hard to do this gig. He's bad-mouthing me all around LA, saying I'm a bitch and too demanding. He's saying I only stayed so long in *O'Rourke's* because I was sleeping with the series creator – I mean, OK, I did once, but that's not why I stayed, it's because the public loved Dolores.'

'So that's why you've been forgetting your lines?' Rosie's sympathy for Ellie was diminishing.

'Well, yeah, plus . . .'

'Plus what?' Rosie asked gently. So *this* was why Ellie had been so hard to work with. Did Jake know about her dad? Maybe then he'd be more sympathetic. 'Plus what?'

Ellie swallowed. 'Well, two years ago I made this cute movie called *Watertown*.'

'Oh God, I loved it – it's your greatest work.' Rosie was proud of herself for remembering to say 'work'. Jake had told her actors adored that word, because it made them feel they deserved their millions simply for falling out of bed and learning a few lines. Ellie smiled, dimples creasing at the corners of her mouth. She was *so pretty*. How could genes conspire to make someone so perfect?

'I think I saw that film,' Becki said musingly, then cleared her throat, clearly about to launch into a lecture on the pros and cons of *Watertown*.

'So you made *Watertown*?' Rosie said encouragingly.

'Yes—' But they were spared this nugget by loud knocking at the door.

'Come in!' Ellie shouted.

The door opened and a burly suited man – presumably a bodyguard – stood there, holding out a mobile. 'Ms Lewis. Mr X is on the phone for you.'

Ellie's eyes widened. 'Oh my gosh, he said he wouldn't call! Ladies,' she said. 'I'm really so sorry, but would you mind leaving? I just have to be alone now to talk to . . . er, someone. Do you mind coming back in half an hour? It really is urgent.'

'Sure,' they both said.

'So sorry, ladies, so sorry, but it's an emergency.' She virtually snatched the phone from the bodyguard, who ushered them out of the room.

They went down to the bar and – why not at this stage? – ordered champagne.

'Imagine, all that stuff with her dad and I bet there's some hidden boyfriend,' Becki mused. 'God, I can't wait to tell the girls.'

'What girls?'

'Well, you know. All the gang at school.'

'You mustn't do that!' Rosie was horrified. 'She told us all that in confidence.'

'I won't share the juicy details, just give them the gist. And it'll only be the girls, I'm not going to put it on Facebook or Twitter or anything. I mean . . . if I wanted to I could probably call the papers and make a few hundred quid with what she's told us.'

How did Becki know about calling the papers? thought Rosie uneasily, hating herself for this paranoia. Did that explain how obscure photos of Jake had ended up in the *Sunday Sun* or whatever?

'More champagne?' she said. They had another couple of glasses, talked about the kids and telly, and were just getting nicely tipsy, when the bodyguard interrupted them.

'So sorry, ladies, but I'm afraid Ms Lewis has had to cancel her dinner with you. She sends her profuse apologies but she is very, very . . . er, tired and she's had to go to bed.'

'It's nine o'clock!' exclaimed Becki. 'I don't want to go to bed and I've got four children. What's with her?'

Rosie shrugged. She was disappointed; she liked Ellie and she'd been on tenterhooks wanting to know what she'd reveal next. But she was an actor. You couldn't trust any of them, apart from her husband.

'Just have to eat in the dining room.'

'Famous people, eh?'

'Tell me about it,' Rosie said. Suddenly this seemed very funny. She started to laugh and so did Becki. They clinked glasses.

'Thanks for coming,' Rosie said.

'Thanks for asking.' Becki smiled. 'I really appreciate it.'

Rosie's heart overflowed with happiness. Perhaps it was all worth it – Jake's long hours, the intrusion, the weird new life in the Village – if they could treat their loved ones. She'd do the same with Nanna soon. Maybe, even, if she could track her down, take her mother.

'Cheers.'

'Cheers.'

21

When Rosie woke the next morning a note had been slipped under her door.

> So sorry about last night, Rosie. Things are so crazy . . .
> I'd love to see you again some time soon. I'll get my
> assistant to call and arrange lunch for a day when
> I'm not needed in rehearsals.
>   Ellie Xx

After their final mega-blowout at the breakfast buffet, she dropped Becki at the station.

'I'm going to look into some other weekends away for us,' her sister-in-law informed her. 'There's this lovely place in the Lake District we could check out.'

Rosie drove home happily. She'd really treated Becki, which was what it was all about. As she hit the M25, she put her foot down. She couldn't wait to be home again, to hug the boys, and to eat lunch to the sound of them biffing each other over the head, rather than the genteel clink of cutlery and Becki musing whether she'd have dessert. She'd go to sleep with Jake beside her, snoring and hogging the duvet, rather than Becki snoring softly.

She opened the front door, glancing up at the clock. An hour until she needed to pick up the boys; just time to unpack, do emails, go through post. Then she stopped. She looked around. Things had changed. The hall walls were an unappealing shade of dark salmony pink and covered with gloomy black-and-white photos of what looked like woodland. It was impressive – but utterly soulless, as if it had been designed by one of those Stepford women you saw in adverts, chatting with her friend in the kitchen about the new wonder cleaning fluid.

The tatty photographs of the boys in the frames from Tiger that she'd placed on a side table had vanished, along with the old Mexican mask she'd picked up in Cancún. Instead, a tidy pile of post sat in a silver tray. Rosie picked up the first fat envelope with a King's Mount stamp on it and was about to open it when . . .

'Surprise!' Jake bounded down the stairs.

'Hey! What are you doing here? Don't you have a rehearsal? What's happened here, did David work all weekend or what?'

'No rehearsal until the afternoon,' replied Jake, ignoring her last question. 'They're doing one-on-one emergency work with Ellie this morning, after she buggered off on one of her Ellie-time weekends without warning.'

'I know, I saw her, she . . .' But Rosie hadn't a chance to say more, her husband was pulling her by the arm, dragging her into the lounge, sorry living room, which now contained new white sofas identical to Patrizia's, and over to the window.

'Look!'

She looked. The garden with its lush green lawn was now a filthy sea of Somme-like mud. A pit sat in the middle, surrounded by piles of bricks, and two builders in overalls sat on a heap of timber drinking tea.

'What have you done?'

'Put in the foundations for a pool,' Jake crowed. 'I stayed here over the weekend to supervise. We kept it a surprise from you, because we know you had a few doubts but we knew once you saw it you'd love it.'

'But it looks horrible.'

'Of course it does now. But when it's finished it'll be amazing. We've got plans. David's mocked up these photos of how it's all going to look in a few weeks. The boys and I are so excited and you will be too – come, look!' He pulled her out of the room and downstairs to the kitchen. 'Oh, and I've got something else for you too. Because I missed you.'

'Oh, yeah?' Despite her annoyance at being bamboozled like this, Rosie felt a surge of affection. She put one hand inside Jake's jeans pocket. 'Anything to do with this area?' Tradition had it, after all, that when he'd been away for more than a couple of days, the first thing they always did was jump each others' bones, rather than study architect's plans.

But Jake shrugged her off, opening one of the kitchen drawers. 'Look.'

He handed her a black box. She opened it and took out a heavy gold necklace. Its thick chains quilting into one another. It was like something Rihanna would wear, the most un-Rosie-like creation she had ever seen. It must have cost a fortune.

'Thank you. Wow. It's lovely.'

'Do you like it? Me and the boys picked it out with some help from Mum.'

'Right.'

He pecked her on the cheek. 'Just to show our appreciation. When you go away it's not the same.'

'I'm glad you noticed.' Rosie folded her arms across her chest. 'But you could have bloody consulted with me about the pool. I still don't think it's a great idea with the boys so little. It's not just them, it's their friends. Suppose some stranger's kid drowns in it, and what about the living room? Did you tell David a white sofa was OK? Because I definitely told him it was not. And what are those photos in the hall all about? Where are the pictures of the boys?'

'Relax,' sighed Jake in a way that Rosie found intensely patronizing. 'The photos in the hall are by this prize-winning Finnish photographer. Apparently they're limited edition, very rare; we're lucky to have them.'

'They're photos. He can print out as many as he wants.'

'I thought you'd be pleased.' Jake's bottom lip curled now and he slumped down in one of the kitchen chairs – at least *they* hadn't been changed yet. 'I thought it would be fun to surprise you.'

Rosie looked at him sceptically. She doubted this. She was pretty sure Jake just couldn't be bothered to argue his case and had decided to pull the rug from beneath her feet. It was the side of Jake she saw occasionally, the ruthless one that was determined to have its own way, a side she didn't like at all.

But she didn't want a fight. Not now. She turned her back, so she couldn't see his face and, as she was filling the kettle, said as calmly as she could, 'So are you going to ask me how the weekend went? You know, with your sister?'

'Hey, don't sound like that. I was going to. But later. Tonight. Because I need to leave in a second.'

'Oh. Right.'

'Bean.' Jake put his hand on her bottom, but she pushed it away. 'You're being so bloody grumpy. I thought you'd be pleased.'

'I really wish you'd asked me first.'

The buzzer went. 'That's my car. We'll talk about it later, OK? See you.'

He was off, running out of the door, leaving her alone by the Aga, feeling as if she'd been hit round the head by a brick. All the benefits of the doubt she'd been allowing him vanished. 'Sneaky fucker,' she said aloud. 'He pulled a fast one on me.'

'Are you OK?' asked Dizzy in the doorway, a bandanna round her head.

'Oh! Hi! I'd forgotten you were here. Yes, I'm fine. Just practising . . . er, some lines for a speech I have to give at nursery. Thanking Wendy. On behalf of the mothers. You know.'

'Right.' Dizzy clearly didn't believe a word. 'Loving what David's doing with the house.'

'Are you?' Rosie tried not to sound too sarcastic.

'Oh, yah. Getting rid of all the clutter, it'll be great. So much easier to dust.' Her iPhone rang. 'Oh, sorry, Rosie,' she said as if she were the employer, dismissing an underling. 'I've got to take this.'

'Be my guest.'

Rosie opened the letter from King's Mount. INFOR-MATION PACK she read on the front of a red folder. Out fell a stack of papers. TIMETABLE. School dates for the next three years, with a note saying parents were strictly forbidden from booking holidays outside these times. REGULATIONS. CLUBS. UNIFORM. PARENTS' SOCIAL CALENDAR. *Social calendar?*

'The uniform list's at fucking Harrods!' she exclaimed.

'Excuse me?' Dizzy held her phone away from her ear.

'Sorry, Dizzy, nothing.' She carried on reading in horror. *Parents' ball. One hundred and fifty pounds per head, to include a glass of champagne on arrival.* 'I should think so at that price,' she muttered to herself. *Autumn Bazaar, donations needed.* She continued to read. *Last year parents generally gave gifts such as an iPad, a week in their holiday villa, a crate of vintage brandy.* There was a pile of forms that needed to be filled in. Toby's health. Their religion. Their occupations. *Occasionally we love parents to come in and talk to the children about their work, do tick the box if you'd be up for it!*

Rosie ticked the box. Jake would be furious, but if he declined, their son might be blacklisted and he'd never make it to a good uni. Her phone rang. She grabbed it, sure it would be Jake, calling to apologize, but no, Christy.

'Sorry about the background noise, I'm just walking down the Strand on the way to pop in on Jake's rehearsals. I'm *so* busy. So what did you think?'

'Well, duty done by Becki.' At least someone wanted to hear about her weekend. 'I mean, she drove me up the wall, but we had a couple of laughs too. And you'll never guess who was staying there.'

'I didn't mean that,' Christy said impatiently. 'I meant what did you think of the necklace. I told Jake to buy you something to soften the blow of the swimming pool. I know you're being all health and safety about it, but you're going to love it.'

'Right.' Rosie felt as if she'd been stamped on. Jake. Christy. Their plotting to buy more fabulous things that she didn't want. Tears of self-pity pricked at her eyes. Why was it that no one she loved seemed to recognize what was important any more?

'Jake said you were a bit peeved. But seriously it'll be amazing. And listen . . .' she continued, as Rosie computed that Jake must have called her to whine as soon as he got in the car. 'I've got a fancy invite for the both of you. Jake's presenting an award at the Top TV bash next Thursday. Do you want to come with?'

'I guess.'

'You don't sound very excited.' Christy seemed put out.

'Sorry, just busy.' She should say how she felt, but once again she didn't want a row. She and Christy never fought; it was always so much easier just to do what she said. But at least Christy had always wanted to hear what she had to say in the past, now she no longer seemed to have the time. She realized with a jolt that she was feeling the absence of Christy's friendship even more acutely than she was feeling Jake's lack of affection. Rosie didn't like confrontation. 'Just busy.' To her relief, the other line started bleeping. 'Christy, I'll call you back.'

'Please! I want to hear how it went with Becki.'

'Sure. Hello, Nanna.' She felt as if she'd climbed into a deep, hot bath after a walk in the rain. Finally, the person who would want to listen. 'I've been meaning to call, but I just got in and Jake's done all this stuff . . . Well, anyway, I'll tell you about it in a minute. But I survived the weekend. Actually, Becki and I got on quite well. And I've got some other amazing news: we met Ellie Lewis. She was staying there! We hung out with her!'

'Oh,' said Nanna.

Her voice sounded as thin as rice paper. A drum thudded in Rosie's chest. 'Nanna, are you OK?'

'Fine.'

'Are you *sure?*'

There was the faintest pause, before Nanna said, 'Well, I need another scan, a more detailed one. They think there might be a lump in my brain.'

'*What?*'

'That's why I've been so shaky lately. Not really a surprise, is it?'

'Oh, Nanna.'

'But they say nothing's certain. I have to have a scan next week – an MI5 or whatever it's called.'

It was like jumping on to a moving carousel. Rosie's thoughts were twirling.

'I'll come and see you,' she said, grasping on to her first thought like a pole. 'I'll be with you in a few hours.'

'Don't be daft, lover, what about the boys?'

'I'll call Dizzy; she can look after them until Jake gets home. I'm on my way.'

22

Later Rosie found she could remember nothing of the drive to Bristol, except she'd done ninety nearly all the way. She didn't cry, instead she was numb all over – the same kind of dead, cold sensation she'd had when they'd given her the epidural for George. She didn't believe what she'd heard. Nanna couldn't have a lump. Nanna was indomitable: she couldn't go and leave them.

She was approaching Bristol, when the phone rang. Christy. She jabbed speaker.

'Hey. Jake just told me. I'm so sorry.'

'Yes.' Irritation broke through the dullness. Jake had told her. Were they ever going to communicate directly with each other again?

'Is there anything I can do? I've sent her flowers already.'

Despite herself, Rosie smiled. 'She'll like that. Thanks.'

'You know there's a lot you can do for her now with Jake's money. Private care for a start.'

'I guess.' Rosie hadn't even begun to think practicalities. All she could think of was Nanna suffering, Nanna being pumped full of drugs, Nanna eventually leaving them.

'I'll start looking into it immediately,' Christy pronounced.

Nanna opened the door to her, looking exactly the same as she had a few weeks previously. Rosie hugged her tight.

'You are ridiculous,' her grandmother said, tutting. 'Why have you come? What do you think phones are for? What'll the boys do?'

'I told you, Nanna, Jake is perfectly capable of looking after them for one night. What about you? I need to hear about you.'

'I'll be fine,' Nanna said briskly. The wobble that had been in her voice earlier had vanished. 'I've an appointment with a specialist next Tuesday. We'll take it from there.' Rosie looked aghast, but she continued: 'It'll work out fine. Jean from the community centre had a breast lump. Did the chemo, was a bit poorly for a while, but last weekend she did a sponsored run. Had to give her twenty quid, but at least it was for cancer research, so a good investment as it turns out. Honestly, love, there's so much doctors can do these days. Now have a cup of tea. Calm down.'

'Next Tuesday?' Rosie was still taking it all in. 'Can't it be sooner? We can have it done privately.'

'Nonsense, lover. Nothing wrong with the NHS.'

'But I'll come with you.' Rosie calculated. Dizzy could look after the boys for the afternoon. Tuesday. Not a problem. 'Do you want me to stay until then? Have you told Mum yet?'

'No, love. You know what she's like. She'd have to find the money to come and visit; she hasn't got that now.'

'But I'd pay!'

Nanna shook her head. 'You can't change everything just by dipping into your wallet, love. People stay the same. If Marianne really wanted to come, she'd find the cash. But you know most of the time your mother likes to keep her distance.'

'Oh, Nanna.' Suddenly Rosie was exhausted. Tears filled her eyes and she slumped down on the battered sofa. Her grandmother put a bony arm round her.

'Come on, lover. It'll all be all right.'

'I'm meant to be comforting you,' Rosie sobbed.

'It doesn't work that way. Come on, love, don't cry, don't cry.' Rosie gulped loudly and reached wildly for a tissue. Nana handed her a sheet of kitchen roll and laughed. 'Oh, all right then. Cry if you want to.'

In the morning, the way forward seemed far clearer. Rosie had stayed up late googling in her old narrow single bed with the orange duvet cover they'd bought at Matalan and the faded patches on the wall where she'd Blu-Tacked her posters of Take That. She'd read plenty of cheering stuff about miracle cures, mistaken diagnoses, wonder drugs. A lot of gloomy stuff too, but she wouldn't dwell on that.

'So there's a really good chance this lump might be benign,' she burbled over the bacon sandwich that

Nanna had insisted on rustling up for her. 'It might be fine to leave it and even if it isn't we can make sure you have the best treatment available to remove it.'

'That's right, love.' Nanna sounded as if she were talking about picking up some shampoo for her in Superdrug.

'So I'll leave today, but come back next week for the scan.'

Nanna reached out and took her hand. 'Listen, love, don't take it the wrong way, but I'd rather you didn't. I'd prefer to go with Maureen.'

'Nanna! Of course I'm going to take that the wrong way.'

'I thought you might. But it'll be easier for me with Maureen there. I won't feel I have to keep strong with her around, but with you I will.'

'You can weep and wail, Nanna. I won't care.'

That was obviously a lie and Nanna laughed. 'Has that ever happened?' Rosie shook her head like a little girl. 'Hell'll freeze over before it does. I want to go with Mo. I need to be the strong one for you. And now I want to go down to Iceland with you and for you to help me carry my bags back and then I want you to go back to London and your family and await further instructions.'

'I'll be checking up on you all the time.'

'I will answer the phone to you only once a day. So don't go crazy. You've got your boys and your hubby to look after. They're what's important, not an old lady like me.'

'Oh, Nanna, don't be such a martyr. I love you. I want to be with you.'

'I've told you, love. I love you too, but for now I need space from you. I can't be wasting energy worrying about you, I need to putting all my effort into fighting whatever this lump might be. My friends'll be there for me. You know I have good friends.'

'Jake and Christy are saying we might have to move to LA,' Rosie blurted out.

Nanna nodded. 'Well, that would be the logical thing, wouldn't it, love? It's where the work is for actors.'

'Would you come with us? You'd love cruising up and down Sunset in a convertible.'

Nanna laughed. 'What did I just tell you? I have my friends here. I love St Pauls. It's a dump, but I was born here and I'll die here. I don't want to spend my twilight years dribbling and hobbling around in some hot foreign place where I'm the only person with wrinkles and they all eat nothing but tofu.'

'Think of the sunshine,' Rosie tried, but Nanna laughed.

'You know I'm not a fan of sunshine. I burn too easily.' She leaned forward and her gnarled hand brushed Rosie's cheek. 'But you must stop fretting about me, love. You need to do what you want to do.'

'But this isn't what I want to do. It's what Jake wants to do. And bloody Christy. I don't want to be any richer than we are already; we already have too much. I don't want to be five thousand miles away from you. I don't want the boys growing up with American accents and modelling for Burberry.' She stopped. 'I know it sounds nuts, but I sometimes wish none of this had happened. I wish I could turn back time to the day Jake went to that audition for *Archbishop Grace*. I wish the tube had broken down or that he'd had a stye and he'd never been offered that part and that he'd decided acting was a waste of time and become a teacher or something. Then we'd still be in Neasden and we'd be happy.'

Nanna shook her head. 'But how would Jake feel?'

'But it's not just about Jake. It's about the whole family.'

'Lover, I know it's hard. But the boys are happy. Jake is stressed in the run-up to this play, but he'd rather be stressed because he's achieved his dream than trudging along teaching drama or whatever, thinking "What if?" So the issue here is not Jake, it's you. You've always been a homebody. You've never enjoyed new situations. God knows, you've spent most of your life cowering behind that Christy. Maybe it's time to be a little more adventurous, to embrace all these new happenings.'

'Even if it means leaving you behind?'

'You won't leave me behind. We can Skype every day. We can email. It'll be no different from you being in London, really.'

'I guess,' Rosie said. The unspoken truth remained: sooner, rather than later, Nanna might not be around to chat to at all. Nanna was telling her to move on, that she needed to live her life without her.

Nanna thumped her fist on the table. 'Now tell me all about that beautiful Ellie Lewis.'

So Rosie told her and Nanna laughed and rolled her eyes at Becki's pushiness.

She drove home feeling a little bit better. When she got home, she couldn't stop hugging the boys: her children, Nanna's great-grandchildren, her DNA.

'Get off, Mummy,' said Toby. 'I can't see Mr Tumble.'

A Question of Scruples with Jake Perry, You Go Magazine

Would you accept the leading role in a show opposite an actor you hate?

Of course. I'm an actor, a professional. It's not a scenario I can really envisage, though. The truth is I've always been much more likely to fall in love with the actresses I worked with than hate them.

A drunken friend offers you a lift home. You will be unable to get a taxi for at least three hours, do you accept?

Never. I value my life.

You discover a terrible secret about your wife's best friend. Do you tell her?

Definitely not, I believe ignorance is bliss.

You are offered a lucrative film that will pay off all your debts, but it involves full-frontal nudity. Would you accept?

No one would pay to see me nude, so the question would never arise. But if pressed – yes, why not? I'd be playing another character. it wouldn't be me nude on screen; it would be whoever I was inhabiting.

You find £50 in the street. Would you keep it, hand it to the police or give it to charity?

Give it to charity.

Your advisors tell you the best way to maximize your earnings is to go into tax exile. What would you do?

Refuse! I don't want to spend the rest of my life in somewhere soulless like Monte Carlo. And I don't believe in tax avoidance anyway. This country has given me so much I'm proud to give back.

You are offered a fantastic job in an American TV show but your partner doesn't want to go to America. What do you do?

I would go because I believe if your love was strong enough you could bear the separation. It would make your love life exciting jumping on planes to see one another.

You are at a party and everyone is smoking joints. You are handed one, would you smoke it?

No, because I've never smoked joints.

You wake up with a terrible hangover and you know you will miss the beginning of your show. Do you ring up and tell the truth or do you invent an excuse?

I'd invent an excuse. Admitting I had a hangover would be so unprofessional. The only time that has ever happened to me was when I was in my early twenties used to go out clubbing a great deal. Today I am incredibly professional and I am always punctual if I have a show.

23

Rosie sat in her chair at Melly & Lyne hairdressers on the Brompton Road, gaping in outrage at her copy of *You Go*. She couldn't believe this bloody questionnaire. Jake had never smoked dope! And bears used portaloos in the woods.

'Oh sure, Mr Clinton, you just didn't inhale,' she muttered.

Give the money to charity, yeah, right – he'd once found a hundred pounds in the pocket of a coat he'd bought from a charity shop and it hadn't occurred to him to take it back. Instead they'd gone for a posh Chinese. Not that Rosie had complained; in fact, she'd encouraged him – something she felt bad about now, but then she wasn't spouting away to a national newspaper colour supplement about how charitable she was.

He'd had affairs with loads of his co-stars. Oh, nice. Rosie knew this was long before they'd met but the readers of *You Go* wouldn't.

But worst of all was this about going to America. If it came to the crunch, he'd go without her. It would keep their love alive.

'Like fuck it would,' she hissed, scratching her head, which was oddly itchy today.

'Hello there,' said a bright voice behind her. 'I'm Helen. I'm afraid Lori who you saw last time's off sick. What can I do for you today?'

'Oh, hello, Helen. I'm Rosie.' Bright smile, even though she was fuming. Helen was about twenty and shockingly beautiful, with huge eyes, perfect (well, you'd hope so, wouldn't you?) blonde hair brushing her bottom and an Angelina Jolie mouth. She fingered one of Rosie's locks and eyed it dubiously. 'So are we going somewhere special tonight?'

'The Top TV Awards.' Helen still looked bored. 'I think I only need a couple of inches off.'

'All riiight.' Helen examined her hair again, like Emilia Fox inspecting a cadaver in *Silent Witness*. 'You could go a bit shorter, you know. You have amazing bone structure.'

'Really?' Rosie flushed with pleasure. No one had ever told her that before.

'Really. I reckon a good six inches could come off. And we could do some colour too.'

'No time for colour. Got to pick my children up from nursery. But another time. Six inches?'

'No offence,' said Helen. Rosie braced herself. This phrase was never expressed without the kick-in-the-behind 'but'. 'No offence, but at your age short hair is always more flattering unless you're Elle Macpherson. I promise you, you're going to be transformed.'

Rosie headed off to have her hair washed and made small talk about the junior's boyfriend. Then back to the chair, where she braced herself for an in-depth discussion of Helen's weekend plans. She'd avoid this by making no eye contact, she decided. She stayed engrossed in her copy of *OK!* as Helen pulled off her head towel and began yanking at her wet hair with a pink Tangle Teezer, then snipping at corners. Oh, look, Brunhilde von Fournigan still looking as if she were smelling a dead cat attending the opening of her friend Countess Blixheim's new toy shop. Rosie was enjoying this.

'Oh!' Helen exclaimed. Rosie looked up from the article about a soap star's wedding.

'Sorry,' Helen said, looking as if Rosie had dangled one of George's used nappies under her nose. 'But this appointment can no longer continue.'

'Excuse me?'

She bent down and whispered in Rosie's ear. 'You have nits!'

'What?' Rosie clawed at her scalp.

'I'm so sorry. I don't want to embarrass you. It's not me, it's health and safety. If we see any creatures in clients' hair, the rule is we must ask them to leave immediately.'

'But we're halfway through the haircut!' Rosie cried.

'I'm sorry.' She didn't look it. She looked as if she couldn't wait for Rosie to leave so she could have a bloody good laugh with her mates. 'You have to leave, and we have to sterilize all the equipment. Of course when you return I'll finish the haircut.'

'Do you think I'm going to return? You're kicking me out on the street with half my hair missing?'

Heads were turning. Helen hissed: 'Go to the chemist. Buy nit-killing shampoo. Go home and wash and then comb and comb and comb until the little fuckers are all dead. Then come back. I'm sorry. But it's health and safety.'

'You again, is it?' smiled the lady in the chemist across the road. 'Still infested, are we? Threadworms can be hard to treat. I hope your little boys are washing their hands.'

'It's not threadworms. There's an outbreak of head lice at nursery, so better safe than sorry.'

'Oh yes?' A disbelieving look. 'You're not having much luck, are you?'

Rosie smiled serenely, as a voice behind her said: 'Hello!'

'Hey, Patrizia!'

'Are you OK? What are you buying?'

'Nothing,' Rosie said hastily, as the chemist said: 'Lice shampoo.'

Patrizia's hands flew to her sleek helmet of hair. 'Oh my God, not another epidemic!'

'I gathered there was one at Wendy's. Better safe than sorry. Ha ha.'

'Indeed. It won't have come from our house. Everyone, even the adults, is combed every day with an electric comb. You should buy one. They don't sell them here. I'll send you the link.' She eyed Rosie warily. 'So, I'm organizing a baby shower for Bella.'

'Oh, how lovely.'

'I've sent you the email. I do hope you can come. Bring a gift. I found her the cutest cashmere blanket at that lovely little shop on the corner.'

'Right.' *But I've only known Bella two minutes*, she wanted to protest, but she knew better. She knew her gift had better be something pretty darn fine.

The door pinged as she shut it behind her.

'So two bottles of Hedrin and another comb, that'll be thirty-two pounds forty-five,' exulted the chemist. 'I hope it works. Nits can be an absolute nightmare to get rid of. They say they prefer clean hair but in my experience that's a myth. By the way, hope you don't mind me saying, but that's a rather unusual haircut you have. Only being honest.'

Rosie had expected Jake to die laughing when she explained her new haircut. But instead he looked worried.

'There are going to be all these important people there tonight. And you're going to look weird.'

Rosie exploded. He cared about all these anonymous people, but he didn't care about her. 'Thanks for bloody nothing! I've spent all afternoon with this foul stinking gel on my head and then combing for hours and then I had to do a DIY job with the kitchen scissors. I'll never

268

dare go to that hairdressers again and all you care about is whether I'm going to let you down in front of the important people. Sod you.' She turned to the mirror. 'Oh, this is awful! I'm going to have to wrap a scarf round it.'

'No, you'll look like you have leukaemia.' Jake stood behind her. 'Sorry, Bean, it's just . . .' He saw her glare and thankfully changed tack. So have you chopped off the boys' hair too?'

'No, just spent two hours combing it through while they screamed the house down. There were creepy-crawlies all over the place. Actually, killing them was quite satisfying.' Could you admit to that? Was that what families did for fun in the olden days, crushing lice between their thumbs and forefingers, instead of staring hypnotized at the X-Box?

Jake's hand flew to his hair. 'Shit. Do you think I'm OK?'

'Probably not,' Rosie said unkindly.

'Look, look.' He bent down. Rosie peered at his scalp.

'Oh yes, my God! It's enormous.'

'What? Help!'

'There's nothing,' she said crossly, though she'd hardly looked. 'What about me? What can I do? So as not to let you down,' she added with even more venom.

'Can you pin it up or something?'

'I think I'm going to have to.'

Jake tugged at his collar. 'How's the shirt? I ordered it from Mr Porter.'

'It's great,' Rosie said, staring distractedly into the mirror and jabbing in hair pins. 'I look like I'm an extra from *Prisoner Cell Block H*. A prisoner with a head full of creepy-crawlies.'

'Whatever. We need to get going.' Jake looked at his phone. 'The car's been waiting fifteen minutes.'

Traffic was slow and Rosie realized she had her husband at her mercy. He'd have to discuss all her concerns. But before she could launch into them, he said: 'So there'll be this complete knobhead from Disney there tonight called Sean. He's the producer of this kids' franchise. He's sniffing around me, working out if I'm marketable enough.'

'What, so they can sell mugs with your face on?'

'In the Disney Store this Christmas,' he said, pulling a stupid face that normally would have made her laugh. But now she said nothing and after a second he continued: 'Anyway, just warning you. He's an idiot.'

'Right. Warning taken.'

'So what's the latest on Nanna?' he asked. About time too.

'She's chipper. She's had the scan. She said it went fine. She'll get the results –' Rosie gulped – 'today or tomorrow. She wants to hear all about the awards, what everyone was wearing, that sort of thing. She was cross with me for wearing the gold dress again, said I should have tried something different, I—'

'Yeah, you're not really meant to wear the same dress twice.'

'Are you for real? When did you start caring about things like that?' She turned to the window and folded her arms over her chest, fuming.

'Bean! Don't be like this.'

'I'm not being like anything,' she snapped, even though she clearly was. What was happening to her? What was happening to Jake? Had he always been so selfish? Well, yes, he had actually. Think of that time when she'd had food poisoning and had been puking her guts out and he'd just lain on the bed beside her banging on and on about whether he should take a part in a fringe comedy in Swindon. But she'd been so besotted she'd overlooked it, excused it.

Only now that she was well and truly linked to him forever was she beginning to understand exactly who her husband truly was. Not a bad person, but undoubtedly a different person from the man she'd fallen in love with: steelier, far more self-obsessed. Why hadn't she noticed when there was still a get-out clause? The chemistry between them had blinded her to the details. She glanced at him fearfully, as if he could read her thoughts, but he was looking at something on his phone and chortling.

'You won't abandon me tonight, will you?' she asked, as Jake finally put it down. 'Because I feel such a lemon standing there on my own.'

'Don't be daft, Bean. Of course I won't.'

24

The Top TV Awards were taking place in the Grosvenor House Hotel's Great Room. Before the ceremony there was a drinks reception on the mezzanine overlooking the huge space below, which was filled with dining tables.

'It used to be an ice rink down there,' said Christy, appearing out of a group where she'd been laughing uproariously. She was wearing a sleek black dress with a zip down the front that Rosie had a dim idea she'd spotted in one of the hairdresser's magazines. 'The queen used to have skating lessons there. The machinery that kept the ice cool is still under the floorboards.'

'Oh. Right.' Rosie looked around. Despite his promise to stick by her side, Jake was surrounded by sycophants and she felt utterly surplus to requirements. She'd tried to cheer herself up by celeb-spotting and so far had managed a couple of people from *Made in Chelsea*, but really – so what? A night at home in front of old *West Wing*s was beginning to seem extremely appealing. She shouldn't have come.

'Hey.' Christy squeezed her arm. 'You OK?' She wasn't looking at Rosie, though, her eyes were darting about, no doubt trying to work out who the most important person in the room was.

'Fine,' she lied. Not so long ago, she would have been able to tell Christy exactly how she felt, but now her best friend was behind a wall, in which she was trying to find a chink to communicate with her.

'And how's your nanna?'

Well, this was something they could still talk about. Rosie told her. Christy listened, looking very serious.

'You just have to keep checking up on everything that's happening to her. Pay for second opinions on everything.'

'It's not only about that. It's about being there for her. I've been thinking maybe we should move back to Bristol, to be closer to her.'

Christy's expression changed, only slightly, but enough for Rosie to notice. 'That'd be tricky, wouldn't it? When would you see Jake? Even if he doesn't go to LA, and the negotiations are all in place, he'll be working in London. Do you want him commuting every day?'

'No, but I also don't want my grandmother getting frailer and frailer and being all on her own. And she won't move to London before you ask.'

Christy looked her straight in the eye. Rosie stared back.

'Look, I know you don't consider me a relationship expert, and you're probably right, but you need to be careful here. Jake's world is being turned upside down and he really needs you there for him. He needs to know that whatever shit's thrown at him on the Internet you'll support him. That if he gets a major role, you'll be cheering on the sidelines. He needs to know if he gets home late from filming, you'll wake up for him. He—'

'I can't believe you're telling me this,' Rosie interrupted furiously. 'You know I look out for Jake. But this is the twenty-first century, you know. Women have rights too.'

'Ladies and gentleman,' said a fruity voice through the loudspeaker. 'Please take your seats for tonight's fabulous event.'

Christy squeezed Rosie's arm. 'Sorry, I didn't mean to give you a Stepford lecture. Just, I know how much Jake needs you. Listen, I'm sitting over there. I'll see you later.'

Rosie was relieved to have something to do, but everyone seemed to take forever to sit down. She randomly chose a seat and removed the glossy goody bag from it. As she sat down, she surreptitiously examined its contents. A paperback tie-in to a reality soap about a stage school. A key ring. A miniature bottle of wine. She didn't dare dump all the booty on the table, so she switched her attention to reading and re-reading the laminated order of ceremonies, while everyone else milled around greeting each other flamboyantly. Rosie fiddled with the straw in her cocktail glass. Occasionally she'd catch Jake's eye but he'd look right through her.

'Rosie!'

She turned. There was Ellie, looking more like Grace Kelly than ever. Golden locks, bare feet in golden strappy sandals and a green silk dress with an enormous flared skirt. Bodyguard behind her.

Rosie jumped up, stumbling on her stilettos. Ellie held out her arms.

'Rosie. Great to see you again!' A puzzled expression crossed her face. 'I like your hair. It's . . . different.'

'Thanks!' Rosie said breezily.

'Right.' Ellie was silent for a second, clearly horrified at the damage Rosie had inflicted on herself. 'So great to see you, I wanted to get in touch before now but I've been working every day and at night I'm just so tired . . . Still, now we can catch up.' A man tapped her on the shoulder. 'Oh, Sam, hi. Excuse me a minute . . .' Ellie turned and was swallowed into a group.

'Ladies and gentlemen,' cried the disembodied voice of the DJ from the seventies, 'please take your seats.'

There was no seating plan at the table itself, so there was an undignified scramble for places, with everyone except Rosie trying to sit beside someone important. She ended up with Jake on her left and a disappointed-looking man in a pinstripe suit – very un-awards ceremony – on her right.

'Hi, I'm Rosie.'

'I'm Sean,' he said with a bone-crunching handshake, immediately returning his gaze to the BlackBerry in his other hand.

'Oh. Right.' Jake was chatting away animatedly to Ellie. Rosie had thought he hated her. 'Um, so what brings you here, Sean?'

'I'm from Disney,' he barked. 'No!' he screamed at a hovering waiter trying to fill his glass. 'No wine.'

'Red, please,' Rosie said with gratitude. Sean from Disney. The guy who was checking Jake out? Was she meant to charm him? Was he meant to charm her? She turned instead to her smoked salmon salad. Everyone at the table was talking animatedly. She felt utterly alone again.

'So what do you do, Rosie?' Sean asked eventually, pushing the salad around his plate.

'I . . . er . . . well, I'm Jake's wife. I used to work in IT. Right now, I'm not working. I have two small boys, you see, and . . .'

'Ah.' Instantly, he turned away from Rosie to the woman on his other side, a woman a million times more glamorous and sophisticated than Rosie.

Rosie ate the rest of her starter slowly, trying to look as if it were the most fascinating salad in the world. Snatches of conversation floated across the table.

'So after the opening weekend it totally bombed . . .'

'She quoted one hundred and ninety k but we quickly got her down. So greedy.'

'Of course, it's wonderful, but there'll never be another Freddie.'

She was grateful when – after the starters – the awards bit finally started, but they turned out to be

276

almost as dull. Prize after prize: best reality show, best newcomer, best supporting actress in a drama, best supporting actor in a comedy. They were all awarded to people Rosie had never heard of – that was what came of watching so many box sets – and they were all preceded by endless speeches and clips, and followed by gushy acceptance speeches.

She could see Christy two tables away, blatantly reading her iPhone, and most people seemed to be talking loudly, and increasingly drunkenly, to their neighbour, paying little attention to what was happening on stage unless the award concerned their table.

Finally, the time came for Jake to make his presentation. He bounded, grinning, up on to the stage, exuding Perry charm. The room went wild at the sight of him. *If only they could see him tucked up in bed with zit cream dabbed all over his chin*, thought Rosie, glancing at her watch.

'Wondering how long you have to go, before you can head home and catch an episode of *Homeland* before bed?' asked Ellie, slipping suddenly into his empty seat.

Rosie turned and smiled. 'Something like that.'

'I'm so glad to grab this chance to talk. So glad to see you again. I felt so terrible making you and your mom leave my suite that night, but . . . someone was on the phone and then I was just so zonked I couldn't stay awake a second longer. I felt terrible.'

'Not to worry,' said Rosie. 'How's your dad?'

A strange, pained look crossed Ellie's face. 'It's so

sweet of you to ask. Thank you for remembering. He's OK. I mean, not perfect, but OK for now. I speak to his carers every day. I'm so touched.'

'That's OK,' Rosie said, a bit embarrassed. She added: 'Um, I know a bit what it's like. My nanna – I mean, my grandmother – isn't that well either.'

'Oh, honey.' Ellie took her hand. 'I'm so sorry. Tell me about it.'

So Rosie told her. She hadn't had a chance to talk to anyone properly about it yet, and it was such a relief to get it all off her chest. Ellie really listened. She asked questions. Rosie felt close to tears. 'Thank you for being so nice.'

'Hey, you've been so nice to me. It's not easy finding friends when you're me. Girls are kind of freaked out – I know that makes me sound crazy and vain, but it's true. They think I'm going to be some kind of snotty princess.'

'Oh, I'm sure they don't,' Rosie said guiltily. She smiled. 'The funny thing is my nanna would be so chuffed if she knew I was talking to you. You're her idol. She's nuts about *O'Rourke's* and she thinks you're the most beautiful woman in the world. If we'd had more time with you at Cliveden, I was actually going to get a photo of us together for her.'

'Well, bless your ... nanna, is it?' Ellie looked delighted by this exotic English word. 'Will I meet her at the first night?'

'I hope so.'

A small woman tapped Ellie on the shoulder. 'Your presentation is next, Ellie.'

'Oh. OK. Thank you!' Ellie stroked Rosie's arm. 'Wait for me. I'll be back!' She sat up straighter and smiled at the room. Her name was called and, with an even broader smile, she stood and began wiggling towards the stage to huge applause.

'All right?' Christy said, slipping into her place as if by magic. 'What's that airhead saying to you?'

'She's really sweet,' Rosie protested.

Christy shook her head firmly. 'She's so mad, she'd eat your bedroom.'

'If you say so,' Rosie said indifferently.

'Why are you sounding so sniffy? I'm warning you, Rosie. She's a fruitcake. Be careful.'

'Hi, gang.' It was Jake, just returned from backstage. 'What's up?'

'I'd better get back to my table,' Christy replied. 'One of my people's awards is coming up.'

Jake grinned and plonked himself down in the empty chair. Immediately he turned to Sean and said something quickly. Sean's head tilted back, laughing uproariously. Oh, so this was how her husband talked to the man he called an idiot. Hypocrite. Not knowing what to do again, Rosie delved into the goody bag and pulled out a huge tub of some skin cream she'd never heard of. Well, that was something at least; she could maybe give it to Dizzy for her birthday.

'Hey, it's me again!' Ellie had returned. The room

279

was applauding the best animal, squealing with delight as Pretty the Cat was led on stage on a lead by her owner, who two years previously had won *Big Brother*. 'So sorry. I just had to do my duty. So where were we?'

A small woman's head appeared between the two of theirs. 'Time to go. We've done a sweep. The car's waiting.'

'Oh! Oh, Sharon, do I have to?'

'But the ceremony's just ending,' said Rosie, looking around and realizing dinner – guinea fowl with mashed potato – was being served by teams of silver-service waiters. 'You're not going to eat?'

'Shit, no!' Ellie laughed. 'We . . . I mean people like me never stick around for the food part. I just came to have my picture taken at the start and to present the award. I'll eat back at my apartment. My chef will have prepared something . . . healthy. Then lights out by nine.'

'Oh. I see.'

'We have to go,' insisted the minder. 'The sweep's been done. We can't keep the car waiting.'

'Oh my God, Rosie, I'm so sorry. I'm so boring. I've loved talking to you. You're even more incredible than Jake said.'

'Jake said?' Rosie looked dubiously at her husband.

'He's always talking about you and your little girls. Listen, Rosie, we won't stop here. Sharon, find Rosie's number, we'll do that lunch.' She bent down and Rosie found her nose pressed in Ellie's bony cleavage, her nostrils assaulted with a sharp citrussy scent. She leaned forward to kiss, but then realized Ellie was doing the American hug thing and ending up banging cheeks with her. Still, she thought wryly, there was no doubt Ellie was being a better friend to her right now than anyone else.

'Jake, see you tomorrow,' Ellie said.

'See you, Ellie.' Jake didn't even bother making eye contact.

Two other bodyguards appeared from nowhere and Ellie was hustled away.

From: Patriziaandgary@ghytr.com

Heading: Baybee Shower

So, girls, don't forget Wednesday night is Bella's baby-shower night. Everyone dress either for team 'pink' or team 'blue', and don't forget to bring pink or blue (preferably silk) ribbons for 'measure the bump'. And BRING A GIFT. 7.30 p.m., my place.

Patrizia

xxxx

25

An incontrovertible law of nature is that the later you go to bed, the earlier your child will wake the following morning. On this occasion, George excelled himself by crawling into their bed at half past five – a whole hour earlier than usual.

'Georgie, it's still the middle of the night.'

'No, it isn't, the sun's shining outside.'

Jake groaned and scrambled around for the iPad. 'Here, watch this for a bit.'

'Really?' George clapped his hands in triumph.

'Oh, Jake, no. Now he'll think that every time he gets up early, he can watch cartoons.'

'Needs must. It's either that or me dying of sleep deprivation.'

'Just don't tell your brother,' Rosie said, as George gazed raptly at the screen. She tried to go back to sleep, but she was wide awake, already worrying about Nanna and what she was going to say to the specialist. Would she listen to his advice? Or maybe she was right to ignore it? Why wouldn't she let Rosie accompany her to the appointments? Oh God, how was she going to cope on so little sleep? She'd have to somehow get the boys to nursery and then she'd go home and crawl into bed and snooze until pick-up time.

When she returned from drop-off, Dizzy was in the kitchen. The air was full of the noises of builders hammering and drilling, and radios playing as all the work on the house sped ahead.

'Hey, have you seen this week's *Heat*? There's a photo of Jake looking really spoddy. "Geek of the Week" it's called. Here.'

Dizzy handed over a copy of the magazine. There, indeed, was Jake, ringed in a close-up of a school photo. He was wearing huge glasses – not cool like his current pair but truly geeky. He was wearing a wing collar and a long coat, his hair was plastered greasily to his forehead and there was what looked like a boil on his nose.

'Pretty bad, huh?' Dizzy guffawed.

Rosie was torn between amusement at the unflattering picture and hurt that someone would have sold it to *Heat*. Who? Surely not Bosey. That was a paranoid thought. Jake's school was huge; it could have been anyone. Still, it showed someone really didn't like her husband very much. How horrible.

Her phone rang. Number withheld. 'Hello?' she asked nervously – withheld numbers always meant bad news, usually from the bank.

'Hey, Mrs Geek of the Week. It's your old friend, Patty. Remember me? Or are you too famous now?'

'Don't be daft. How are things?'

'Well, not great at the moment to be honest. Heidi's only gone and got exhaustion or some such bollocks, not at all related to that dodgy boyfriend of hers, oh no. Anyway, the doctor's signed her off sick and we've got this huge project coming up and we'd love you to come back for a few weeks and help us out or we're totally screwed and the company will collapse and we'll all lose our jobs and starve to death.'

Rosie laughed. 'Are you being just the teensiest bit over-dramatic?'

'Possibly. But we really need you back. For a bit. As soon as possible. Say yes, say yes, say yes, say yes.'

Rosie glowed. It was lovely to be wanted. But she knew what kind of deal this would be. 'Will it be super-long hours?'

'We . . . ell.'

'Tell me.'

'Yeah, we'd be talking eight-to-eight days as standard. Probably a bit more work to take home.'

That meant seven to nine, plus extra work all week-end. It was always that way when they were trying to impress a new client. It was one of the reasons Rosie had had to give up the job. All the same, she was tempted. She'd be back in the Disneyland that was work: tasty Pret lunches rather than cold fish fingers, unsticky sur-faces, being able to drink a whole cup of tea rather than rediscovering it hours later, milk curdling on the surface. There'd be people who didn't wear nappies and only cried in private in the toilets. Who talked about last

night's telly, rather than baby showers. And Jake, well . . .
Jake would have started the play so he'd be free until six
most days, so he could do some childcare, with a bit of
help from Dizzy. Not that he'd been thrilled to pick up
the baton in the past, but now the boys were older he
might be a bit more cooperative. Yolande could help out
a bit, and they could stay for lunch at Wendy's. It wouldn't
be forever. Before she knew it, she was actually starting
to take the idea seriously.

'I'll have to run it by Jake, but . . . maybe.'

Patty whooped. 'You are a fucking superstar. Tristan
is going to be well made up. Let me know ASAP?'

'I said maybe.' The other line was going. 'Thanks so
much for asking, Patty.'

'Hey, no worries. You must know you'll always be
our first choice.'

Rosie was smiling, but then she stopped, as if
thumped in the stomach. Nanna said the caller ID.

'Hi,' she exclaimed, trying to sound breezy. 'Do you
have the results?'

'Do you want the good news or the bad news?'

Ohnoohnoohnoohno. 'The good!'

'I haven't got cancer.'

'What?' Rosie sat up straight. 'That's brilliant. Amazing.' A tear of relief ran down her cheek, but then . . .
'And the bad?'

'Apparently, I'm in the early stages of sodding
Parkinson's.'

*

285

She was waiting for Jake to return home like a runner, desperate to leave the starting blocks. As soon as he was through the door – just after seven, not too late for once, she cornered him. 'Jake, I've had horrible news.'

'Shit, that is horrible,' he replied when she'd told him, opening the fridge and examining the contents, a disapproving look on his face.

'I've been googling all afternoon. There's loads they can do. It may take time for the disease to really kick in. So it's not all bad. But of course it means we can't move to LA now.'

'Why?' He picked up a pot of hummus. 'What's the sell-by date on this?'

'Jake!'

'Sorry, but I'm starving. I need to eat something before I can think straight. Why can't we move to LA?'

'Well, because of Nanna.'

'You just said it won't kick in for ages, and there's masses we can do.' The boys came whooping into the kitchen. 'Hey, guys, how are you?'

'Boys, go and watch telly.'

'We've already watched loads,' Toby said primly. 'We don't want to get square eyes.'

Jake laughed. 'Brilliant, boys. Quite right too.'

'It's a Wednesday,' Rosie tried. 'Square eyes don't happen on a Wednesday.'

'Mummy, no! I don't want square eyes.'

'Nooo!' George agreed gleefully.

'OK,' Rosie snapped. 'Then you give them their bath, Jake, and read them a story. Then we'll talk.'

'What? Me do bath?'

It had been ages, not since they'd moved in, Rosie realized. 'Why not? I'll fix us dinner.'

'Daddy do bath!'

'We'll splash you, Daddy.'

'Go on, then. Go up and get undressed.'

They headed up the stairs, yelling and punching each other. Rosie glared at her husband. 'You know I don't want to go to LA.'

'It may not happen,' Jake retorted. 'But stop closing doors that haven't even opened. Talking of which, I've been thinking. Maybe we should start going a bit easier on all the decorating.'

'How do you mean?'

'I think we should tell David and his team to give it a break for a few weeks. So we can decide what we really want.'

'But they're in the middle of installing that den you wanted and they're putting in the fake grass you were so keen on tomorrow. Do you really want all that to stop?'

'Just take a breather.'

He turned back to the fridge. 'Is any of this gluten-free? Rolla says I need to start eating gluten-free.'

'Of course, sodding lettuce and a pot of hummus is gluten-free. Why do I have to tell David to stop? It was you who wanted all this in the first place. If he downs

287

tools like that we'll still have to pay him and the place'll be chaos, worse than it is now.'

'Tell him to take a few days' break, while I think about what we really need.'

It wasn't the moment, but Rosie, furious, decided to go there anyway. 'Well, while we're changing things, Patty from Tapper-Green called. They want me back at work for a few weeks to cover a big job. I thought I'd say yes. I mean . . .' she faltered seeing Jake's expression. 'Just for a while.'

'That's absurd,' he exploded. 'I'm working every hour God sends. You can't go back to Tapper-Green. What would we do with the boys? Put them in nursery full-time?'

'We'd work something out. Dizzy would cover it, if it was short-term.'

'You hated your job. I gave you the chance to leave it.'

'I didn't hate it. I hated things about it.' *I didn't appreciate everything that was great about it, at least not nearly enough.* She knew really that she was being ridiculous, that she'd dreamed of staying at home. Most importantly there was Nanna. Whatever would she have done if she'd still been a wage slave at Tapper-Green when that bomb had started ticking? Still, she didn't care. She wanted to show she counted in some way, that she wasn't only an appendage to Jake and his increasingly barmy whims. 'But anyway . . . they need me. I've told you, it's not a permanent thing, just while they have this crisis.'

'What about my crisis? What about the fact the play's about to start?'

Oh fuck you and your play.

'I need to know you're at home for me, that the boys are settled, and not have us both rushing about like loons all the time. I helped you stop working. I thought it was what you wanted. Now you're throwing it back in my face.'

'You never asked me what I wanted,' Rosie said, turning on her heel. Anger was bubbling through her body. She hated him. She wished she'd never laid eyes on him.

'I try. I just don't get you, any more, Bean. I don't know what you want. You say you don't want to go to America because of your nanna, but then you want to leave the boys at home all day with a nanny.'

'And you want to install swimming pools and then remove them. You're insane.'

'You're crazy.'

'Are you getting divorced?' George said conversationally from the doorway. They both jumped.

'Why do you ask?' Rosie snapped.

'How do you know what divorce is?' asked Jake.

'Wendy talked about it at nursery. She said lots of parents did it and not to worry if it happened to ours.'

'If you got divorced, you could get married again,' Toby said thoughtfully, standing naked behind him. 'You could be on *Marrying Mum and Dad*. Kids plan their mum and dads' wedding. We could have one for you with Gary Guitar.'

'And Peppa Pig.'

Normally Rosie would have laughed, but she was too upset. She was also too angry to slap down divorce suggestions. 'If we got divorced, we wouldn't marry again,' she said. She wondered shakily what was happening to her marriage and with a cold slap of realization knew it had never been as perfect as she'd fooled herself, that there'd always been signs of Jake's flaws. 'Now go up. Get in the bath. Jake, go up with them. And don't expect any dinner. I'm off to the baby shower.'

26

Five years ago

Jake had proposed at the hospital, just after they'd had the twelve-week scan, causing the sonographer to shed a small tear at the romance of it all. They married, when she was six months pregnant, at the Chelsea Physic Garden, a magical oasis tucked between the Thames and the King's Road and, cheesily, Rosie really did consider the day the happiest of her life. Christy (who organized nearly everything) was bridesmaid, so was Sandrine.

Luckily Rosie didn't find pregnancy hard, because it was a long commute to work. Tapper-Green had taken on a big project and she was starting early and finishing late. Meanwhile, Jake was unemployed. He went to audition after audition after audition, but nothing ever came of anything and much of his time was spent sitting in cafés in Soho with other rejected actors, complaining about how tough life was.

Time after time after dinner he'd implore Rosie not to bother with the washing up, to come to bed and ravish him, that he'd clear up in the morning. But she'd arrive home late, lugging Sainsbury's shopping bags, to find the bed rumpled and last night's dirty dishes in the sink.

Once or twice she'd hinted that she'd like him to do a bit more and he'd been abject, saying of course he would, that he was a lazy idiot, that he didn't deserve her. He'd improve for a day or two, but then things would slip backwards.

But Rosie didn't mind really. Jake was the most wonderful man in the world and she couldn't believe she'd actually married him. At night, she'd lie beside him, one hand on her growing stomach as the baby wiggled and kicked, gazing at him sleeping, wondering like Maria in *The Sound of Music* what the 'something good' was that she must have done to have bagged him.

He was so handsome in his geeky way, he was funny, he was bright and he loved her. All right, he had no money at all, but she was earning enough for them to get by.

Right at the end of the pregnancy, when she was off work but too fat and exhausted to go anywhere, Jake began to pull his finger out. He would make her breakfast in bed and then snuggle up next to her and they'd spend all day watching box sets: *The West Wing*, *The Sopranos*, *Sex and the City*.

Everyone warned them gloomily that once the baby arrived, they'd descend into hell. 'You won't know what's hit you,' Becki kept saying happily.

But the first six months of Toby's life were some of the most precious of Rosie's life. Yes, she was exhausted, as Becki had warned her; yes, her nipples were in agony; yes, she was confused about everything from routines to how often to change a nappy and whether buggies were better than slings, but she had Jake at her side, jogging up and down the room with little Toby pressed to his chest, singing him silly songs, laughing at the baby's excruciated expressions when he did a poo, sleeping with little Toby lying across his chest.

They succeeded at keeping Yolande pretty well at bay. The flat was too small for her to stay the night as she would have loved to, and Rosie became expert at turning a deaf ear to her advice on breastfeeding ('Waste of time, I never bothered.'), car seats ('We didn't have them and all our kids survived.') and crying ('Just leave them to it.').

She and Jake went for long walks with Toby in the sling or the buggy, exploring hidden corners of London. They attended mum and baby screenings, taking turns to jiggle him on their lap, while *Gone with the Wind* played out on the big screen. They marvelled over each stage in his development — smiling, laughing, the moment when he no longer needed burping. He was four months old when Rosie decided to broach the subject that had been preying at the back of her mind.

In hindsight she could have chosen a better venue. They were staying at Yolande and Rupert's for the weekend, and Becki, Dave and their four children were also there and running amok.

'I'm going to have to go back to work quite soon; I'm already only on half pay,' she said to Jake in a sudden quiet moment in the cluttered but cosy living room.

'That's a shame. Yes, who's a beautiful little boy? You are. You are!' He blew a raspberry on a delighted Toby's tummy.

'So I was thinking. What will we do about childcare? I'd been wondering about nursery, but you're having such a great time with Toby, I thought . . .'

'You thought what?' Something in Jake's tone changed.

'I thought you could look after him.'

'Be a nanny?'

'No, not a nanny. Be his dad.'

'You must be joking!' Jake looked horrified.

Rosie was baffled. 'Why would I be joking? You're so brilliant with him.'

'I can't be a stay-at-home-dad. A SAHD. A sad. What about work?'

'But there isn't any work. At the moment. Obviously if there were we'd think again.'

'I need to be available at the drop of a hat for auditions. I can't be looking after a baby. And I need to be doing workshops: comedy, the Alexander technique. I was planning to brush up on my riding, always useful for costume dramas . . .'

'Oh.' Already Rosie knew she was going to lose this argument. 'OK. So Toby will have to go to nursery?' Even though her heart was breaking, she struggled to keep her tone unemotional.

'You always said that was the plan.'

'That was before I realized how expensive it is. When we take away the fees from my salary there's going to be hardly anything left. We'd just about cover the bills, but there'd be no fun money.'

'I'll get a break soon,' Jake said breezily.

'Really?' Rosie felt sick. She should have thought all this through before she'd fallen pregnant. She was an idiot.

'Of course I will!' Jake's voice was so loud it frightened Toby and he started to cry.

Yolande was not at all impressed at the idea of her precious grandson going into a nursery. 'Won't he catch all sorts of bugs there?' she demanded when the subject came up over dinner of over-boiled potatoes and pork chops. 'And the girls that work in those places – they're all sixteen, not a brain cell in their heads. They all leave them to cry while they're on the phone to their boyfriends.'

'Oh, that's good to know.' Rosie failed to keep the sarcasm out of her voice. Could this become any more stressful?

'All the studies show babies are better off with one primary carer,' said Becki firmly. 'I was lucky Dave was so supportive and I could take all that time off work, wasn't I, darling?'

Dave grunted.

'Mum, you're not seriously suggesting I become a nanny?' Jake had snapped.

'Of course not, darling. You're an actor.'

'But he isn't working right now,' Rupert, who had been silent until now, pointed out politely. 'Rosie is the breadwinner.'

'But that's the way it is for all actors. His luck will change. But it's not going to help if he can't make the right contacts because he's pushing a buggy round the place, changing nappies.' Yolande turned to Rosie. 'I feel for you, darling. I loved those baby years. I was very lucky not to have to work, to stay at home and supervise my babies' development. Let's face it, nothing else is as important.'

'But I like work,' said Rosie. And she did. A little part of her was looking forward to returning to the office, to being in control again. But that little part was blotted out by the dark cloud of leaving Toby with strangers. Plus, she'd been unnerved by Jake. For the first time she'd spotted another side to him, a side that was fiercely, ruthlessly ambitious, that didn't care about how his choices might affect his loved ones.

So she went back to work but it was far tougher than she'd anticipated. After the nursery fees they had no spare income at all. Jake did actually contribute a bit, picking up Toby most days, but nonetheless it was galling hearing how he'd spent the afternoon having a pint with the boys when Rosie had been strap-hanging on the Bakerloo line, heart thudding like a woodpecker in anticipation of being reunited with her little boy. She tried to talk to Christy about it, but for the first time in their friendship, it was clear her loyalties lay elsewhere.

'Jake's right, he has to be available!'
'But he wanted this baby.'

'Of course, but he still has to work.'

Rosie gave up. Christy couldn't be less interested in Toby, that had been clear from the start. Rosie understood the risks of becoming a baby bore, but all the same, just a question here or there about how she was finding motherhood, how Toby was developing, would have been kind. Christy simply didn't get it: had no idea of the earthquake-like fault that had turned her life inside-out.

'So, no offence, but have you set a timescale for this?' Patty asked, after one incident when Jake was an hour late to pick up the boys because a 'networking' meeting with a producer overran.

'Timescale for what?' Rosie asked snappily, eyes on her monitor.

'For Jake actually making it? I mean, at some point is he going to accept it just isn't going to happen?'

'It will happen,' Rosie had responded loftily, annoyed because Patty was only voicing her fears. 'Jake's very talented. Cream rises to the top.'

'I bloody well hope so, because otherwise you're going to end up in an early grave.'

The first pregnancy had been an accident but the second one was planned minutely, though she didn't tell Jake that. She needed a break, she needed time off work and another baby was the only way she could engineer that.

She'd never forget that night when she returned from work early with the pregnancy test in her bag. Jake was in the tiny kitchen, spooning a jar into Toby's mouth – initially Rosie had been determined to go down the Annabel Karmel puree road like Becki, but when would she ever find the time to source, boil and mash an organic swede?

As soon as she entered the room, he turned, face glowing. 'Christy's got me an amazing audition. It's for a new sitcom on the BBC. I'd be playing this gay vicar.'

'That's fantastic!' But all Rosie wanted to do was run into the loo and pee on the magic stick that was burning a hole in her bag.

'I really think I have a chance. Christy says I do.'

'Of course you do. You're so talented.'

'I knew it, Bean.' He planted a sloppy kiss on her cheek. 'The tide's turning.' He opened the fridge and removed a bottle of champagne. 'Look what Christy sent us. To wish us luck.'

'Oh! How sweet.'

'We'll drink it tonight and then we'll go to bed and I'll do very bad things to you.'

'I don't know if I can drink it!' Rosie had yelped.

'Why not?'

'Because I think I'm pregnant.'

'No!' For a second, Rosie felt as if she were on the operating table in *Grey's Anatomy*, and a team of doctors had just defibrillated her chest. Jake sounded horrified. He didn't want another baby. Well, too bad.

'No! That's brilliant.' Jake grabbed Toby out of his high chair and swung him in the air. Toby squawked in delight. 'Boyo, you're going to be a big brother. How about that, eh?'

'You're pleased?'

'I'm bloody ecstatic. Oh my God. Maybe it'll be a little girl who looks just like you!'

'Um, I haven't actually done the test yet.'

'Sorry?'

'I haven't done the test. I was going to do it now. But I'm sure I'm pregnant. I can feel it: my boobs are tender and bigger and—'

'Oh goodie,' Jake said with his best Leslie Phillips leer.

'I'm going to go into the loo now and pee on the tester and we'll know in five minutes.'

She was pregnant. They both stared at the stick, delighted.

'It's the best thing that's ever happened to us,' Jake crowed. 'I want loads of babies with you. We can afford them now. I'm going to get this part and I'm going to be famous.'

Yeah, right, thought Rosie. Although she'd badly wanted another child, now the reality was here, she felt very nervous. Patty was right: Jake's ambitions were a pipe dream. He wouldn't get this part and life would be even tougher.

27

Rosie stormed out of the house and across the Green, the silver gift bag containing her present to Bella – a cashmere cardi that had cost about the same as a Bentley – swinging by her side. As she walked to Patrizia's, she was fuming to herself.

'Bloody bastard, why can't I do the job? He gets to have all the fun. I *miss* Tapper-Green.'

'Are you OK?' asked a voice behind her.

Rosie jumped. 'Oh, Caroline! Hi. Um, just . . . practising a little speech I might make at – er – at Jake's first night.'

'Oh. Right.' Caroline stared at her curiously. 'Are you sure you're OK? You look upset.'

To her horror and fury, Rosie started to cry. 'Jake and I have just had the most horrible row,' she choked out. 'I don't know what's going on. We don't seem to talk to each other any more and he's become so hard. He won't negotiate anything. He's earning the money, so it all has to be how he says.'

Caroline nudged her towards a bench on the Green. 'Hey, hey,' she soothed. 'Sit down. Hey, it's OK. Men, eh? Christ, they're so annoying. I should know.'

Oh shit, she'd forgotten she was talking to Caroline,

divorcee extraordinaire. Sure enough, she was off. 'Johann was exactly the same. He thought because he earned the money, he controlled everything I did – my friends, what I wore, what I watched at the cinema. It was crazy. I used to be an independent woman, then I marry a man I love and, just because he's rich, he thinks he's also God.'

Rosie sniffled. 'Jake's not that bad, but he's just so, so . . . .'

Caroline squeezed her hand. 'Hey, hey. It's tough. I know. But you have friends, Rosie. You really do.'

'I . . .' Rosie was about to start blubbing again, saying she didn't, that Parvaneh was on the other side of town and always too busy to take her calls, and Sandrine was far away in Hebden and Nanna was sick and Christy, who was normally the first person she'd have turned to, was now unavailable because she only cared about her husband's career.

She tried to calm herself, as Caroline said, 'You know we're here for you. We were talking about you the other day, saying we wondered why we didn't see more of you.'

'But I never see you!' Rosie gulped, trying to bury all the unkind thoughts she'd nursed. 'You're never there. I mean, you're never at Wendy's.'

'Well, we're busy women. What with our charities and all that. But we're always around for a friend. In the Village, in the cafés, hanging out in the shops, having lunch together. Hey, I'll text you next time we're having coffee. We'd love you to join us more.'

'Thank you,' Rosie sniffled.

'Great.' Caroline stood, and clicked her fingers as if she were Mary Poppins. 'Come on, or we'll be late.'

Indeed, Patrizia – rather than a servant – was standing at the door of the Conifers, tapping at her Georg Jensen watch. 'Guys, hurry up. I was about to send out a search party.'

They hurried into the room, where all the usual crowd, plus a few unfamiliar faces, were waiting. The maids were busy circulating, holding out trays with slices of pink and blue cake.

'Choose a colour,' Patrizia urged. 'Hold it up at the gender reveal.'

'What's that?' Rosie asked.

'Gender reveal,' smiled Bella, who was sitting back on the uncomfortable white sofa, still-tiny bump prominently displayed, surrounded by pastel-coloured gift bags attached to silver heart-shaped helium balloons. 'I had my scan, but I asked the nurse to put the sex in an envelope and we're just about to open it and find out.'

'Oh. Right. Does your husband know?'

'Uh-uh. He likes a surprise, so all you ladies are sworn to secrecy.'

'Are we ready?' Patrizia was jumping up and down in excitement. 'Shall we see the colours? Who wants Bella to have a boy?'

'Me!' yelled several guests. Gingerly Rosie raised her blue card. This wouldn't turn out well.

'And a girl?' Another larger group whooped and waved their pink tickets.

Bella held up a silver envelope. 'Shall I?'

'Yeeeah!'

She tore it open, her expression like Sue Perkins about to announce the *Bake-Off* winner. Her face fell. 'Oh!' Then, like a losing actor on Oscar night, she rapidly altered her expression to one of manic joy. 'I mean, yes! How fantastic. A boy.'

'Aaah,' cooed team pink in disappointment.

'Fantastic,' Patrizia said hastily. 'A little playmate for your Ben. And my twins.' She coughed. 'So now, moving on – time for the urn.'

A maid appeared bearing a huge Grecian urn. Bella leaned back on the cushions, her face a study in disappointment. Rosie remembered how guiltily flat she'd felt when she'd discovered she was having a second boy, horrible and spoiled to be gutted but still gutted she'd never be able to indulge in her dream of reading *Ballet Shoes* aloud to her daughter, that she'd never be able to go crazy on the party-dress front, that the toilet seat would remain up for the rest of her days.

She sat down beside her. 'Two boys is the best thing,' she said. 'You'll feel like a goddess, the only woman in your domain. And boys are just so . . . squidgy somehow. So soft. They adore their mummies.'

Bella smiled ruefully. 'I know. Thank you.'

'Pick out a piece of paper, ladies!' Patrizia called out. 'You'll see a number. You're going to write a letter to

303

the baby, for him to read when he reaches that age.' She turned to Elise, who was standing by the door, virtually jogging on the spot in her impatience to leave. 'Els, you're not going? It's so early.'

'I have to get up at five to catch a flight to Glasgow,' Elise explained.

'Just hang on a bit longer! You have to write the letter. It's to Bella's unborn child.' Patrizia grabbed Elise's arm and pulled her into a chair. 'Bring Elise some paper, please, Romy. She needs to get writing.'

Reluctantly Elise accepted a Montblanc ballpoint from a jar. Rosie had picked 'twelve' from the urn. She stared at that number. She barely knew Bella. She had no idea what advice to offer a twelve-year-old boy. The only one she'd ever known, and then only barely, was Barron. 'If you want to be a girl, think carefully. It's a big step to take.' Yes, that would go down well. She accepted a pen and a piece of thick, creamy Smythson writing paper and, kneeling on the hard wood floor, so she could lean on the driftwood coffee table, tried to work out what to say.

This was like your worst exam nightmare ever. Everyone else seemed to be writing busily. One woman even stuck her hand up. 'Can I have more paper, please?'

'*I hope you're enjoying school,*' Rosie tried. '*Remember, exam results aren't everything.*'

'Excuse me,' said a woman kneeling beside her. 'Sorry to bother you, but you're Jake Perry's wife, aren't you? Patrizia pointed you out.'

'I . . . ah . . .' Out of the corner of her eye, she could see Caroline dabbing her eyes, clearly deeply moved by her words to the unborn child. What? Rosie would have given anything for a peek.

'I'm Laura Regan, I'm currently head of PTA at King's Mount.'

'Oh, lovely!'

'I have a little one in year three and my second boy – I've five, I know, crazy isn't it? – is going to be starting reception in September with . . . Tobias, is it?'

'Toby, just Toby.'

'Super. Toby. Anyway, I wanted to touch base because I wondered if we might possibly beg a little favour of you, which is to help with the getting-to-know-you tea party. It's in a couple of weeks. You'll no doubt have the date in your diary but so many people will be off on their summer hols and it would be tremendous if you would be able to lend a hand.'

'Right. Well. I should be able to, I'll have to check my diary, I . . .' Then she remembered. 'Oh, I may be back at work by then!'

Laura brushed this aside. 'Mrs Benzecry, the reception teacher, always attends the picnic and she *always* takes notes of which parents have helped out.'

'I'm sure it'll be fine. I'll just have to check, but—'

'Oh, you are marvellous. And another thing, Rosie. We – that's the committee and I – well, obviously we know who your husband is . . .' Laura giggled girlishly.

'Ye . . . e . . . s.'

'Well, he is so marvellous and we all adore him, so I had a couple of requests. First, do you think he might be so kind as to ask Ellie Lewis to autograph some box sets for our raffle at the autumn fair? I know it's not for ages, but I believe Ellie – am I allowed to call her Ellie? I feel like I know her. Have you met her? – won't be in town for that much longer. And, second, do you think your husband would open the autumn fair?'

'I can ask,' Rosie said cautiously.

'Would you? The school look so kindly on children who participate in these ways, I find they often are chosen for leading parts in school plays. Anyway, Rosie, you're going to love King's Mount. It's a fabulous school, so much more relaxed than Gadney's. They're all four-by-fours there. We're far more chilled – and we're not all City bods. There's quite a few arty parents, the kinds who if they had a few spare quid would spend it on an old master, not a yacht, do you know what I mean?'

'Uh . . .' Rosie said faintly.

'So I'll put you down for the picnic!' Laura said, as Patrizia clapped her hands.

'Papers in now, ladies! Oh, Bella, where are you going? C'mon, be a sport. We're going to play guess the size of the bump now.'

Rosie looked around for a glass of blue champagne. It was going to be a long night.

28

For the next couple of weeks, Rosie hardly saw her husband, as rehearsing intensified, and that was just as well as everything about Jake made her fume. When they were in the same room as each other, they seemed to do nothing but squabble.

She'd thought things would improve after she'd reluctantly called Tapper-Green and told them the job wasn't going to be possible, because she just couldn't see how to make the logistics work, but instead she felt even angrier, unable to let go. She was filled with resentment towards Jake for simply refusing to understand this or to discuss any future compromise. When she tried to talk to him, he blanked her. He could only focus on the play. Normally at this stage a big West End production would be previewing, and members of the public could buy tickets cheaply so the director could try out various approaches on them. But this time things were being done differently. So great was the buzz surrounding Ellie's debut on the London stage that no one was allowed an advance peek.

'It's a nightmare,' Jake would groan, looking at his morning email from Simon listing all the changes he wanted them to incorporate that afternoon. 'It's bloody impossible to sit through it, with Ellie forgetting all her lines and then cracking up giggling, like she doesn't even care.'

'She's just nervous,' Rosie said, soothing him. 'She'll pull it together on the night.'

'She'd better or the ship's sinking with her.'

Rosie couldn't really find it within herself to care. She was busy with the house – David Allen Robertson hadn't taken the news he was temporarily to down tools at all well and kept ringing up asking when he could start again. Every weekend she drove the boys to Bristol for a day to visit Nanna, while Jake stayed at home 'resting'. After her initial panic about the Parkinson's diagnosis, Rosie had calmed down. There was plenty of comforting information out there about how the condition could be staved off for years with the right drugs and Nanna seemed absolutely fine, much better than she'd been for ages now she'd started taking the prescribed pills. So there was hope. There always had to be hope.

Nanna was coming to London for a press night this week – the official opening – and Rosie was far more excited about her visit than about her husband's performance. The plan was that she'd stay on for a couple of days and Rosie was going to treat her like a queen, taking her out for lovely meals and a shopping trip.

'So I'm all sorted for Thursday,' Nanna had told her. 'Train ticket booked. I got Maureen to help me do it online.'

Rosie sighed. 'I told you not to catch the train. I'll send a car and driver.'

Nanna snorted. 'Don't be ridiculous. Train is fine. Just a taxi to pick me up at Paddington, that's more than enough luxury for me.'

The week sped by and before they knew it the big day had arrived. It was nearly ten in the morning and Jake was lying on the bed groaning. 'I am going to vomit in a minute. I can't take this.'

It wasn't attractive to see your husband snivelling and whimpering at the prospect of some harsh words from a handful of middle-aged critics. Weren't husbands only supposed to be frightened of leopards in trees and woolly mammoths?

'Poor you,' she said unconvincingly, laying a soothing hand on his brow.

But Jake pushed it away. 'The reviews are going to crucify us.'

'Don't read them then. Ellie says she never does.'

'That's because Ellie *can't read*,' he snapped. 'Or barely. I could try not to read them, but word'll get back to me anyway. Mum'll tell me, or Twitter, or Facebook. So I'll have to man up.'

'Why don't I make you a boiled egg and soldiers?' Rosie said. 'To soothe your stomach.'

'I can't eat eggs at the moment. They're not on my nutritional plan, remember?'

The aggrieved way he said this meant an end to all sympathy. 'OK, I'll just let you get on with it then,' she said as calmly as she could. She had plenty to do around the house. Rupert and Yolande were attending the premiere, natch, and would be staying the night afterwards, so she would put fresh flowers and some magazines in the second-best spare room. The best magazines and the best room, with its view over the garden, were reserved for Nanna.

But as she thought it, her phone rang.

'Nanna, I'm just getting your room ready. I've got all the gossip mags for you. *OK! Hello! Heat.* Are you about to leave for the station?'

'Lover –' Nanna sounded far away – 'I've got bad news. I can't make it.'

Rosie felt like she was leaning over the edge of the Niagara Falls. 'What's happened?' she managed.

'I had a bit of a turn in the night. Went all wobbly, totally lost control. The doctors want to admit me for a day or two. I told them I have to go to London, but they say it's out of the question.'

Normally Nanna's tone would have been defiant, suggesting that these bloody doctors didn't know what they were talking about. But now she sounded defeated.

'I'll come and see you.'

'If you do, I'll never speak to you again, I mean it. I want you to go to that first night and be there for your husband and call me in the morning and tell me all about it.'

'But . . .'

'No buts now. I'm disappointed too, you know. Tell

Ellie Lewis from me she's a goddess. I'm going now and I'm turning off my phone, because otherwise I know you'll be pestering me forever and I want you to be thinking about Jake's big night.'

The rest of the afternoon was a daze. The hair and make-up lady Rosalba had booked for Rosie had turned up at four and made her look glamorous (and mercifully didn't find any nits). A couple of months ago, she'd have been bubbling over with excitement; now she just felt queasy, as if she were watching herself from a great height.

'Not that old thing again, Mummy!' yelled George, after she zipped herself into the gold dress.

Rosie laughed for the first time since the phone call. 'Who do you think you are? Suri Cruise?'

'I like it, Mummy,' Toby smiled.

'I think you're perfect!' George said. Rosie smiled. Motherhood was so flattering sometimes, when the children weren't wiping their hands on her skirt or coughing directly into her eyes. She kissed them both on the head. 'Now be good for Dizzy,' she said, then wobbled her way out of the front door and down the steps to the waiting car.

Traffic was heavy, and the driver wasn't chatty. Rosie said a little secret prayer to whoever was up there to make the play go well that night. If it was a success maybe Jake's tetchiness would finally abate and she'd get her old jolly husband back. If it was a flop – well, it wouldn't be. It had sold out on Ellie's name alone for the entire run, so that was the definition of a non-flop, whatever the reviews might say. But Jake would be inconsolable. The thought of the amount of hand-holding and 'there, there-ing' he'd expect made her feel indescribably weary.

They arrived at the theatre in a little alleyway behind St Martin's Lane with just minutes to spare. It was like the premiere all over again, but in a more confined space, with the barriers, the shouting, the photographers, the assorted passers-by and autograph hunters.

This time, Rosie didn't linger on the red carpet, but hurried straight to the door.

'I'm on the guest list,' she told a young woman in eight-inch heels with a clipboard. How could she bear the discomfort, Rosie thought – another indicator of imminent HRT and a new passion for the Country Casuals catalogue. 'Rosie Prest.'

She shook her head. 'I can't see you.'

'I'm Jake Perry's wife.'

'Why didn't you say? Go on in!'

In the foyer she immediately spotted Yolande in floor-length turquoise, fanning herself with her programme, looking around avidly to spot the celebs. Beside her, Rupert was in a slim-fitting pinstripe suit, clearly purchased for the occasion, hands in pockets, looking shy. Behind them, Becki in a black-and-white dress that Rosie had spotted in the Phase Eight in the Village, and Dave in a grey suit. Rosie was touched he'd made an effort; Dave hated suits.

'Rosie!' cried Yolande, reeking of Coco Mademoiselle. 'How are our lovely boys?'

'*Great*, thank you.'

'Bless them. What did they eat for their supper?'

Cheese on toast for George. A lump of cheese for Toby. One carrot each. 'A little bit of calves' liver with some green beans and mash,' Rosie said, smiling.

'Oh good Lord.' Yolande's hands flew to her bosom. 'How wonderful.'

'Best to give them two different kinds of veg,' said Becki firmly. 'But still, well done, Rosie. Definite progress. We were all beginning to despair, weren't we, Mum?'

'Hey, hey!' Christy was approaching briskly, with slim black trousered legs and a drapey red top, looking only slightly agitated. 'Rosie! Yolande! Becki! Dave! Rupert!' Christy was always brilliant at remembering people's names. 'Excited for our boy tonight?'

'More excited at the Disney rumours online,' said Yolande.

'Rumours, schmumours.' Christy diluted this dismissal with a broad wink. She was nervous, Rosie could tell. God, maybe the play really was as bad as Jake had been saying. 'All will be clear very soon.'

Before Rosie could ask exactly what that meant, a piercing bell rang.

'Well, shall we?' Christy asked.

Three hours later, the six of them stood crammed into Jake's dressing room with its stench of greasepaint and musty costumes, waiting for him to return from the post-show debrief. Everyone looked worried. Voices were hushed. Smiles were strained. None of them dared admit it, but they all knew they'd just endured the theatrical equivalent of dog's vomit.

Now Rosie understood why Jake had been so stressed these past few weeks. His performance had been *fine*. Not his best, but passable. The rest of the cast, however, were dire – and Ellie's was the worst by a long way. Her expression was glazed throughout, as if she'd been hypnotized. She'd forgotten half her lines and needed nearly continuous prompting. Rosie's face had blazed every time she stepped on to the stage. She hadn't been so embarrassed since the time Belinda Crighton had caught her crooning 'Blue' by Joni Mitchell while making soulful expressions into the mirror in the school toilets.

'Lovely flowers,' Yolande said nervously. 'Really. So kind. And all these cards. Aren't people wonderful, eh, Rupert?'

Before Rupert could concoct a response, the door opened and there stood Jake in a sage-green dressing gown, his face, ashen under his heavy make-up.

'It was shit, wasn't it?'

'*You* were fantastic,' Rosie said firmly.

'It was brilliant.' Yolande's tone took no prisoners.

'I didn't love it, I have to be honest,' said Dave, clapping him on the shoulder. 'But you were OK. I didn't get a lot of it. Why did they all have to sit in the *Big Brother* chair and . . . ?'

'I'm not sure the director had fully thought it through,' said Becki.

Christy pushed into the room, a huge smile on her face.

'Brilliant, Jake! Absolutely spot on. I don't know how you do it.' She patted him on the shoulder. 'You're a star. You really are. Shall we all go and celebrate?'

There was a second's pause, then Rupert, catching Christy's eye, took her cue and exclaimed: 'Absolutely. And well done, my boy.'

In silence, broken only by Dave continuing to ask puzzled questions about the *Big Brother* theme, they walked the short distance up the road to the Hospital Club, where the after-party was taking place. Outside a line of photographers waited.

'Hey, Jake, why do you think Ellie forgot all her lines?'

'Jake, is your career dead in the water?'

Jake smiled and waved, and Rosie tried to look as if she couldn't hear them.

'These people are horrible,' Yolande wailed. 'Can't the police do something?'

'They have a right to free speech,' Dave pointed out.

Inside, everyone headed straight to the bar as if it was the *Titanic*'s last lifeboat.

'None of the Disney people have come,' Christy muttered in Rosie's ear. 'Can't say I blame them. Did you see that bit when ... Oh shit, your husband's coming.'

As Jake approached, Christy started bowing and scraping in an 'I'm-not-worthy' gesture. 'The star of the night!' she exclaimed.

Rosie glanced at her in irritation. She was so two-faced. Didn't she get tired of the perpetual fawning?

'Have the Disney people all left?' he asked. 'Because before the reviews come in I need to get utterly shitfaced.'

'Hey, Jake,' said one of the bartenders.

'Hi,' Jake replied in that embarrassed way he'd adopted when strangers addressed him.

'Jake, it's me! Nick!'

'Nick?'

'Nick Jacobus! From drama school.'

'Nick!' Jake held out his hand. 'Hey, man! Great to see you! It's been ages. So. How are you doing?'

A tiny pause. 'Well, I'm a bartender, so could be better.'

'Oh. Right. Hey, but didn't you do that BBC drama with Romola Garai? That was amazing. Such a witty script. You were brilliant, really sinister.'

'Yes, but it was eight years ago. Nothing since. Hey, but what about you? Congratulations, man. Everyone's so jealous.'

Jake shrugged. 'Really, you know it's just been luck. You were always more talented than me. And you know, after tonight, it's probably all over. The show's bombed.'

'Oh, I'm sure that's not true,' said Nick. He was a very handsome guy. Talented too. Rosie remembered him now in the BBC drama. He didn't deserve to be pouring drinks. It could so easily have been Jake standing there, and Nick being the man of the night. It was all so unfair.

'Hey,' snapped an elderly man behind Nick. 'Guests need serving.'

'Later, then,' said Nick, raising a wry eyebrow.

'Yeah, later. Let's have a drink some time . . .' But Nick was already at the other end of the bar. Jake's family surrounded him in a pincer movement, though all the other guests seemed to be backing away from him.

Rosie held her head high. 'It wasn't that bad,' she said firmly.

'It was a very strange decision to move it to contemporary times,' said Becki. 'Those canapés look nice. Hey, Dave, look.' She turned to Jake. 'Listen, while we have a moment . . . because God knows you're not easy to get hold of these days, I was wondering if there's any chance you could open this fundraising event for the local cats' home in September. All you'd have to do is make a speech — a funny one — and cut a ribbon, and then maybe hang around for a bit to sign autographs. It would mean so much to the cats; they've had such hard lives.'

'I'd love to, Becks, you know I would.' Jake had got so much smoother at this kind of answer, not so long ago he would have stumbled and stuttered. 'But it may be tricky. I've no idea what I'll be doing in September — I could be filming, I could be in America . . .'

'I doubt that,' Rosie said firmly, as Becki said even more firmly: 'We can be flexible. We could move the fete, so it fits in with your timetable. Rosie, keep me posted.'

'You should really have a word with Christy,' Rosie said. 'She's in charge of the diary.'

She snatched a glass of champagne off a passing tray. There was no other way to get through the night. In the distance she saw Simon the director looking thunderous and Brunhilde von Fournigan stony-faced, although still shockingly beautiful. They had four children, Rosie knew from hairdresser gossip mags, so no wonder she looked a bit stressed out. All that wealth and beauty was no protection against worrying if your kid had fallen out with his best friend or had a high temperature.

'You OK?' Christy asked. She looked tense, slightly edgy, obviously wondering how to deal with the fall-out.

'*I'm* fine. I'm just wondering how I'll deal with Mr Grumpy once we get home.'

'*I'll* deal with him. It's not the end of the world. His performance wasn't the problem; it's the whole production that was idiotic. And as for Miss Ellie over there . . .' She glared in the direction of Ellie, who was standing surrounded by gay men, laughing uproariously and clapping their hands together like seals, a radiant smile still plastered over her perfect features. Rosie had once or twice tried to catch her eye and wave, but she appeared not to have noticed her. 'She could have at least bothered *trying* to learn the lines.'

So if the production was so doomed, why did you push Jake to do it? Rosie thought. Instead, she asked, 'Is that the end of his glorious career?' How would she feel about that? Not as bad as she ought to. God, she was a terrible wife.

'I shouldn't think so for one millisecond.' Christy's tone was firm, but suddenly her expression changed. Her olive skin grew paler, her brown eyes even more anxious and she stood on tiptoes, eyes focused on something in the far corner.

'Are you OK?' Rosie asked, turning to look, but all she could see was a crowd of guests pretending to enjoy themselves.

'Yes,' Christy snapped, holding her glass so tightly Rosie thought she might crush it.

'Is it the married man again?'

'No,' Christy said unconvincingly. Rosie's head shot round. Who was he? But the room was packed and she'd didn't recognize most of the people.

'Rosie!' said a soft voice behind them.

Rosie turned and Ellie stood there, arms out-stretched. 'Ellie! Hi!' Kiss, kiss. This was more like it. 'You were . . . wow.'

Ellie shrugged. 'I stank. I lost the plot.' She didn't sound remotely bothered.

'Not at all! And you look amazing.'

Ellie smiled. 'Thank you. You too. Is that the Vivienne Westwood you wore to those other events? Good choice to recycle; it really suits you. So where's your . . . nah-nah, is it? I've been so looking forward to meeting her.'

Rosie's eyes filled with tears. 'She couldn't come. She wasn't well enough.'

'Oh my God, I'm so sorry to hear that.'

'She was really looking forward to meeting you.'

'Don't worry,' Ellie said briskly. 'We'll go to meet her.'

'Sorry?'

'We'll visit her. I'll tell Sharon. Take her out for lunch, or tea or something.'

'Oh . . .' It was a lovely gesture but Rosie didn't actually believe a word of it. Ellie had promised lunch already. It would never actually happen.

'I mean it,' Ellie said firmly. 'This *will* take place.'

'That would be . . .' Her husband was standing, glowering, behind them.

'*Hey*, Jake. How are you?'

'The first review from the *Guardian*'s gone online,' Jake said. He looked like he had that time he'd eaten the dodgy prawn from the Bengal King.

The party started emptying out pretty much immediately. No one wanted to be around when the reviews were arriving. The handful of hardy souls who remained frowned at their phones as if they had just been presented with the obituary of a loved one.

'The best bit about it is the third act, which is far shorter than the preceding two,' Yolande read disdainfully from her iPhone.

'Everyone's taxis have arrived,' cried Christy. 'Shall we get going?'

At home Yolande instantly set up her iBook on the kitchen table and started googling incoming reviews.

'This one says "Perry is acceptable,"' she said brightly, peering through the bifocals, which she only donned when utterly necessary.

'The Disney people will read it! I'll never get the job.'

'It was all the director's fault and they'll know that,' Yolande affirmed. 'They shouldn't have cast that silly starlet. It was a gimmick. It misfired.'

'Shall we go to bed?' Rosie tried.

'Come on,' said Jake.

In their tiny bed in the huge room, they lay very still.

'This bed is so claustrophobic,' Jake snapped. 'When are we going to replace it?'

Rosie said nothing. Still, they lay. She couldn't bear it, knowing they were both awake, unhappy, beside each other. She reached for his hand.

'Don't!' he snapped.

'I'm trying to be nice to you,' she exclaimed. 'Don't push me away.'

'Everything's ruined,' he said numbly.

'No, it's not. This play's been cursed. The run will be curtailed and then you'll be free of it.' She yanked at his underpants. 'C'mon.'

But he wiggled away. Almost instantly he was snoring. But Rosie lay awake for a long time staring at the ceiling. She wished that their life together had a rewind button, that they could return to the time when they were poor, struggling, dull. But happy.

Oh, they'd been so happy. When they'd squabbled it had been over Jake putting wooden spoons in the dishwasher and the way she left coffee granules on the work surface. Inconsequential nonsense. Whereas now the canyon between them seemed to be widening every day. Perhaps that was it. Perhaps they'd had their happy time together and they'd never be able to capture it again.

Twelfth Night – *Felt Like It Was the Two Thousandth Sleepless Night of My Life, Criffon Theatre, Review*, Sunday Comet

If you've always felt guilty about your lack of exposure to Shakespeare – don't worry! This revival can safely be missed. Set in a contemporary Big Brother-*style house Simon Barry's production of the Bard's great comedy was supposed to run for three hours; it seemed like thirty.*

The setting is as delicate and pretty as an upmarket soap wrapper, but the cast cavort around like elephants on an ice rink. Flash-in-the-pan discovery of the week Jake Perry is acceptable as Malvolio, but Ellie Lewis as Viola is in quite another category. It's true she looks ethereal and perfect, but when she speaks we're down to the level of the Artful Dodger.

She spoke all her lines as if they were on an autocue slightly too far away for comfort – and on several occasions the prompter had to step in and help her. Scientists devoting their lives to discovering if dolphins can talk would be put to better use enquiring whether producer Jeremy Frank can actually think. Because if he could he'd never have resorted to this dire bit of stunt casting.

Verdict: Avoid 0/5

29

After tentative overtures, summer had descended in force. Everyone said 'Hot enough for you?', because their brains had mushed like ice cream and they simply couldn't think of anything more sophisticated.

It was definitely hot enough for Rosie. No one was sleeping well – why hadn't Samantha and Louis thought to put in air conditioning? David was on at them, asking when he could resume work, and Nanna's doctor said she needed to slightly rejig the prescription, as she was concerned the drugs were no longer working well enough.

Rosie kept trying to ask Jake for his opinion, but Jake was acting like a wounded ... not lion, that was too noble a word, Rosie thought crossly, more like a ferret who'd trapped his paw. As more and more terrible reviews appeared, he was spending longer and longer locked in the bathroom. Rosie *knew* he was masochistically studying Twitter feedback and examining his bald spot in the mirror. When she asked him about money, he brusquely told her not to spend anything.

'The play's still a sell-out, so it really doesn't matter,' Christy said. She was calling about five times a day to check on morale.

'I don't think Jake sees it that way. He sees it as the end of his career.' Rosie was beginning to feel really rather anxious.

'He's got plenty in the diary. One lot of bad reviews will make not a jot of difference to all the other stuff that's lined up. Relax.'

'*I'm* relaxed,' Rosie lied. 'It's everyone else that's stressed.'

Somehow Jake had struggled through the play's second night. His parents had stayed the weekend, with Yolande loudly berating the reviewers and Rupert disappearing for long walks on his own. Rosie didn't blame him; she'd have joined him if she could possibly have escaped cooking for everyone and supervizing the boys. But, mercifully, they had departed on Sunday night. Now it was Tuesday morning and Jake – just back from a two-hour training session with Rolla – was slumped morosely on the sofa googling theatre forums.

'Like it's my fucking fault Ellie couldn't learn her lines!' he shouted, chucking the iPad to one side.

'Shhh,' Rosie snapped. 'Calm down.'

'What time is it? Ten thirty? Great. Only another six hours until the car comes and leads me off to the hell-hole. All these disappointed people, who spend zillions on their tickets, are going to sit there bored out of their skulls, listening to the prompter give that dingbat her lines.'

'It won't be so bad,' Rosie chivvied. 'Why don't we go for a little walk round the Village? We could pick up the boys early from nursery, maybe have a picnic? It would be fun.'

'People will stare,' Jake said. 'It'll stress me out.'

'It's not always about bloody you!' Rosie snapped again. She turned her back on him. She thought of how Jake used to love going for picnics, having fun, being spontaneous. That seemed so far away now. He stood up and walked into his office, firmly shutting the door. She flicked a V-sign at the mahogany panels. Probably Jake would be announcing soon they should dismantle them and sell them on eBay.

He emerged as she was about to head off to the shops to run a few errands before pick-up. 'You know, I've been thinking. I don't think this private-school idea is a good one,' he said gruffly.

'*What?*'

'I think you're right. I think Tobes'll be just fine at the school down the road. Why fork out all that money for Latin lessons?'

Rosie exploded. 'But the school down the road doesn't have a place! And I haven't looked anywhere else, because you and your mum insisted on King's Mount. And we've paid the first term's fees. They won't give them back.'

'Losing one term's fees against paying for thirteen years is OK,' Jake said. 'You were right. It's not disastrous to go to a state school. I mean you turned out OK. I know the school down the road's full, but there must be other ones.'

Rosie couldn't believe her ears. 'There aren't! We looked into all this when we moved.'

'And I've been thinking about the decorating. We shouldn't carry on. We don't need a pool and fake grass and all the other gyms and saunas and whatever. It's ridiculous.'

'The boys will be so disappointed.' Despite herself, Rosie had come round to the pool idea.

'The boys will get over it,' Jake snapped.

'What's wrong, Jake? I know the play had bad reviews, but you've all this work lined up. Do you have a secret gambling habit I don't know about?' She tried to keep her tone jokey, but she was genuinely suspicious. But before he could reply, someone buzzed at the gates.

'Oh, who's that now?' Rosie wailed, noting the relief on his face. Probably another flower delivery. Even though the play was a failure, flowers kept coming, though perhaps not at the rate they'd arrived after *Archbishop Grace*. She went to the entryphone. On the screen she saw a big man in a black suit. Shades. Earpiece.

'Hello?'

'Mrs Perry?' asked a booming male voice.

'Er, she is no home,' Rosie squealed in what she hoped was a squeaky foreign accent. Who was this? The Mafia coming to collect Jake's debts?

'Is she close by, madam? Because Ms Ellie Lewis is waiting for her outside the gates. She wants to go and visit her grandmother.'

'Wha—? Jus' one second,' Rosie gabbled. 'I go find

her. She be right down.' She turned to Jake. 'I'm going out. You pick up the boys from nursery. I'll text Dizzy and tell her she's babysitting.'

'What?'

'I won't be back late.' She couldn't be, Ellie was in the evening's performance. But what a chance for Nanna to meet her idol! Rosie couldn't pass it up for anything.

Nanna wasn't at home.

'Ah,' Rosie said after she'd buzzed on the door four times and left three messages on the mobile, which was going straight to voicemail. 'Um, what shall we do?'

'Where else is she likely to be?' Ellie stood beside her on the pavement in a bright blue sleeveless blouse and pedal pushers.

'I don't know. Bingo? The community centre?'

'Let's try bingo and the community centre then,' Ellie said firmly. 'Where are they?'

'Um.' Rosie tried to remember. 'I think you turn right and then . . .' But then it came to her. Tuesday. Today was Tuesday. 'She does pensioners' aqua aerobics on a Tuesday.'

'Oh? Well, then. Let's go to the health club.'

Rosie smiled. 'It's not exactly a club, it's the public baths.'

'Whatever, let's go.'

The blacked-out car was an incongruous sight making its way through the back streets of St Paul's. Tired mums pushing buggies stopped to stare, as did teen-agers on street corners and old men leaning on sticks.

'This kinda reminds me of Cleveland,' Ellie said, staring through the darkened glass at a burnt-out pre-cinct. 'Your nah-nah really likes it here?'

'It's what she knows. All her friends are here.'

'I guess.' Ellie shrugged. 'I've lost touch with all my friends from home. I tried, but it just became too hard. They envied me for being famous and they couldn't see I kind of envied them for being ordinary.'

'It's the same with Jake,' Rosie said, as the limo drew up outside the leisure centre. They walked in through the sliding plate-glass doors and up to the desk, where the shell-suited receptionist was watching a music video on her phone. She looked up. She did a double take.

'Er, we're here to find my grandmother,' Rosie said. 'We think she's in the OAP Aqua Zumba.'

'You'll have to buy two tickets to use the pool.' Her Bristol accent was so strong Ellie gawped in confusion.

'We don't want to use to the pool, just to go in and surprise my Nanna.'

The receptionist folded her arms over her ample chest and stared at them grimly. 'That's the rule.'

'How much are tickets?'

'Two pounds fifty unless you're eligible for a concession.'

'Um.' Rosie realized she'd come rushing out of the house without her purse. 'Do you have five pounds?' she asked Ellie.

Ellie looked blank. Like the queen, she clearly never travelled with money. 'I'll have to go and ask my driver.'

After all this time despising the don't-you-know-who-I-am card, it was time to play it.

'Oh for God's sake!' Rosie exploded at the receptionist. 'This is *Ellie Lewis*. You recognize her, I know you do. My nanna is sick. She's come to take her out for tea. Just let us go to the poolside and wave at her.'

'I . . .' Before the receptionist could say more, Rosie pushed through the barrier and Ellie followed. Down the hot corridor stinking of chlorine they went, through the harshly lit women's changing room, with its shabby green tiles and smell of shoes, full of half-naked women, wet heads turning incredulously as they passed. The receptionist followed, yelling, 'I'm going to tell my boss!'

From the pool came the sound of thumping Latino music. 'OK, ladies,' boomed a woman's voice. 'Shake those booties. And – a-one, a-two, a-three.'

'Oh,' squeaked Ellie. They'd reached a little puddle of chlorinated water that had to be waded through to reach the pool. 'Quick!' She pulled off her red-soled Louboutins and ran through it and over to the poolside. Rosie followed. There was Nanna in the water, a plastic cap framing a gaunt face, her limbs scrawny in the fifties-style swimming costume she'd so excitedly bought from Primark the previous year. Her arms were waving in the air, but Rosie could see she was struggling to keep up with the rest of the group.

'Nanna, Nanna!' she called, her voice bouncing off

the walls, but she couldn't be heard above the music. Ellie stepped forward and started waving her arms in the air. One by one, the Zumba class stopped dancing.

'Nanna!' Rosie yelled, stepping forward. 'Ellie and I have come to take you out to tea.'

An hour later, they were sitting in the lounge of a Marriott hotel drinking tea (green for Ellie). Rosie and her grandmother nibbled at scones piled high with thick yellowish cream and strawberry jam, Rosie also managed a couple of sneaky biscuits from the tiered cake stand. Nanna's hair was still wet and sticking out wispily at crazy angles, but her expression was one of dazed delight.

Ellie was in apologetic mood. 'I'm sorry this is the best we could find to take you to, Marjorie. Apparently Bristol has no five-star hotel.' She looked as if she couldn't really believe this news. 'Even Cleveland has a Hyatt.'

'Really,' Nanna assured her, wiping some crumbs away from her mouth, 'this is more than perfect. I can't believe this is happening to me. I'm having tea with Ellie Lewis. It's better than meeting the queen.'

'I hardly think so,' Ellie said, laughing. She took Nanna's hand. 'You know, this is just as much for my benefit as yours. My dad is so sick and I can't be with him, so you're going to have to be my adopted grandmother for the duration.'

Nanna laughed. 'I'll see what I can do, lover. Are you finding it lonely here?'

'*So* lonely,' Ellie said passionately, tears welling in her eyes. 'I've been working so hard, and I know I've ruined the play for everyone, but there's been all this stuff going on in my life. I didn't use to let personal stuff affect me but this . . .'

'With your dad,' Rosie said knowingly, taking another cucumber sandwich.

'It's actually not just with my dad,' Ellie said. She smiled and then said: 'I'm pregnant.'

'Pregnant!'

'Nearly four months gone.' She looked uncharacteristically shy and very proud.

'By your agent?' Rosie asked stupidly.

Rosie laughed. 'No, silly. By Simon, the director.'

'Simon who's married to Brunhilde von Fournigan?' Rosie screeched. Bloody hell. That innocuous little man shagging two of the most beautiful women in the world? No wonder he always looked so pleased with himself.

'Shh. No one must ever know,' Ellie implored. 'We've agreed that. It was just a stupid fling. But I'm going to keep the baby – it's a little boy – and I'm going to call him Volcan. Simon will have nothing to do with it. But, oh, it's been hard. I'm so tired all the time and I was feeling so sick.'

Rosie shook her head. 'No wonder rehearsals were so difficult.'

'It hasn't been easy.'

Nanna's face was a picture as she took it all in. 'I don't advise married men, love,' she said. 'My daughter got involved with a few, messed up her life nice and proper.'

'You're so right,' Ellie agreed. 'It's all over now. I've learned my lesson. But what can I say? I'll have a baby. I've always wanted a baby.'

'Well, you're rich,' Nanna said. 'Always helps. You can have a nanny from day one.'

Ellie laughed. 'I'm not rich.'

'Oh, yeah?'

'No! I mean, I'm comfortable, sure. But not rich like Henry Malvion, you know my co-star in *O'Rourke's*? He always travels private; I go commercial, even if it's first.'

Nanna looked utterly baffled. Rosie glanced at her watch. 'Ellie. It's gone four o'clock. We need to be getting back. You're doing the show tonight.'

'If you say so.' Ellie shrugged. She took one of Nanna's hands. Blue veins jutted through the translucent skin. 'Do you want to come with us? See the show?'

'In all honesty,' Nanna said, 'it's a very kind offer, but the reviews haven't been that great. So if it's OK with you, I'll take a rain check. I'm a little tired anyway. Must be all that swimming.'

'Let's just do a selfie,' Ellie said, kneeling next to Nanna and holding her iPhone in the air. 'Smile for the camera.'

Click. Flash.

'Now we'll always have a souvenir of our time together. I'll email it to you.'

*

'That was so kind of you,' said Rosie for the umpteenth time, as the car nudged along the M4 outside Swindon. It was half past five and she was a little anxious that they'd make it in time, but Ellie seemed unbothered, fiddling with a phone. Rosie looked around, drinking in the leather seats, the television, the bar. But who could she describe it to? If she told Christy she'd just shrug and say Jake could have a limo of his own, if only he moved to LA.

'My guru says you should commit a good deed every day. I reckon this was mine for the week,' she said contentedly, stroking her completely flat stomach. 'Did you breastfeed, Rosie? I can't decide if it's a good idea or not. It's meant to be fantastic for shifting pounds but I don't know if I could face another boob job when I'm done.' She glanced again at her phone. 'Oh, that's so cool! I've had two thousand and forty-three retweets.'

'Of what?'

Ellie handed Rosie the phone. 'Of me and your nah-nah. Look.'

There, on the little screen was vital, glowing Ellie and drawn, but very obviously chuffed, Nanna. Having fun with an old lady friend of mine, Ellie had written. #bekindtooldpeople

'You've made my nanna go viral!' Rosie wasn't at all sure how she felt about this. She didn't like the idea of Nanna being used as a publicity stunt, but then again Nanna would probably be thrilled.

The driver spoke into the intercom. 'Ma'am, I'm sorry but the traffic is gridlocked. I can no longer guarantee arrival in central London for half past six.'

'Oh?' For the first time, Ellie looked faintly alarmed. 'How about we take another route?'

'The motorway is blocked solid, ma'am, we can't reach an exit. When we do, I can try that, but everyone else will have the same idea.'

'Oh, right.' Ellie bit on her lip. 'Ah. OK, I'll call Sharon.'

Sharon – on speakerphone – was clearly not happy at all to hear that her boss had gone AWOL. She politely informed Ellie there really was nothing she could do. If Ellie had allowed Sharon to plan the itinerary and accompany them, she would have made sure none of this would have happened, but never mind, yes, looking at the traffic reports they were in big trouble, because there'd been a multiple pile-up a couple of junctions ahead, and, no, regrettably Sharon had failed at her job as PA because they could not send a helicopter to land on the packed motorway and deliver Ellie to the West End in time for a seven thirty curtain-up. 'I'm so sorry, Ms Lewis, but all I can do is notify the producers that there is a potential problem and we may have to delay curtain-up. Alternatively your understudy can perform.'

'OK.' Ellie had bitten one of her nails right down. 'Tell them I'm really sorry.'

'Of course I will. Don't worry about a thing.' Sharon sounded as if she were telling Marie Antoinette to relax about stepping out on to the scaffold. 'I'll be back in touch.'

'Well,' said Ellie brightly, looking out at the static traffic. 'Shall we play *I Spy*?'

30

To the audience's understandable outrage the play went ahead with Ellie's understudy.

Sharon called Ellie to tell her.

'I goofed. What can I do?' Then she'd shrugged, leaning back in her limousine seat. The driver had turned the engine off now. Around them, people were sitting on their car bonnets, chatting to each other and enjoying the evening sun. No one was going anywhere in a hurry, so why not sit back and go with the flow?

'Are you OK about it?' Rosie asked. 'You seem so calm.'

'I don't know what's going on, don't know if it's the hormones or what, but I just don't care about anything except this little thing.' Ellie patted her pancake stomach. 'All my energies are invested in it. I refuse to engage with anything else – especially not all this meaningless showbiz bullshit. So I missed a performance? Will I remember that on my deathbed? That's what my guru, Astral, always asks and she's right. It's all meaningless.'

'Jake would have been freaking.'

'Five years ago, I would have been freaking. Jake's on the verge of the enormous time – he's already hit the big time, so he doesn't want to blow it. You don't get to be this successful without the occasional meltdown. And a core of steel.'

Rosie sighed. 'Jake certainly has that.'

'Anyone who makes it to the top has. You've got to be ruthless. Not just with other people, with yourself. I remember when I started out waiting tables until two in the morning so I could afford elocution lessons in the daytime, I knew that would give me the edge. Other girls in my drama class weren't prepared to push themselves that hard. I lost so many boyfriends on the way, because I wasn't at their beck and call.'

'I think Jake loves us deep down, but at the moment he barely seems to notice us,' Rosie said.

'I know he loves you. I told you, he talks about you guys all the time. But he loves himself too.' Ellie laughed. 'We're actors, it's part of the job description.'

'I didn't really know him when I married him. We were both carried away by this tsunami. It was all so romantic. Now I wonder if he was acting.'

Ellie squeezed her hand. 'Oh, honey. Don't be hard on yourself. We all get carried away when we fall in love. Look at me and what an idiot I've been with Simon – though in a funny way it's all worked out. When the first wave of love subsides, you just have to get to work building a raft, so you have something solid, instead of drifting around in the sea. I mean, that's never going to happen where I'm concerned, but you and Jake can do it. You *have* done it. He's just a little preoccupied for the moment.'

'I hope it is just for now.' Rosie nibbled at a cuticle.

Ellie yawned. 'Forgive me, honey, it's nearly my bed-time. Let me shut my eyes for five minutes.'

It was gone ten when Rosie finally walked through her front door. The boys were asleep, and Dizzy was watching a gory DVD while simultaneously tapping into her iphone. Everything was eerily calm.

'Everything OK?'

'Not so sure about Jake, he puked a couple of times before he left for the theatre, but that's normal for him, isn't it? And the boys haven't been too bad, though I did have to confiscate Toby's monkey because he kept hitting his brother round the head with it.'

Rosie would normally have gone straight to bed, but she knew she'd better stay awake until Jake got home. He was going to be furious. He'd accuse her of having led Ellie astray, of trying to sabotage this already gigantic turkey even further. Rosie's mouth was dry at the prospect of the fight that lay ahead. Rows with Jake were horrible. He could be so cutting, so cold. Why had she married someone like that? Why hadn't she stuck with wimpy Richard, whom she'd gone out with for five months in her mid-twenties, but dumped because he'd always wanted to stay in and cook? What had she been thinking of? Now she and Richard could be living in his cottage in Muswell Hill, enjoying his gourmet dinners, curled up in front of a box set together, instead of finding herself alone night after night, surviving on lumps of cheese, dreading her husband's moodiness on his return home.

Her phone pinged and she grabbed it nervously. It was a text from Nanna. Rosie beamed as she read it.

> Thank you so much for today, lover. Think it was truly the highlight of an eventful lifetime! I'm a star on Twitter! *Evening Post* wants to interview me. Won't breathe a word about the love child ☺ ☺ PS Cucumber sandwiches were a bit rank, tho. Bristol deffo needs a five-star hotel.

> Highlight of my lifetime too, Nanna. See u soon.***

So there, Jake. Yes, their outing might have messed up your precious play even more, but it had made an old woman very, very happy.

She picked up the iPad. While she waited for Jake to come home, she'd see what Twitter was saying. That might prepare her a bit better for the explosion.

She put her husband's name into search. All the usual abuse appeared.

> U think ur so grate, @Jakepezz, but you is a penis. Suck mine.

> As u like it, wrst play I ever saw. @Jakepezz makes me want to puke.

> @Jakepezz, you think you're all that but you're not.

Christ. No wonder Jake was so grumpy when he had to endure this all the time. She needed to remember that.

> You slate the tax dodgers, but you're no better @Jakepezz

Here was a retweet from some journalist or other. Read the *Sentinel* tomorrow for startling news about @Jakepezz, the so-called 'caring' actor.

Rosie stared, puzzled? What startling news? But then she heard the front door opening.

She rushed into the hall. Jake stood there, looking tired, but not angry. 'Hi,' she said meekly.

'So what happened?' he asked. He didn't sound angry either, more amused. Relief whooshed through Rosie like a brisk wind.

'I'm sorry. Ellie just turned up and wanted to see Nanna and I had to let it happen, you know how she loves Ellie, but then we got stuck in traffic. I mean, it wasn't my fault, I tried to get Ellie to leave but . . .'

'It all worked out for the best,' Jake said with a little laugh.

'Sorry?'

'It all worked out for the best. Lauren took the part and she was stellar. She got a standing ovation.'

'But that's brilliant,' Rosie beamed.

'It is. It was so much more fun working with her. Now the producers think they may extend the run with Lauren in the lead. A star has been born.' He pulled Rosie to him. 'So hip hip hooray. Your nanna may have totally, inadvertently saved the day. Good for Marjorie, the woman is a superstar.'

'That's fantastic,' Rosie exhaled as if she were in a Lemsip ad. 'And great news for Ellie too. She needed an excuse to . . .' She stopped herself. She wasn't going to reveal any details of the pregnancy.

'Bean, Bean,' Jake crowed. 'Something's gone right again. God, I can't tell you how different it was acting with Lauren. I felt like I was a rusty machine who'd been oiled. We all felt it.' Despite his obvious relief, he still looked pale and somehow tense. Before Rosie could celebrate with him, the buzzer went.

'Who's that?' Jake looked positively panicked.

'Jehovah's Witnesses. Leave it.' Rosie slipped her hand under his shirt.

But there was that zuzzing again. 'I'll just go and see who it is,' Jake said.

'Oh, whatever,' Rosie sighed as he went to the door.

'Christy!' he exclaimed.

'Christy?' Irritation rushed through Rosie's veins. 'What the *hell* is she doing here?' He was buzzing her in. 'Why don't you tell her to sod off?'

'It's urgent,' Jake said, ashen.

Rosie was filled with a burning fury. 'Why doesn't she give us any peace? Why can't she just email you? Or better still, let it wait until morning.' She strode to the door and opened it. 'Christy, please would you go away? This can wait. My husband and I want some time on our own.'

Christy shook her head. 'Sorry, but it's urgent.' She began to push past her. Furiously Rosie tried to push her back out of the door.

'Ro, what are you doing?'

Rosie stepped back. She couldn't shove Christy around; she'd never behaved like this with anyone in her life.

'I'm sorry. I know I'm a pain in the arse, that you're never shot of me. But I just need a quick word with Jake. It's really urgent, I swear. Really.'

They stood, staring at each other for a moment, then Rosie said, 'OK. But please don't be too long.'

'Sorry, Ro!' Christy said. Jake said nothing. 'Shall we go into your study?' Christy said to him. It was a command, not a question. They retreated into the David Allen Robertson wooden-panelled sanctuary.

The door shut. Rosie stood there for a second, stunned.

Slowly she climbed the stairs to the bedroom. Sod him, she fumed, as she undressed and – deliberately – dug out her frumpiest pyjamas. She dabbed his spot cream all around her face. She lay under the duvet, fuming with indignation until finally Jake poked his head round the door.

'There you are! What the hell was going on? Why do you have to talk to Christy all the way through the bloody night?'

'Bean,' said Jake, sounding distinctly shifty. 'We're going to be up a while longer. It's quite a big deal.'

'What?'

'I . . .'

'Is it about this Disney deal, or going to LA? Because I'm not going. I've uprooted my life once and I'm not doing it again to go and live far away in a weird place

343

without Nanna and where I never see you because you'll always be on set or hanging out in the Skybar or wherever it is you go and—'

'It has nothing to do with LA. We have to work on some damage limitation.'

'On some *what*? What's going on?' Rosie felt dizzy, like a diver on the top board. 'Have you been having an affair?'

'No! Nothing like that. Look, I'll tell you in the morning. I'd tell you now only—'

'Tell me now!'

Christy appeared in the doorway. Rosie glared at her. 'Look,' Christy said rapidly. 'There's a bit of an issue. The papers want to print a story in the morning about Jake's tax.'

'His tax?'

'Mmm. You know Yolande does his accounts? Well, she's found this loophole, so all your money was going in and out of some island in the middle of the Atlantic, meaning you've basically been paying something like three per cent tax, instead of fifty per cent. Which is why you've had quite a lot of surplus cash and been able to build the pool, do all this decorating and send the boys to posh schools.'

Rosie stared at them both. Her head was swimming, like that time she was coming down with flu.

'Don't worry,' Christy continued hastily. 'Jake hasn't done anything illegal. Technically. But it's just a bit unfortunate, as he's been giving all those interviews about how much he hates tax dodgers, so we're worried he may be in a spot of trouble.'

'How could you let your mum do this?' She tried to sound calm, but her voice was shaking.

'I didn't really know what was going on,' Jake said. 'She just made me sign the various pieces of paper.'

'You didn't ask her? Fucking hell, Jake. How much more of a baby can you be?'

'I'm sorry,' Jake said.

Christy dived in. 'Look, it may not make the papers. We've lawyers on to them now, arguing about it. They were going to put it online around now, and they haven't, so that's already something. And Jake and I are working on some defence strategies, should things not work out.'

'Defence strategies. Is this fucking NATO?' Rosie's Bristol accent was very strong now.

'It will be all right,' Christy intoned. 'I suggest you get some sleep and in the morning we'll take a review.'

'You sound like a zombie, Chris. You don't sound like my . . . friend any more.'

'Ro. We have a lot to get done.' She tugged lightly at Jake's arm and Rosie bristled. 'Come on.'

Rosie heard them hurry back down the stairs. Someone's phone was ringing. She stared after them in disbelief. *Tax scheme, Caribbean, Yolande. This was how they could afford so much, so quickly. This was why Jake had recently been worrying about the swimming pool and the schools. They were going to be a laughing stock; he'd never work again.*

345

She knew she wouldn't sleep a wink, and she knew in the morning she would need to be strong. Without hesitation, she walked into the en suite and took Jake's emergency sleeping pills from his manky toothpaste-smeared wash bag. Pity they hadn't upgraded that before this news had broken because now they never would. They were going to be poor again, poor and hated and rightly so.

She swallowed the bitter pill with a glass of water from the tap. Sleep still took a while to come, but then out of the blue it whacked her like a truncheon.

My God, you poor thing! I read all about it in the *Sentinel* this morning. You should have had Gary to advise you; he is much more competent. Is there anything I can do to help, darling? Do you want to borrow our house in the Greek islands until it calms? Patrizia Xxx

P.S. I'd love to know more details of the scheme.

31

It took five seconds from Rosie opening her eyes to Rosie remembering what had happened last night. Jake's half of the bed was unslept in and George was prodding her.

'Mummy, Mummy, the door keeps buzzing.'

'Wha—' Rosie sat up, her head muzzy. She pulled her son to her. 'Darling, did it wake you up?'

'No, I was awake anyway. Where's Daddy?'

'Downstairs?' Rosie guessed. The buzzer went again. She felt sick, her mouth was dry and hollowed out, her vision bleary. She shouldn't have taken that sleeping pill.

'Mummy!' Toby was standing at the door, looking terrified. 'What's happening?'

'Darling.' Now she was hugging both boys as close to her as possible. 'It's OK. Some people just want to talk to Daddy.'

'Not the police?'

That would have been funny, were it not also kind of true. 'No, not the police.'

'Rosie! Morning, boys.' Christy was standing in the doorway, looking pale and distinctly dishevelled. 'Good. You're up. So, listen. We've a plan for you today. No nursery, instead you're all going on a trip to see Sandrine.'

'Sandrine!' exclaimed Toby joyously, as George began to wail.

'No, Sandrine. I want to go to nursery. It's Gary Guitar day. Want to go to Wendy's.'

'Shhh, shhh, sweetheart. What's happening?' Rosie asked Christy over the bedlam. 'Toby, don't poke your brother.'

'But he's annoying me!'

'The *Sentinel* have printed the story,' Christy said. 'If you look out of the window, you'll see the house is surrounded by press. So we think the best thing is for you to disappear entirely for a while until this all calms down.'

'What about Jake?'

'Jake has to do the show. He'll probably go and stay with his parents.'

'How long—'

'It'll just be a couple of days.' Christy said, opening a cupboard. 'Do you keep your suitcases in here? Calm *down*, George, you'll have a lovely time with Auntie Sandrine.'

'Where's Jake?'

'Asleep in the spare room.' Christy was now briskly rifling through Rosie's knicker drawer. 'I told him to grab at least a couple of hours, since he'll have to do the show as normal tonight.'

'Oh, how caring of you.' George was still wailing. 'Shh, sweets. We're going to have an adventure.'

'I'll pack your jeans. Do you have wellies? You need them up there.' The doorbell buzzed twice, as Christy's phone pinged. 'I'd get packing for the boys, if I were you.' She turned and took Rosie's hand. 'I'm so sorry about this, Ro; I tried to stop it, I really did. But someone told the papers just when I was beginning to get Jake to listen to me.'

'It's not your fault,' Rosie said, after a second's pause.

Two hours later, Rosie was sitting in the back seat of yet another limousine being driven up the M6, while the boys gaped at a Disney DVD that had been the key to persuading George to stop wailing about missing Wendy's. At least he hadn't been sick yet. Usually on motorways he was fine; it was the winding Hebden Bridge roads that might spell trouble.

She tried to take in what was happening. Texts had come flooding in from all the Wendy's mums, full of sympathy. Rosie felt terrible for every mean thought she'd harboured about them. She couldn't bring herself to google the story in the *Sentinel*, to read the pages of vitriolic readers' comments. She called Nanna. She needed reassurance that everything was all right, and that it was a storm that would quickly pass.

'Sure you're all right, lover?' Nanna sounded far more anxious than she did when talking about her Parkinson's. 'They're all calling me up, knocking on the door, wanting to know what I have to say about it.'

'Ignore them.'

'Oh, I do. It's funny really. Nothing like this has ever happened to me in my life. But it's not funny for you. Are you sure you're OK?'

'I'm fine, honestly, Nanna. We'll have a few lovely days in the country with Sandrine and when we return everything will have blown over.'

Rosie hung up, furious. Nanna's flat surrounded by reporters. Brilliant. How could Jake have done this? How could he not have known what Yolande was up to? Been so lazy as never to ask her any questions about what was going on? When a journalist first started sniffing around several weeks ago, Christy had told Rosie while helping her pack, he hadn't thought to confide in her, but just grown snippier and snippier.

But she'd been an idiot too, she berated herself. Why hadn't she asked more questions about how they could buy that house outright, about affording David Allen Robertson's schemes? Oh God, she'd better stop that right away. The school — she'd need to inform them Toby wouldn't be starting in September after all — and somehow find a new place for him, poor little thing. Would they have to pay back loads of tax? Presumably not if the scheme was legal. But they'd look terrible if they didn't.

She stared at the back of the yellow lorry in front of her. Red lorry. Yellow lorry. Red lorry. No husband. How had this happened? How had her and Jake's relationship changed so much in the space of less than six months?

How could they have gone from mad, devoted love to this situation where she felt like a footnote to his glossy life? She'd seen so many different, new sides to Jake this past half-year, sides she wasn't sure she could tolerate for another six months, let alone for the rest of her life.

It wasn't just Jake's behaviour – the Mariah Carey moments, the ruthless disregard for what everyone in the family wanted, it was the way their lives had gone completely out of synch. Everything Jake had done until now had brought in money and was in the public eye, so was therefore important, while Rosie seemed to do nothing of significance.

Yes, she looked after Jake and the boys, and made their lives easier, but no one really appreciated what hard, thankless work that could be. Being the family linchpin, the wind beneath everyone's wings, sounded idyllic – it was what women were supposed to do – but it wasn't working. Somehow, along the way, Rosie had lost sight of herself and who she was – and everyone else had too. She wasn't the woman Jake had fallen in love with and that had placed another wedge between them.

She would talk to Sandrine about it. Sandrine would calm her down, cheer her up, make her work out a way forward. A grim way forward, Rosie thought, because she couldn't see any happy ending to all this, but at least a plan to cling to.

Her phone was ringing. She glanced down. Christy.

She ignored it. If it were really important she'd leave her a message. Sure enough, up pinged a text.

Rosie, so sorry. Managing this as best we can. Have told
Sandrine to look out for wellies in your size. xx

'Fuck off, Christy,' said Rosie, glancing guiltily at the boys, but they were gazing raptly at the screen. It would have been nice if Jake had contacted her, but throughout the journey she didn't hear a word.

It was ages since she'd been to Hebden. She'd forgotten how beautiful the approach was along winding roads flanked by tree-studded hills. Old stone bridges crossed trickling streams. York stone houses with smoke billowing from their chimneys. A wide sky glowering above them. They drove into the town, past noticeboards advertising rebirthing workshops and second-hand dulcimers, vegan cafés, boutiques selling stark German designer clothes. It was like the Village redesigned by a hemp-weaving hippy.

'Do you feel OK?' she asked George every three seconds, but he assured her he was fine.

Sandrine's B & B was in a cobbled side street, with pretty pastel-coloured Victorian cottages along one side and a stream flowing on the other. The door was surrounded by flowerpots and painted a delicate mauve. SANDRINE'S PLACE read a ceramic sign hanging from a nail beside the old-fashioned brass doorbell.

'Hang on a second!' Sandrine called in her booming

voice. The door opened and she was standing there, wearing possibly the world's most unflattering pair of dungarees.

Rosie launched herself into her arms.

'Hey! Hey!' Sandrine patted her gently on the back, as Rosie sniffled.

'Sandrine!' The boys were yelling. 'Can we go and see horses? Can we live here forever?'

'Why don't we all have some lunch first and then we'll make plans. You must be starving.'

They sat in Sandrine's cosy kitchen, the boys scoffing ham sandwiches (Toby's hatred of bread having mysteriously vanished), while Rosie drank proper leaf tea from a pot. 'The guests love it like that,' Sandrine said, smiling.

'Oh God, your guests! What are they going to make of these two little darlings?'

'Luckily we're quiet the next couple of days. June's visiting her mum in Guernsey, so we didn't take any bookings for the duration. But thanks for asking.' Sandrine's lips pursed wryly. 'Christy didn't bother, just told me you were coming. So we can have plenty of fun together. We'll go for a lovely walk through the Dales. Visit Haworth maybe? Have you ever been? It's where the Brontë sisters grew up. I love it. I think Emily Brontë wanted to be a man.'

'In your dreams,' Rosie laughed. Already she felt so

much better, but Sandrine's company was a plaster trying to hold together a huge gaping wound.

They spent the afternoon walking across the moors, sun blazing on their uncovered heads. The boys whooped and cheered, gathered sticks, poked in streams and rolled in the grass.

'This is heaven, Mummy!' yelled George. 'Let's live here always.'

'Yay,' Rosie agreed wholeheartedly. 'London stinks.'

'London stinks,' they chorused, giggling. 'London stinks. Poo! Urgh!'

'What do you think?' Sandrine asked Rosie.

'I love London. I didn't think I could ever tire of it. I thought the Village was the perfect compromise for a family – lots of green space, but a quick hop on the train into all the noise and filth. But now . . . I don't know. I never go into the centre anyway, unless it's for one of Jake's shows and . . .' Suddenly the bridge of her nose tingled. She wiped away a tear.

'Hey.' Sandrine's huge hand was on her shoulder. 'It'll all be OK.' Her phone started ringing. 'Hang on, one sec'. Oh!' Her expression changed. 'Just a minute. Yes. Yes, Christy, she's with me . . . Well, she probably doesn't have a signal on the moors . . . I'll put her on if she wants to talk.' She mouthed at Rosie. 'Do you?'

'I want to talk to Jake,' Rosie said.

'She wants to talk to Jake.'

'He's in a meeting,' Sandrine relayed.

'Well, then I'll wait until he's out of meetings.'

'Christy wants to talk to you.' Poor Sandrine looked horribly stressed.

'I'd rather talk to Jake,' Rosie snarled, her stomach twisting and cold.

They walked the rest of the way down the hill in near silence, apart from Rosie occasionally begging the boys not to run too fast or touch dog poo. They had just reached the foot and were turning towards the town – the plan being tea at the chippy, when Jake called again.

'Hi. Sorry. It's all been . . . horrible.'

'So does the whole world hate you?' Rosie asked coldly. She was sure that was all he cared about.

'I'm taking a bit of a battering. But I can survive that. I need to know you're all OK.'

That was more like it.

'We're fine,' Rosie said stiffly, trying to ignore her heart, like a frozen river, slowly turning back to slush. 'The boys are having a great adventure.' Indeed, they were carousing around her, as light drizzle began to fall.

'Kiss them from me. Tell them I'll see them soon. Bean, I'm really sorry, I have to go now. I have to have a meeting with a PR company about how they're going to deal with this. But we'll talk later, OK? I love you.'

It had been so long since he'd said that, that once again Rosie felt tears in her eyes.

'I lo—' she began, but he'd gone.

*

'So how did the papers find out?' Sandrine asked. The boys were in bed after nine stories and a very splashy bath and the pair of them were sitting at the kitchen table, a half-drunk bottle of Sauvignon Blanc and a curry ordered in from up the road in front of them.

'They think someone at the tax office snitched on him to the *Sentinel.* Kind of fair enough, given how vocal Jake's been about other people doing exactly the same thing. *The moron.*'

'So what will happen?'

'Well, put it this way, we'll be moving to Hebden sooner than you'd expected.'

'Oh, Rosie.'

''S OK. I mean, we probably won't be moving here, but we're going to have to sell that house. Which is fine, because I never felt right there anyway.'

'You can stay as long as you want, you know that?'

'Thanks, Sandy. I don't want to outstay our welcome, though.'

'You could never do that.'

'You know what I've missed so much?' Rosie said passionately. 'Having good friends like you around. People I can really talk to. Ever since we had children that side of my life has slipped away, and since we moved to the Village and I stopped working it's almost all gone. We've got – well, we had – all this money, but if there's no one to share it with, it's meaningless.'

'What about the mums at the nursery?'

'They're OK. They're lovely, actually, today's made me realize that. I was all chippy about them being rich, as if I weren't too. But the thing about the Wendy's mums is we just don't have any shared history. I had Parvaneh and we moved from her. I had my work mates, people who knew me. I had Christy! That's all gone and I feel so lonely.'

'Mummeeee!' came a call from upstairs, before Sandrine could say anything. 'Toby told me I'm a smelly poo.'

Rosie couldn't sleep. Jake was at the theatre. He'd emailed her, saying they'd speak in the morning and make a plan. His tone had been so abrupt, so business-like, compared to their earlier brief but emotional conversation, it had sawed at Rosie's heart. Then he'd sounded close to her, now he sounded in tunnel-vision, survivor mode.

She wished she'd stolen his sleeping pills. She refused to check the time because she'd only freak out seeing how near it was to morning, but she guessed it was about two. Rosie rolled out of bed and made for the little bookcase in the corner of the room. These personal touches were one of the things she loved about Sandrine's place. She squatted down and surveyed the shelves, searching for something mindless to read for half an hour, something that would hopefully send her to sleep.

There was various chick lit, but she wasn't in the mood

for happy ever after. Instead, she picked up one of what Christy called Sandrine's 'hippy-dippy' books: *Where God Begins to Be: A Woman's Journey Into Solitude*. This looked dull enough to work like Mogadon on her. Grinning, she climbed back into bed, and began flicking through the pages when a postcard fell out, a picture of the Empire State Building. She glanced at it, then noticed Christy's handwriting. Well, it was a postcard. Anyone could read them.

Hi Sandy,

    Returning the hippy-dippy book. [Rosie smiled. 'See!'] Didn't help me, I'm afraid. Told ya. But thanks for the pep talk about Mr Perry. Promise you, I really am going to quit him this time. I'm addicted and it's tough, but I'll do it. Because you're right, it's all far too close to home and he needs to be with his wife. Speak soon.

    Love,

    C xx

Rosie felt as if she'd plummeted from a bungee cord. She began to shake. Through narrowed, incredulous eyes, she read the postcard again, then again. *Mr Perry. Wife. I'm addicted.*

Christy had been sleeping with Jake. When? Recently? Still? Christy and Jake. Bloody Christy. Bloody Jake. No wonder she was all over him.

Why couldn't Rosie have seen it? Her husband was the mysterious married man. How could she have been so stupid not to have spotted it ages ago?

She felt as if a great hand were pushing on her head. She couldn't breathe. She wondered if she was going to vomit. She lay on the bed, looking up at the ceiling, willing tears to come, but they stayed obstinately absent.

My Daughter, Her Tax-dodging Celebrity Husband and How Fame Turned Both Their Heads

Amid the bundles of letters I keep in an old shoebox, I have a copy of a letter I wrote to my daughter, Rosie, who's married to tax-dodger Jake Perry. Sent two years ago, as my son-in-law's fame and wealth were on an upward curve, it was normal maternal advice.

Don't get too big for your boots, girl. Never forget where you came from.

Alas, it seems she didn't listen. Yesterday I watched with great sadness as my adored daughter was driven into hiding after it was revealed by the Sentinel that her husband had been using a legal tax-avoidance scheme to pay only three per cent of his earnings to the Treasury.

Rosie and I always shared a special bond. A single mum, I was only nineteen when I had her, but I used to say she was the best mistake I ever made. Throughout her childhood and teenage years, we were inseparable. We lived in a council flat in the St Pauls area of Bristol, where I also cared for my elderly mother. Times could be tough. I had to work hard as a barmaid to make ends meet, but we had each other and that was more than enough.

But after she met Jake she cut me brutally out of her life. The last time we saw each other was four years ago, when my grandson Tony was born. I arrived at her flat, laden with gifts, over the moon about becoming a grandma, but after only half an hour Rosie told me she was tired and had to go and rest.

Since then, nothing. I've laughed, like everyone, at Jake in Archbishop Grace *and joked with my friends, 'Not on my patio.' But not a word from Rosie. No replies to my many calls, postcards, emails. Even my birthday's now forgotten.*

I've seen the photos in the papers of Rosie's new five-million-pound home in London, a home where a swimming pool's being installed, and which – we now know – was bought with ill-gotten gains.

I can only conclude that there was no space in her glossy life for her old mother. For reasons inexplicable to me, however, she seemed content to stay in touch with my mum, recently visiting her in St Pauls with her new celebrity buddy, Ellie Lewis.

Why she chooses to see her grandmother but shuns me is impossible to answer, though I wonder if the fact that Ellie tweeted about their meeting, ensuring it was seen by her one million seven hundred and sixty-five thousand followers, made Rosie think it was a good idea. Maybe she knew her husband's lucrative career was about to go up in smoke and she needed to remind the world of her humble origins, hoping they'd think she hadn't changed.

Sadly, I can attest, she has. But she's still my daughter and I still yearn for any word from her. So, Rosie, if you're reading this, I'm here for you. You didn't use to be too proud to cry on your mum's shoulder when you stubbed a toe or a boyfriend dumped you, so call me now and I'll be waiting, with all your mistakes already forgiven.

32

Sun streaming in through the curtains roused Rosie from a brief and troubled sleep. Birds were singing, while from the kitchen came the noise of the whistling kettle. It was going to be another beautiful day, and for a moment she was happy. But then she remembered and gasped.

'Mummy!' the boys chorused, leaping on to the bed. 'Bouncy, bouncy, bouncy, *we're full of beans* . . . Waargh. Get off! Get off, Georgie!'

'Mummccc! What will we do today?'

'We're going back to London,' Rosie said firmly.

'Oh no!'

'No, Mummy. We love it here. Stinky London.'

'Stinky London,' George agreed.

'Well, we won't actually be going home. We might stay in a hotel for a bit.'

'At Disney?' Toby asked hopefully. 'Like Santos and Michael did at half-term?'

Rosie picked up her phone and turned it on, ignoring the dozens of texts and missed-call icons, and called Patrizia.

She answered straightaway. 'Are you OK? God, this

stuff in the paper is horrible. Did you know anything about what Jake was doing?'

'I knew nothing. Listen, I'm out of London, but I have to come back. If I leave the boys with you for the night, will that be OK?'

'Of course. I can call in two of the extra nannies. I'm sure they'll be happy to help.'

Despite herself, Rosie smiled. 'Thank you, I'll tell you everything later. I have to go now. I'll text when I'm near.'

'No problem,' Patrizia said warmly. 'By the way, your mum looks good for her age.'

'Nee-naw, nee-naw, I'm a fire engine,' George yelled, making Rosie think she'd misheard.

'What?'

'Your mum in the *Sentinel*. She's been speaking to them about how you don't talk any more. Maybe you should call her.'

'Er, thanks, Patrizia.' Rosie hung up. Her chest was churning so much she felt like a fizzy drink. She wasn't quite sure what her plan was beyond leaving the boys with Patrizia for the night, but she knew she had to be out of Hebden. Sandrine must have known about Jake and Christy and the thought that she'd been hiding this secret from Rosie was the most sickening discovery yet. She was climbing out of bed when her phone rang. It was Jake. Reluctantly she picked up.

'Bean, I'm so sorry,' he said instantly. 'I've been awake all night. I should have told you all this before, told you as soon as I found out Mum had signed me up to this stupid scheme. I should have warned you. I –'

'I'll talk to you later. I'm not talking to you now.'

'But, Bean!'

'The boys are here. I am not talking to you in front of them.'

'Can I speak to the boys? Are you OK? What's happened?'

'I'm going to get the train back to London today with them. I suggest you book a hotel room and I'll meet you there tonight after the show. We need to talk properly.'

'But . . . Don't bring the boys back to London. They can't go home, the house is surrounded.'

'They'll stay at Patrizia's. I don't want them here any more.'

'With Sandrine? Why ever not?'

'Boys! It's breakfast time!' Sandrine called. 'Bacon sandwiches.'

They ran whooping from the room.

'OK, they're not listening now,' Rosie hissed. 'So I'll tell you why I'm coming back. It's because I need to talk to you. I've just found out another little secret you were keeping from me. You and Christy.'

'You're mad, Rosie! What are you talking about?'

Rosie. He only called her that if something was very serious. 'You know what I'm talking about.'

'No, I don't. You've lost the plot.'

Liar. 'I have proof. Written proof.'

'I have no idea what you're on about.'

'I think we need to talk face to face,' said Rosie. 'I'll be back later this afternoon.'

'OK,' Jake agreed miserably. His defeated tone made Rosie feel as if she were hanging from a tree branch in a high wind. Scared, vulnerable and utterly defeated.

She didn't eat breakfast, just muttered something about not being hungry. She couldn't bear to look Sandrine in the eye, didn't want to speak to her, because she knew any conversation about Jake and Christy would make her emotional and she needed all her strength preserved for later. All these years Sandrine had pretended to be her friend when she'd known what her sister was getting up to behind her back! God, only last night, bitching away to her about him and Christy and their plotting and Sandrine had known. She'd bloody known.

'Are you all right?' Sandrine asked, looking concerned. What a cheek.

'Just tired. Didn't sleep well.'

'Oh, you poor love.'

'Well, whatever. I'll survive.' Rosie stood up. 'So, listen, there's a train in half an hour. We'd better get going.'

'You're leaving?' Sandrine looked shaken.

'I have to get back to London and talk to Jake.'

'But you could leave the boys.'

'Yeah, we'll stay here!' crowed George, as Toby wailed: 'Don't leave me, Mummy.'

'I want the boys with me.'

'Are you sure you're OK?' Sandrine was watching her questioningly.

'Fine.' Rosie couldn't make eye contact. She'd never so desperately wanted to escape somewhere in her life.

The train journey back to London via Leeds was a testament to the invention of the iPad. Rosie plonked headphones on the boys and pressed play on the first of many kids' movies she'd had the luck to download a couple of weeks ago. An earth-mother type who was encouraging her three children to colour a child's version of the *Odyssey* glared at her. Rosie glared back and once her head was bent over one of her children's drawings she gave her the finger.

She stared out of the window. The weather was no help at all; it was far too perfect today, mocking her agonies. They were whizzing past green fields, the trees were in full bloom. The world was beautiful but Rosie's heart was black, like something rotting at the back of the fridge.

Surreptitiously, on her phone, she read about her husband, though it was tricky on such a tiny screen – why had she never bothered upgrading to an iPhone? Now they'd probably have to sell every electronic gadget they owned to pay the tax bill.

Squinting, she read how her husband, with a taste for 'Armani and Prada' was living in a five-million-pound house in one of London's most exclusive suburbs, how the battered car in the driveway – they'd never got round to upgrading that either – masked a fondness for luxury restaurants. She read how he was planning to send his children to private schools, how his career had suffered what many suspected was a body blow after appearing in a 'shambolic' *Twelfth Night* with Ellie Lewis. How his wife, Rosemary, forty-four, didn't work.

She couldn't bring herself to read the interview with Mum or the comments below the article. But she did call up her husband's Twitter page. U c*nt, Perry. Stealing criminal. Living in the lap of luxury while the rest of us do an honest day's work. U disgust me. Always hated him. Grasping chavs.

'Oh, look, there's Daddy!' screamed Toby, even louder with the headphones on. He pointed at a man opposite reading the *Sentinel*. On the cover was a photo of Jake looking particularly shifty, like a villain in a Victorian melodrama.

'Shh, now, Toby,' Rosie hissed. 'Voice down.'

'But what's he doing?'

'Shhh.' Every head turned. 'Watch the film.'

'I think we've watched enough film. You told us if we watch too much telly, we'll get square eyes.'

'That doesn't count when you're on a train,' Rosie said hastily. Out of the corner of her eye, she could see a couple of passengers trying not to laugh.

'Let's play a game.'

'Watch the film,' she said softly. 'And I will give you

a packet of chocolate buttons each when we get to London.'

'Ooh.' They immediately turned their attention back to the screen.

They took an expensive, slow-moving cab from King's Cross to Patrizia's, who actually opened the door herself, rather than delegating the task to a retainer.

'Hey, guys. Welcome. The twins are so excited you're coming. Elena! Jana! Kasia! The visitors are here. I've only managed to call in one extra nanny, but I hope that will be enough.'

'Santos!' bellowed the boys, dashing through the hallway into the garden. 'Michael!'

'Thank you so much.'

'It's my absolute pleasure. Are you OK?' Patrizia asked.

'No . . . Er . . . Not really.'

Patrizia's big brown eyes were full of sympathy. Rosie hated that. Everyone feeling sorry for her at school, because she was scruffier than the rest of them. Now the Wendy's mums. She wouldn't cry in front of her. She wouldn't.

'It's fine. Thank you for this, Patrizia. I'll pick them up from Wendy's tomorrow. There's everything they need in their suitcases.'

She turned and stumbled down the steps.

'I can recommend a great divorce lawyer!' Patrizia

called after her. 'Caroline used him. Oh, and by the way?'

'Yes,' Rosie said, turning.

'This tax scheme. Sorry to keep asking, but please let us know more about it? Only Gary's really interested. He's going to sack his accountant for not putting us on it.'

An hour later, Rosie was walking briskly through the backstreets of Soho. It was weird to be back in her old stomping ground, this playground for the unencumbered, for adults enjoying a prolonged childhood. Nothing had changed – there were still the scribbled signs on doors offering massages with busty Thai girls, still the quirky boutiques selling patterned sundresses, with tattoo parlours at the back. Still the boys walking arm in arm down Old Compton Street and Lina Stores standing on the corner of Brewer Street with its vast chunks of Parmesan in the window and musty salamis hanging from the ceiling.

Christy's offices were down a shabby side street, flanked by a shop selling bolts of bright fabric and a sandwich shop. There was the shiny black front door (it had been a flimsy, peeling MDF number when Christy had taken the premises over, but as the money had come rolling in – *Jake's* money – she had tarted everything up). Rosie pressed the buzzer.

'Hello,' Rosalba's voice crackled.

'It's Rosie.'

A pause. 'Rosie who?'

'Rosie Prest,' Rosie spat. 'Christy's oldest friend. Your favourite client's wife. Favourite until today that is.'

'Oh, hi, Rosie.' Rosalba sounded as warm and friendly as ever. 'But Christy's not here. She's working at home today.'

Rosie turned and stuck out a hand.

'Taxi!'

The taxi carried her down the Mall, round Hyde Park Corner and down to Victoria, then wiggled through the back streets of Belgravia, before swooping round Sloane Square and heading off down the King's Road, with its array of chain stores and jumble of shoppers: old women in thick Loden coats, even on this hot summer day, emerging from Waitrose with their sunglasses perched on their noses. French-looking women in sundresses talking animatedly into their mobiles. Lost-looking Chinese tourists.

Then it moved on, down towards World's End. The shops were different now: charity shops, newsagents, boarded-up façades, sleepy-looking antique shops. Pensioners pushed shopping trolleys, while mums in vest tops slumped on their buggies.

'It's just round the corner,' Rosie said. The taxi turned left and pulled up outside the block.

She buzzed on Christy's door. No answer. She tried again. Nothing. 'Bugger.'

Rosalba had said Christy was working from home.

Of course Rosalba could have got it wrong. She could have been lying, expressly trying to put her off the scent, though she couldn't know what Rosie had just discovered. She pulled out her phone, ready to call her former friend, but then she thought again. If she reached Christy on the phone, she'd merely fob her off and for the first time in her life Rosie was craving confrontation. A thought occurred to her. She still had the keys on her fob from way back when they'd shared the flat. She could let herself in and wait for Christy to return.

Her heart thudded. It was such an un-London thing to do, to let yourself into someone's flat, the equivalent of striking up conversation with the person next to you on the tube, or standing on the left on an escalator, even if that someone was your so-called oldest friend. But she had to have this out with Christy. Her life had backed itself into a corner and she needed to do whatever it took to manoeuvre it out again.

She stepped into the lift and it whisked her up to the fifth floor. Down the corridor and she stood, heart beating, outside the front door. Christy hadn't double-locked it. That wasn't like her. She'd always been on at Rosie to safeguard her place and keep burglars at bay. Nervously, Rosie stepped inside. She was beginning to change her mind. She could be waiting for hours. Christy might not come back at all, or she might come back at midnight after wining and dining a client, or she might be en route to Australia in search of new talent.

She might be with Jake.

Rosie was going to wait. After all, she had nowhere else to go.

She stood, undecided, in the hallway, then turned back towards the door. Dumb idea. She'd just have to go and sit in a café and hope Jake got in touch with details of where they were meeting later. Assuming he did get in touch. But then, behind her, Rosie heard a noise.

She froze, straining to listen. Yes, she'd heard a footstep. Her heart beat even faster and a dribble of sweat ran down her front. A burglar. She hadn't been prepared for this. She looked around for something heavy and saw a copper vase on the table. She picked it up and slowly turned round. From the bedroom, she heard voices. Then laughing.

Oh bollocks. It wasn't a burglar. It was Christy and some man. The slut. Oh God, and it might be Jake! In her confusion, she put down the vase heavily so it banged on the table. She began creeping back towards the stairs. She was an idiot to have come here. But a male voice behind her shouted: 'Stop! What the hell do you think you're doing?'

Rosie turned, face flaming. And then she gasped.

Standing there, looking just as shocked as she was, was Rupert in grey silk underpants.

Her father-in-law.

***Prime Minister Brands Perry's Tax-avoidance Scheme
'Morally Dubious'***

*The Prime Minister today described the tax affairs of
'Not on* my *patio' actor Jake Perry, best known for his role
in* Archbishop Grace, *as 'morally dubious'.*

*Breaking off a meeting with German Chancellor Angela
Merkel, the Prime Minister told reporters, 'This is clearly
wrong.'*

Perry, 35, is currently starring in Twelfth Night *in London's West End, alongside actress Ellie Lewis. The
production has received negative reviews. He was recently
discovered to be avoiding tax through a legal loophole, despite his vocal criticism of others who behaved in the same
way.*

Calls to Perry's agent have not been returned.

33

Rosie ran from the building, too shocked even to say a word to Rupert, or to Christy, who emerged from the bedroom behind him in a silk dressing gown, shouting: 'What's going on? Rosie! Rosie! Come back! Come back now!' She sounded as if she were calling back a naughty dog.

Rosie dashed down the stairs, stumbling over her feet and out into the street. At first she ran, but she quickly, because she was totally unfit, slowed to walking pace. Things were just getting more and more ludicrous. Christy had been having an affair with her husband and now it turned out she was also sleeping with her husband's father. *Rupert* – reticent Rupert, who wore golfing jumpers and had a passion for jazz – was the mysterious married man. If it wasn't so grotesque, it would be hilarious.

But then everything recalibrated, like a picture coming into focus. *Mr Perry*. Christy hadn't been shagging both men, just the father. Relief made Rosie suddenly dizzy. She stopped and leaned against a lamp post. Jake hadn't been unfaithful to her. Her oldest friend hadn't been shtupping her husband. But still, still . . . It was all too weird to compute.

Her phone buzzed and she snatched it, expecting it to be Christy once again on a damage-limitation exercise, but it was Patrizia.

> Boys are having a great time, excited about the sleepover. Take care. PS Don't forget to let me know details of tax scheme. xx

She looked up, blinking, and then turned as she heard running behind her. Aha. Christy, wearing . . . not pyjamas, surely? Not Christy who never had a hair out of place?

'Ro!'

'Are we on dress-down Friday?' She couldn't help smiling at what a state she looked. Christy glanced down at her outfit impatiently.

'I just grabbed whatever I saw. I had to talk to you.' She stood panting.

'Why didn't you tell me, Chris?'

Christy stared down at her bedroom slippers. 'I feel such an idiot. I've been trying to pluck up the courage for ages to tell you about me and Rupert, and then you had to find out like this.'

'You lied to me,' Rosie replied shortly. 'How long has it been going on for?'

'Years, on and off. Since your wedding.'

'*Our wedding?* Jesus, Chris.'

'I know.' Christy's head hung. 'I'm sorry. I kept trying to end it, but there was just something about him. It's been agony.'

'Well, I don't know what you were thinking, but you

have to finish it properly. Right now. Or you'll end up my stepmother. In-law.'

They caught each other's eye and suddenly started laughing and laughing, unable to stop, as all the stresses of the past few days and a flood of memories were released. So many, she thought, wiping away tears of hysteria. She and Christy running together on sports day at the back of the race, singing songs from Bros. Shrieking with cold in the local swimming pool. Paddling canoes along the Bristol Channel on their outward-bound day. Calling up boys from Carlsedge and slamming down the phone when they answered. Reading *J-17*. Worshipping Hugh Grant. Sharing huge bowls of ice cream topped with Ice Magic. Screaming at *Friday the 13th* on DVD. Sneaking peeks at the top-shelf magazines in the corner shop. Dancing to 'Let's Talk About Sex', complete with risqué gestures. Laughing. They'd always laughed so much.

'I'm not going to be your stepmother-in-law. It's over.' Christy said when they finally calmed down. 'I've just told him to get out for good. Seeing your expression was the nail in the coffin.' She paused and said, 'But at least Rupert told me about the stupid tax dodge. Yolande had told him. It was how Jake could afford to buy that house with cash – *I* didn't understand it. I knew he was doing well but not that well. It's why I was so desperate to get Jake the LA job. I could see it might turn nasty and I wanted him in a safe berth five thousand miles away. Protected. But it didn't work out.'

Rosie shook her head. 'It certainly didn't.'

'He'll come out the other side, you know,' Christy said. 'He needs to grovel a bit, make it clear he had no idea what he was getting involved with – that his wicked mum pulled the wool over his eyes.'

'He'll have to pay back all those taxes he dodged, though.'

'Afraid so. It's the only way if he's going to earn back any of the respect he's lost. And he'll have to be whiter than white in future. It's insane. Everyone tries to dodge taxes, but unfortunately your husband got caught. Well, not that unfortunately – actually he was set up.'

'Who by?'

'You haven't heard?' The usual I-know-everything look from Christy. Oh well. She'd always be that way. 'It was Stella, his daft school friend's po-faced girlfriend.'

'Bosey's Stella! No!'

'She works at the tax office. She became suspicious, she looked at his files, and she grassed him up to the papers.'

'Does Jake know this?'

'I haven't told him yet. Not sure if I should. We can't prove it.'

'I wonder if Bosey knows.'

'I hope so, so he can dump the little cow.'

'Why do you care so much?' Rosie asked suddenly. The question had been bothering her for ages, but there'd never been a right time to ask. 'I know he's your client and I'm your friend, but you seem so *invested* in us.'

Christy shivered as a chilly wind blew down the street. She wrapped her arms round her thin cotton top, as she shrugged. 'I just owe you. You were the only one that was kind to me, and kind to Barron – you and your nanna taking him in like that when he had nowhere to go. Never laughing at us, like everyone else. I was so chuffed when I introduced you to Jake and you got it together, when things started going well for you. I could see a way of making all that nastiness in your childhood go away. Giving you the life you'd always wanted.'

'That I thought I always wanted,' Rosie contradicted. 'All those stupid magazines. I didn't need any of the stuff: the house, the interior decorator. The life I had already was just perfect. Well, not perfect, but good enough.'

'Your mum was perfect?'

'She's not great. In fact, she's probably the worst mum in the world. But she's kind of irrelevant. Nanna was the important person. And you.'

'Oh shut up. You sound like a fucking Hallmark card,' Christy said, then swallowed and continued: 'I'm sorry, Rosie. Really sorry I tried to control you like I did. I pushed you and Jake together because I thought he was perfect for you. I pushed his career so he'd have enough money to look after you properly. I was an idiot to try to be so controlling. I should have just let you do what you wanted to do.'

'But I wanted to be with Jake. You weren't wrong.'

'Still . . .'

'Listen. I love Jake. Loved him? Love . . . Oh, I don't know!' Rosie cried. 'The point is you were right. Jake and I were a great team. Jake is a fantastic actor and he deserved to make the big time. It's not your fault it all went tits up.'

'Don't say "went". Don't say "loved". You can fix this.'

'I don't know,' Rosie said. 'I really don't.'

'Oh come on, he made a daft mistake trusting his mum. You know what an idiot she is. Surely you can forgive him that?'

'It's not that, it's deeper. It's the person he's become. Probably the person I've become too. I just keep thinking we rushed into things too quickly, that we each thought the other person was something they weren't.'

'Don't say that, it'll make me so sad.'

Rosie couldn't help smiling. 'With the greatest respect, Christy, love, it isn't always about you.'

34

The hotel where Jake was staying was just off Piccadilly. Christy and Rosie had gone out for a pizza to kill time before the show ended and they could meet there.

'Good luck,' Christy had said. 'Do you want me to come with you?'

Rosie had laughed. 'No thanks. I really think I need to be alone for this.'

So now she was fumbling her way down a dimly lit corridor – *why* did hoteliers always think that finding a hotel room should be a challenge akin to something on *The Crystal Maze*? – trying to find room four-two-nine. Ah, no, not that one – she'd taken a wrong turn. Back again, squeezing past the trolley with all the mini soaps and shampoos on it – would the temptation to stop pinching them never go away? – ah, here it was, right at the end.

She took a deep breath, then knocked.

Jake opened the door, head bowed. 'Hi.'

'Hi.'

Their heads weaved awkwardly, noses clashing, as they pecked each other on the cheek. Glumly Jake ushered her in. It was a suite – through an open door, Rosie could see an unmade bed and a messy room-service tray. She thought her heart was going to break.

'Sit down,' he said, nodding at a beige sofa. She sat. 'How are the boys?'

'Fine, they're staying the night at Patrizia's. They seem pretty oblivious to what's going on.'

Jake sat in the armchair opposite her, looking down at his hands clasped between his legs. 'Good.'

There was a long pause, then Rosie blurted out: 'I don't think we can carry on like this.'

He said nothing.

'It's not about this tax business,' she continued, her chest hollowed out with sadness. 'Though that hasn't helped. It's about how we've been together. We're not happy any more. Something has to change.'

Still, silence.

'Please look at me.' Slowly Jake rose his head so his eyes met hers. He looked agonized. Rosie winced. She squeezed her nails into her palms to stop herself crying.

Jake looked away, then back at her. 'What do you want to do?' he asked wretchedly.

Rosie felt as if she were underwater. 'I don't know.' Then she gulped. 'Maybe we need to separate.'

Jake looked astonished. 'But, Bean, is it really that bad?'

'I think so.' She felt as if she were walking on the moon, cut off from reality. 'We haven't been happy, not since we moved to the Village. I feel like I don't know you any more. You've been so angry all the time, so preoccupied. You didn't tell me what was going on, and

I keep reading these articles about you where you're like a different person. I think we need some space.' Oh, God! She sounded like a character from *EastEnders*. Next thing she'd be saying 'Cannaverword?'

Jake was still silent.

'Are you going to say anything?'

'What would you like me to say?' He was emotionless. Flat.

'What do you want? How do you feel? What do you think?'

'You've already decided,' he snapped. 'So what can I say?'

'I haven't decided anything. It's just a suggestion. What do you want?'

'What I want appears to be irrelevant.'

'No it isn't. What do you think? You haven't been happy either?'

'No, but it's not our marriage that's the problem. It's my job, all the stress. I knew you didn't understand.' He paused for a moment, then said, 'I wasn't about to throw in the towel.'

'We're not throwing in the towel. We're not divorcing.' The very word made her feel faint. 'But maybe we need some time alone to . . . reconsider. We've been ships that pass in the night for so long now and—'

'And the boys?'

'What do you mean?' Rosie asked, though she knew very well. She felt sick. This was going to break their hearts.

'Well, you're going to want to stay in the house with them, aren't you?'

She swallowed. 'I know it's your house. I know your money bought it.' She refrained from adding it was money that should have been given to the government. 'But yes, I think, for now, the boys should stay in their home.'

'And I'll take them out at weekends?' He snorted ruefully. 'What a fucking cliché.'

'You can take them out whenever you want,' Rosie said. She was tingling, as if she were coming to life again. The truth was sinking in. They'd spent months barely speaking and now they were finally communicating again it was to mark the end of their marriage. Like that. Gone. She blinked back tears. She'd put out the separation idea purely as a suggestion, but Jake had immediately embraced it. She wondered what she'd been expecting. Yelling? Heated debate? That they'd talk and then he'd come home with her and in the morning everything would have magically rewound to where they were six months earlier?

Who had she been kidding? She'd failed. Just like her mum, she couldn't keep a relationship going. She'd always known Jake was too good for her and that it could never last.

'Maybe we should talk some more,' she tried, but Jake was shaking his head.

'Let's not prolong this. I can stay here for the rest of the play, then I'll move into somewhere near the

Archbishop studios. Maybe you could pack a suitcase for me tomorrow and I'll get Christy to send someone over to pick it up?'

'OK,' she said miserably.

'By the way, what was that bollocks about me having an affair with Christy? I mean, I know I've been a bit crap sometimes but I have *never*—'

'I know.' She tried to stand, but her legs were jelly. She collapsed back on to the sofa. With a Herculean effort, she forced herself to stand again.

'So you'll be in touch?' she asked, as if he were a work contact.

'Very soon.' And then Jake started to cry: huge, shaking sobs ripping through his body. Rosie started to cry too.

He held out his arms. 'Come here,' he said and for a moment he was holding her against his chest and they were weeping together. She could hear his heart beating through his shirt, feel the outline of his ribs. It was the first time they'd held each other in ages. He'd lost even more weight. The collapsed-marriage and career-on-the-rocks diet. Never fails. It was so tempting to keep standing there, to comfort each other, to gloss over everything, to say they'd start afresh, but Rosie knew it wasn't go to be so easy. She forced herself to step backwards.

'We should probably have some counselling,' she tried.

She expected arguments, but he nodded dully.

'*I'll* sort it out,' she said. 'Not Christy.'

There was hammering on the door. 'Turn down!' called a maid.

'I'll be off then,' Rosie said. 'Bye.'

'Bye.'

At the door she turned. 'Can't we make it work?' she bleated.

'I don't know,' said Jake. 'We'll see.'

She made it to the lift before the tears started up again. She hailed a cab to take her back to the village. A few cars were parked outside the gates and when she waved the tag to make them open automatically, photographers jumped out and started banging on the windows. She ducked her head and ran up the front steps, hands shaking as she opened the door, but no one followed her – it would have been trespass, after all.

The house seemed huger than she'd remembered. The dark staircase echoed with her footsteps as she made her way up to bed. In their room the first thing she spotted was their wedding photo in its silver frame, a gift from Jake's Aunt Clarissa. They looked so happy, so carefree. What an idiot she'd been then, all lovestruck, unable to believe her luck.

Carefully she picked it up and put it in her top drawer. It didn't help to remember what they'd once had; it had all been a chimera. With every passing second she was more and more sure that she and Jake could never retrieve that happiness. The hurt had been too much. They'd moved too far away from each other.

This was how it would be, she thought as she climbed under the sheets. Going to sleep alone, every night, forever more. She'd never meet anyone else, she didn't want to. She'd downsize, and find a three-bedroom flat, ideally with a small garden for the boys. No need for cleaners and gardeners or David Allen Robertsons.

Jake could live close by; she wouldn't deny him access to his sons. She'd do her best to keep relations between them civil, and she'd let him see the boys whenever he wanted.

The final thought was too much. A fat tear plopped on to Rosie's pillow, followed by another. Rosie bawled her eyes out.

35

The other mothers all gasped when, the following day, she appeared at Wendy's gates.

'Rosie, you're so brave.' exclaimed Caroline. 'You didn't need to come, you know. We would have taken the boys.'

Rosie smiled behind the dark glasses. 'Thanks, but it's time to take them home.'

Caroline squeezed her arm. 'Don't take this the wrong way,' she muttered. 'But if things are going bad with hubby, you have me to rely on. We'll be single girls together. We'll have a blast.'

'Right.' Rosie took a step backwards. She didn't identify herself as a single mum. Not yet! She wasn't sure she'd ever be able to do that.

Caroline saw her body language. 'I know,' she said softly, over the noise of shrieking children as, one by one, Wendy let them out of the room. 'You think it'll never happen to you. But think about it: it's far better for the kids to have two happy parents under different roofs, than two under the same roof who loathe each other.'

'Mummeee!' George and Toby hit her like a tornado. 'I poured water on Sabina's head and Wendy said, "Naughty!"'

388

'Oh dear,' Rosie said. Caroline was swallowed up by her children. All the way home, Rosie thought about what she'd said, the boys burbling happily about all the fun they'd had at the sleepover, as if nothing in the world had changed. Maybe she was right. If Jake were still just a boyfriend, if the boys hadn't been born, they would have split up by now. The children were what was keeping them together. How could she deprive the boys of a mother and father, of a happy family, of the thing she'd never had?

But for a while now they hadn't been a happy family, she thought as they hurried past the photographers and let the gates swing shut behind them. Were things really going to change? Or was the truth that her children would never grow up in the unit she'd always dreamed of providing them, that even if she and Jake stayed together their home would be filled with rows and silences and tears? She'd survived with Nanna just fine. She'd love the boys, Jake would love them, Nanna and bleeding Yolande and Rupert would love them too. They might not all be together, but they'd all be united in wanting the best for them. Perhaps that wouldn't be so bad.

'Mummy, you almost stepped in a dog poo!' George yelled.

There were so many awkward conversations to be had. With King's Mount, who politely said they wouldn't charge her the first term's fees, even though it was their contractual right, as they had such a long waiting list.

With David Allen Robertson, who was less gracious, muttering about how he still expected to be paid, despite Rosie's constant reassurances that he would be. The boys were asking where Jake was, saying they missed him. Rosie said he was away for work and they accepted this, but they still asked every night when he would return.

He called to speak to them every day, just before he went on stage. At the sight of his name on the caller ID, Rosie's heart would start racing with fear, hope, excitement, confusion.

She was yearning for him to say it had all been a terrible mistake, but too proud and scared to say it herself. But he always sounded so emotionless. 'How are the boys?' he'd ask coldly.

Rosie could do brisk too. 'They're fine,' she'd reply.

'Good. I miss them.'

'Of course. They miss you too.'

Only on Friday, did he add. 'So did you find out about counselling?'

'I'm looking into it.'

'We have to be really careful about it. After all this, I do not want our marital problems in the papers.'

All he cared about was his sodding reputation, not about saving his marriage. 'I'm sure none of this will end up in the papers,' she said, trying to keep her cool.

'So I'll see you on Sunday morning. I'll take the boys out. About nine?'

'Great.' Rosie was shaking as she put her phone back in her pocket.

She had an hour to kill before pick-up, so she decided go down to the Village, stroll round the duck pond, window-shop – anything that could take her mind off her worries. She walked down to the Green and began her familiar routine – the posh charity shops, the gift shop, where she bought a stupidly expensive bar of rose soap, immediately regretting it. The deli, where a box of macaroons, a snip at eight pounds, was about to go in her basket when she became aware of two women muttering to each other.

'That's her, I know it is! Look at what she's about to buy. Bloody disgraceful, isn't it, when her husband's basically stealing from ordinary people?'

Hot-cheeked, Rosie put the macaroons back on the shelf, as Patrizia and Caroline burst in.

'Hey, Rosie! Darling!' They both hugged her. 'What a piece of luck. We were just talking about you. In fact, we were about to text to ask you to come and join us and then we spotted you. Come on, let's go and have a coffee and cheer you up.'

They whisked her out of the shop, the women's jaws dropping. 'We'll pick up Minette from the shop, she gets so bored in there,' Caroline announced, pushing open the boutique's doors. Minette, who was engrossed in her copy of *Junior* magazine, jumped up.

'Come on, darling, we're going to have a latte – decaf for you, obviously, and cheer poor Rosie up.'

'Rosie!' Minette exclaimed. 'I actually have just the thing for you. It came in today and I thought of you instantly.' She ran to the racks, and pulled out a floaty orange blouse.

'Orange?' Patrizia said dubiously.

'I was a certified House of Colour consultant before I met Adrian. It'll look great on her.' She held it up to Rosie's face. 'See how it brightens her up. Because you're looking pretty pale, darling, no offence.'

'She's right, it does!' the others cooed.

Rosie turned to the mirror. Minette was right, the orange made her face seem bathed in sunlight. Who would have thought it? She smiled tentatively at her reflection and the reflection smiled back. If she wore this, she might at least be able to fool the world into believing she was functioning, even if she was doing nothing of the sort.

'You have to have it,' cried Patrizia, and the others murmured assent.

'I can't.' Rosie shook her head as she looked at the price tag. 'I can't be seen splashing cash right now.'

'We're not going to grass you up to the papers,' said Caroline indignantly.

'I'll give you a ten per cent discount?' Minette added hopefully.

Rosie laughed. She knew this was the last extravagant purchase she'd ever make. From now on, it would be back to Primark, TK Maxx and Matalan. She wouldn't mind. She'd never wanted the designer clothes in the first place.

'Twenty per cent?' Minette urged her.

She'd wear it tomorrow when Jake picked up the boys. He'd see her and . . . again, this was nonsense. She'd ended things. She didn't know if she wanted him back. But then all the more reason to look glamorous, in control.

'Thirty per cent?'

'Say fifty and we have a deal.'

At ten to nine on Sunday morning she was in her jeans – they were far looser than they'd been for months, another result for heartbreak! The flattering orange top was on, and she'd threaded huge dangly earrings through her lobes and her skin glowed under her foundation and her lips glistened under their application of lipstick. She twirled in front of the mirror, practising her smile again.

What on earth was she doing?

She reached frantically for the baby wipes and scrubbed at her face. She pulled out the earrings and yanked the blouse over her head. She was pulling on an old sweatshirt as the doorbell rang.

'Daddy!' the boys cried ecstatically.

Rosie hurried down the stairs. She was an idiot. She wasn't even sure she wanted Jake back, she certainly didn't want the Jake of the past six months, yet she still wanted him to want her. She was being juvenile and immature she reprimanded herself, as she buzzed him through the gates. Buzzing her own husband, the father of her children, through the gates of the house that he owned. It was a horrible concept.

He stood there looking even skinnier in a new bomber jacket – *where* had that come from? – and jeans. Perhaps she should have kept the make-up on? At least worn the blouse.

'Hello,' she said, her mouth suddenly so dry she could hardly speak.

'Hi.'

The boys were dancing around his legs. 'Daddy, Daddy!' Toby thunked into George. 'Eee-aaagh!'

Rosie couldn't stop staring at her husband. She'd forgotten how attractive she found him. She should have kept the make-up on.

'Here are my keys,' he said, reaching in his pocket and handing over the Fripley and Farquhar key ring. Rosie remembered the day they'd moved in, him excitedly trying to work out which key went in each lock. Another stab in the heart.

'You could have used them,' she said.

'No, I couldn't. It wouldn't have been right.' He clapped his hands. 'Come on, then, boys! We're going to McDonald's!'

The boys screeched with joy.

'Jake! Really?'

He shrugged, his face completely closed down. 'I'm

394

a cliché now. I'm going to do what clichéd divorced dads do with their children on Sundays. Next week . . . the zoo.'

'The zoo!'

'Jake . . . I . . .'

'Got everything? Right, then.'

Rosie knelt down and hugged the boys tight.

'Ow, Mummy, that hurts.'

'I love you. I love you so much.' She looked up and her eyes met Jake's. She buried her face in George's shoulder. He wiggled. She jumped up and started leafing through the coat stand.

'They don't need coats, it's tropical out there.'

'Sure. You're right. Well. Have fun.'

The door shut behind them. Rosie watched them trotting across the drive, yabbering away to their father. So this was how it was going to be. Jake wasn't showing the faintest inkling of wanting a reconciliation. They reached the gate and Jake pressed the red button to open it. Her precious family disappeared from view.

36

Their marriage-guidance counsellor, when she eventually found one, was a man, which threw Rosie, because, chauvinistically, she'd assumed this was a woman's job. His name was Julian, and he was very skinny with a shaved head and big brown eyes. He was a bit of a dandy; Rosie became fixated on the silk spotted handkerchief that could always be seen peeking out of his breast pocket. Which was all wrong, because she shouldn't have been concentrating on Julian's get-up, she should have been concentrating on saving her marriage.

Julian asked them to take turns talking and for the other one to listen. Rosie went first, because she'd organized the sessions.

'I feel I don't know who you are any longer,' she said, sitting in her beige upholstered chair – very David Allen Robertson – wringing her hands. 'We used to be a team, but since the move and the play and all this secret tax stuff, I've felt we haven't been communicating at all. Everything seemed to be about you: your career, your problems. The boys seemed irrelevant. I seemed irrelevant—'

'That's not true!' Jake exploded. 'I was doing it all for

you. The hard work, the tax stuff, the stress, it was all to give you the life you wanted.'

'But I never said that was the life I wanted! I was happy how we were. You didn't seem to realize that. It just showed how we didn't really know each other.' She'd been thinking a lot about this: their whirlwind courtship. They'd still been on their best behaviour when they married, they hadn't yet had the chance to see each other's faults.

Jake was arguing his side. 'I'm an actor. I'm ambitious – I always was. If I did well, I had money. That's the way it goes in my profession. It's famine or feast and we had the chance to feast.'

'We didn't have the chance to break the law.'

'Oh for Christ's sake.' Julian raised a long, warning finger. 'Sorry. Sorry, Julian.' Jake continued: 'But, Ro . . . it wasn't breaking the law. I just didn't ask enough questions. I was lazy and let Mum do everything. I've told you that a million times. And because I was stupid, I've lost everything: my career, my house, maybe you. I can't apologize enough. I can't do any more.'

'Mmm.' Rosie hesitated and then said. 'You didn't want to go for walks in the park any more. We used to love our walks in the park.'

'And box sets. We were in the middle of *Breaking Bad* and suddenly you weren't there any more.' Then she giggled, because she knew this was mad.

'People recognized me. It wasn't fun any more.'

Rosie cleared her throat, trying to think of the least inflammatory way to say the next bit. 'Do you think perhaps you should have listened a bit less to your mother?'

'Yes.'

'Do you think perhaps you're too much under your mum's thumb?'

'Leave my mum out of it, all right?'

With that explosion they were back at square one. 'See what I mean?' she said, appealing to Julian. 'He's just stopped being able to communicate like a normal person.'

'Oh, sod off,' Jake said, standing up, and he stormed out of the room.

Rosie looked at Julian. 'Well, didn't that go well?'

After that, Jake wouldn't go back to counselling and Rosie barely had time to dwell on how she felt about this, because so much else was going on. The house was on the market and since a quick sale seemed likely, they had to find a new place to live before term began. Rosie was ringing round every primary school in London, seeing if they had vacancies, hoping she could then rent a flat nearby, but the only schools with free spaces were schools whose Ofsted reports said things like: 'There is not nearly enough good teaching in any area of the curriculum.'

Rosie thought of how dismissive she'd been about King's Mount with its acres of playing fields and science

398

labs and wanted to kick herself. Then she thought of the lovely little primary school up the road in Neasden where Toby had been accepted just before they moved and she wanted to weep.

The summer holidays had arrived and Rosie was having to take each day as it came. Once again the Wendy's mums were proving a godsend: suggesting outings, inviting the boys over for the day so Rosie could have some free time to pack up the house – no luxury fleets of removal men, this time.

At least the photographers had left the gates, bored with endless snaps of Rosie coming in and out wearing a tracksuit. No one seemed to have twigged that Jake was no longer living there, they assumed he'd discovered a secret way out – plus they had a picture of him looking upset and an apology. The story was dying, just like Christy had said it would.

The play had finished. Ellie had returned to the US, visibly pregnant in the paparazzi shots, resolutely refusing to name the father. Rosie knew she'd never hear from her again.

Whenever Jake was with the boys, she drove down to see Nanna. She was on a new combination of drugs and responding well to them.

'So what's going on with you and Jake?' she'd asked on the latest visit, like every time. 'I'm not happy seeing you apart.'

'We made a mistake getting married,' Rosie said. 'I think we were in lust, not in love. I think I was stupid and got pregnant accidentally and I think we never really knew each other.' She'd rehearsed this speech endlessly to herself and was starting to believe every word of it. Her heart was broken, but Jake didn't even want them to try to get back together, so somehow she had to justify it to herself.

But Nanna tutted. 'Well get to know each other now.'

Rosie thought of Jake storming out of the session and shook her head sadly. 'I think it's too late. Even if we did get to know each other, I'm not at all sure we'd like what we found.'

'Nonsense. I know Jake's a good guy. He's just got a bit of a daft mum. Talk to each other.'

'That's what we were doing in the counselling. But he walked out.'

Nanna's expression made it very clear what she thought of counselling.

'I know, Nanna, but it's the modern way. Anyway, it's not working. I'd like to give it another go, but Jake's making it clear he's not interested. He must have given up on us before I did.'

'I don't believe you. Jake loves you. That's always been clear.'

'I'm really not so sure.'

Returning home from Bristol, heart full of sadness, she wasn't exactly delighted to pull in through the gates and find Yolande's Range Rover parked there.

'Hoo-bloody-ray,' she muttered to herself, jumping out of the Passat.

'Yolande!' she said brightly. 'What brings you here?'

Yolande looked far older than Rosie remembered. She was wearing as much make-up as always, but Rosie couldn't remember the deep lines above her mouth or the etchings round the eyes. Perhaps they'd just not been so pronounced, or perhaps she'd had to give up on the Botox. Rosie thought of Rupert and Christy, and to her annoyance felt a huge pang of sympathy for her mother-in-law.

'I needed to talk to you.' Her outfit, at least, was as vibrant as ever: a violet trouser suit. But as she walked towards the front step, she stumbled in her stiletto boots. Rosie realized that she'd never see her mother-in-law as the unstoppable matriarch again. She was human, frail, vulnerable.

They sat in the kitchen, making small talk about the boys.

'I was rather hoping to see them. Perry didn't tell me they were with him today, but he has a lot on his mind.' She frowned at her coffee. 'Hmm. Perhaps a touch more milk.' OK. She hadn't changed beyond recognition.

For a while, they only talked about the boys. Rosie simply didn't have the nerve to bring up the marriage, so they skated round it as she broke the news that on the plus side Toby had started eating broccoli. On the minus, he'd given up carrots.

'But they both seem very happy at the moment, even though . . .' Rosie's voice trailed away.

'Even though their parents are no longer together,' Yolande said.

'Well, er . . .'

Yolande sighed heavily and once again looked every second of her sixty-eight years. 'Look, I take responsibility for this. I made a bad mistake and didn't inform my son about the choices I was making on his behalf. So I hold my hands up.'

There was so obviously a 'but' coming. Rosie sat and waited.

'But in my day you married to stick at things. For richer for poorer, for better for worse.'

Right. Something your husband obviously subscribed to. Rosie nodded politely, looking in her coffee cup.

'Jake misses you so much, you know,' Yolande said suddenly.

Rosie's head jerked upwards. 'Sorry?'

'He misses you. He's in terrible pain.'

'He's not showing it!' Rosie cried, forgetting to keep up her guard and then added softly. 'God, I miss him too. So much.'

'Do you?' Something changed in Yolande's expression; she looked instantly softer, happier, eager.

'Of course!' Rosie exclaimed and then added, dejected, 'But I don't think he's bothered about us.'

'What are you saying?' Now there were tears in Yolande's eyes. Seriously, would wonders never cease? 'Of course he's missing you. He's wretched.'

'He's not showing it.'

'Oh, Rosie,' laughed Yolande in the way that normally made Rosie want to deck her, but which now she suddenly found oddly reassuring. 'That's just Jake, you know. He was always like that, even as a little boy. So ridiculously *proud*. And he's an actor, remember, he knows how to hide his feelings when he has to. He thinks you don't want him any more, so he's trying to show he doesn't care.'

Now it was Rosie's turn to try to hide the huge surge of optimism that shot through her. 'I'm still upset with him,' she warned. 'He hasn't been a great husband recently and the tax thing was the last straw.'

'I take full responsibility, I told you!' Yolande cried, holding up her hands. 'He wanted to tell you when it first all looked like it was going to blow up, but I expressly told him not to. I said the less people who knew, the better. We hoped it would never get this far.'

Rosie's head was reeling. Yolande was admitting she was wrong. Far more importantly, Jake missed them. She couldn't help the little smile that crept round the corner of her lips.

'I have a lot to think about,' she said.

'We all do.' Yolande stood up. 'I don't think Jake should continue to be represented by Christy.'

Silence fell. Rosie stared at her. She *knew*.

Yolande continued: 'I know she's your friend, Rosie, though really I've never seen what you had in common, but she's not done wonders for Jake. Telling him to do that ridiculous play. I think she's bad news.'

Now her pale blue eyes bore straight into Rosie.

Rosie smiled up at Yolande. 'That's up to Jake to decide.' Christy will always be my friend, she wanted to add, but she knew better. The battle lines would be drawn again and she needed Yolande to pass on the message. 'Please tell Jake I . . . I do want to talk to him at least.'

'I will.' Yolande moved towards the door. 'Goodbye, Rosie.' A soft cheek was offered for a kiss. The familiar smell of Coco Mademoiselle. 'We'll be in touch.'

37

The following morning, the boys were playing at Elise's house, supervised by her new handsome Slovenian manny. Rosie was singing along tunelessly to Daft Punk on the radio while packing their belongings into crates. A plastic tractor intoned, 'I. Am. Coming. To. Find. You,' in a creepy robotic voice whenever you pressed the red button. Maybe she'd accidentally lose that. They wouldn't have room for all these toys in the new flat anyway.

The buzzer went. Rosie went to the door. It would be a meter reader. People kept arriving to shut things down and turn other things on, in preparation for the tenants: a Venezuelan banker and his wife.

'Hello?' she said into the entryphone.

'Hi,' said a familiar voice and her heart jolted as if she'd put her hand on an electric fence.

'Hello. What do you want?' It came out very abruptly.

'Charming,' Jake snapped, but then in more placatory tones: 'Sorry! Sorry.'

'No, I'm sorry. Do you want to come in?'

She buzzed. On the little screen she watched him walk across the drive. His gait was much jauntier than usual. Rosie's heart dived. Had he met someone else?

She opened the door, her head spinning at this horrible prospect. They stood and looked at each other.

'I've come to take you out for lunch,' he said.

'Is this Christy's idea?' she asked. 'Or your mother's?' Then immediately she hated herself for her snippy tone.

'No, it's not! It's mine. I've been thinking about how we used to be, what we used to like doing, before . . . before everything changed, and I wanted to try to do that again.'

'Oh.'

He beckoned to her. 'Come on, let's go.'

Outside the gates a rickety-looking moped was parked. Two helmets hung from the handlebars. Jake handed her one.

'Are these your wheels now?' she asked in surprise.

He nodded. 'I know you like going on the bus or the tube, but people do stare a lot so . . .'

'Do you know how to drive it?'

He laughed. 'Of course I do. It's a bike with a motor. How hard can it be?'

Nonetheless, Rosie was nervous, sitting behind him, as they bumped off along the road and swept round the corner past the Village Green. There was Patrizia jogging by the pond, Minette was outside her shop, looking quizzically up at the window display, Bella was walking her dogs. None of them spotted her.

'How do I stay on?' she yelled, as they turned into a corner.

'Lean into it. And hold on to me.'

Reluctantly she leaned forward and put her hands round her husband's waist. He was skinnier even than before, but his body felt warm. As they hit the road that led to the common, he sped up and she buried her face in his jacket. He smelled so . . . Jake. Slightly spicy, slightly sour. It was that smell that had intoxicated her the first night she'd met him and as a flash of how she'd felt when she'd caught his eye swept over her, her knees turned to jelly.

Stop it, Rosie.

They bumped and jerked and occasionally sped through south London, round busy roundabouts, along stretches of green covered with bodies – no longer pasty, but tanned from the long hot summer, past red-brick mansion blocks, imposing stucco houses, sprawling council estates, over railways lines and overtaking buses, until they pulled up in a car park on the edges of Tooting Common.

'What are we doing here?'

'There's a restaurant where Simon and I have been hanging out. It's fab. No one recognizes us. I want to show it to you.'

'Simon the director?'

'Yup. Brunhilde's left him. He's living in a little rented flat just up the road.'

'She found out?'

'You knew?' Jake was surprised.

'Ellie told me.'

Jake shook his head. 'She's a minx, that one. Simon's desolate, but he buggered up. Brunhilde's going to make sure he only sees those kids once a month. She has him over a barrel.' He turned to Rosie. 'You'd never do that to me, would you?'

'Of course not!' she exclaimed.

'Good. Only ... Simon cheated on Brunhilde. I never betrayed you. I've always loved you.'

Rosie's head was turning swimmy again. 'Yes,' she said idiotically and then, confused, pushed open the restaurant door. It was Lebanese: a small, cosy place with a huge clay oven in the corner blasting out heat that was having to be counterbalanced by whirring fans. The room was full of men and women at small Formica tables, who were clearly Lebanese too, talking and laughing. Forks clattered and singing floated through the open kitchen door. The room smelled of herbs and freshly baked bread. Rosie's stomach rumbled. 'This is lovely.'

'Wait until you try the food,' said Jake, as they sat at a corner table. 'Will you let me order?'

'How long will it take for you to make up your mind?' Rosie teased.

He smiled. 'I know the menu off by heart.'

Rapidly a plate of mixed mezze arrived. Rosie dipped her bread into a bowl of mashed broad beans and groaned in delight as the earthy, garlicky, lemony flavour exploded in her mouth.

'Oh, yum. This is fabulous.'

'It's the kind of place you like, isn't it?' asked Jake, smiling at her.

'Mmm-waargh.'

He smiled. 'I got you wrong, Bean. Christy did too. We thought you wanted fancy restaurants and jewellery and swimming pools and Range Rovers, but you didn't, did you?'

She shook her head, still unable to talk.

'You pig,' he laughed.

'Are you going to eat something?'

'I'm too nervous,' he replied and suddenly her stomach flipped and she was too nervous as well.

They stared at each other.

'I was an idiot,' he said. 'I've said it before, I'll say it again, I was an idiot to think money was so important to us, when it never had been and it never will. I was a dumbass to prioritize my career over spending time with you.'

She nodded.

'I was a fool to be so proud, to go all cold on you when you suggested this separation. I was a moron to walk out of counselling.' He gulped, then continued: 'I miss you and the boys so much. I can't bear it any more, Ro.'

'Is it me you miss or the boys?'

'All of you! You come as a package. You can't have one without the other.'

He reached out and touched her hand. She put her other hand on top of his. They looked down at the pile of fingers.

'You don't know how much I wish none of this had ever happened to me,' he said. 'Everything was easier before *Archbishop Grace*. I mean, I know you were working hard, but we had so much more time together. I saw the boys so much more. I didn't have to spend my spare time with a freaking personal trainer. I didn't feel under so much pressure to succeed the whole time.'

'You shouldn't have felt that pressure. It was silly.'

'I know, but I did.'

'I'd have loved you whoever you were. I'd love you if you were a dustman.'

'Would you?'

'Of course!' Rosie said firmly. 'Idiot.'

'I'm sorry, Bean. It's all become so frightening. It used to be just me and my dreams, reciting Willy Loman's big speech to myself in the mirror, hanging out with my mates who weren't getting anywhere either, but it didn't really matter, because everyone had warned us how tough acting was and how we didn't stand a chance. And then I got lucky and suddenly there was all this stuff I was never prepared for, never wanted, like dinner with producers, and interviews where I don't know what to say and it all came out wrong. I'm sorry.'

'Everything OK with the food?' The manager was hovering over them, looking worried.

'It's fine,' they chorused. 'It's delicious. It's . . .'

'Just give us a moment,' Jake said.

Rosie made a huge effort and dipped the bread into

a bowl of charred aubergine, speckled with pomegranate. 'Ooh, this is delicious too!'

They carried on eating. It felt surreal sitting at a restaurant table together, yet at the same time utterly mundane, something they'd done a hundred times before, as if they'd nipped out to their local caff, like they used to in the good old days. Without either of them saying anything, Rosie knew they were back together now, that they'd overcome this hump and without having to say anything more they were able to gasp over the crisp pastries containing melting feta and lemony spinach and squabble about who was going to have the most of the grilled chicken order, and who was going to settle for second best with the beef.

'Me, I guess,' Jake said with a shrug.

'I should think so too.'

They were back to normal. Well, not the old normal, that had been lost the first time *Archbishop Grace* was aired, but a new kind of normal and they'd deal with that.

Once they'd scoffed their way through the pastries and had a cup of bracing black coffee, they wandered hand in hand across Tooting Common.

'You were saying we didn't go for enough walks in the park,' Jake said.

'I was. We weren't.'

'We'll do it now,' he promised.

Tentatively he reached out and touched her face.

Slowly she touched him back. She stood on tiptoes, as he bent down towards her. She felt his forehead warm against hers, his breath warm on her face and they were kissing with even more passion than that first night they met, that night when they hadn't actually known each other, just had the strongest feeling that it was all meant to be.

Their second first kiss: the kind of kiss you forget all about a few months into a relationship, because you become assailed with an uneasy feeling that you're imitating something you saw in a film and, anyway, there's a box set to watch. They'd have to both try harder to recapture that feeling, to make it last, to recognize that sometimes it wouldn't be so strong, but if they still paid attention to each other and respected each other, it need not mean the end of everything.

38

Six months later

They lay in bed, the sheet was tangled around their feet. From the garden, Rosie heard the scream of mating foxes. She was breathing heavily, but her mind was whirring into a different gear.

She ran over her to-do list for the following day. Tesco online shop. RSVP to various birthday-party invitations (boys, of course, her social life was as dead in the water as ever). Double-check with the consultant about what he'd said to Nanna at her hospital appointment. (Though to be fair, Nanna seemed to be doing pretty well on the drugs she was taking.) Try to call some painters for quotes on having the living room repainted.

They'd moved back to Neasden, though in a bigger house this time, with four bedrooms and a smallish garden. Thanks to a schmancy new free school round the corner, which offered Latin from reception, last-minute places had opened up at the other local school for Toby in reception and George in nursery.

Jake was slowly rebuilding his career. He'd sucked up the abuse, grovelled madly to various interviewers, and appeared on a few panel shows making jokes about himself. After four months of unemployment, having filmed the second series of *Archbishop Grace*, an offer had come in for a big part in a BBC drama.

The production company had made it quite clear to Christy that he'd be contractually obliged to give three interviews talking about 'taxgate', but since Jake was genuinely contrite, there was no problem with that. Rehearsals kicked in in a month, at which point life would become more challenging in terms of child care, but Rosie had a lovely childminder lined up, who was also a mum at the school, so she was quietly confident that they'd wing it.

Christy's career was thriving, she'd impressed several 'in the business' with the way she'd handled Jake's upset and her client list was growing. She'd sworn to Rosie that the affair with Rupert was over, and although Rosie was finding it very difficult to look her father-in-law in the eye any more, she hoped one day she'd have almost completely forgotten what she saw. She and Christy were friends again. Not friends like the way they were at Brightman's, or when they'd shared the Chelsea flat, but Rosie had realized you couldn't recapture the ingredients that made those times so special. For the time being, day to day, other people would be more important in their lives, but that didn't devalue what they had had in the past and the affection they'd always feel for each other.

Rosie herself was back at Tapper-Green, doing four days a week. There'd been no choice but for her to return when Jake's future was so dubious and this time he'd stepped up to the plate and done the childcare. But in her absence from work, her Village period as she called it in her head, she felt in a weird way she'd grown up.

She'd realized so many things. That it was OK to have rows with Jake, to disagree, to want different things at different times, to have periods when they didn't actually like each other very much. It didn't mean it was all doomed to failure.

She'd realized that, with a mother like hers, she'd been trained at a subconscious level to expect nothing to work out, to throw in the towel at the first bump. She'd also realized that she'd felt so honoured at some level to have been chosen by Jake that she couldn't believe their relationship could truly last.

But it didn't have to be that way any more. They'd had a bumpy patch, endured some life-changing experiences, and they'd come through. For now. There'd be bumps in the future too, of course. The LA question still hovered on the horizon. But for now, in their semi on a quiet road, just off the high street, with a patch of garden big enough for a mini trampoline, they were happy. Again.

Now she rolled towards Jake. He was indulging in his favourite fantasy.

'So, I think a boiled egg on soda bread, with some Maldon salt.'

'You're obsessed with breakfast,' Rosie grinned. He always loved to plan his next meal far in advance.

She nuzzled her head against his chest. 'I love you and the way you're obsessed with breakfast.'

'I love you and the way you're always trying to chuck out newspapers I haven't read.'

'I love you and the way you get all obsessed with mad things – like no-cheese diets.'

'I love the way you'd never even countenance a diet,' he said, squeezing her bottom.

'Hey!'

'Sorry, Bean! I love your bottom. I love the way you don't need to diet and you don't pretend you do, like most women. I love the way you don't realize you moult in the shower.'

'I love the way you tell me we've run out of orange juice after you've finished the carton.' She hauled herself up and kissed him hard on the lips. 'I love you, Jake Perry.' She hadn't said it for way too long. Once they'd said it to each other two, three, four, ten times a day.

'I love you too, Rosie Prest. Goodnight.'

Psst
want the latest gossip on all your favourite writers?

Then come and join us in . . .

THE BOOK BOUTIQUE

. . . the **exclusive club** for anyone who loves to curl up with the latest reads in women's fiction.

- All the latest news on the best authors.
- Early copies of the latest reads months before they're out.
- Chat with like-minded readers as well as bestselling writers.
- Excellent recommendations for new books to read.
- Exclusive competitions to get your hands on stylish prizes.

SIGN UP for our regular newsletter by emailing
thebookboutique@uk.penguingroup.com
or if you really can't wait, get over to
www.facebook.com/TheBookBoutique

He just wanted a decent book to read ...

Not too much to ask, is it? It was in 1935 when Allen Lane, Managing Director of Bodley Head Publishers, stood on a platform at Exeter railway station looking for something good to read on his journey back to London. His choice was limited to popular magazines and poor-quality paperbacks – the same choice faced every day by the vast majority of readers, few of whom could afford hardbacks. Lane's disappointment and subsequent anger at the range of books generally available led him to found a company – and change the world.

'We believed in the existence in this country of a vast reading public for intelligent books at a low price, and staked everything on it'
Sir Allen Lane, 1902–1970, founder of Penguin Books

The quality paperback had arrived – and not just in bookshops. Lane was adamant that his Penguins should appear in chain stores and tobacconists, and should cost no more than a packet of cigarettes.

Reading habits (and cigarette prices) have changed since 1935, but Penguin still believes in publishing the best books for everybody to enjoy. We still believe that good design costs no more than bad design, and we still believe that quality books published passionately and responsibly make the world a better place.

So wherever you see the little bird – whether it's on a piece of prize-winning literary fiction or a celebrity autobiography, political tour de force or historical masterpiece, a serial-killer thriller, reference book, world classic or a piece of pure escapism – you can bet that it represents the very best that the genre has to offer.

Whatever you like to read – trust Penguin.